Gutter Road
You Can't Stop Me
ROBERT SILVERBERG

Stark House Press • Eureka California

GUTTER ROAD / YOU CAN'T STOP ME

Published by Stark House Press
1315 H Street
Eureka, CA 95501, USA
griffinskye3@sbcglobal.net
www.starkhousepress.com

GUTTER ROAD
Originally published as by "Don Elliott" and copyright © 1964 by
Sundown Readers. Copyright © renewed 1992 by Agberg Ltd.
Reprinted by permission of Agberg Ltd.

YOU CAN'T STOP ME
Originally published under the title *Lust Lover* as by "Dan Eliot"
and copyright © 1963 by Pillar Books. Copyright © renewed 1991
by Agberg Ltd.
Reprinted by permission of Agberg Ltd.

Foreword copyright © 2023 by Robert Silverberg

All rights reserved under International and
Pan-American Copyright Conventions.

ISBN: 979-8-88601-025-1

Cover design by Jeff Vorzimmer, ¡caliente!design, Austin, Texas
Text design by Mark Shepard, shepgraphics.com
Proofreading by Bill Kelly
Cover art by Rudolph Belarski

PUBLISHER'S NOTE
This is a work of fiction. Names, characters, places and incidents are
either the products of the author's imagination or used fictionally, and
any resemblance to actual persons, living or dead, events or locales, is
entirely coincidental.

Without limiting the rights under copyright reserved above, no part of
this publication may be reproduced, stored, or introduced into a retrieval
system or transmitted in any form or by any means (electronic,
mechanical, photocopying, recording or otherwise) without the prior
written permission of both the copyright owner and the above publisher
of the book.

First Stark House Press Edition: April 2023

7
Foreword
by Robert Silverberg

9
Gutter Road
By Robert Silverberg

115
You Can't Stop Me
By Robert Silverberg

223
Robert Silverberg
Bibliography

FOREWORD

You will note from the copyright notice that these books were written more than sixty years ago. The world has changed quite a bit in the past sixty years, and I ask you not to hold me to account for having failed, in 1963, to have my characters live up to the moral standards now being set forth by the inhabitants of 2023, who were not even born when I wrote these stories. I have written, among other things, a great deal of science fiction, but these two were not science fiction books and I made no attempt to predict the future in them. They are novels of their time. Please read them as that.

Robert Silverberg

Gutter Road
ROBERT SILVERBERG

CHAPTER ONE

Bauman's first really bad mistake was to stop the car and pick up the attractive, breasty chick who wanted to hitch a ride.

It was the sort of thing any man might have done, Bauman told himself. Even a sensible man like Fred Bauman, who was thirty-eight years old and more or less loved his wife and didn't usually think about stopping his car to pick up strange women.

But it was a miserably rainy spring night, with distant thunder booming like muffled drums, and the occasional wild crackle of lightning splitting the black sky. Bauman had been working late at the office, which was an accounting firm in midtown Manhattan, and he was heading uptown in his car, figuring to take the Queensboro Bridge at 59th Street across the river to Queens, where he lived in the middle-class residential district known as Forest Hills.

Ordinarily, Bauman would have driven down 42nd Street and used the Queens Midtown Tunnel, but the tunnel had a toll charge. Bauman had spent a little too much on lunch for himself that day—and, being something of a thrifty guy by nature, he was making up the extravagance to himself by going a little out of his way and taking the bridge. You saved a dime here, you saved two bits there—it added up, Bauman liked to think.

The girl was standing in the shadows at the approach to the bridge on 59th Street where Second Avenue crossed it. Bauman saw her standing there, when his car was stopped for the traffic light. He gave her the kind of automatic appraisal any man would give. There was nothing wrong with Bauman's hormones. He looked her over, and wondered what she was doing there in the rain, and he couldn't help feeling at least a tinge of attraction toward her.

She was young, and good looking. *Very* good looking. He could see the clean, even lines of her face, and the jutting lines of her figure, her high breasts sticking out in front of her. She was wearing a flimsy plastic raincoat huddled up around herself, but despite it she was getting good and wet in the soaking downpour. The way it looked, she was planning to walk across the bridge into Queens. That was one hell of a walk, even in dry weather.

The idea struck him then.

It was an uncharacteristic idea, maybe, something left over from his early, long-buried Boy Scout days. Be kind to women. Help old ladies across the street. If you see a pretty girl, offer to carry her books to school

for her. Be chivalrous.
   Was it chivalry that stirred him now?
   Or something else, something you didn't get a Boy Scout merit badge for? Some stirring deep in the metabolism, some unvoiced indeterminate hope that by taking a step now, he might get himself involved in an adventure that would brighten an all too monochromed life?
   Bauman wasn't sure. Bauman didn't really understand why he did it. Probably, he decided later, it was a mixture of things: partly just a good-natured wish to be helpful, and partly the buried hope that his kindly act would pay a dividend of some sort for him.
   Bauman leaned across the front seat and quickly rolled down the window on the right-hand side of the car. A cold April wind whipped in at him and chilly rain sprinkled his face as he peered out.
   "Miss?" he called.
   She looked up suspiciously. Dark eyes gleamed as she stared at him.
   Grinning to show that he meant no harm, that he was no rapist or sadist or kidnapper, Bauman added immediately, "Hi, there. Can I help you out with a lift, maybe? I'm driving across the bridge."
   Instantly, the suspicious look on the girl's face vanished, and her eyes lit up. "Oh, would you?" she asked. Her voice was soft and deep and pleasant to hear. "I'm so wet! If you'd just take me across—"
   "It would be a pleasure, Miss."
   Bauman twisted the door handle and shoved the car door open. The girl skittered away from the building against which she had been huddling and stepped lithely into the car, bringing with her a little of the chill of the spring storm. She dosed the door behind her and snapped down the thumb-lock.
   The light turned green.
   Bauman started up again and nudged the car forward, onto the bridge approach.
   As he drove, Bauman veered his attention away from the slippery roadbed of the bridge long enough to steal a glimpse at her from the corner of his right eye. She was young, all right, twenty-two, or maybe twenty-three at most. Just a kid, Bauman thought from the vantage point of his own elderly-sounding thirty-eight years. She was just a kid.
   A good-looking kid, though. She had brown eyes and brown hair, the latter plastered rather prettily to her forehead. A clear-skinned, alert face, with a pert, saucy nose and full lips. Strong chin. Sharp cheekbones. And what looked like a first-rate pair of breasts pushing the front of her raincoat outward.
   Bauman's insides began to churn with strange sensations. He was very much a middle-class married man, and he couldn't remember when

the last time was that he had been alone in his car with a strange, attractive single girl. It was a novel situation for him, and a pleasant one.

She was sitting quite close to him, too. He could feel the warmth of her near his side as he drove. He gripped the wheel more tightly than he needed to.

Feeling he ought to say something, he said, "Lousy night, isn't it? Lousy night for girls to be walking along bridges alone."

"I had to," she said simply.

"Oh."

After another moment or two Bauman said, "How far into Queens are you going? I'm heading for Forest Hills myself."

"I'm going all the way out to Jamaica," the girl told him. "If it's okay with you, you can drop me next to the Forest Hills subway stop, and I'll get there the rest of the way myself."

"Sure," Bauman said. "Be glad to."

She said, "What's your name?"

He frowned slightly; something seemed to be a little out of key in what she was saying, but he didn't worry much about it.

Until she moved a little closer to him. Now she was sitting practically jammed up against him, the way the teenage girls did when their boyfriends took them for a drive in their cheap jalopies. Pressed tight. Knee to knee.

"Ah—"

He didn't know what to say in a situation like this. He fell silent.

"Bauman. Fred Bauman."

"My name's Joanne," she said. She didn't give the second name. Bauman didn't ask for it.

They were off the bridge now, and driving through the dark, silent streets of Queens. Outside, the rain continued to pour down, keeping the windshield wipers busy, but within the car everything seemed warm and cozy, a world sealed off from the raw, nasty wetness outside. Like a traveling motel room, Bauman thought suddenly. Bauman felt the first powerful stirrings of a strange desire that shocked and astonished and pleased him all at the same time.

Her hand slipped to his knee. Her touch was like the touch of a branding iron against him. Bauman reacted automatically and unthinkingly. Keeping one hand on the wheel, he brushed her hand off.

"Please," he said.

"What's the matter?" she asked, her voice a soft, sensuous purr. "Don't you like me, Fred?"

His face blazed. He was so stirred up he could hardly see the road. In a voice that sounded strange in his own ears, Bauman blurted, "I—that is—listen, please don't do that."

"Will your wife object? You *are* married, aren't you?" She was watching him sharply, out of shrewd young brown eyes.

"Yes, I'm married," Bauman told her, a little impatiently. Tension roared through his eardrums.

What sort of girl had he picked up, anyway? He was starting to wonder more and more. Why had he picked her up? What did she want from him? Why was she sitting so close to him now? Bauman was regretting the whole thing now. He wished he had never stopped the car for her. She represented danger, adventure, romance. He was afraid. He wished there was some way of getting her to leave the car, right now, before something unfortunate happened. But he couldn't think of any way to get rid of her.

"I'll bet I can show you some things your wife doesn't know," she said slyly "Don't be afraid of me. Fred. I'm not going to hurt you."

She put her hand back on his knee, her fingertips digging lightly into his kneecap. This time Bauman did not brush the hand away.

She started to move it. Northward up his leg. Inch by inch by inch, until it was practically at the top of his leg. Bauman felt a sizzling sensation all through his body. What if she moved the hand another six inches, he asked himself? What if—

He drove on. He gripped the wheel as though he thought it might break loose and go flying through the roof of the car. He was having a hard time focusing his eyes. The rain-shiny streets seemed to blur and shift before him.

She said, "Why don't you park over there, Fred? Just for a couple of minutes. It's dark there—right next to those trees, over there where I'm pointing. Nobody will see us."

"No," Bauman said.

But he found himself swerving the car toward the dark sidewalk anyway, guiding it into a parking spot under the big trees, heavy with their new spring foliage. "What's happening to me," Bauman wondered. "Why am I doing this," he asked himself.

He pulled up and stopped the car. Joanne reached laughingly across him and yanked back the handbrake. As she bent forward, Bauman felt the firm hills of her breasts pressing for a moment into his knees.

Then she turned to him and her lips sprang to his like iron springing to a magnet. She clung to him a moment in the front seat of the car, and despite the annoying interference of the steering wheel she moved lightly against him.

Bauman kissed her uncertainly. He wasn't sure how much of a kiss to make it. Passionate? Yes, that seemed to be what she wanted. Her mouth was demanding. He slipped his arms around her body and kissed her the way he had once kissed girls in automobiles on rainy nights long ago, before he had slipped into the routine of marriage and middle-class respectability.

She kissed artfully, provocatively, teasing and tempting. Her lips were tender, and the smell of her cologne in his nostrils was sweet and sensual and provocative. Through his spring jacket and through the plastic of her raincoat Bauman could feel the firmness of her young breasts against his body. His brain was seared by a sudden imaginary vision of what those breasts must look like—high and hard and round, with sharp red tips and a deep, alluring valley. Her lips darted against his; her hands convulsively tightened on his shoulders.

Bauman felt a wild pounding of lust. There was a furious ache within him, everywhere. Thunder in his ears and a different thunder in his brain, and the savage frenzy of lust in his body.

The kiss went on and on. Bauman let his hands work between their bodies, and cupped them over her breasts. Her breasts felt soft. It seemed to him that she must not be wearing a brassiere underneath her blouse and raincoat, but that the round globes of her breasts were naked in there, easy to reach, easy to touch. She—

Then she broke away from him.

Her eyes glinted like beacons in the darkness. Her voice was thick and husky as she said "Okay, Fred. We can drive on now."

"No," Bauman grunted, stunned by the unexpectedness of her words. "No!"

"No?" she repeated. "No, Fred?"

Her eyes danced mockingly before him. Shaken by a desire wilder than any he had felt for many years, Bauman reached out for her, tried to pull her toward him.

He locked his arms around her. He forced her legs.

"Don't hold me like that!" she said, almost whimpering, as she fought to get loose.

"You—damned—tease—" Bauman muttered hoarsely. He was inflamed now—not far from being a madman. The interrupted caresses had done their work. He wanted more, now.

He wanted everything.

She fought, but his strength prevailed. Despite her repeated outbursts of "No, no," she gave ground steadily, her resistance weakening, her words lost in sobs. Bauman got her raincoat open. Beneath it she wore a coffee-colored blouse and he tried to fumble the buttons open, but they wouldn't cooperate with his tense, trembling fingers, so he simply ripped. Buttons went popping into every corner of his car. The blouse opened.

She was naked underneath it.

Bauman saw her breasts in the faint light. They seemed to gleam with a light of their own. They were everything he had imagined they would be. They were round and firm, high and close together, with small dark nipples that were standing up straight and tall. The fact that her nipples were erect made Bauman all the more excited, spurring him onward. That meant that she wanted him, that her struggle was not really serious.

He got his hands to her bare breasts, enjoying the tips like little pebbles against his palms. His fingers dug at the firm, ripe flesh. Her breasts were hard and soft all at once. They were resilient, not saggy or droopy but taut and firm, and yet at the same time they were soft, wonderfully soft. Bauman heard his own ragged gasping in the car as he grasped her breasts.

Then he let her breasts go and grabbed her knees.

He jammed her dress up. She was nude underneath. What the hell, didn't she wear underwear? Her eyes adjusted to darkness now, saw the slender columns of her legs and the flat drum of her middle revealed a complete bareness as he got her skirt out of the way. He touched her legs, savored the cool nudity of them.

Then he moved toward her.

Even as he drew her to him and positioned her, Bauman's mind kept asking quietly, "Why am I doing this? Have I gone crazy?"

He didn't answer himself. Her body was a lure he could not resist. Bauman pressed himself against her. She was so warm, so soft, so very young, and eager, now. She was eager for him, he realized.

He took her.

That wasn't easy maneuvering in the cramped confines of the automobile, but Bauman was carried away by his own wild lusts and hardly stopped to worry about convenience. He moved again and again. To his great jubilation, she had stopped resisting and had begun to cooperate. The movements of his body were met by responses of her own. He was almost brutal in his excitement. She was so warm, so vibrant, so exciting

He trembled with passion. He heard her gasping against him. He pushed his face against the apples of her bosom, took one breast with his mouth, held it with his lips, played with the nipple.

Ecstasy seared him. In half a dozen blazing, searing sighs, Fred Bauman found the acme of his stolen pleasure.

And now, finally, everything was over. Bauman drew back, awed and shocked at what he had done. In the aftermath, as sanity returned to him, he felt strangely alone, dazed, as bewildered as a man who has for no reason at all pressed the button that detonates all the H-bombs on Earth and who is now waiting for the fiery moment of global destruction to arrive.

After a shaky moment Bauman looked at the girl. He was expecting to see her bowed in shame and terror, cursing him, sobbing. She wasn't.

She was smiling.

She sat there comfortably, watching him. She was leaning against the window, her blouse still wide open, her breasts still impudently bare, her skirt still pushed up and hunched around her hips to reveal her cool nudity.

She said, "In this state, Mr. Fred Bauman of Forest Hills, Queens, that offense you just committed is known as the crime of rape."

Her voice was under control, as if they had merely been holding hands five minutes before. There was nothing panicky or hysterical about her. She wasn't behaving the way one would expect a rape victim to behave.

She went on, "You must be aware of the act you just committed, Mr. Bauman. You violently compelled me to participate with you. What an immoral act, Mr. Bauman! To force yourself upon me—to violate an innocent girl—what a thing to do! Tell me, what would your wife say if she learned you had done an awful thing like that to a young girl like me?"

Bauman swung round in his seat and stared wildly at her. His hands were shaking, and not from desire any more, either. He grabbed the wheel. The note of irony and sarcasm in her voice baffled him as much as anything.

"What are you getting at?" he rasped.

"Money," she told him sweetly. "I want money for keeping quiet about this dastardly deed of rape. You wouldn't want me to go to the police and inform them of your discourteous behavior, would you?"

"You couldn't prove anything."

"My blouse is torn," she said. "All the buttons are off. There are marks of a struggle on me. A medical examination will show that I've been had this evening. It'll be your word against mine, sure, but what of that?"

"I'll tell them that you picked me up. That you provoked me, you put your hand on my leg, you sat close to me, you kissed me—"

"Prove it," she said. "I was going to Queens. You gave me a ride and you stopped the car on the other side of the bridge and raped me. All the evidence will be on my side. And so will the jury. They'll throw the book at you, Mr. Fred Bauman. Maybe you'll be lucky and get off with only a couple of years—but even a short sentence for rape wouldn't do your name much good, would it?"

Horror clutched at Bauman. "What do you want from me?" he asked thickly. "How much?"

"Five thousand dollars," she said. Her voice was completely calm.

"Five thous—"

"You heard it the first time, Mr. Fred Bauman of Forest Hills. Five thousand clams. Cough it up or I'll go to the police."

Dazed Bauman fumbled for words. "I don't have any such amount of money."

"Find it somewhere, then," she told him crisply. "You don't think you can rob me of my virtue and get away, do you?"

"But—but you led me on! You tempted me!"

She smiled. With a cheerful gesture she pulled her skirt down over her knees. Her bare breasts still were on display. She said, "You heard me yelling 'No' when you got serious, didn't you? Did that sound like my willing consent to you?"

Bauman moistened his lips and tried to stay calm. He had to admit to himself that he'd, in fact, forced her, at least technically. But how had he known that this would happen? She had seemed like nothing but an easy-minded tramp who wanted a little quick fun on a rainy night. How could he have possibly known—?

"This is the end of the ride for me," she said. "I'm not going any further with you. Suppose you let me have your business card."

"What for?"

"So I can get in touch with you at your office," she said. "Or would you really prefer to have me telephone you at home to make arrangements for payment?"

Bauman thought of Ethel at home, perhaps picking up the telephone and hearing this girl's voice ask for him. Ethel was so touchy about things; she'd be sure to ask a million questions, and not to believe him even then, no matter what kind of denials he made. Fred Bauman's suddenly shattered world spun in dizzy pieces around him.

The girl was waiting. She sat there with bare red-tipped breasts showing. There was something dreamlike about the casual display of her nudity, just as there had been something dreamlike about the sizzling, unforgettable moment of passion in which he had taken her.

She had him. He didn't even have room to wiggle.

"Come on," she said. "I don't have all night. Give me your card."

"Here it is," Bauman said in a harsh whisper. He took one of his cards out of his wallet and shoved it at her. She grinned at him and pocketed it.

"Thanks, sucker."

She drew the sides of her blouse together and closed the raincoat over it. Then she unlocked the door, sprang lightly out, and trotted off into the darkness. In a moment she was out of sight.

Bauman's first thought was for the buttons. That girl's blouse buttons, scattered all over the car. What if Ethel saw them?

He got the flashlight out of the glove compartment and got down on his hands and knees and hunted around for the brown buttons. One, two, three, four—was that all of them, he wondered? He didn't see any others. To hell with the buttons, Bauman thought. Straightening up, Bauman flung the buttons out the window, into the night.

Suddenly he realized that he had very much more serious problems now than the explaining away of strange buttons on the floor of his car.

The rain was still coming down.

CHAPTER TWO

Shivering a little in the cold rain, Joanne hurried through the quiet streets toward the subway. She grinned as she remembered the sight of the sucker's face as the bite finally sank into him.

"What a dope," she thought. "What a goop!"

She pulled her raincoat close around herself. Glancing down, she eyed the front of her blouse, wondering how much bosom was going to show as she rode in the subway. The idiot had pulled off all her buttons! She hadn't expected that. And she was without a bra, too.

She didn't wear underclothes on expeditions like this. They got in the way at crucial moments. At least once, a promising setup had been spoiled because she was wearing panties when she shouldn't have been. But she hadn't bargained for losing her buttons. The plastic raincoat didn't hide much. She'd have to keep herself tucked together on the way home, and not let a boob or two go peeping out into view. The last thing she wanted was to get picked up by a cop for indecent exposure or vagrancy or some crazy thing like that.

With luck, she wouldn't. She might draw some stares on the subway, but she figured she could keep things together for a while.

She reached the subway. She dropped a token in the slot. She went out on the platform and waited. It was a pretty lonely platform. She could stand here with her bare boobs hanging out, she thought, and nobody was likely to come along and point a finger. But she kept covered up, all the same. Ten minutes went by, and two or three people appeared and joined her on the platform. Then a train for Manhattan arrived.

Joanne got into the first car and stood by the window looking out. That way she didn't have to worry too much about the parts of her that showed. Her chest ached a little. She hadn't had enough to be fulfilled, of course. Just a couple of minutes of clumsy shoving and mauling. So she was uncomfortable now. Bauman had excited her by necking with her and then by having her, but he hadn't given her satisfaction, and so she was still a little excited.

What the devil, Joanne thought. She could stand a little discomfort at that price.

Besides, in half an hour she'd be home, and there'd be someone stopping over to fix her up and give her what she needed most now.

She thought about Fred Bauman as the train zoomed toward the city. The poor twerp. Not a bad-looking guy, really. But he had that worried, harried look that you got when you were married too long. Probably he had a mortgage to wrestle with, and a wife who wanted furs and trips to Europe, and kids who needed ballet lessons and teeth-straightening jobs and eight weeks of camp in the summer—

Well, now Fred Bauman had a new expense on his back. A big one.

Joanne didn't really think she'd collect five thousand dollars from Bauman. That was just a convenient figure to name. Her experience in this sort of thing told her rather that she was more likely to get eleven or twelve hundred dollars or so before the mark rebelled. Still, that was pretty good money. And there were ways of keeping the deal alive. You didn't need to strike many marks a year in order to keep yourself ahead of expenses.

It was a living, Joanne thought.

And fun, besides. In a way.

She grinned at her reflection in the mirror. Then she shivered a little. She was cold in her light clothing, and she missed having underwear on. The train barreled along. Her breasts ached.

She was twenty-three years old. It had been a pretty busy life for not so very many years of existence, all things considered. She had gone on her own at the age of sixteen, when her mother died. She had already been pretty experienced at that age. Since then she had been mixed up in a variety of enterprises. She had worked for a year as a stripper, and she had worked for eleven months as a dime-a-dance girl in a 48th Street emporium. She had also put in a stint of close to a year as a plain old streetwalking prostitute, which had been the most profitable of all, but she had hated that life too much to continue.

She had had other adventures, too. She had done some Lesbian stuff, and she had been for six months the mistress of a masochist who had to be whipped before he could enjoy the act of love, and she had been for at least one night the mistress of a sadist who preferred to be the whipper and not the whippee. Joanne hadn't cared much for that gig, and she had never gone back.

Now she was in the fake rape business. She was a professional blackmailer. It meant some scenes with strange men, but she didn't mind that—at least, not on an occasional basis. She couldn't stand to peddle herself five times a night, but that was different. Love now was just incidental to the main operation of trapping suckers and making them cough it up.

It was a living, Joanne thought.

A very healthy living—cash-wise, at least.

The train pulled into the Times Square Station. Joanne got out and went up the stairs, and then up the next stairs, and up still more stairs, and out into the street. Her breasts, bare beneath the buttonless blouse, jiggled as she hopped up the stairs. She kept her raincoat clutched tight at the bosom for the sake of preserving her modesty. You could get away with a lot in Times Square, but you couldn't walk around with your boobs showing, for sure.

It was still raining. Somehow, here, amid all the gaiety and neon brightness of Times Square, the storm didn't matter so much. You didn't have the forlorn, dark, soaked-to-the-skin feeling that you got from standing around over near the Queensboro Bridge approach, or out in Queens. Here, the life and vigor made the rain seem almost imaginary. People still walked around on 42nd Street, though they walked a little faster than they would have in good weather.

Even so, you could get wet. Plenty wet. Joanne hustled along, up to 45th Street, and turned west. Rain came into the collar of her raincoat and worked its way under her blouse to her nude breasts. She felt cold raindrops crawling along her nipples. She shivered. The sensation wasn't altogether unpleasant, though. Her breasts were bruised and sore from the excitement of the rape, and the cool trickle of rain tended to soothe them.

She crossed Ninth Avenue and went into her building, a ramshackle tenement that had seen better days when Teddy Roosevelt was in the White House. Joanne didn't mind living in a beaten-up old dump, on a fourth-floor walkup. Her mind wasn't attuned to luxury. She didn't need—the way some call girls seemed to need—the $500-a-month apartment near Sutton Place, the fancy dresses, the posh sports car. She was content to take the subway, to live in a $60-a-month dive, to wear simple clothing that she could buy in Macy's or Klein's or Alexander's. What was money for? Money, thought Joanne, was for stashing away in the bank, against a time when you weren't pretty enough or alluring enough to earn it in the ways you were accustomed to earning it.

She had a lot of money stashed away, for a girl of twenty-three. Four different bank accounts, including one out in California. She wasn't exactly a rich girl, but she had a nest egg, and the nest egg grew every week by a few dollars. Joanne had seen how a girl could come apart at the seams at forty-five, or forty, or sometimes even thirty-five. It was handy to have something put by.

She let herself into her apartment. Not much of a place, just two rooms. "Buddy?" she called. "Buddy, you here?"

No answer. Nobody home. Joanne looked at her watch. Past ten o'clock. He was usually here by this time. But maybe he had stopped off somewhere to wait for the rain to stop. He wore expensive suits, and he didn't like to get them rained on.

Closing the door behind her, Joanne walked through the combined living room and kitchen and into her bedroom. She glanced at herself in the mirror, and laughed.

"You look like a wet poodle." she said to herself.

Her hair, usually fluffy, was straight and slicked down and dripping. Her face was wet. She looked like something the cat had dragged in.

She went into the bathroom took her raincoat off, and hung it up over the radiator. The view underneath wasn't much better. Her blouse hung wide open, and the pale curving flesh beneath was damp with the rain that had crept through the raincoat. The blouse was a mess—torn as well as missing buttons—and there were some marks on her flesh where Fred Bauman's lust-panicky hands had grabbed her too hard. Joanne shrugged, took the blouse off, and threw it onto the rag pile. It wasn't worth repairing. She wriggled out of her wet skirt and draped it over the radiator to dry.

Naked, she confronted herself in the mirror.

The view wasn't bad. She was tall, just a shade over medium height at five feet seven. She had a good bosom, with deep, steep-rising breasts tipped with small reddish-brown nipples rising out of smooth dark aureoles. Below the double thrust of her bosom, Joanne's body was lean and taut until the sudden ripeness of her hips, broad and flaring and sensual. She had good buttocks, she knew, firm and succulent, and her legs had always been first-rate. It was the kind of body that men found attractive, to say the least.

She was *built*.

Smiling appreciatively at herself, she fluffed out her hair and wrung some of the water out of it. The gesture of lifting her arms made her breasts rise all the more steeply, the tips pointing ceilingward. Joanne liked the effect. She spread her hands out over her breasts for a moment, cupping them and squeezing them. Then she began to move the twin mounds of taut flesh in a slow rotary motion, rubbing them against each other.

That sent sensations of excitement through her. She let out her breath in a low hiss, and pressed her knees tight together, and closed her eyes till they were only slits of smoldering lust.

She wanted him. She needed him. Not wild groping in a parked car, but the real thing, loving on the scale that a woman could appreciate.

She would just have to be patient a little while longer, she told herself. Buddy would be here soon. Buddy would take care of her.

She stepped into the cracked, yellowing shower tub and turned the water on. Warm. The best antidote for the cold shower she had had before, out all evening in a miserable lousy rainstorm, was a hot shower now. The faucet sputtered and reluctantly began to disgorge hot water. Joanne laughed, began to sing.

"I've been working on the railroad,
All the live-long day
I've been working on the railroad—"

Her husky voice rang in the small bathroom. As she sang, Joanne soaped herself up. She soaped her breasts, her legs, her buttocks, and rubbed vigorously. She wanted to be fresh and clean and sweet-smelling when Buddy arrived. Nothing but the best for Buddy, she thought.

Hot water pattered against her breasts and waist. She turned her face upward and let the water hit her lips and eyelids. It ran down her body.

"There," she thought. "Now I feel better!"

She stepped out of the shower and toweled herself dry, going at it good and hard, until her flesh gleamed a rosy pink. Her breasts jiggled wildly as she put the towel across her buttocks and yanked it rapidly from side to side. She dried herself off, and then, pink and fresh and well-scrubbed and naked, she stepped out of the bathroom and went into her living room.

A man stood there.

Joanne wasn't surprised. Buddy had a key of his own, and he came and went as he pleased. Now he stood in the middle of the living room, a dapper and handsome figure, helping himself to some of her Scotch. As she walked into the room, he smiled at her and looked her over from head to toe, eyeing her naked body appreciatively.

"Hi there, keed," he said. His voice was deep, resonantly virile. "You're a sight for sore eyes in that birthday suit of yours, you know that?"

"You just get here, Buddy?"

"Five seconds ago."

"What took you so long?"

He lifted an eyebrow. "What do you mean, so long? It's only quarter past ten."

"You said you'd be here at quarter of."

"So what's half an hour?" He laughed amiably. He was a big man, six feet three, and he dressed with crisp Ivy League elegance. He looked like a stockbroker, like a television executive, like a banker—like anything but the part-time procurer and full-time hoodlum that he was. "How about a kiss hello?" he asked.

"Sure," Joanne said. "Come and get it."

He put the bottle down and walked toward her. His big arms enfolded her. He still had the chill of the rainy outdoors on his clothing, and as his jacket touched the tips of her breasts, Joanne shivered a little. He ran his hands down her bare back to the ripe globes of her buttocks and gripped them firmly as he pulled her close.

His hands were cold too. So was his belt buckle against her warm flesh. But the moment he put his lips to hers, Joanne felt the climate beginning to change.

She clung to him. He was sure, strong, masterful. No clumsy, uncertain kiss like Fred Bauman's, but a lingering, passionate fiery kiss. She let her breasts crush against his cold lapels. Her nipples grew rigid again and began to ache with need. Her body moved against his, aware of the power of him disguised by the dapper suit. After a moment he let go of her, and she stepped back, a little dizzy, her head pounding. Buddy had always had the power to set her on fire with a single kiss, even a single glance, the way no other man ever had.

A little shakily, Joanne crossed the room and sank down on the old couch. The corrugated upholstery rubbed against the bare skin of her back and buttocks, but she didn't mind that, never had.

"You want a drink?" he asked her.

"As long as you're pouring."

"As long as it's your booze," he said. He poured her a good healthy shot of Scotch, ran some water from the tap into the glass, and brought it over to her. He sat down next to her on the couch. He was still fully dressed, jacket and tie and all, and Joanne was completely naked. She found it exciting to be sitting there naked when he still had all his clothes on. Her body ached with need. But she held herself in check. Let him make the first move, she thought. Right now she needed the Scotch, too. She took a long, deep drink and let out her breath in satisfaction.

"Well?" he said. "How did it go tonight?"

"Good."

"You mean you found someone?"

"I sure did," she said. "I think I shot me a bullseye tonight, Buddy."

He grinned. "No fooling! Do tell!"

"There was this guy in the car at the approach to the 59th Street Bridge," she said. "Name of Fred Bauman. Sort of maybe fortyish, married-looking type. Picked me up, took me over the bridge. He wanted me so bad I could practically hear him saying so. We parked the car and I pawed him a little and then he took me."

"You work the rape routine like I told you?"

Joanne nodded. "What else? I got him all eager, and then I tried to cut him off. Naturally he was like a wild man. Ripped all the buttons off my blouse, the stinker. He took me and then I took *him*, with the blackmail pitch, right between the eyes."

"What did you ask for?"

"Five."

"C's?"

"You joking? Five g's, Buddy."

"Think you'll get it?"

"Who knows? I'll get something out of him, that I'm sure of. I've got his business card. I'll call him tomorrow and put the needles into him."

Buddy grinned. He moved closer to her on the couch and slipped his arm around her shoulders, passing it all the way around so that his hand came out over her far-side breast. His hand was big, even bigger than her breast, so that he could cup practically the whole fleshy globe. He grasped it gently, then not so gently. Joanne caught her breath as excitement stirred for her.

"You're a smart little cookie," he said.

"Am I?"

"My best pupil. You're an ace, keed."

"I bet you say that to all the girls."

"That's unkind."

"Is it? Who were you with tonight, Buddy?"

"I deny that accusation!" he said with a look of innocence. "I come to you with clean hands!"

"Sure you do," Joanne said. "But you've still got a black heart."

"Come on, come on—"

"I know you're cheating on me," she said, half seriously, half teasingly.

"Me? Why would I do a thing like that?"

"Because you're a wolf, that's why."

"Listen," he said, "I'll prove to you that I haven't been to bed with anybody since I was last with you. Let's go to bed and I'll love you, and you'll see I haven't done any loving all day. Obviously, if I'd loved anybody else today, I'd be too exhausted to be any good for you."

"Obviously," she said with heavy sarcasm, "That's why I've seen you take me three, four times the same night. Because you tire easily."

"Well, can I help it if you're suspicious?" he said. He finished his drink and put the glass down. He waited moment until Joanne had finished her drink too, and took the glass from her. Then he turned to her. His arms went around her. His lips went to her mouth, and then to each of her breasts in turn, and in a moment she was gasping and panting in ecstasy.

"Come on," she whispered hoarsely.

They ran into the bedroom. She helped him out of his clothing, and he carefully draped everything over a chair. He was so fussy about the creases in his clothes, she thought, as he got out of them.

Then he was naked. His lean, hairy body moved toward hers.

They tumbled down together onto the bed.

Joanne closed her eyes. She gave her lips to him, and he kissed her with a direct, hard, brutal pressure of mouth to mouth. Joanne twisted and gasped and panted.

His hands were roaming her, now. Touching her, exploring her, setting her on fire. Cunning fingertips toying with the soft flesh.

She was wild for him, now.

It didn't take much to excite her. Especially after her escapade in the car. Now she was hungry for him, famished for him. Her body began to tremble and shake.

He reached for her. He pulled her to him. Her arms opened.

He took her.

Joanne gasped in pleasure. That moment was like the sudden crescendo of a symphonic orchestra within her brain, a blare of sensation that radiated dazzlingly over her entire being. Her body began to move with his. His hard, flat chest crushed the tender globes of her breasts. She loved that.

He got his hands under her buttocks. Squeezed the firm cheeks.

Harder, faster.

Ecstasy blazed for her. Her body pinwheeled and went wild, twisted and flailed. She moved in a wild, crazy dance of passion to the drumbeat of encroaching delight, a savage, fierce melody of ecstasy.

Then the moment of total bliss arrived. Colors blazed behind Joanne's closed eyelids, and skyrocketing passions zoomed over her. Somewhere far away, distantly, she heard the hoarse grunts of his pleasure, and then she knew that he too was experiencing the ecstasy, and she was happy for him but happier for herself, because of the power and drive of what she had experienced.

Afterward, they lay still. Side by side, his arm around her, his body touching hers, his big hand spread out over the hillock of her breast.

Joanne felt content. Fulfilled. Radiant. It was wonderful, she thought, how the right man could light up your entire body, give you thrills far beyond anything you ever dreamed was possible. Joanne had slept with who-knew-how-many hundreds of men in her short life, even some women, too, yet none of them had ever turned her on the way Buddy Castillo did.

Which was why she put up with the things he made her put up with.

Which was why she was willing to give him money.

Which was why she was willing to take almost anything from him—so long as he was coming back, and giving her more of what she craved.

He reached across her for the pack of cigarettes that lay on the nightstand. He took one from the pack and put it in his mouth.

"Light one for me," Joanne said.

"Sure, baby." He took another, touched it to the tip of the first, then popped it between her lips. He squeezed one of her breasts affectionately. Joanne lay back against the pillows, feeling relaxed and happy now. She wondered how Fred Bauman felt about things at this precise moment. Outside, cold rain beat against the dirty window panes.

"So you lined up another sucker today," he said after a while. "Good girl."

"Another day, another dollar."

"Speaking of which, did you collect from your guy Miller today?"

Sid Miller was one of Joanne's other blackmail victims. He had kicked through with plenty so far—and she wasn't through with him yet.

"Yeah," she said. "I collected."

"You cash it?"

"Yep."

Buddy leaned closer to her. He ran his free hand down the length of her body, lingering for a moment over the smoothness of her waist, over the satiny tenderness of her hips. His expert fingers reawakened the slumbering desires in her. Joanne felt passion trembling in her nude form, and she knew that soon he would have her again, and that she would feel new rapture in his arms.

He said, "I need about thirty bucks, baby. Can you spare it?"

"Sure, Buddy."

"I need it tonight."

"The money's in the top dresser drawer," she told him, as his hands moved in narrowing circles around her slender waist as he moved to kiss her, beginning the passion-game anew. "You just help yourself, Buddy. You know that you can have anything you want from me. Anything. *Anything.*"

CHAPTER THREE

Numbed by what had happened to him, Bauman pulled the car away from the curb and drove shakily off homeward. Only now, minutes after the girl had left him, Bauman was fully beginning to realize what had actually taken place. Even if he hadn't sensed it earlier, the girl's final words—*"Thanks, sucker!"* gave the whole show away.

The entire thing had been rigged.

Bauman saw it all now. The girl had been waiting there by the bridge approach in the rain—how long? half an hour, maybe?—for a man driving alone to come along in a car and offer to pick her up. Once she was safely inside the car, she had made use of a series of skillful questions to find out whether he was married or not, what his name was, where he lived. Meanwhile she had been moving closer and closer to him, exciting him.

Then she had stirred him to action with an intimate caress, a long, lingering kiss—and by refusing at the critical moment to let him consummate his passions, she had cunningly led him on to commit what had actually been an act of rape.

But her attitude was completely businesslike right afterward. The rape hadn't shaken her up at all. Forthrightly, she had asked for money—a tremendous amount of money—and she had taken his business card, so she'd know where to find him and haunt him.

That had all been rigged.

He had been played for a fool.

And it was going to cost him five thousand dollars.

That was the chilling, numbing, jolting, killing fact that hit Bauman like a meat cleaver in the skull. Five thousand dollars! If he didn't pay, she'd go to the police with her rape story, and who was going to believe his side of it?

He would lose his job, his wife, his home. Everything. He would go to jail.

Thirty-eight years of quiet, law-abiding life, Bauman thought. And everything undone because some shrewd girl with the morals of a snake climbs into your car and uses you as the unknowing, unwitting actor in an unrehearsed little drama of passion.

As he drove, Bauman gripped the cold plastic of the steering wheel tightly with aching fingers. He reviewed the whole scene over and over again in his mind, seeing the white hills of her bare breasts with their rosy tips, the smooth columns of her legs, the taut youthful flatness of her waist, the moist fullness of her lips. He realized now how this had been done to him, how she had led him on, how she had artfully inflamed him into committing this one mad act that marred all the structure of the life that had gone before.

He realized that if he had any brains he would have smelled something peculiar right at the outset. If she was going all the way out to Jamaica—far toward the eastern end of the borough—as she had told him, what in creation was she doing walking across the Queensboro Bridge in the rain? Did she intend to walk the miles and miles to Jamaica? Of course not.

She didn't intend to walk anywhere.

She had just been lying in wait, like a black widow spider crouching and waiting for its prey to come along down the garden path.

Well, he had come along. And now the spider's fangs were hooked deep in his throat.

Keeping his eyes fixed to the road in front of him, he drove slowly home. He got there about twenty minutes to ten. The rain had doubled its intensity, hammering malevolently on the hood of his car. Bauman parked the car outside the apartment building where he lived and went upstairs, to the four-room apartment where he and Ethel had lived for all the seventeen years of their married life.

His hand shook a little as he turned the key and let himself in.

"Fred, that you?" Ethel called.

"Yeah," he said, his voice ragged and hard to keep under control. "It's me."

She was sitting in the living-dining room, wearing an old housecoat, watching television. *Ben Casey*. She was the world's biggest *Ben Casey* fan, Bauman sometimes thought. He looked at his wife with new eyes when he came in. She was thirty-six years old. He had never thought of her as being particularly old, but she was middle-aged, almost, from the viewpoint of the girl he had picked up and raped this evening.

It was a little hard for Bauman to remember the slim, passionate nineteen-year-old girl that he had married so long ago. Ethel's hair, once a lovely auburn, was starting to go gray around the edges. She was getting a little plump and the skin around her throat was loosening up a bit. She was still an attractive woman Bauman thought, but he found himself automatically adding the qualification, *for her age*. Ethel was getting along. The bloom of youth was off her now. She wasn't the teenager he had married.

Bauman hadn't really noticed any of these things before. He had simply accepted the little signs of aging as being—part of, well, Ethel. After all, he wasn't the same hotshot he'd been seventeen years ago, either. The years had worn him down just as they ground everyone else between the turning millstones.

Now Bauman found himself comparing his pleasant plumpish, thirty-sixish wife to that slim, hungry, lean-waisted, taut-breasted girl he had encountered that evening. No matter what that was going to cost him, he thought, it was almost worth it just to have held that girl and squeezed her firm cool breasts and—

Bauman felt a tingle of shock at what he was thinking. He hung up his damp coat in the hall closet and walked into the living room. It seemed to him that the signs of his guilt gleamed like searchlights all over him. The scarlet letter and so on.

But Ethel looked up from the shimmering screen only for an instant, to smile at him and say, "Did you work hard today, dear?"

"Yeah," Bauman said thickly. "It was a tough day, Ethel. I'm beat."

He dropped down into the soft chair near the window and eased his shoes off. His whole body ached. There was a stiffness and a soreness in his back from the cramped position he had had to take with the girl in his car. He was still aware of some of that pounding, violent moment of passionate action.

He tried to relax.

Five thousand dollars, he thought. That was a pretty damn expensive thrill.

Five thousand dollars! What will I ever do?

That was a good question. But he had no good answers to it.

He sat there limply, staring at the screen without actually making any sense out of the flickering images. The tension didn't ebb from him. It stayed right where it was, a cold lump in his chest.

Ten o'clock came. The program ended, and Ethel's hypnosis broke. She got up, turned the television set off. Her housecoat fell apart a little way as she leaned forward to snap the knob, and as she turned around Bauman saw some of her bosom. She had full, heavy pale breasts. Maybe too much bosom, now. Starting to get a little flabby—just a little. Ethel had always had wonderful breasts, full and firm and round. He would never forget the feeling of pure joy that surged through him the first time he opened her blouse and saw her breasts, white and perfect by moonlight. He had been twenty years old, and the moment he had seen those two snowy hills of flesh, he had known he was going to marry her.

Almost half a lifetime had gone by since then. And now he was an adulterer. A rapist. A blackmail victim.

She said, "Should I make a snack for you, Fred?"

"Don't bother. Where's Karen?"

"In her room, doing homework."

"Can't she come out to say hello when her father comes home?"

Ethel shrugged. "She probably didn't hear you come in. You know how it is with high school kids—they're all wrapped up in themselves. Anyhow, she's got studying to do. Midterm exams next week, or something."

"All right," Bauman said. He pulled himself up out of the armchair. "I'll say good night to her myself. I'm going to bed."

"It's only ten o'clock, Fred."

"I can't help that. It was a long, rough day. I'm knocked out. I want to get some sleep."

Five thousand dollars, he thought numbly. *Five thousand dollars!*

Karen Bauman lay sprawled out across her bed, flat on her stomach, staring at her Spanish textbook and trying to make some sense out of irregular verbs.

She muttered in a low voice:

"*Tuve.*"

"*Tuviste.*"

"*Tuvo.*"

"*Tuvimos.*"

"*Tuvisteis—*"

It was no use. She couldn't keep them straight in her mind. Karen had the uneasy feeling that she was going to flunk the upcoming exam, and not just flunk it by a couple of points. She was going to bomb.

It scared her. She had always been a good student, an honor roll student, right at the top of the class. Now she was in real danger of flunking two of her courses, and she wasn't exactly doing well in the other three.

Men, she thought.

Men. That was the whole trouble. That was why she couldn't keep her mind on her schoolwork.

Karen was fifteen years old. She was a short girl, only five feet three, but she doubted that she was going to grow any taller, because her body was already fully developed. She had the lush, ripely mature figure of an adult. Her breasts were heavy but firm, so taut and well-muscled that when she was naked they jutted out straight instead of drooping and dangling the way some big-breasted girls did. Her hips were broad, her legs solid, her buttocks voluptuously feminine.

And she was still a virgin.

All this voluptuous maturity had come to Karen quite recently. She hadn't even started to develop until she was about thirteen, when some of the other girls she knew had been wearing brassieres for more than a year and a half. Those were the days when she had been a skinny bookworm, making up for the flaws in her figure by academic success.

Then her body had started coming on like gangbusters. She would never forget that dizzy year of growth, that year of seemingly endless change, as her body blossomed and bulged and firmed. It was the springtime of her womanhood, a year of growing pains.

She wasn't growing anymore. The violent growth had tapered off. Now she was as she would be in adulthood, full-breasted and full-hipped, a strikingly handsome redhead with a graceful posture, fluid motions, a voluptuous come-hither sort of body. Hers was a body made for love.

But Karen hadn't had any yet. It was all too new, this body of hers. She was too young. She was bursting with new desires, but she felt that she had to move slowly into this strange world of flesh.

She simmered with needs. She could hardly sleep at night, but lay awake, dreaming of what it was like to lie naked with a boy, to want him and to know that he wanted you, to participate with him in the mysterious, delightful adult act of love. In imagination, Karen had been had a thousand times. In actuality, nary a once.

Her schoolwork was suffering. She was confused and troubled by her body's needs, and it was impossible, during this time of torment, for her to concentrate on Spanish irregular verbs. She wanted to do well in school, and go on to college, Radcliffe or Bennington, one of the better schools. But right now college was ages away, and her needs were immediate and insistent.

She lay flopped out on the bed, peering hopelessly at the lists of irregular verbs. Karen was wearing a pair of old pajamas, pajamas left over from her thirteenth year. They were about four sizes too small on her now, and clung to her body shamelessly, molding the contours of breasts and legs, hips and buttocks. They were filled to seam-splitting abundance. Her mother had told her to give them to the next charity drive, but Karen had refused. She liked to wear them. She liked the feeling of tightness, the almost straitjacket-like snugness of the pajamas. She liked the way they hugged her buttocks and her legs and her aching-nippled breasts. She enjoyed the very discomfort of the tight pajamas.

Her head swam with thoughts of passion. She bit her lip, went on muttering Spanish:

"*Ponga.*
"*Pongas.*
"*Pongamos—*
"*Ponga.*"

There was a knock at the door, breaking the stream of her thoughts. "Come in," she called.

Her father pushed the door open. Karen flipped over, aware of her undignified buttock-upward position. She felt a little flustered this way, with the heavy apples of her breasts jutting against the taut-stretched fabric of her pajamas so hard that the nipples made an impress in the cloth. Her father seemed a little surprised by her immodest appearance too, because he quickly lifted his glance to her face.

"You just get home, Dad?"

"A little while ago. You didn't hear me come in?"

"I've been busy with these irregular verbs. They're driving me batty!"

"I never saw you have so much trouble in school before, Karen."

She shrugged. "I guess it just gets harder as you get older, or something. A person gets to have more problems as he goes along. You know how it is."

Fred Bauman nodded. "Yes." he said. "I know how it is, Karen."

His face looked lined and pale. Karen said, "You aren't sick or something, Dad?"

"Sick?"

"You look kind of worn out."

He smiled faintly "I worked late tonight. It gets harder as you get older, as you say. I'm tired, that's all. Nothing else. I'm going to sleep. Good night, Karen."

"Good night, Dad."

She got to her feet and padded to the door to kiss him good night, her breasts going bounce-bounce-bounce under the pajamas as she walked across the floor. She was very self-conscious about the good night kisses, these days. When she was younger, she used to hug him and kiss him on the lips, but Karen felt that it wasn't quite right to do that anymore, not with these big breasts of hers sticking out, and now that she was old enough to have men and all.

So she kissed him chastely on the cheek. Close up, she could see the strain and worry on his face. She wondered, as he went out of the room, whether something special was eating him. It wasn't like him to look so troubled.

The door closed.

Karen flopped down on the bed again, and peered gloomily at the Spanish book. After fifteen minutes more, she knew she was going to have to give it up as a bad job, at least for tonight. Her head was swimming. She couldn't concentrate. The most useful thing she could do now was to go to bed.

Besides, there were special attractions offered by going to bed.

Bedtime was the time of day she most enjoyed, these days.

She cleaned up her schoolbooks, getting everything ready for the morning. Then he ducked into the bathroom to brush her teeth and shine up her face a little. Finally, she returned to the bedroom. She closed the door all the way, so that no sounds would escape her room. She snapped off the light.

She got into bed.

She lay there quietly in the darkness for perhaps five minutes, getting into the mood of things. It was a warm, mild, stickily humid night, and the rain pattering against her window helped to set a properly romantic tone for things. Karen closed her eyes.

She began to imagine.

There was someone climbing up the fire escape outside the building, she told herself, slipping easily into one of her most favorite fantasies. Someone handsome, someone clean-cut and agile. He was about nineteen years old, which made him old enough to have had some experience, but not so old that he was part of the strange, alien, adult world. In her fantasies, Karen had met him that afternoon, had been fascinated by him, had given him her address.

"Come to my bedroom at night," she imagined she had told him. "Climb up the fire escape. I'll leave the window open."

And now he was mounting the iron step, rung by rung. He was up to the fourth floor and crawling along the ledge toward her open window. And now he was swinging himself lightly through the window and into her bedroom. Karen began to stir and twist in the bed.

She let her hand go to her waist and tugged at the snap that held the pants of her pajamas together. It yielded. The pajama bottom popped open. Karen began slowly to push the top of her pajamas up, inch by inch, baring first her waist to the darkness, then the lower curves of her breasts, then the rigid, taut tips, then the entire swelling mounds of her breasts.

She lay there in the blackness feeling cooler air going across her sensitive nipple. Her pajama tops were around her throat now. In her mind's eye she could see the handsome stranger standing by her bed, looking and smiling as he stared at her bare breasts and told her how beautiful they were.

Now he was moving onto the bed.

She smiled. Her breath began to come a little faster. Her nostrils flared, and her breasts rose and fell more rapidly.

She lifted her right hand and poised it in the air. Then she brought it down.

Gently, slowly, she lowered it until it was at her left breast. She grasped the firm fleshy mound tightly, fingertips digging. She used her wrist to move the breast around, and then she brought her fingers inward until they had found the nub, holding firmly.

She began to gasp and pant.

To her fevered mind, the hand at her breast was the hand of the handsome stranger who had climbed through her window. It was his hand caressing her silken softness, it was his hand toying with the rigid tip, it was his hand cupping and hefting and savoring the full opulence. And now the other hand was there too, at the right breast. She crisscrossed her hands across her chest, taking a handful of flesh with each, pulling her breasts close together. There was a dull ache. She began to twist impatiently as the intensity of her need grew.

If there had been anyone in her bedroom with her, she knew, he would be drawing down her pajama bottoms, laying bare the smooth flesh of her legs. Then he would be stroking her knees, kissing her eager lips, making her ready for the ultimate passion. And then he would take her and she would dissolve in bliss.

But there was really no one there.

So Karen had to do all the work herself.

Slowly, languorously, she let one hand slip from her breasts across the satiny skin of her chest and waist to the pajama bottoms, brushing them away, baring her hips. She continued to envision her imaginary lover—how gentle he would be, yet how insistent.

He was ready now, and so was she.

The last moment of breathless anticipation. And then—he would take her.

Karen's young body trembled and tingled in ecstasies of passion. She held her own breast and all the while imagined the lean, hard masculine chest pressed to her, taking ...

Passion rose for her. This substitute was the best she could manage, under the circumstances, but over the last few months she had come to respond quickly and easily even in this second-best way. Her pulse pounded. Her brain reeled. Wild currents of ecstasy surged over her.

Her entire body began to move. Hips pistoning, her whole being churning and flailing in ever more violent movement. The bedsprings creaked. Could they hear her, in their bedroom down at the far end of the apartment? Most likely they were asleep by now. Karen hardly cared. She had her needs to care for.

She clamped her teeth tight on her lips now. She snorted for breath, rolled her head, squeezed her breast mercilessly. The moment of complete ecstasy was approaching, now. Closer ... closer ...

Yes!

Fulfillment surged through her. She shivered and shook and rocked as she was hit by wave after wave of pounding bliss. Which swept over her like the inexorable tides. That went on for a long moment.

And then ended.

Everything was over. Karen was alone, in the strange disappointed solitude that followed the supreme moment. Now was the moment of truth, the moment when all pretense ended, the moment when she realized that she was still a virgin, just a lonely, curious, eager fifteen-year-old in a darkened bedroom on a rainy night.

Still, even considering all that, she felt pretty good. At least the worst nagging of the inner need was done away with, for a while. Not for another day or two would the urge return to plague her. She had postponed a little of the anguish—until the time when it would be necessary to do this once again.

She was sweating from her exertions. The air blowing through her window cast a chill over her bare breasts, her waist, her legs. She pulled the pajama tops down and tucked them into the bottoms. She fastened the snap. She pulled the covers up as high as her ears, and settled against the pillow.

Her fantasy was fast fading now. Her mysterious imaginary lover had kissed her tenderly good night, and had slipped out, through the window, down the fire escape and into the darkness outside. She was alone. The fire had been quenched for a while.

She bit her lip in loneliness.

This wasn't a good enough substitute! That was the whole trouble. There were girls in her class who had more, she knew. They didn't have to give themselves pleasure this way. They could do things the right way, in the arms of a boy, doing the forbidden thing that Karen craved so desperately and so eagerly.

She knew the time was coming when her substitute love would no longer satisfy her. That time could not be very far off, either. She was fifteen. Her breasts were full. They ached with need. She wanted to give herself to a boy and find the great jolt of ecstasy that only a true loving could provide.

Soon, she promised herself. Soon.

Very soon.

She closed her eyes. She tried to imagine, for a moment, what that would be like—the real thing. Would that hurt? Make her cry? Would she really enjoy love as much as she hoped she would?

Questions. Too many questions. Life was a mystery. Growing up frightened her.

She pulled the covers even higher. After a while, sleep took her.

CHAPTER FOUR

Sid Miller picked up the cognac bottle, scientifically poured an inch and a quarter of cognac into the snifter, and nodded in satisfaction. He put the bottle down, grasped the snifter, cupping it in his hands to warm it and make fumes rise from the cognac.

He walked slowly over to the window and looked out at rainswept New York. It was a good view. His apartment was on the seventeenth floor of a plush new co-op on Central Park South, and from where he stood he could see the long dark strip of the park, stretching for three miles or so in front of him to the remote place where it met the slums up near the edge of Harlem. Lights formed a gay ribbon through the park, marking out the circular roadway that ran around it. To the right, Miller could see the upper-bracket splendor of residential Fifth Avenue. On the left was the slightly seedy but still impressive array of old apartment buildings on Central Park West. From the window, Miller could see billions of dollars of real estate, and the apartments of people who themselves were worth untold millions of dollars.

Somehow, he didn't find that a very cheering thought at this moment. Because he had been a pretty well-heeled man himself, with a six-figure bank account, a safe bulging with stocks and bonds, and a table reserved for him every night at one of New York's most elegant restaurants, not to mention his $5,000 apartment on Central Park South and his glamorous, jewel-bedecked blonde wife.

Well, he still had the apartment. It was mortgaged right up to the hilt, but he still had it.

That was about all he had.

The bank account was a joke. The stocks and bonds had long since been sold. The blonde wife was down in Florida, collecting $1200 a month in alimony from him and spending it on lawyer's fees to make his life even more miserable than it already was. As for the elegant restaurant, he had run up a tab of close to a thousand bucks there, and didn't dare set foot in the place now for fear that they might oh-so-gently hint that they'd like to see some dough out of him.

As if all that weren't bad enough, Miller was a blackmail victim. A sexy, long-stemmed cutie name of Joanne was hitting him up for a hundred bucks a week, and that was really killing him. He was breaking his back to make those payments, digging down deep.

But he couldn't stop. If he ever cut off the blackmail boodle, Joanne would hurt him in the worst way anybody could possibly hurt Sid Miller.

She would make him lose the part-time custody of his kids.

Right now, Alice had the three kids six months out of the year, and Miller had them the rest of the time. Alice had tried to get year-round custody, but Miller had fought it and had been able to win. Alice's case was that since he was an adulterer and a general lowlife, he had no right to be allowed to raise small kids. Miller's lawyer had built up an elaborate case to prove that, whatever Miller's past sins were, he was a virtuous and law-abiding citizen who deserved the right to bring up his own children. The judge had agreed. Even though the marriage had been dissolved, custody would be divided.

That had been a big victory for Miller.

But what would happen if this Joanne Harris now came forward and said a thing or two to Alice's lawyer? Suppose she said, "I have documentary proof that even while Mrs. Miller's ex-husband was telling the judge how virtuous he was, even while the divorce trial was going on, he was having relations with me practically every night—and he was carrying on in a pretty unnatural way."

What then?

Alice would start a new custody suit. And with Joanne as chief witness, she'd win. Miller would never get to see his kids again.

He had known, at the time that he got himself involved with Joanne, that there was potential danger in it for him. He couldn't help himself. He needed a woman. The tension of the divorce trial was too much for him. Miller couldn't live like a monk while that was going on; his business affairs were collapsing at about the same time, and the double strain was driving him crazy.

So he took a mistress—right in the middle of the divorce trial. He picked this Joanne girl up in midtown Manhattan, and brought her home, and told her what he wanted her to do for him, and she did. And continued for week after week.

Miller hadn't dared to tell his lawyer about Joanne. How could he, when the lawyer was standing up there in court every day bragging about his client's virtue? So now that he was in a mess, he couldn't run and ask his lawyer to get him out of it. This was something of his own doing, and he was stuck with it, and nobody else was going to help him.

If only he hadn't let Joanne in on the truth about his situation, everything still might have worked out all right. But, thinking it was for his own protection, he had told her the truth. Sincerity is always the best policy, so they said.

"Look," he had told her. "I'm mixed up in a tough divorce suit and it could be murder for me if my wife's lawyers found out I'm carrying on with a girl. You've got to be absolutely hush-hush about this. When you come visit me, come up the freight elevator so the doorman won't see you. And don't mention my name to anybody for any reason at all. Okay?"

"Of course," she had said. "I understand."

Sure she understood. She understood terrifically. She had waited until the divorce trial was over and until the custody decision had been made. Then—while Miller was still way up in the clouds, jubilant because the judge had given him custody half the year—Joanne let him have it. She wanted a hundred bucks a week to keep silent. Otherwise, she'd let Alice's lawyer have the full story, with dates, affidavits, the works.

Her voice had been sweetly matter-of-fact as she dropped her bombshell. Miller had known there was no escaping. The clever little witch!

In the old days, a hundred bucks a week wouldn't have mattered a bit to him. He spent more than that on cognac a week, for himself and his friends. What was a lousy hundred?

Nothing, then. Plenty, now.

Miller was in the real estate business. He was a developer, a builder. His specialty was putting up shopping centers in places like New Jersey and Long Island. He wasn't interested in operating the shopping centers: he just built them, got them rented, and sold them after a year or two. Not much of his own cash needed to be tied up in deals like that. He could get a whopping construction-money mortgage from the banks, because of his past reputation as a successful builder. So he'd erect the shopping center on perhaps fifty thousand bucks of his own money and a million from the bank. Then, after benefiting from juicy depreciation rates for a while, he'd find a syndicate of buyers who'd take the property off his hands for perhaps a quarter of a million more than it had cost him to build it. They assumed the mortgage, of course. He was out, free and clear, with a profit of two hundred g's or more on an investment of fifty grand—and all of it capital gain.

It was an excellent way to make a living—while it lasted.

Inside of eight years, Miller had made himself a millionaire a couple of times over, simply by building and selling shopping centers. Then had come the big stock market crash of 1962. He was on the verge of closing a good transaction when the market blew up. His buyer got cold feet.

Suddenly everybody had cold feet, all at once. Miller was getting margin calls on his own stock speculations, and he needed cash to settle up. Finally he had to dump a shopping center at a loss, simply to keep above water. That had saved him from bankruptcy proceedings, but it had also ruined his credit rating with the banks. He was no longer Sid

Miller the Magician. He was just another over-extended speculator.

They began to worry about those big loans. They started to call them in.

Miller had to sell things to satisfy them. One bank simply took possession of a center, eating up an investment of 65,000 of Miller's money. He had to get rid of his stocks, his bonds, his private holdings, his savings account—bit by bit, he had to give up everything that could be liquidated.

The carnage was just about over, now. Miller was down to rock bottom. He had sold off everything but a few tiny properties, and whatever he had was mortgaged. Right now he was living off money that he had stashed away in a Swiss bank account; each month he withdrew a couple of thousand, and made that do. But it was melting away fast. Joanne's weekly blackmail take didn't improve matters any.

Miller still had hopes of getting started again. All he needed was one banker with faith in him.

He had made the rounds, seeing them all. "Look," he kept saying, "I'm down, but I'm not out. I didn't go into bankruptcy, did I? I met all my obligations one hundred cents on the dollar. Was it my fault that the market crashed just when I was over-extended? If it had crashed in November instead of May, I'd have been home free with millions of dollars in capital. Will you back me on a new project? Will you let me get started again?"

So far he had a lot of sympathy but nothing else. You couldn't build real estate with sympathy. Miller was discovering a bitter fact of financial life: money goes to money. When you're riding high, the bankers flock around to lend you all you need. When you're on the floor, they stomp on you to make it a little worse.

Time was running out. Those Swiss accounts wouldn't last forever. Pretty soon he'd be penniless. Then what? Go to work as a bookkeeper? Find somebody to take him in out of pity at eight grand a year?

Miller shook his head sadly. He downed his cognac, peered out gloomily at the rainy city outside.

The doorbell chimed. A delicate, tinkling, moneyed chime. The chime was mortgaged, but at least he could still listen to its soothing sound.

He went to the door.

A girl stood there, smiling at him. She was stunning. She was a leggy blonde, close to six feet tall, but delicate and fragile-looking. She was about twenty-one. Her eyes were blue, her eyebrows a thin arch, her nose high-bridged and slender, her lips firm, kissable. She was elegantly dressed in the highest East Side fashion, a slim, soft silk dress showed off the tapering flawlessness of her legs. Magnificent was the only word for her. A real thoroughbred. A girl with class.

"Mr. Jones?" she asked, in a polished, finishing-school voice.

"That's right. Come in."

"I'm Natalie," she said. "My, what a lovely apartment you have!"

"Thanks," Miller said.

He took her coat from her. She was an expensive girl, expensively dressed. Nothing but the best for him, even now. If he was going to go broke, Miller planned to do it in style, he figured.

It was costing him fifty bucks for this girl's services—for about two hours of her time. That was the standard fee. He used a number of different organizations. Having been bitten by the blackmail bug once, he didn't intend to let himself in for more trouble by getting involved on a regular basis with one girl. He never saw the same girl twice. It was too bad, in a way, because a lot of the girls were knockouts that he wouldn't have minded seeing again. On the other hand, this way he got plenty of variety in his life.

Even now, with his back to the wall, Miller couldn't let the girls alone. Once a week—or, when he felt he could splurge, twice a week—he had a girl visit him. She was always an elegant, refined, cultured-looking girl like this Natalie. And she did just what he wanted her to do, because that was how she earned her upper-bracket living.

"Would you care for a drink, Natalie?" Miller asked "Some cognac?"

"I'd love some," she said.

No sense rushing things. Miller poured drinks, and they sat down genteelly in the living room to sip them and chat a while. She sat on the couch, he on the facing armchair. Everything was done quite respectably. She was expert at small talk; that was one of her skills-in-trade, as much so as bed. A successful call girl had to know how to put the client at ease, how to provide a tone of respectability and propriety for the action. A call girl wasn't just a tramp, after all. You went to bed with a streetwalker in a quick, contemptuous way. A call girl made every trick a work of art.

Miller let about fifteen minutes slip by in relaxed chit-chat. Then he said, "Well, shall we—?"

"Of course," Natalie said.

They got to their feet. Miller liked tall girls. He was a big, rangy man of forty, with dark hair just starting to turn gray, and he had no use for any woman shorter than five feet five. Natalie qualified with inches to spare. She looked so young, he thought. Fresh out of Vassar, probably. But not a novice, by any means.

He got the whip from the closet. It was a flexible length of cane, with a little ivory handle at one end. Miller had paid a hundred and fifty dollars for it in happier days.

Natalie didn't flinch as he got it out. She had no way of knowing, of course, whether she was going to be beaten or going to do the beating, but her professional poise was capable of taking both in stride.

Miller smiled easily and said, giving the whip a few experimental whicks through the air, "You've used one of these before, haven't you?"

"Yes," she said. "Is there anything special you'd like me to do?"

"Just whip me. Until I yell, 'No more.' Then we'll love. I imagine you've had clients of my sort plenty of times."

Her smile was answer enough. She said, "Any preferences about my clothing?"

"Garter belt and stockings," he said. "Nothing else. Let's get undressed."

He didn't suggest that they go into separate rooms to strip; and so of course she began to peel right before him. Which was what Miller wanted. He undressed himself, keeping an eye on her as she stripped.

Like most girls of her trade, she made a fine art of the simple act out of taking her clothes off. Every motion was calculatedly graceful; every act a luscious one. Off came her blouse, to reveal a lovely yellow bra; off came her skirt, and the yellow half-slip. Her legs were long and shapely, slender and tapering away to tiny ankles. Miller liked his women to have that kind of leg.

The general slenderness of her frame didn't seem to have any harmful effects on the development of her bosom. The yellow bra came away to reveal two full, firm, high-crested breasts, very pale, very round, very good to look at and probably even better to touch. Smiling she artfully rolled her lacy panties down, to show a youthfully lean waist and two sensually globular buttocks.

She was a delectable dish, Miller thought.

She wore nothing now except her garter belt, cutting deep at the flesh of her hips and upper buttocks, and the sheer nylon stockings that set off the tapering flawlessness of her legs. High spike heels completed the outfit.

Perfect, Miller told himself. Absolutely perfect.

He looked her over. The white round breasts with the rosy nipples; the dark straps of the garter belt knifing along the pale satin of her legs; the lush opulence of her buttocks; the perfection of her legs. Everything first-rate.

He stood naked before her. His own body was not in its usual trim these days; he was drinking too much, exercising too little. For reasons of economy, he didn't stop in at the steam room of the athletic club anymore. So his fortyishness was beginning to show. But only beginning.

He was still pretty lean and agile.

"Go ahead," he said. "I'm ready."

She hefted the whip, got the balance of it. Then smiling serenely, she let him have it across the back and Miller caught his breath with a hiss. The whip stung but would not break the skin unless the girl gave him a really demonic slash. He found it invigorating rather than painful. He enjoyed getting whipped. It was something like a Finnish sauna to him.

But there was more to it than that, he knew. It wasn't just the sensual feeling of the whip against his skin that turned him on. It was the *idea* of it all. The idea of a nearly naked girl whipping him strenuously, sweat rolling down, her bare breasts joggling. That was what really excited him.

He wasn't really able to enjoy love without these preliminaries. Oh, he could love the ordinary way, but that was as flat as stale champagne to him. One of the reasons for his divorce was that Alice had refused to play his little game. As a result, he had little interest in sleeping with her, and the marriage had crumbled.

Natalie, though, knew just what to do.

Whick! Whack!

Flick! Flack!

She chased him around the sumptuous apartment. They were both laughing and giggling wildly. She whipped him across the shoulders, the small of his back, the buttocks and the legs. She let him feel the sting of the whip on his chest, his waist, his arms. He was glowing all over.

And she seemed genuinely to enjoy her work. Her lush body was shining with perspiration. Each stroke of her arm made her bare breasts leap and bobble around in a way that Miller found unutterably attractive. Her lean, nimble body moved agilely, the long legs prancing like a ballerina's in the high heels.

They went on and on. Until finally Miller got to the critical moment where he knew he had to have her.

He stopped being chased, and did the chasing. He turned on her, and as she lifted the whip he lunged and caught her arm.

Laughing insanely, Miller grasped her by the wrist and forced her arm up, so that the whip pointed toward the ceiling. He got closer to her, so that their naked, sweating bodies all but touched. Another step and her hard-pointed breast tips were grazing his skin. Another step and her round firm breasts were being crushed by his chest.

He put his mouth to hers.

The whip dropped to the carpet. Their bodies locked in a tight embrace. With her heels on, she was just about the same height he was, so that they stood face to face. Her breasts seemed to blaze against his skin. He was aware of the faint roughness of her stockings against his legs. Her mouth was good to kiss.

His arms went around her. His hands pressed the soft flesh of her back, and descended, down the bare middle of her back, over the strap of the garter belt, to the rising, jutting mounds of her buttocks. His fingers pulled her against him.

Slowly he forced her backward, down onto the carpet. They were both gasping with excitement, and as with all these call girls, he was unable to tell whether or not hers was an act. Did they fake excitement to give the client a good time? If they did, they were awfully good actresses. When a ten-buck tramp went to bed with you, you could bet that she hated every minute and that any enthusiasm she showed was strictly in hopes of landing a tip. Things were different with these girls, Miller thought.

His mouth fastened hungrily to hers, and his hand groped between her firm, high breasts, teasing and caressing. She was gasping, warm and ready to go. Of course. Who ever heard of a frigid call girl, anyway?

Miller didn't bother taking off the garter belt or stockings. He preferred them. She was somehow more nude this way than if she were completely naked. He liked the difference in textures between the oh-so-soft skin of her breasts and upper body, and the roughness of her stockinged legs.

Her body went wild for him.

Miller took her.

He took her roughly and savagely, ridding himself at last of all the frustrations and disappointments that this last week had created for him. The girl met his assault with energy and vigor.

Her rhythm was perfect. That was another thing Miller liked about these call girls. With an ordinary, non-professional woman, there were always some awkward moments the first time, as you got attuned. Not with these girls. They had an innate sense of rhythm, it seemed, so that they could glide easily and readily to the gyrations of a passionate embrace.

Miller clung to her. His passions, already wakened to fever pitch by the whipping, soared high and higher with each ecstatic move of his body. The girl raised her arms, locked them about him. She was all softness and warmth and fire; for a moment Miller forgot the troubles crowding in on him.

He caught his breath as a surge of ecstasy ripped him. The girl doubled and redoubled her activities. Miller gripped her, pressed himself against her, and let the burst of passionate fulfillment roll over him. At the supreme moment, he heard her gasps of excited satisfaction.

For a long time after that was over, Miller did not move. He enjoyed the warmth of her, the nearness of her, and he kept her body close to his. Then, at last, he got shakily to his feet. He looked at her lush form as she sprawled on the carpet. Extending a hand to her, he helped her to her feet. Her breasts swayed enticingly as she rose.

She smiled at him. It was just the right kind of smile: a grateful smile, the smile of woman well-loved. Did she mean it? Would she remember him tomorrow night? Of course not. But for the moment, at least, she was perfectly in character, playing the role of beloved mistress, not of hired toy.

"There's a bathroom just through there," Miller said. "You can get yourself tidied up."

She thanked him and went out. He eyed her as she left, the trim back, the sensual buttocks framed so perfectly by the garter belt and the stocking tops. He began to dress. When she came back, perhaps five minutes later, he was in his clothes.

She looked cool and refreshed in her nudity now. Miller stood to one side, watching in pleasure as she put her clothes back on, her panties, her bra, donning the slip, the skirt, all the rest. In short order she was clad again—once more the sleek elegant girl-around-town, probably with another call or two to make yet this evening before her working night was over. She fluffed her blonde hair into place and she was all set.

Miller showed her to the door. No money changed hands; that was too crass for such an operation. He'd send his check, made out to a dummy account, in the morning. As she left, she smiled warmly at him, took his hand a moment.

"This has been a lovely evening," she said.

"For me too, Natalie. Thanks ever so much for coming over."

"I enjoyed this. I hope I'll be seeing you again."

"Who knows?" Miller said. "Let's hope so."

And then she was gone. He knew he never would see her again, because it had to be that way. Women were dangerous. One blackmailer was enough. Natalie would never get a chance to know him well enough to be dangerous to him. For two unforgettable hours she had brightened a dark life, and now she was forever part of a closed chapter.

Miller's gloom returned. He was more relaxed now, but hardly happy. He had two big appointments tomorrow. If both of them fell through, he was just about finished—wiped out at the age of forty, with no one willing to help him replenish his capital and start anew.

He poured some more cognac for himself. Then he walked to the wide picture window overlooking the park, and bleakly watched the rain come down.

CHAPTER FIVE

Joanne woke.

She was alone. Buddy had loved her a couple of times, and then he had left, about one in the morning. He rarely spent an entire night with her. There was always a poker game for him somewhere, or a deal to close some kind of shady business operation having to do with gambling or jukeboxes or vice of some kind.

Joanne didn't mind it when he spent his time at things like that. What hurt her was when he went to his other women. She knew he had them. She tried to be all he would need, but it didn't seem to work. No matter how much time Buddy spent in bed with her, no matter how energetically she gave herself to him, he was always creeping away to love other girls in his spare moments. He was that kind of guy, and there was nothing Joanne could do.

She got out of bed. Naked, she walked to the window and threw open the blinds.

The rain had stopped, sometime during the night. Now it was a bright, clear spring morning. The slum street outside seemed freshly washed, almost clean after last night's downpours. Golden sunlight streamed down now. Joanne stood by the window a long moment, breathing deeply, stretching, filling her lungs with air. The high-tipped spheres of her breasts rose voluptuously as she inhaled. Happily, she put her hands over them, cupped them, squeezed them tight and let out her breath.

She was in a good mood. She had been well loved the night before, she had some money in her purse, and she had a new sucker on the string to take care of today. Fred Bauman. The guy who had been so eager to have her last night, and who was going to start paying through the nose for the privilege as of today.

Joanne went into the bathroom and got under the shower. She turned the water on full force. She loved the feeling of fresh water flowing over her body, over her bare breasts and waist and legs and buttocks. She stood under the shower a long while. Then she got out, toweled herself dry, touched her toes with her fingers twenty times just for the heck of it. Her breasts bobbed and jiggled every time she bent forward.

Yes, she thought. She was in a good mood. An excellent mood. A fine day for blackmail.

She was generally in a good mood these days. It hadn't always been that way, not by any means. It was hard for Joanne to accept the fact now, but only four years ago she had been right on the edge of suicide—not merely contemplating it but actually standing there with the razor blade in her hand.

Of course, things had been a lot different then, she told herself.

She had been nineteen, and already pretty experienced. She was working as a stripper at the time, and she was very much in love with a guy named Mack, who was the bartender at the club where she peeled every night. Mack was thirty years old, with Latin features and dark curly hair, and Mack was hell on wheels in bed. They had been talking seriously about getting married. At least, Joanne was talking seriously about it. Mack was doing a lot of thoughtful listening, but he wasn't saying much.

Then Joanne discovered that she was expecting.

She was in her third month, so that didn't interfere with her strip routine, except for the minor fact that she felt nauseous as hell just about all the time. However, she knew that in another five or six weeks she'd have to take a leave of absence.

So she went to Mack. "I got great news," she told him. "We're going to be parents."

"You mean *you're* going to, honey."

"Huh? So are you, Mack!"

"How the hell do I know that? A girl who stands up there every night, before a whole mob of people, how I'm supposed to know that I'm the only one?"

"Mack, no! I swear, you're the only one! There hasn't been anybody else for six months, Mack!"

Mack smiled. "So you want me to marry you, is that the pitch?"

"Well, sure, of course."

Mack smiled, showing his pearly white movie star teeth. In his deep, romantic baritone voice he said, "Go to hell, Joanne."

The manager of the strip club was even more blunt about it, if possible. The day after Mack broke the news to her about her real status with him, Joanne went to the manager to explain her situation. She informed him that in another few weeks she would have to leave the club. However, she didn't intend to quit permanently. What she wanted was a one-year leave of absence, without pay, of course. Then she would return to the club and go back to stripping. Would he hold a slot open for her until then?

The manager's reply was a simple one:

"You're fired."

That was all there was to it. So there was no room in the operation for Joanne any more. As for the leave of absence, who ever heard of a thing like that? A year from now, if she felt like working again, she was free to come around and ask for a job. If there was a slot open, she'd be hired. If not—well, tough situation, kiddo.

It was a tough situation right now. Joanne was nineteen and alone in the world and practically broke. It didn't seem like a very promising outlook. That was when she picked up the razor blade and figured that the simplest thing for her was just to end it all right now. She came within an inch of doing it, and then she put the razor blade down.

She decided to take her chances on an operation.

She had contacts among her fellow strippers who could put her in touch with the right people. The next day, she had a name and she had the price: five hundred bucks.

Joanne's liquid assets amounted to a shade under $150. And every day that she waited longer made things more dangerous. Where was she going to get the money? Borrow it? Don't be silly. Steal it? From where? Earn it? But she had just been fired.

She earned it.

It was the rock bottom moment of her life. She went out on the street. Ten dollars, fifteen, whatever she could get. She wore a blouse that left her breasts practically bare, and she went running up to men on the street, asking them if they wanted a good time. She was insistent about it. Once when another girl tried to cut in on her territory, Joanne knocked her down and kicked her until she agreed to clear out.

It was pure hell. Sick, disgusted by the grimy, foul-smelling men, Joanne drove herself. She found as many as eight customers a night, sometimes. She charged as much as they'd give her, and she gave that all she had, hoping to boost her tips. She half hoped that in all that franticness, she might lose the baby and not need the operation.

No such luck.

After two and a half weeks of full-time effort, Joanne was exhausted and had lost ten pounds, but she had managed to earn close to a thousand dollars. That gave her five hundred bucks for the operation, and some money to live on in the weeks that she was recuperating. So she made her appointment and went to get the problem taken care of.

The doctor's office was in Brooklyn. Of course, the "doctor" wasn't a doctor, at least not anymore, and the "office" wasn't an office, but just a loft in a dismal building on the Brooklyn waterfront. There was no nurse, no shining array of surgical implements. The doctor didn't have a white uniform on; he wore old clothes, and dirty clothes at that. He hadn't shaved in a couple of days, and there was a faint smell of alcohol on his breath. Joanne didn't know his name. She never was to find it out.

"You got the fee?" he asked her. "In cash?"

Joanne paid him. He counted the money through, bill by bill, even examining a couple of bills closely as though he thought they were counterfeit. Then he put the money away and said, "Okay, strip. Everything off."

Joanne peeled away her clothes. When she stood naked before him in the drafty room, he pointed to the table and told her to lie down. She did.

So did he.

"Wait a second," Joanne said. "I—"

"You want an operation?" he asked. "Then first you pay the rest of the fee. Come on, baby. You're the prettiest one that's been in here in a long while. I want some fun first."

He meant it. He began to squeeze her breasts. What could she do, report him to the A.M.A.? If he felt like taking advantage of her for his own amusement, she couldn't do a thing except walk out of there, and that wouldn't solve her problem.

She relented. Why not? She had slept with untold dozens of men so that she could afford to come here in the first place. It didn't make sense to turn virtuous now.

That was quick, a short experience of rapid, selfish energy, and after a few minutes that was that. He sent her into an adjoining room to wash herself up while he sterilized the instruments.

The anesthetic consisted of a pill of some kind and a shot of whiskey. It didn't make Joanne unconscious, but it did make her groggy and woozy. She sprawled out on the rough, uncomfortable operating table, and was dimly aware that he was reaching for a scalpel. She felt pain, but not unbearable pain. After a while, that was all over.

There was lots of blood, for weeks afterward. She felt miserable. Finally, worried about herself, she went to a public health clinic, and told a young and good-looking and obviously concerned interne what had happened, and he examined her and told her that she'd be okay, but that she wouldn't ever be a mother.

After that, she tried to find work as a stripper. But the stripper market had gotten very tight, all of a sudden. So Joanne continued as a hooker, right through to her twentieth birthday. Hardly a day went by when she didn't think about killing herself.

But she didn't. And now all that terrible era was years behind her. She had money. She had Buddy. She had her health back. She didn't have to peddle herself to anybody she didn't want to. She had come a long way since that dark time of her life.

And now, she was getting her own back on the world that had been so rough on her back then. Blackmail was a pleasant way of getting even. Let the Sid Millers of the world squirm on the hook, she thought. Let the Fred Baumans fry. Who had come forward to help her, when she needed help the most? Nobody. Nobody. Men had used her, but they hadn't *helped* her.

Joanne smiled cheerfully.

She went to the telephone, to start making Fred Bauman's life miserable.

Somehow, Bauman had fallen asleep that night. It hadn't been easy. There had been the drumming of the rain outside, and the drumming of fear within himself, and the nearness of Ethel.

Ethel had wanted to love that night. He knew that because she came to bed nude, and she only did that on nights when she wanted him. Ordinarily, he was glad to cooperate. But not tonight.

Bauman wasn't sure that he was physically up to loving his wife two hours after Joanne. But he was certain that psychologically he wasn't. He was shaken to the core, and he didn't want to touch Ethel while he still remembered Joanne so clearly. He couldn't. The whole idea made him weak.

So he watched his wife cross the bedroom naked, still a good-looking woman with her big round breasts and her full hips. She was a little too fleshy now, but not really bad. She got into bed next to him. She pressed herself against him, her breasts touching his back. Bauman just lay there.

After a long while Ethel said, "Is there something wrong, Fred?"

"I'm very tired tonight, Ethel. I had a lousy day at the office."

"This night work! It's wearing you out."

"I can't help it. It's income tax time, Ethel. You know that's always the toughest time of the year for an accountant."

She let him be. She hid her disappointment and rolled over and went to sleep. Bauman wasn't so lucky. He lay there, feeling like a hell of a heel for having refused his wife.

There had once been a time in his life when refusing to sleep with Ethel would have been as unimaginable as refusing to accept a million dollars tax free. That had been when he was young and wildly in love. He was twenty, and she was seventeen, and she had been a virgin until one blissful night when he took her, and as she lay gasping and crying her ecstasy in his arms Bauman knew that this was the woman for him.

That had been a long, long time ago.

He had been faithful to her for all the eighteen years since then, and so far as he knew she had been faithful to him, but the spark of passion that had blazed so brightly once now burned rather fitfully. They had grown accustomed to each other. Attractive as she still was, Ethel didn't hold the same magnetism for him as she did when he was a kid, and it seemed to him back then that her legs and her breasts were the most magnetic things in the world.

He still loved her, he thought. But not in the old way. And certainly he hadn't been such a terrific husband tonight, picking up a strange girl and letting himself be pushed into raping her.

Why had he picked up the girl?

Bauman knew why: it was because somewhere in the back of his mind he had halfway been hoping to have an adventure with her.

Well, he had had his adventure. And now he was about to have a different kind of adventure, a less pleasant kind of adventure. A blackmail adventure.

Somehow, finally, he got to sleep. And somehow he woke up the next morning, and he ate a tasteless breakfast and drove back to Manhattan. If he seemed preoccupied, Ethel didn't say anything about it. She was simply taking at face value what he had told her last night: that he was working too hard, that he was tired.

But he was beginning to realize that. Ethel never looked too closely at him anymore. She took him for granted. Well, Bauman thought, she was going to find out a few things about him that would surprise her, unless he coughed up the five thousand bucks. She was going to look awfully startled when the police came and got him and booked him for a charge of rape.

He settled in at his desk. Somehow, it felt better to be back in the office. The office, at least, was real to him. What had happened last night was more like a wild dream.

Bauman was in the middle of a complicated tax case preparation, and he was having a tough time with it because the image of the full-breasted brown-haired girl in the rain kept coming between him and the dull figures on the long yellow sheets of paper before him, when the telephone rang.

The time was quarter after eleven in the morning. Bauman's first reaction, as his hand went out automatically to grab the receiver, was puzzlement. The only person who ever called him at the office in the mornings was Ethel. And Ethel always called at twelve noon on the dot, never any earlier.

Who was calling him at quarter after eleven, Bauman wondered?

"Hello?" he said.

"Mr. Bauman?" came a woman's voice.

A deep, husky, provocative voice.

Her voice.

"Who is this, please?" Bauman asked, fighting hard and not very successfully to keep the quiver of nervousness out of his voice.

"You know damned well who this is, Freddie-boy," she said. "Don't try to play dumb now. It won't get you anywhere, and you ought to know it."

An image blazed into Bauman's mind: the girl named Joanne in his car, leaning against the window, with her blouse open and her skirt pushed up around her hips and her breasts and legs shamelessly naked as she told him how much she was going to blackmail him for. There was a sudden savage pain of terror.

"What do you want with me?" Bauman asked.

He was speaking in a low, conspirational tone of voice. There were other men in the office, and their desks were not very far from his. They were all bent over their own work and probably weren't paying any attention to what he might be saying. But he couldn't be sure of that. In his present jumpy mood, it seemed to him that everyone around him had grown giant ears to listen in.

"You know exactly what I want with you," came the level reply. "Don't waste words. I want five thousand bucks, Freddie-boy. Cash on the barrel, or else I go to the police."

Bauman was bathed in cold sweat. He gripped the receiver tightly. "I told you last night I don't have that kind of money," he said.

She laughed huskily. "Believe me, you aren't going to like it in jail, lover."

Bauman brushed the beads of perspiration out of his eyebrows. He fought desperately to control his panicky emotions. What he wanted to do was hang up the phone and get out of the office and run for it, run to California, run to Brazil, run anywhere where they couldn't find him. But he knew that that was crazy. He had to stay here and face the music. He had a family to think about. He had a job. He had responsibilities.

After a moment of silent lip chewing he said, "Can't you make it less?"

"Five thousand smackeroonies," she replied evenly. "You willfully and wantonly assaulted me, buster, and I can make that stick in court."

She had him. Bauman knew that.

He felt like a speared fish, wriggling and writhing on the gaff.

He gave in. In a dead, defeated voice he said, "How long do I have to raise the money?"

"I want it by tomorrow afternoon."

"You might as well ask me to swim to the moon. I can't do it."

"Tough," she said. "If I wait much longer than that I won't have a case. I can't very well yell 'rape' two months after the event and expect it to hold up. You realize that, don't you? So I have to know right away whether you're going to ante the dough or whether I'll have to talk to the cops ... and to your wife."

Bauman was silent again for a minute, groping for the words that might get her off his back. At length he said, "You don't seem to understand that if I could pay you, I would. Anything, just to get rid of your threats, to let me forget the thing that happened last night. But I'm not made out of money. Believe me. Whatever you may think, I can't just pull five grand out of the air. If I took anything like that out of the bank, my wife would want to know all about it. It's a joint account."

"Maybe we can arrange terms," said the girl thoughtfully.

Hope rose in Bauman's chilled heart. "What kind of terms?"

"Listen, can you put your hands on a thousand bucks in a hurry?"

Would she really settle so cheaply? Bauman wondered.

He considered it. "Yes," he said. "I could get a thousand, I imagine. It wouldn't be such an easy thing to manage, but—"

"Good. Here's how we'll work it. You deliver a thousand dollars to me tomorrow, and then you pay me a hundred bucks a week till the end of the year. Every Wednesday, say. That'll come out to five thousand, just about, and we'll call it quits."

Bauman, with his accountant's mind, made the automatic computation: it would actually be only $4700 that she'd be extorting from him. There were just thirty-seven weeks left to the year. Very merciful of her. Well, whatever the figure was, he'd be well rid of her at the price, Bauman thought.

"Okay," he said weakly. "I'll do it. Somehow. How do I get the money to you?"

"You mail it, chum. Box 356, Times Square Station, New York 36. Address it to Miss Joanne Harris. That's the name the box is rented under, and it'll get to me. Got that? Box 356."

Bauman jotted it down. "I'll send you the thousand right away."

"You better," she said, and hung up.

Bauman lowered the phone slowly into its cradle. His hands were shaking.

A thousand dollars by tomorrow!

A thousand dollars!

Bauman shook his head. He felt like a dead man. He wondered how he was going to swing it.

CHAPTER SIX

It was eleven in the morning, a bright, sunny morning, and Ethel Bauman was just about finished with her household chores. There was never much to do, in any case. Make the bed, tidy up Karen's room, whisk around here and there with a dustmop—that was about it. She did her marketing once a week, and this wasn't marketing day. So she was finished. She had the rest of the day to herself, until it was time to get dinner going.

Fine.

She could devote the next five or six hours to cultural pursuits. She could read James Joyce, or she could practice the cello, or she could divert herself with differential calculus, or she could play Beethoven on the hi-fi, or she could get onto the train and go to the city and visit an art gallery or museum.

Sure, she could.

Except that she didn't know a thing about any of those subjects. She didn't know Beethoven from Bach, didn't know a cello from a mouth organ. Her reading was confined to women's magazines and novels from the lending library. Ethel Bauman was an intellectual lightweight, and she knew it, and she wasn't happy about it.

It was too late to do anything about it, though. When other girls getting out of high school were going on to college, Ethel was meeting Fred Bauman, and sleeping with him, and marrying him. She was engaged at eighteen and married at nineteen, and a mother at twenty-one, and that hadn't left much time for her intellectual development. First she had had to work, when Fred was starting out on his career, and then she had had a baby to bring up, and by the time Karen was old enough to be spending most of the day at school, Ethel didn't know how to develop the intellectual interests that could fill up the empty hours of the day. If she had lived in a house with some land around it, she could use up time puttering around in the garden. But they lived in an apartment house. What could you do in an apartment house?

Ethel was bored.

Every day, between noon and five o'clock, she went half-crazy from boredom.

She was bored in other ways, too. Bored with her marriage. Fred was a nice guy, he took care of their needs, he didn't earn any fortune but it was enough to stay ahead of the bill collectors. All the same, she was losing interest in him. Bed-wise, that is. And he seemed to be losing interest in her. He didn't have much desire to sleep with her. When he did, he was mechanical, dull, leaving her feeling vaguely dissatisfied.

Ethel had never slept with any man in her life but Fred Bauman. So she wasn't certain whether there was more to be had out of love than she was getting lately. All she knew was she was enjoying bed a lot less than she remembered enjoying in the old days.

"What is it?" she asked herself. "Am I getting old? Is he?"

They were only in their thirties. That wasn't so old. Ethel didn't *feel* old. True, she had gained a little weight lately, but she still had her figure, she was still an attractive woman. People saw her and Karen together these days, they thought they were sisters. And they weren't just saying it to be complimentary, Ethel thought.

So what was the trouble?

Last night, for instance. She had wanted Fred to make love to her. She had gone naked into the bed. That was her way of saying, "Let's love." She didn't like to come right out and ask for him—not in words, anyway; but leaving her nightgown off had been a pretty shameless way of telling him what she wanted.

So what had happened?

So nothing.

She had lain there with her bare breasts throbbing with need, with her heart stirred by yearning, and Fred had rolled over and ignored her.

"I'm tired," he had said. "I'm working hard these days, Ethel. It's tax time."

So? So couldn't he spare a little love for his wife, who was still pretty good-looking, and who was bored crazy with her life?

Ethel sighed and shook her head. Then she went into the kitchen to get her private boredom medicine. She kept it in the broom closet, down on the bottom, with the cleaning fluid and the shoe polish and all the other odds and ends. Fred would never dream of looking in there. In all the years of their marriage, he had never once poked his nose into the broom closet.

That was where Ethel kept her vodka.

There was always a quart bottle of good cheap unbranded eighty-proof vodka in there. Ethel bought it by the quart because the bottles lasted longer that way; she bought unbranded vodka because vodka didn't have much taste anyway, so what was the sense of paying extra money for name brands? She bought eighty-proof vodka because it was cheaper than the hundred-proof kind, but she could get just as drunk on that.

The vodka that she bought cost $3.39 a quart. She saved the money out of her household expense fund. There were ways of cutting corners— buy a slightly cheaper cut of meat, buy in the chain store instead of the little grocery—and every nickel Ethel could put by went into her booze kitty. She bought almost a quart a week. That was a lot of money: better than $150 a year for vodka. And Fred didn't know anything about it. They kept some bottles of other stuff in the house for entertaining, but Ethel never went near that supply during the day.

The vodka helped her get through the day. It was her one vice. She drank a good deal, and somehow it seemed that she had to drink more and more to achieve the same degree of relaxation. Naturally, nobody else knew about her drinking. Not even Karen. Ethel took care to have all her lushing out of the way before Karen came home from school.

Now, she carefully fixed herself a drink. She poured about four ounces of vodka into a water tumbler. She added about two and a half ounces of orange juice. The orange juice gave the drink some flavor. She dropped an ice cube in for refrigeration.

She drank.

She didn't gulp. She drank steadily, a sip at a time, the glass always moving from the table to her lips, back down to the table again, then to her lips. She drank while she read the paper, she drank while she watched the afternoon television programs, she drank while she stood staring out the window with her mind a blank. She belted away plenty of the stuff.

Ordinarily, Ethel didn't start drinking this early in the day. She tried to keep away from the vodka until at least noon. At noon each day she called her husband at his office, and then she fixed a light lunch for herself, and then she poured her first drink. Today, she had more than an hour's head start on herself. But she was still pretty sober when she called her husband.

"Anything new?" he asked, as he always did.

"Not with me," Ethel said.

"Any mail?"

"Nothing interesting. Will you be working late again tonight?"

"I don't think so. I'll be home for dinner."

"Okay."

That was the extent of their conversation. With that chore out of the way, Ethel was free to drink more liberally. And she did.

Soon she was in a wonderfully relaxed, carefree mood. She didn't feel bored anymore. She still felt a little hungry for love, a hangover from last night. The thought struck her that it would be fun to take off her clothes. So she did. She peeled off her house clothes.

She went into the bedroom and stood naked before the full-length mirror in her closet. She looked herself over from head to toe.

Not bad, she thought. Not bad.

Twelve pounds too much flab. She could put her hands on her hips and feel the loose flesh. But her breasts were still good. Turning sideways, she looked at the profile of her buttocks, patted them, grinned as they jiggled. So she had some weight on her. What was wrong with that? A man didn't like his woman to be all bones. It wasn't as if she were fat or sloppy.

But she was going to waste. All this good body, and Fred hardly ever made use of her anymore. Once a week, sometimes twice a week—not any more frequently than that.

She wanted a man.

She needed some love.

She cupped her hands over her breasts, letting the tips peep through. Curious chills of excitement ran through her body. She clamped her soft knees together and kneaded the flesh of her breasts.

What if a delivery boy were to come in now? What if the postman came with a special delivery letter? Anybody, ringing the bell—finding her nude, half pickled, keyed up and ready for love—

The thought of sleeping with a man who was not Fred excited her tremendously. She had always been faithful to him. For many years, it simply had not occurred to her to think of going to bed with anybody else. He was her husband, and she had vowed to love, honor, and obey, and that was all there was to it.

But these days, as the needs grew stronger for her, and as Fred's attentions grew less, the thought was coming to her more and more often. Why not? Fred would never have to know. He didn't care about her body anymore; why not let some other man try? She was curious. Maybe there were other ways of making love, things Fred never did with her. New thrills, new excitements.

But she held back cautiously. The man she chose as her lover would have to be a stranger, certainly not any of the men they saw socially on a husband-and-wife basis. She didn't want a scandal or any kind of trouble. Just someone who would come to her and make love to her and then go away again without starting trouble.

Ethel, standing naked in front of her mirror, pictured the man who would be her lover. Someone tall and lean and handsome and young. And virile. He'd bowl her over. He'd take her in his arms and drive himself to her, and she'd gasp and twist and shake in ecstasy. It would be her little secret, just as the drinking was her secret now. He would touch her breasts, and make the tips go hard, and pass his hand down the front of her body, and kiss her—

Yes, maybe he'd kiss her, as Fred had never done. He would send her over the edge of ecstasy. And she in turn would do the same to him. Fred thought that was disgusting, but Ethel wasn't so sure. There were so many things she and Fred had never done—so many intriguing things she wanted to try.

With somebody. Mister X.

She laughed at her own romantic stupidity. Then he took another look at her naked body, her plump, thirty-six-year-old body, and she began to feel depressed all over again. In another few years she'd be middle-aged. Who would want her then? Who would risk anything to be the lover of a middle-aged married woman? It was now or never. Be unfaithful now, or forget about it. And the more she thought, the more it seemed that such a thing could never happen.

She turned away and covered her body again. Her mood was ruined. She got her glass, poured some more vodka into it, and some orange juice.

She took a sip.

And another.

And another.

And another.

And gradually the long afternoon of loneliness and boredom melted away, the way they all eventually did.

It was quarter to four in the afternoon. Karen's school day was over. Her last class ended at ten minutes to three, but then it was time for extra-curricular activities. Those students who were interested in the recreations the school had to offer stayed around, some of them to work on the school newspaper, some of them to wash test tubes in the biology lab, some of them to sing in the glee club, and so on.

Karen had always been active in the extra-curriculars. Her position as a top student had left her with plenty of free time, since she had never had to muddle over her homework the way the slower students did. This was the first year that she had ever had trouble with her studies, but by now the extra-curricular habit was part of her, so that she still stayed after school even though she ought to be home boning up on her Spanish.

Today's activity was the United Nations Club. It was a club that distributed U.N. leaflets in the school, sponsored fund drives for things like UNESCO, and otherwise furthered the cause of the world organization. It was a good, socially useful activity, the kind of thing that would look worthwhile on a college application.

Karen was co-chairman of the United Nations Club. She shared authority with a boy named Dick Stearns, who was one year older than Karen, and two terms ahead of her in school. He was a good-looking boy, serious and scholarly, with a thick mane of brown hair, dark eyes that peered out from behind his glasses, and a clean-cut face. He was going to be a lawyer, and probably he would be a very good one. Karen liked him. He was short, only five feet eight, but she didn't mind that because she was short, too. They had been dating each other since January. He was rather shy, she thought. He had a lot to learn about girls.

He had a perfect opportunity to do some learning today. The United Nations Club was having an executive session, which meant that nobody was there except Karen and Dick, the two chairmen. The meeting room was a cubicle way up on the top floor of the school building, in a wing that was used chiefly for storage. The room was a conference room, meaning that instead of desks and chairs, it had a round table, and several couches. It had a lock on the door, and a shade that could be pulled down.

It was a very private situation indeed.

And there they sat, at quarter past four in the afternoon, the sixteen-year-old boy with the glasses and the sober expression, and the fifteen-year-old girl with the full breasts, the tight sweater, and the blaze of sensual desire in her heart. There they sat, looking over some press releases for United Nations Week. No teachers present as faculty advisers. No one else on the floor of the building. All, all alone.

And Karen had an idea.

She waited as long as she could, while they went through the formal business of the session. Then, when her patience was just about exhausted, she reached across the table and took Dick's glasses off.

He blinked and squinted at her. "Hey, why did you do that?"

"Because you look cuter without them."

"Aw, come on, Karen, we've got work to do."

"Let it go, huh? It's nice and cozy here Dick. We don't often get this private."

He looked at her strangely. "I guess you aren't in a mood for working."

"I guess I'm not," she said. She turned, giving him her profile view, and took a deep breath that thrust her spectacular bosom out to maximum effect. She heard him give a little sigh of appreciation, and knew that she had scored a point.

On their dates, he was the soul of propriety. But he was warming up. On the last date, he had gone so far as to fondle her breasts—through her clothes, of course. Karen had been yearning for him to go beyond that point, but he hadn't cared to.

Maybe now, though. Here, alone in this locked room where no one could find them.

On that comfortable leather couch. Maybe—maybe they would go all the way! Maybe the moment of which she had dreamed so long was at last at hand! If only she could make him see how much she wanted him. How desperately she craved the experience of love! Didn't he? Most likely he was a virgin too, unless she judged him all wrong. What better opportunity would they ever have?

"Come here," she said huskily. "Let's sit down on the couch for a while."

"Karen—"

"Come here," she said.

As though hypnotized, he followed her. She took him by the wrist, drew him down next to her on the couch.

"The door's locked," she told him. "We're all alone and nobody can disturb us. And I've had enough U.N. stuff for a while. I just want to relax." She reached out, ran her hand up his cheek to his earlobe, fondled it a moment. "Come help me relax, Dick. Don't you like me?"

"Of course I do."

"Then come close. Put your arms around me. I won't bite you, I promise."

He grinned, shyly, self-consciously. Then, as though making an effort to enter into the spirit of the moment, as though not wanting to seem a prude and a square in the presence of a willing girl, he slipped one arm around her shoulder. Karen guessed that he would much rather be muddling through United Nations Club business right now. But she didn't think his resistance would last long.

They kissed. His lips met hers, and she kissed him with a fiery passion, pushing her tongue forward, forcing him to respond to her demand. They had kissed that way Saturday night, though he had taken long time to work his way around to a real kiss. Now, Karen's fervor and insistence seemed to be contagious. He met the command of her lips and tongue with a passionate kiss of his own.

Karen's body pounded and churned with lust as his kiss set her ablaze. Yes! That was the way to begin! Now go on from there, she thought.

He did. Without being prompted, he brought his free hand up and let it rest on the jutting globe of her left breast. Karen tingled in satisfaction. She smiled, purred, kissed him more fervently.

His hands roamed over the front of her sweater, gripping the firm globes, squeezing them, waking them. Karen thrilled with delight. She rubbed her cheek against his, nibbled his earlobe, felt a dryness in her throat as the excitement took hold of her.

"Put your hands inside my sweater," she whispered. "Open the bra."

"Karen—"

"Now!" she said sharply.

His face was bright red. But he obeyed. He tugged her sweater up out of her skirt, and ran his hands up, across the smooth bare flesh of her waist, toward the bra. But he didn't seem to know where the catch was. He fumbled around for a moment without getting anywhere.

"In back," she told him, "Silly!"

His hands slid around behind her. Even so, he couldn't manage the complicated catch of the bra. After another moment, Karen's impatience got the better of her. She slipped one hand up behind herself and unsnapped the bra herself. The cups fell forward, allowing him room to get his hands inside and caress her breasts.

But he hesitated. Karen had to take the lead again. She grasped his hand, pushed it toward her breasts.

"I want you to," she said. "Please!"

His fingers slid into place. Karen nearly went wild. At long last a boy's hands were actually touching her breasts. He was cupping them, his fingertips were digging into the resilient swelling firmness of them. He had found the tips, he was playing with them—!

Oh, God, that was good! Oh, yes!

She gasped and sighed. She kissed him again a hard, biting kiss, putting into the kiss all her pent-up desire and lust. She wanted him to push her backward, full length on the couch, shove her skirt up around her hips, pull her panties down, and have her. Right here. Would he?

They were both gasping, now. He didn't want to let go of her breasts, now that he had finally reached that stage. He kept squeezing them, caressing them. Karen twisted restlessly on the couch. She reached out, put her hand on his knee, moved it. He gasped in sudden passion. She let her hand linger. She felt her own cheeks flaming at the shamelessness of what she was doing, but there was no turning back now. That was what she wanted. She wanted him to take her, to go all the way past childish innocence to the forbidden adult game.

But he didn't seem to want to go beyond playing with her breasts. Once again, Karen saw that she would have to take the initiative. If she got herself ready there would be less for him to do, he could more easily be seduced into loving her.

So while he caressed her breasts in a delirium of passion, Karen reached down, found the hem of her skirt, and began to draw it up. Up over her calves, over her knees, past the straps of her garters and the tops of her stockings. He didn't seem to notice. She pulled the skirt up until it was bunched around her hips.

Then she began to take her panties off.

She tugged at them, yanked them down an inch or two. Her heart pounded. Down over the fullness of her hips, down over her navel, over her hips, over her garters, over her stockinged legs. Down and off. The panties dropped to her ankles. She kicked them away somewhere into the middle of the room.

"Go on, Dick—" she said in a strangled voice "Take me! Now!"

For the first time, he became aware of what she had done. He looked and got the full view: her legs, her bare hips, the straps of her garter belt, and the nudity between her stocking tops and her waist. His eyes seemed to bulge. His face was crimson.

Karen shifted her legs, wantonly. She reached for him, tried to pull him closer to her. The throbbing in her heart was agonizing. She was breathless. He just had to help her.

"Dick—please, Dick—"

He leaped back as though she had suddenly turned radioactive. Wrenching his hands away from her breasts, pulling them out from under her sweater, he jumped to his feet and stood there, wildly gasping, staring at her. He couldn't seem to take his eyes away from her.

"No," he said. "Karen, this is crazy! What are we doing?"

"I want you to love me, Dick!"

"We mustn't! We're only kids!"

She laughed quotesquely. "Listen to him! You may be a kid, but I'm not! I need you, Dick. And you want me. Come on!"

She would not allow him to leave her tortured by the fit of lust that racked her. She caused a terrible scene, begging him, urging him desperately, and waited for him to step forward and take her. That would be so easy for him.

But he didn't.

He staggered back from her, eyes still riveted to her. He shook his head. Sweat was rolling down his face. He was shaking.

"I don't know what's wrong with you, Karen!" he said in a thick voice.

"Nothing!" she cried hysterically. "Absolutely nothing! I'm all right! What's wrong with you?"

"You've gone berserk. You're only fifteen! It isn't right for you to want this yet. Or me. We aren't adults. We—"

"You disgust me," she said suddenly.

"I'm not the only disgusting one," he snapped back at her. "Cover yourself! I don't want to have to look at you!"

"Am I so ugly? You've never seen a woman before, have you? Come on, Dick!"

He shook his head. He seemed terrified of her. "Cover yourself," he said again.

Karen realized that there was no hope. He wasn't going to take the virginity that she hated. Dazedly, she got to her feet. She was crazed with lust, on the edge of collapse. Her brain reeled. She was disheveled, a mess, her bra hanging loose, her skirt around her hips, rumpled and brazen. She stood there, deliberately delaying in covering her nudity, After a moment she reached under her sweater to fasten her bra. She picked up her panties and stepped into them. She let her skirt drop back into place.

She was still disheveled-looking, but at least she was decent now. She was trembling. Her body blazed with unfulfilled lusts.

She walked up to him. The boy stood frozen in his tracks, an expression of wonderment and disbelief and shock on his face.

She spat at him right in the face.

"Chicken!" she cried. "Dirty stinking lousy chicken!"

Karen grabbed her schoolbooks. Then she turned, fiery tears of shame and rage coursing down her cheeks, and unlocked the door and bolted from the room, fleeing wildly down the deserted corridors.

CHAPTER SEVEN

Joanne put down the telephone and smiled a satisfied smile. Bauman had sounded scared, genuinely scared, and she had no doubt but that he would kick in the money she had asked for.

A thousand bucks now—and then a hundred bucks a week for the rest of the year.

Quite a windfall for one itty bitty little rape she thought. She'd give some money to Buddy of course—a "loan," they would call it, but they'd both know better. And she'd put some money away in her bank account, and let it pile up more money for her through the wonderful magical device they called compound interest. And she'd squander some, not much, on riotous living.

Oh, yes, it was a good life—now, The old hardships hardly seemed to matter anymore to Joanne. The knocks and rebuffs of her adolescence were like memories of bad dreams, products of an uneasy night, vanishing in the bright clear light of morning.

She began to get dressed. It was a beautiful spring day; time to go out and get some fresh air. She and Buddy were having dinner together at six-thirty. Then they were taking in a movie, and afterward she expected that he'd come back to her apartment and make love to her a couple of times. But that gave her the next five or six hours free. A good brisk walk was one way of spending the time. Get out into the sunshine, get some good fresh filthy New York City air into her lungs.

She went downstairs. It was warm, mild, springy. She walked eastward along 45th Street till she came to Eighth Avenue, then turned south. She went past the Greek restaurant where she and Buddy often ate, and waved to the waiter who stood near the door. He waved back and winked. He thought she was a showgirl, and he was always asking. "How's about some free tickets?"

She went on, past some bookstores that made their pile not by selling books, but by peddling in perfect legality the German and Swedish nudist magazines that ran absolutely unretouched photos of German nudists. As always, there was a crowd of men in the stores. Joanne often wondered what would happen if she walked in, picked out a man at random, and offered herself to him.

"Come on," she might say. "Come home and go to bed with me, instead of thumbing through those pictures of naked girls."

Joanne had a pretty good idea what would happen. The man would bolt and run in terror. The sort of guys who crowded the Times Square stores preferred their kicks in the vicarious way. They were safer that way than getting involved with a real live girl, it seemed.

She laughed and walked on. She rounded Eighth Avenue and turned onto 42nd Street, stopping near the corner to buy herself a hot dog. Then, munching the frankfurter, she strolled slowly down 42nd Street, past the myriad movie theaters with their sensational marquees.

She knew that the effect she was causing was pretty sensational itself. She was wearing a turquoise polo shirt that clung voluptuously to the ripe cones of her breasts, and a pair of ruby-colored pedal-pushers which modeled the outlines of her hips, waist and buttocks as snugly as a skin graft. Even on a street that wasn't exactly noted for its sedateness, Joanne was causing a stir. She could practically hear the creaking of vertebrae as men swiveled their heads round to stare at her as she sauntered past.

Good thing I put a bra on this morning, she thought pleasantly. She hadn't bothered with panties, because they would show as a thin line under her tight pedal-pushers. But she knew that if she dispensed with a brassiere, the tips of her breasts would be plainly visible against the taut-stretched fabric of the polo shirt and that would be altogether too provocative for a public street.

She walked up to the corner and stood there, staring up at the shiny Allied Chemical Building and waiting for the light to change.

"Joanne?" a soft voice said.

She turned. And gasped in surprise and pleasure.

"*Becky!*" she cried.

A girl a year or two older than Joanne stood next to her: a tall girl, strapping and full-breasted, with close-cropped red hair, a healthy, vigorous body, a broad grin of pleased surprise.

"I'll be damned," Becky Collins said. "You can meet just about anybody in this city!"

"Especially in Times Square," Joanne said. "God, it's been years, hasn't it?"

"At least four years," Becky said. "Since we worked in that strip shop together."

Joanne nodded. "Four years. It's sometimes been like four centuries. What have you been doing with yourself, Becky?"

"I've been in Vegas, mostly. Showing off my boobs for the tourists. You?"

"Right here in New York, most of the time. I make ends meet."

Becky's face darkened. "I never heard anything from you after your operation."

"It was a success, more or less," Joanne said quietly. "Look, let's go somewhere and talk where it's a little more private."

Becky pointed to the cafe across the street. "How about the Crossroads? Have you had lunch?"

"No."

"Neither have I."

"Let's go, then."

They hurried across. Joanne was still startled by the meeting. When she had been nineteen, and one of the strippers at the club where she had met Mack, Becky had been the star attraction in the show, the long-legged redhead with the giant breasts that all the customers came out to see. Joanne and Becky had become good friends. It was Becky who had loaned Joanne the money to help her keep afloat after losing her job.

Becky and Joanne had also been to bed a few times. Becky was a full-time Lesbian. And Joanne, who wasn't necessarily particular about the gender of her bed companions, had willingly succumbed to the big redheaded girl's seductions.

But since she left, Joanne hadn't been in touch with Becky or with anyone else from the strip club. She had been in such a miserable mood that she preferred to keep that whole part of her life a closed chapter. In a way, she was bitter toward Becky because the doctor she had recommended had turned out to be such a heel—though Joanne knew that that really wasn't Becky's fault. She had done her best. Even so, Joanne hadn't wanted to see or talk to any of the people she had known during that era of her life.

Four years later, everything was different. She was far enough removed from that grim period so that she no longer felt as she once had.

Besides, Becky was one hell of an attractive woman. And, Joanne thought, as they sat down at a table in the cafe, that would be an amusing way to spend the afternoon—in bed with Becky Collins, renewing auld acquaintance.

So this is what it's like to be blackmailed, Fred Bauman thought dully. One thousand bucks down and only thirty-seven weeks to pay.

After finishing his conversation with Joanne, he devoted a few moments to working out the arithmetic of his position. It was pretty brutal arithmetic.

Bauman's salary was $9000 a year. Not bad, not good—just average. His take-home pay was in the neighborhood of $140 a week, after state and federal withholding taxes, hospitalization insurance deductions, and things like that. And he was supposed to divert a hundred dollars out of his weekly hundred and forty into the pocket of the enterprising little witch who had lured him into raping her that night in the rain.

That didn't leave much margin. He had managed to save about ten or fifteen dollars a week, out of his hundred-forty. The rest went for rent, food, clothing, household expenses, whatnot. There was money in the savings account, but it was a joint account and he didn't dare touch it. Ethel liked to look at the bankbook every now and then. It was supposed to be Karen's college fund, and there were a couple of thousand dollars in it, enough to see him over part of his troubles. But what would he say if Ethel asked him one night, "Why did you take so much money out of the bank?"

No. He couldn't do it that way.

But he told himself that he'd manage it somehow—without Ethel's finding out.

The horses, Bauman thought. The nags. They'll do it for me.

Once, long ago, Bauman had been pretty good at playing the horses. It wasn't that he ran with a fast crowd, or that he was a dedicated gambler. But one day a friend had taken him and Ethel out to the track, and Bauman had paid some attention to the way it worked. With his highly-developed accountant's head for arithmetic and percentages, Bauman had taken the races as a challenge.

He worked out a system. He was cautious and methodical about it, and did plenty of paper work. He had never gone for fancy stuff like the daily double, had never bet on a long shot. He left that kind of business to the plungers and the wiseacres and the fools.

Bauman's system involved always backing favorites, and doing it in such a way that he stood to lose almost nothing and gain a little. With his system, he could never be a big winner, but he wouldn't get badly burned, either. Generally, he could go out to the track with $100 and come back with $109. Nothing very spectacular—except that that was a 9% return on his money in a single day. You couldn't do that well in the savings bank.

Of course, Bauman didn't always come out ahead. But over the long run he did. His annual winnings mounted up to fifteen hundred bucks, sometimes two thousand. Then Ethel had asked him to give up the track. "I don't like you spending so much time at that place. It isn't right. Even if you make money out of it, I don't like it. Besides, what if you start to lose all of a sudden?"

They had quarreled about it for a while—and then Bauman had given up betting, at her insistence, for the sake of preserving family harmony. If it bothered her that much, well, he'd find some other hobby. It was years since he'd last looked at the racing news.

But maybe now he could start again, and pick up the extra cash he would need to pay off the girl. He could find out what the hot horses were, and he could start building up a surplus of cash, without Ethel's ever finding out.

First, though, he needed some money to begin with. And he needed a thousand bucks to hand over to Joanne right away.

At lunchtime, Bauman left his office and went down to the bank on the corner. He had done business there before, both as a private individual and also representing his firm. They knew him and respected him there. There wasn't a reason in the world why they should mistrust him.

Bauman had an interview with Mr. Wilson, the vice-president with whom he had dealt before. Mr. Wilson was plump and pink-faced and very cooperative.

"How can we help you, Mr. Bauman?" he wanted to know.

Bauman told him, trying to look him straight in the eye and maintain a façade of respectability. "I need a general-purpose loan," he said. "Fifteen hundred dollars for about six months."

It was easily enough arranged. Fifteen hundred bucks, the only collateral required being his signature. They weren't afraid of a default. They knew he'd be good for repayment of the loan when the principal fell due in six months' time. They let him have it at six per cent, discounted in advance, of course—one thousand four hundred fifty-five dollars. Bauman knew that his real rate of interest was closer to twelve than six per cent, because of the advance discounting, but he wasn't in a position to haggle. He needed the money, and he needed it fast.

Now he had some.

He had enough now to meet the blackmailer's initial payment, and still have enough left over to see him through a few more weeks' installments to her. He could use some of the money for the horses. If he could make sixty or seventy dollars a week on the nags, he told himself, he'd be able to keep paid up with Joanne, and maybe even put a few dollars aside toward the repayment of the loan. Whatever he couldn't manage to repay when the loan fell due, he'd borrow from another bank, and from another, and another, extending the loans if he had to, until finally he worked his way out of the network of debt.

All he had to do was hit a streak of luck at the races, Bauman told himself, and everything would be okay. A few weeks of winning two or three hundred bucks, and he'd start to gain both on the loan and on the payments to Joanne. And at least this way, borrowing the money from the bank instead of taking it out of the savings account, Ethel would never know a thing about the money. Provided, that was, that he didn't have to pull it from savings anyway when the loan fell due in October. He didn't think he would. He was pretty sure he'd be able to negotiate a new loan, if necessary, with one of the other banks his company did business with.

Bauman had asked the bank to give him the money in the form of a bank check for a thousand dollars, and the rest in cash. The bank check was payable to Fred Bauman. He endorsed the check, slipped it into an envelope, and mailed it to Miss Joanne Harris, Box 356, Times Square Station, New York 36, N. Y. So much for the down payment.

He had better than four hundred fifty dollars in cash. It made a nice thick wad in his wallet. He didn't often carry that kind of money around with him. But, of course, he wasn't going to carry it around for long. If Ethel ever happened to find him with something like four hundred dollars in cash bulging up his wallet, there was sure to be a question session.

So he went back to the office, not bothering to eat lunch, and put the cash in an envelope. He stowed it away safely in a drawer of his desk at the office, and locked the drawer.

He shook his head sadly. And I was being thrifty by taking the bridge that night instead of the tunnel, Bauman thought bitterly. Just to save on the toll. Big deal. I saved two bits in tolls and I threw away forty-seven hundred dollars. Plus interest.

Bauman started to think about petty economies he could make to ease things up and free more cash for Joanne. Not eating lunch today had saved him some dough, but of course he couldn't make a habit out of that. But instead of spending a dollar and a half for lunch every day, as he usually did, he could eat in the Automat for a dollar or less. He wouldn't starve. And that would save him two-fifty a week and up, ten or twelve dollars a month, right there. He could put that money into the blackmail fund without trouble from Ethel. She'd never be the wiser.

There were other ways he could save, too. He could wear his white shirts three or four days, instead of two. If his collars looked a little seedy, so what? That would cut down Ethel's laundry bills by fifty or seventy-five cents a week, and he could channel that off to the girl who had him by the throat. He could ration himself on cigarettes and liquor and new clothes. He could do lots of things to nick money off his expenses.

By the end of the day, his work was hardly done, but the little adding machine in his accountant's mind had computed that he could manage to save, with careful management perhaps twelve dollars a week out of his pocket money. That meant he only needed to find eighty-eight dollars a week somewhere, not mentioning the loan due at the bank. Even with luck at the track, he was going to be hard pressed. It was going to be a lousy year, that was for sure.

If I only had taken the tunnel that night, he thought for the millionth time.

It was too late for that now. He was stuck.

As he drove home that night; he took the bridge route again. The quarter toll at the tunnel was an important hunk of cash to him now. He looked to the right at 59th Street to see if the girl were lurking there, waiting for some other sucker.

She wasn't.

She has made her catch for the week, it seemed, and that was enough.

Bauman wondered how many other men in New York were making weekly payments to her because of a moment's lapse. It all seemed unreal to him. But it was no dream. It was very, very real indeed.

Becky Collins said, "Let me take the check, Joanne. I'm loaded with dough."

"Well, if you insist—"

"I do."

"I'll be graceful about it," Joanne said. "Go ahead. It's all yours."

They had had a good substantial lunch, washed down by a couple of bottles apiece of Danish beer. Joanne was in a relaxed good-natured mood now. She had filled Becky in on some of the ups and downs she had had since they had last met, soft-pedalling some of her more garish exploits. She didn't say a word about the blackmail bit, and she went easy on the prostitution angle. But she got the point across, at any rate, that she was in comfortable financial condition now, and not hard pressed anymore.

Becky seemed to be doing all right too. She had been pretty well off even back in the strip club days, but, as she put it, "I went out to Vegas and some rich Texans adopted me as their girlfriend."

Joanne had the picture: Becky stark naked in Las Vegas hotel rooms, letting wrinkled-faced, drawling oil millionaires do whatever they wanted to do to her—for a price. A damned good price, if she knew Becky.

And now, weary of the western sun, Becky was back in New York, dressed fit to kill, probably sitting on a hefty pile of stocks and bonds, and looking for new worlds to conquer. Joanne was impressed with the picture. It wasn't exactly the kind of setup she wanted for herself, but it was a nice deal anyway, and she had to admire Becky's coolness, Becky's savoir-faire, Becky's all-around level-headedness.

They left the restaurant. It was still early in the afternoon,

"Where are you staying?" Joanne asked.

"At the Woodmere. It's only a couple of blocks from here. Want to come up for a while?"

"I'd love to," Joanne said.

She knew exactly what was going to happen if she went to Becky's hotel room. That didn't trouble her at all. It was many months since Joanne had last been to bed with another woman, and she was in the mood for precisely that kind of entertainment now. Besides, Becky was stacked. Joanne with her ambisextrous orientation, was able to appreciate Becky's beauty just as much as any man could.

So they went to Becky's.

They stopped off first in the Woodmere bar. "I want you to try this cocktail that they serve here," Becky said. "It's made with Aquavit and Benedictine and God knows what else, and it's out of the world."

So they had a couple of Woodmere Specials first. They reacted nicely with the beer Joanne had already had. She began to feel pleasantly giddy—not drunk, just a little tipsy.

They went upstairs.

The Woodmere was a good hotel for thrifty types. It didn't quite offer Waldorf-Astoria luxury, but it didn't charge Waldorf-Astoria prices, either, and the rooms were spacious and clean and well furnished. Becky ushered Joanne in and closed the door. Then she spun around and reached for Joanne. A moment later, they were in each other's arms.

"It's been so long," Becky whispered.

"An age and a half."

"I'm so glad I met you today."

They kissed. Hesitantly, at first, almost like two strangers kissing, but after half a second the old warmth and passion came flooding back.

Joanne's breasts shoved forward against the firm mounds of Becky's, and her kiss grew warmer and more demanding, and their arms tightened about one another. The kiss was a long and lingering one and when it broke they were both gasping from mounting passion and yearning.

"All this clothing—" Becky gasped.

"Who needs it?"

"Get rid of it!"

They stripped quickly. Joanne, because she was wearing less, was naked first. She yanked her polo shirt off and threw it on a chair, and dropped her pedal-pushers. She was nude under the pedal-pushers and Becky's eyes brightened at the sight of Joanne's firm legs and bare haunches. Her eyes glistened even more a moment later when Joanne whipped off her bra to reveal the firm white globes of her breasts.

Becky was built to a different scale entirely—much bigger in every direction. Joanne watched her undress, watched her slip out of the tailored suit, watched her divest herself of slip and stockings, then unhook the bra that confined the mammoth globes of her breasts. Joanne had a big, eye-catching bosom, but Becky's were gargantuan, two huge globes nearly the size of basketballs, firm and white and forward-thrusting, tipped with incongruously small dark red nipples.

Becky's figure hadn't suffered any in the four years, Joanne thought. Her breasts hadn't started to droop or hang yet. Those muscles were still doing a tip-top job of supporting her.

Off came Becky's panties, her garter belt, everything. She stood nude before the equally nude Joanne. Her big body was not gross in any way: it was in perfect proportion, with long limbs and a deep chest to balance those huge breasts and heavy buttocks. She was a six-footer, weighing close to one-eighty. A big girl, that was all. Big and healthy-looking, the kind men would pay big money to see in the nude.

"Come here," Becky said.

Joanne went to her. They kissed again, and this time flesh pressed against bare flesh. Joanne stood on tiptoe. Their tongues met. Their waists touched. Their knees were soft and warm.

They kissed tremblingly, moving slightly, slowly. Joanne experienced a thrill of excitement in her breasts. She ran her hands down the satiny smoothness of Becky's back, down to the lushly abundant ripeness of her buttocks, and grasped the firm flesh. Becky was tanned an olive-brown, all over. No bikini marks across breasts and hips, no white stripes. She had spent plenty of time under the Nevada sun, in the nude, Joanne thought.

They moved toward the bed.

A moment later they were on the bed, hands and arms and lips busy. Becky's knee was touching Joanne's, Becky's hands were on Joanne's breasts. Joanne reached for and found the huge globes of Becky's bosom, and squeezed, and kneaded.

"Oh, yes," Becky muttered thickly. "Oh, yes indeedy, yes!"

She ducked and dove toward the other end of the bed. A moment later, Joanne was aware of Becky's lips teasing and tantalizing her, kissing her in that special sweet way that only a woman knows. Joanne closed her eyes. She lay back relaxing, ready, welcoming the pleasure. She made hoarse little sounds of delight.

Then, after her brain was starting to reel with pleasure, she scrambled into a different position and tugged Becky down so that they could make each other happy at the same time. Becky was incredibly soft against Joanne's cheeks as she sought her goal.

Then they were both gasping, both panting, both clutching for flesh. Breasts and buttocks, arms and knees, all formed a wild tangle on the bed. Joanne lay back, and Becky's body was good against her. Joanne allowed the big redhaired girl's churning, gyrating body to dominate her own, to lead her toward ecstasy.

They soared upward together toward bliss.

This was altogether different, making love the Lesbian way, from making love with a man. Each way had something to be appreciated and enjoyed. With a man, you had the violence, you had the knowledge of surrender, that he was taking you. You couldn't get that from Lesbian love. But this way had special advantages, too: the softness of female skin, the sensualness of two big breasts against your own, the tenderness of a woman, and the expert caresses that only a woman can give.

Joanne was equally disposed toward both kinds of loving. She took everything in her stride.

Now, gasping in frenzied ecstasy she clung tight to the soft, warm body of Becky Collins, pushing her mouth against Becky's in a passionate kiss, then wrenching her head away so she could draw breath into her lungs through wide-open mouth.

She arched from the mattress. She felt Becky's hands gripping her, digging at the firm flesh.

Ecstasy came in a golden sunburst of pleasure.

The universe pinwheeled wildly. Joanne clung tight, shivered in happiness as Becky's smooth body moved against her own.

Together, they went riding far out on a tide of pure delight.

CHAPTER EIGHT

Another day, another step closer to the grave.
Ethel Bauman was still bored.
The days blurred one into the next. Part of the year there was snow on the ground, and then the leaves began to turn green, and then it was hot, and then the leaves started to drop. She was vaguely aware of the change of the seasons. But not the individual days. They all melted into one unending stream of time. Day after day after day, purposeless, empty, dreary.
It was noon. The sun was shining. The chores were done. How to kill another day? How to use up the empty hours ahead?
The bottle. That was the way. The old joy-juice, what else?
Ethel went to the broom closet. She reached in, grasped the smooth cool vodka bottle, pulled it out, studied it. It was still almost half full. Too bad. If the bottle were almost empty, she'd have an excuse for going out, down to the store, buying a new one. That would provide some excitement to break up the day. But there was still plenty of vodka in the bottle.
A hell of a note, Ethel thought. When a trip to the liquor store becomes a big exciting excursion in your life, something to look forward to.
She poured herself a drink. She added the orange juice. She drank.
She turned on the television set for a while, but there was nothing decent on. Just a baseball game. Who cared about baseball? She didn't. Grown men wearing kid's uniforms, batting a little ball around in the afternoon—and getting paid for it, too. Some of them made a hundred thousand dollars a year for playing baseball, Ethel had heard. A hundred thousand! It took Fred eleven years to make a hundred thousand dollars, and here were men who got that much between March and October every year for doing nothing but hitting a baseball around.
It wasn't fair, Ethel thought.
But nothing ever was fair. She consoled herself with more vodka, and thought about what she could do if her husband made a hundred thousand dollars a year.
Get a house, first. No more living in lousy apartments where you could hear every noise the neighbors made. Get a nice house somewhere out in Jamaica or Great Neck, with a lawn and trees.
Travel. Europe, the Caribbean, Hawaii, all the places she had dreamed of. On their vacations they went to the Adirondacks. Big deal. Once they

had gone out to California and Arizona. Big, big deal. What about Paris, Rome, Nice, London, Vienna?

Eat at the fancy restaurants. Ethel had never tasted real caviar in her life. Drink fancy wine. Pheasant, filet mignon, duck in orange sauce.

Oh, you dreamer you!

She poured more vodka into her glass. The stuff was disappearing at a pretty quick rate today. She chuckled. Maybe she'd need to make that trip to the liquor store after all. Another hour or so, at the rate she was guzzling, and the bottle would be empty. But by that time, she reflected, she'd be too potted to go downstairs. It would have meant drinking almost half a quart of vodka in about two and a half hours. That was pretty good going. She'd be in no shape to go to the store after that.

Ethel laughed. She had some more to drink. The drunker she got, the more keen her thirst was. She got up, waltzed around the apartment, her breasts jiggling under the housecoat and gown that were her only garments.

"Waltz me around again, Tilly—" she sang in a wild, off-key falsetto.

Hey, I'm really getting stoned, she thought. She felt a little frightened. What if Fred called up out of the blue and found her like this? I won't answer the phone, she thought. I'll let him think I'm out shopping. What if Karen came home early from school? What if a friend from the neighborhood dropped in for a visit? What if—

What if the doorbell rang, and it was Mister X, coming to make love to her?

That thought both frightened and excited her all at the same time. She felt so tense that she had to have another drink and she picked up her glass again, and drank its contents rapidly now, not sipping as she usually did, but gulping away. It went down so easily, now. Just as though it was nothing but orange juice.

Ethel began to sweat.

She stood up, peeled off her robe and her nightgown, and hurled them wildly away from her. She looked down at her naked body, at the big sensual breasts, at the slightly too fleshy waist, at the firm legs, the big hips. Desire burned in her. Fred hadn't made love to her last night, either. He was still in a moody, preoccupied frame of mind. She was too inhibited to ask him for love. So she suffered.

She ached for a man.

The vodka helped. But just a little.

She drained her glass and put it down. Her head was swimming. She put her hands over her breasts, cupped them, squeezed them. The tips ached. Her whole being was driven by a frenzy of lust.

She swayed. Suddenly she was terribly dizzy. She took two steps, lost her balance, toppled, fell.

Ker-plunk!

She hit the floor hard. With a real crash. She landed on her hip and left buttock, but the pain went right through to the bone, and she let out a yell of surprise and discomfort as she hit the floor. For a long moment she didn't move, for fear that the floor would sway and writhe beneath her a second time.

It seemed to hold steady. After another moment, she began to pick herself up. Her hip and backside ached, and she figured she'd have a black-and-blue mark there tomorrow. But nothing seemed to be broken. What a flop, though! She was still shaky from it. All of a sudden, her legs had seemed to go out from under her. That had never happened to her before. It was pretty scary.

I must be awfully drunk, Ethel thought.

She told herself that she had better steady herself. The best way she knew of doing that was to have another drink, fast.

So she had another drink. Fast.

She stood in the middle of the living room, banging on to the back of an armchair, stark naked, very drunk, swaying back and forth. Her head was spinning, Beads of sweat ran down her body, rolling out to the tips of her bare breasts and dropping off into space.

The doorbell was ringing.

Ethel couldn't be sure how long it had been ringing before her ears tuned in on it. All she knew was that it was ringing right now, an insistent nasty buzz. Somebody was out there, she thought.

It's him! Mister X, the lover she had dreamed of for so long!

It had to be. Who else would come out of nowhere in the middle of the day? It was someone sent in answer to her prayers, someone who would take her in his arms and kiss and caress her, and then make love to her as her husband had never done, someone who would show her how to attain the heights of passion.

The doorbell went on ringing.

"I'm coming!" Ethel yelled.

Stark naked and unsteady on her feet, she began to walk uncertainly toward the door. Her face was flushed and her bare breasts ached with yearning. Sweat rolled in rivers down her excited body.

The doorbell went on ringing. Ethel thought she heard a distant voice, and she thought—she wasn't sure—that the voice was yelling, "Mrs. Bauman, are you all right? Mrs. Bauman?"

"I'm fine," Ethel said.

She threw the door wide open and stood there magnificently, her hands outstretched, her heavy round breasts shaking in feverish agitation.

The day after Bauman had sent the thousand dollars to Joanne, she called him at the office. He winced when he heard her husky, exotic voice whispering to him over his desk telephone.

"I got the dough, sweetheart," she said. "You're a man of your word."

"All right," Bauman said. "Do me a favor, don't call me at the office anymore. It's not so private here, you know."

"You want me to call you at home instead, maybe?"

"Don't call me at all. There's no need to call me. I'll pay you."

"You better," she said. "I'm going to be expecting a check for the amount of one hundred bucks the morning of the 16th. That's next Wednesday."

"You'll get it," Bauman said. He bit his lip. Why couldn't she go away and leave him alone? Why did she have to plague him here in his office?

"And I'll be expecting one check every week after that till New Year's," she continued.

"Don't worry about me," Bauman grated. "I'll give you your money, you she-devil. You're draining me white, but I'll pay you!"

She ignored the bitterness in his voice. "Aren't you even wondering about this installment plan business?" she asked.

"What do you mean, wondering?"

She laughed. "Well, don't you see, I'm killing my own case by accepting installments, Freddy. Suppose you decide not to give me another penny, after today's thousand. What can I do? I can't holler rape now—not when you can prove you had paid me a thousand— it's blackmail already."

"I hadn't thought of that," Bauman admitted. "If you cash that check you don't have much of a claim on me in court, do you?"

"Nope."

"Then why tell me all this?"

"I figured I'd bring it up before you did," she said "Just in case you *did* think of it and tried to freeze the deal. The whole situation is a little different now, but not much. For one thing, you miss a check and I'll yell copper anyway. Maybe the case will get tossed out of court, but you try explaining to you wife that you've been paying me hush-money!"

Bauman winced. "I wouldn't want to have to."

"Besides that, buster, I've got a friend. He's bigger than you are, and he looks out for my interests. You keep paying me or he'll come around to visit you."

"Are you threatening me?"

"Not yet," she said. "Just keep kicking through with your hundred bucks a week, and you'll be okay."

"I told you I'd pay."

"Just make sure you do," she said.

She hung up. Bauman slowly lowered the telephone into its cradle. There was a dull throbbing pain just back of his forehead, and a needle-like sharp stabbing in his stomach. She had him coming and going. There was no escape from her, none at all.

Thousands of people had driven across that bridge that night; only he had bothered to stop and pick her up. Why was he the lucky one?

Let's face it, he told himself sternly: you asked for it. When you picked her up, you wanted something to happen. And something did happen.

And then you got it.

Right where it hurts.

Ethel stood in the doorway, glorying in her nudity. Her cheeks were crimson and she felt wild and dizzy, but she made no effort to hide her bare body.

She tried to focus her eyes.

There was a man standing there. A man who looked familiar. He was gaping at her, his mouth wide as he took in the unexpected sight of her full-bodied, voluptuous bareness.

With a struggle to get her vodka-bleared eyes under control, Ethel recognized him. Mr. Hawkins, the man who had the apartment downstairs. He was a ticket-taker in a Manhattan theater, and he worked evenings, so he was always home this time of day. A handsome man, tall and dignified-looking, maybe forty years old.

He would do, Ethel thought.

He would be her Mister X.

"Come on in!" she gaily cried, "just who I've been waiting for!"

She reached forward, the bare globes of her breasts swaying, and caught him by the wrist. She yanked him into the apartment and closed the door. Then she stood facing him, and as excitement burned away some of the haze of vodka in her brain she was able to see the expression on his face more clearly.

He looked stunned.

But he wasn't hiding his eyes in horror. He was looking right at her, looking her over, getting a good view of breasts and middle and hips and legs.

He said, "I heard a crash—I heard you yell. I was afraid something was wrong."

"Nothing's wrong," Ethel burbled. "I'm having a party. All by myself. Come joint the party. You want some vodka, maybe?"

"No, I'd better—"

"Don't go away," she said.

She hesitated only a moment. Then she flung herself at him. She threw her arms around him, and grabbed him tight, pulling him against her. She rubbed the passion-swollen tips of her breasts against him. That was good—the fabric against her sensitive skin. She touched him with her hips and knees. She put her lips to his, and kissed him violently, but he didn't respond.

He wrenched his lips away. "Mrs. Bauman—"

"Ethel. Call me Ethel."

"You're drunk."

"I know. Isn't it great?"

"This could cause trouble," he said. "We're both married people."

Ethel let go of him. She stepped back and tried hard to look sober. Her breasts were in agitation, and she knew she was blushing violently. She wasn't in the habit of standing naked before strange men.

She said, "I won't tell anybody if you don't tell anybody. This'll be our little secret."

"Mrs. Bau—"

"The name's Ethel."

"Ethel," he said. "Look, you're a very beautiful woman, but I—"

"Damn you, love me!" she shrieked. "What do I have to do, get down on my knees in front of you? Love me! Right now! I need you!"

She had never said words like those to her own husband, or to any other man in the world. But now, as she stood nude before Charlie Hawkins, the words came spewing out of her mouth in an uncontrollable flow. She begged him to take her. She trumpeted her need. She hardly felt drunk anymore. This was a matter of life and death, this was the craving that could keep her from going buggy with boredom.

Hawkins stared at her with bewilderment written all over his face. Then he said, in a low voice, "I never heard anything like this in my life. You want me to—"

"Come on."

Ethel flung herself at him a second time. She began to claw at his clothes. If she could only get him naked, she thought, he wouldn't hesitate like this. She fumbled with buttons and zippers. For a moment, he tried to push her away. But as he shoved, he happened to put his hand against the ripe lush pinkness of one of her breasts, and what had started as a shove ended as a caress. His fingertips curved around the heavy, taut globe of flesh. At the same moment, Ethel's fingers passed over his clothing. She heard him gasp and snort.

The rest was easy.

In another instant, he was pulling his clothes off. His inhibitions vanished with Ethel's wild assault. She helped him, and soon he was naked except for his socks. Ethel looked him over. He was a bigger man than Fred. And he wanted her very much just now.

They didn't go into the bedroom. For one thing, Ethel was a little queasy about taking him to the bed in which she had spent her whole married life. For another, the bed was made and she didn't feel like mussing it. For a third thing, her passion was so overriding that there was no time to go into any other room.

She pulled him right down to her on the floor, and he had her there.

There was no carpet on the floor. Just bare, cold wood. "It's such a handsome parquet," Fred had said, meaning it would cost a lot of money to carpet it. Now Ethel was aware of the handsome parquet against her back. She didn't mind, not at all.

Charlie Hawkins was against her. He was gasping hoarsely, his face as flushed as hers. His hand grabbed for the big globes of her breasts. His mouth hit hers, and he kissed her, hard.

They didn't waste time. A kind of wild frenzy had come over her, and her keyed-up body, which had been waiting for this moment for eternities, needed no further preliminaries. She was ready. She was as ready as any woman had ever been.

He took her.

He was forceful and Ethel went wild at his assault, and she experienced ecstasy at this moment when her dream came true. This was like losing her virginity, in a way. That was a terribly exciting moment for her. She had crossed a border. Until this moment, only her husband had known her. Now she had broken her vows. Now she was free.

Her body, beyond her control, trembled and twisted. A shock of delight went over her. Each moment brought her closer to ecstasy.

He was almost brutal. There seemed to be great strength in him, great endurance. His body worked like a machine, bringing forbidden pleasure to her.

Ethel quivered. Ethel shook.

Ethel exploded with a passion wilder than she had ever experienced before.

Her whole body trembled and went into a convulsion of lust, and she grabbed him tight, her fingers clawing the muscles of his back, and his hands grabbed her buttocks, and he buried his face to the deep hills of her breasts and gasped his pleasure while Ethel found the final peaks of her own.

They were finished. Over and done.

She had sinned, and she had had pleasure from her sin, and now she felt strange and different.

They rested. His hoarse gasping went on for a few minutes. Then he rolled away, and lay by her side. Ethel felt perfectly sober. She knew she had done something wrong, and yet she did not regret having done so, for now her life had a center once again, she had a reason for being alive.

He said, in a strangely deep voice, "This wasn't my idea. Remember that. You practically raped me"

"I know. I don't deny that."

"Why?"

"Because I wanted you," she said. "Do I need any better reason? I'm bored and lonely, and I was drinking to cheer myself up, and I wanted a man. And you rang the doorbell. You were just what I wanted."

He was silent. Ethel got to her feet. She stood naked, looking at him. Her heart still beat thunderously from her ecstasy.

"Do you want a drink now?" she asked.

"I might as well."

She poured vodka for them both. Then she padded back across the room to him and crouched to hand him his drink, her bare breasts dangling forward.

She took a sip of her drink. Then she said, "Isn't it lucky that you work evenings? You're home every day. And so am I. Home and alone and bored. I hope you'll come to visit me more often, Charlie. There are so many things I want to try."

CHAPTER NINE

Sid Miller sat at his handsome limed-oak desk, writing checks. They weren't big checks. He didn't have enough money left for that. They were ordinary garden-variety checks—twenty-five dollars to the telephone company, thirty-five for electricity and gas, the check to his account, to his lawyer, the hundred-dollar blackmail check to Joanne Harris.

They were small bills, at least by the one-time standards of Sid Miller, but they added up. He had better than five hundred dollars' worth of bills to pay, and when all the checks had been written, his account balance would be down to a nice round zero, give or take a kopeck or two. That wasn't so good. But he had a check in his wallet for two grand, just received from Switzerland, and when he got that deposited he'd be in better shape—for a while. The Swiss money was just about at its end. Miller had had a rough week financially. He was getting close to rock bottom now, and he would be sunk pretty soon, unless the deal now in the fire came through.

His head ached. His back hurt. He was dog-tired. He had been drinking on and off all day, to ease the deal. There was a girl coming in another fifteen or twenty minutes, and that would help—a little, But not much. Not enough. Miller was in a bad way, and he knew it.

The telephone rang.

He snatched it up frantically on the first ring—an out-of-character gesture for him, because in his more lordly days he had usually let the telephone ring four or five times before deigning to answer.

"Hello?"

"Sid, Harry here."

His lawyer. The man had been working all day on an attempt to revive Miller's career as a real estate operator, by pyramiding a couple of Miller's small properties into a bigger deal that would get him started again.

Miller said, "Well?"

"Not so good, Sid."

Miller kept calm. "How so?"

"They want an escrow before they'll go anywhere," the lawyer said. "I've been hammering away at them all day. They wanted you to put a hundred grand on deposit as a token of good faith. I told them that it was out of the question. I got it down to twenty grand."

Miller closed his eyes. "That's all, huh? Just a twenty grand escrow?"

"How much of it do you have, Sid?"

"Maybe a hundred bucks. If I tear up a couple of these checks I've just written, maybe about two hundred. That's not enough, Harry."

"No. It isn't."

"Can I get financing?" Miller asked.

"On an escrow deal?" the lawyer said. "Be realistic, Sid. Nobody's going to lend you money to help you stake a performance bond. The whole idea of a performance bond is to show that you're solvent. And you aren't solvent."

"No," Miller said. "I'm not. So where do we go from here?"

"I don't know," the lawyer said. "Sell the properties outright and live off the proceeds, I guess."

"And what do I do after that? Eat up the last of my capital and then where am I?"

"I wish I could tell you, Sid."

"Let me tell *you*, then. I'm nowhere. I'm all through. That's where."

"Listen, Sid, maybe I can stop over, we can talk this whole thing through—"

"Never mind," Miller said quietly. "You've done all you can do, Harry. Call it a day. And send me your bill in the morning. I might as well pay you while I've still got a little left. If you wait till the weekend you may have to get it from the bankruptcy referee."

"Let me come over and talk to you, Sid."

"What's the use?" Miller asked tiredly. "Thanks for everything, Harry. So long."

He hung up. He hunched himself forward and put his head in his hands.

That was it. The finish, the end. He didn't have any resources left. The money he might have used to start again had drained off in blackmail, in alimony, in lawyer fees, in call girl fees, in everything under the sun. He was just about broke now, and no way to get on his feet.

The door chimed. That lovely, sexy chime. Miller answered it. There was a girl there, a girl from the service, a slender, willowy brunette with stunning breasts jutting out against a wine-colored sweater. Miller didn't even bother to be polite with her. There was no airy chit-chat tonight, no pretense of sociability.

"Come on in," he said. "And get your clothes off."

"I'm Nolie," the girl said, looking puzzled by his brusqueness.

"Hello, Nolie. Come on, strip. I don't have all night!"

She smiled uneasily. Obviously she wasn't used to this kind of treatment from her clientele. But, pro that she was, she fell jauntily into the mood. Without protesting or losing any time, she began to get out of her clothes.

Miller watched her. Hungrily.

Off came the sweater and the skirt, the slip, the bra. She had superb breasts, big and white and firm and close together, with small dark nipples rising from their centers. Her body was lean from the chest to the hips, then blossomed out in magnificent hips and legs and buttocks.

"Keep the stockings on," Miller said. "And the garter belt."

He looked her over. The large, squeezable buttocks, the firm breasts, the gently curving waist, the flaring hips—yes, an absolutely delicious hunk of woman flesh he thought. A girl of about twenty-three, in the prime of her seductiveness, darkly beautiful, with glittering, alert, intelligent eyes—terrific. Utterly terrific.

He got the whip from the closet and handed it to her. Her breasts swayed enticingly as she took it from him. Miller began to undress.

"Hit me," he said, when he was naked. "Good and hard."

She whipped him, as he encouraged her to do. His body tingled with each stroke of the flexible cane; within minutes, he was alive with physical excitement. But tonight he did not care to prolong the preliminaries. Another time, he might enjoy half an hour or so of running around the apartment pursued by the girl with the whip, but tonight he was tense and tight-knit, and he wanted only the release that passion could give him.

"Okay," he said, after a few minutes. "That's enough of that."

The girl smiled and put down the whip. She was panting from her exertions, her breasts gleaming with sweat and rising and falling actively. Her nostrils were wide as she gasped; her small, dark nipples were taut. She was ready.

Miller pointed to the carpet.

"Lie down," he said.

She obliged. He lay down with her. He pressed his body against hers. Almost hysterically, he took one of her breasts to his mouth, kissed it, touched the soft, firm, springy flesh against his lips, enjoying the nipple against his lips. He caressed the breast.

Clawing your way up in life, trying to make something out of yourself. And for what? To get kicked in the teeth eventually, anyhow. No matter how high you get, Miller thought, there's always somebody waiting to kick you in the teeth.

He felt like crying.

He lifted his head from the girl's breast. She was ready for anything, a nice cooperative girl. He ran his hand across the smooth coolness of her waist, then along her legs, where the silky flesh alternated with the straps of her garters. He touched her soft knees. She give a little sigh. Good girl, he thought. Put on a show for the customer. Or do you really mean that? Do I turn you on, girlie?

He touched her again. More intimately.

She made a gentle purring sound.

Miller smiled. He almost felt calm now. He pressed his body against hers. Her arms opened for him. Miller took her.

She was willing and ready. He took her, and she gasped and sighed and trembled and twisted. She wrapped her arms around him, as agilely as a contortionist, locking them around his lower back. He could feel her nails digging him. His body moved, and that was great, and he reached to grab her bare buttocks with his hands.

The flesh was firm and cool and good. He dug his fingers at her flesh.

He was trying to take from her a comfort that mere loving could no longer give him. He was very alone tonight, and no matter how luscious the body he held, that could not help enough. Still, she helped a little.

She was sighing hoarsely. Her fingers were raking his body. Miller put his mouth against her shoulder, nibbled, took a gentle bite. Faster, faster, the dizzy throb of passion over him now. She helped him along. Faster and yet faster she worked, to give him the most intense thrill, and Miller began to snort and gasp in growing ecstasy.

The big moment.

He took his pleasure and his shuddering body shook through a long moment of delight, and he was vaguely aware of her shivering, and acting as though she were really enjoying the moment. Then the tide of pleasure passed over him and was gone. Miller lay exhausted.

He rolled away, after a moment, getting to his feet. She didn't budge at first. She just lay there on the floor a delectable-looking creature with her pale skin and her dark hair and eyes. Her feet were apart and her breasts were heaving, and her sparkling eyes were smiling at him as though he were the only man in the world capable of making her happy.

Miller felt like hell.

He said, "That was very good, Nolie. Now get up and put your clothes on and go away."

"I could stay awhile."

"Don't bother. I'm in a lousy mood tonight, Nolie. I'm sorry, but that's the way things sometimes go. Ordinarily I'm a little more civil."

"I didn't mind."

"I feel embarrassed for myself," he said. "But I couldn't help that. You might as well go."

She smiled and got to her foot. Even now, after he had finished, Miller was able to appreciate the smoothly sensual flow of her body as she stood up, her big breasts swaying like bells, her muscles rippling, She went into the bathroom to tidy herself up, and Miller stared after her, eyeing the firm globes of her buttocks with satisfaction, watching the play of muscles in the two firm cheeks that were so attractively outlined by the upper band of the garter belt.

While she was gone, Miller walked over to his desk, where the checks he had written earlier were still lying. He studied them for a moment, then picked up the hundred-dollar check to Joanne Harris and ripped it unhesitatingly in half. The blackmailing witch could do without her money this once, Miller thought. He picked up his checkbook and wrote a new check, also for a hundred dollars, and made it payable to "cash."

Nolie came out. Miller watched her graceful motions as she pulled her panties up over the white globes of her buttocks, as she imprisoned the heavy, stunning thrusts of her breasts in her bra, as she slipped her other clothing on. When she was fully dressed and just about ready to leave, he walked over to her.

"Here," he said. "This is for you."

He handed her the check, folded in half. She took it, without unfolding it, looked quickly down at it, then up at him.

"You didn't have to do that," she said.

"I *did* have to," he told her. "Otherwise I wouldn't have done it. Take it and don't raise a fuss about it, will you? It's the least I can do for you after the way I just treated you."

"I wasn't complaining."

"You should have complained," Miller said. "I used you like an animal. I'm sorry. I feel like a louse for that. The only excuse that I have is that I'm overwrought, and that isn't any excuse. So take the check. Take it and go, Nolie. I'm sorry. I'm sorry about a lot of things."

He was still naked. She stood by the door, fully dressed, and looked at him in an odd way. Then she managed a professional smile and said, "Well, I hope to see you soon. Maybe next time you'll be feeling a little better."

Miller nodded. "So long, Nolie."

She went out. He locked the door of the apartment after her. His head still hurt. His mind blazed with the memory of her, with the image of those long legs, those stunning globular breasts, the picture of her red nipple, the touch of her satiny buttocks against his hands. She had been really a memorable girl, he thought. Too bad he hadn't been in a mood to make the best use of her. Wham, bam thank you, ma'am, and she was gone. With a girl built like that, lovemaking should have been a slow voyage of exploration.

Too late for that, Miller thought.

Too late for everything.

At least he was calling it quits on a high note bed-wise. This Nolie had been a superb dish. Quite a contrast to his first girl, a quarter of a century before. Arlene, that was her name. A fat pig, with ruddy cheeks and boobs like melons and a flabby, thick waist. Miller had had her in a vacant lot one night, down in the weeds and garbage, and that had seemed like the sheerest bliss to him. At fifteen any kind of tramp seems like Helen of Troy.

He shrugged. No use reliving old memories now. He looked at the checks lying on the desk. He looked around the plush apartment. He thought quickly of the good times he had had, and then he thought about how it had felt to go broke.

He walked to the window. He looked out at the dark splendor of Central Park, stretching off for miles to the north. Then he opened the casement. Cool April air blew in. He realized that he was still naked, and he wondered if he ought to put on a robe, at least, before he did it.

He decided not to. He had come into the world naked, and it was appropriate to go out of it that way. Appropriate in more ways than one, because they had all stripped him of his possessions, especially the blackmailer Joanne, and so he couldn't really claim ownership of the clothes on his back. To hell with modesty, Miller thought. When they found what was left of him, they'd throw a blanket over him quickly enough and cloak his nakedness.

He put one leg over the windowsill. He felt very calm, now. He knew that there was no turning back, no imaginable point in staying alive, because he was through, kaput, finished, washed up. If he lived, it would be to spend the rest of his life as a slave to employers and lawyers and blackmailers and grasping wives. Who needed it?

Sid Miller didn't.

He put the other leg over the sill, and let himself dive forward like a swimmer leaping into a lake. The night air rushed up around his sweating naked body. He plummeted downward, hundreds of feet, and all the time he fell he waited calmly, knowing that at long last he was going where nobody could make trouble for him anymore.

Fred Bauman was having trouble, too. Financial trouble, which was not exactly what he needed most at this particular moment.

His scheme of acquiring Joanne's blackmail money by playing the horses wasn't working out so very well. He didn't have time to go out to the track himself, of course, and so he hunted up his old bookmaker and quietly placed a couple of bets. He had studied the form charts endlessly, and had calculated his system from scratch.

All that happened was that he lost eight dollars. A 3-1 favorite failed even to show, which was something that Bauman's system didn't allow for. Trying to recoup that loss, he tossed another eight away. He was out sixteen, now. He started to squirm.

He studied the charts even more closely. His system produced a winning day: a net take of $1.15. The next day, he dropped $5. Things weren't going properly at all. He began to see that it wasn't going to be so simple to recoup his money this way. His system supposedly protected him against big losses, but at the same time it guaranteed that he'd never make a big winning. And a streak of improbably bad luck could really hurt him, since he was fighting against time. He didn't have all that much money that he could use as his stake for wagering. A hundred bucks a week had to go to Joanne. And he knew he ought to be putting aside at least ten dollars a week toward the ultimate repayment of his bank loan.

The following Tuesday, he stopped off at the bank and bought a hundred-dollar money order. He didn't dare send the girl a check drawn on his own account, because there was always the chance that Ethel might suddenly decide to go over the checkbook some Sunday afternoon. That could lead to all kinds of problems. Bauman could see it now: Ethel coming into the living room, checkbook in hand, a mildly puzzled look on her face.

"There's this check made out to a Miss Joanne Harris," she would say mildly, "One hundred dollars. What's it for, Fred?"

Bauman didn't care to risk that. So he sent a money order, even though it was a few cents more expensive than a check, and involved making a special trip to the bank. He mailed the money order off.

One payment down and thirty-six to go. Strain lines began to appear in his face as the days crept along. A second week passed, and another hundred-dollar money order went off. Bauman tried to pretend to his business friends, to his wife, to their occasional guests, that everything was all right.

"Sure, I'm a little tired," he said. "The tax season—it was really rough this year. But I'll pick up. Wait till summer."

He started to look worse and worse, though, instead of better and better. People started to tell him so. It was May, now, and the weather was sunny and bright, but he walked around with a shrunken, waxy winter pallor. The head of his firm even suggested that he take a couple of weeks off, with pay, a kind of early vacation.

It was a tempting idea. He could collect his pay and maybe get another job for the two weeks. He'd leave home at the usual time every day, and Ethel would never be the wiser, and at the end of the two weeks he'd have earned an extra hundred fifty bucks or so. But then the summer would come, and Ethel would say, "Where are we going for our vacation this year?" and he'd be in a mess.

He'd have to tell her. "Oh, I took my vacation in the early part of May, didn't you know? I was holding down a temporary job to make a little extra cash so I could pay my blackmail money."

Sure. Great.

So he had to turn the idea of the early vacation down. He just went plugging along. Every Tuesday he mailed off his money order for a hundred smackeroonies.

But it was getting tougher and tougher. Whatever magic touch he had once had with the horses seemed to have disappeared. He had a little luck with the beasts, but not much; so far, through the first couple of weeks, he showed a net loss of forty dollars on his bets. That wasn't helping him very much toward surmounting his deficit.

The trouble was that there was too much at stake. He had his back to the wall, and couldn't let up. In the old days, when he played the horses, he had felt relaxed and confident. He could give his system full rein. But not now. Now that he had to produce, now that it was vital to show a net profit, he was pressing too hard. Fiddling around with his system. Not trusting it. He was going for bigger killings now, in the hopes of reducing his earlier losses—and the overall result that he was adding to his losses instead of decreasing them.

He had started with about four hundred and fifty left over from the bank's loan after paying Joanne her initial thousand dollars. By the end of the third week, that surplus was just about used up. He had sent three hundred dollars to Joanne, with another hundred due to go on the following Tuesday, and he had dropped money on the horses, and he hadn't so far put aside a red cent for amortization of his loan. He was getting into very deep and very hot water now. He would have to start channeling money from other sources.

He squeezed some cash out of his weekly paycheck. Ethel didn't keep such close watch on him, and he was able to slide five or ten dollars out of his take-home without raising a storm at home. He nibbled a little out of his savings account, ten dollars here, fifteen there. The rest came from his lunch money and his cigarette savings and the tunnel tolls that he no longer paid.

Somehow he made the next payment, the fourth. And the fifth. But there was Number Six coming up, and he wasn't sure how he'd manage.

There were thirty-two payments still to go, all told. Each week, Bauman knew, he was going to have to go through the same grim process, scrabbling and scraping around to come up with the necessary C-note. And when October arrived, the bank was going to want fifteen hundred more from him on that loan. Would he be able to refinance it? Would he have to turn to another bank? He didn't know. He saw chaos ahead.

The decision crept up on him slowly. Bauman didn't know when the thought first entered his mind, his dreams, whispered suggestions in his ear as he worked.

The sixth week he put down twenty on a sure thing at five to two. The good odds were tempting. It went against Bauman's system to stake so much money on a single bet, but he had studied his form charts carefully, and despite the relatively long money, he had concluded that the other horses in the race were duds. His nag would walk home easily, and he'd pick up fifty dollars for his twenty, and that would put him a long way back on the road to recovery.

Everything went fine, except that the horse forgot to win. It finished fourth on a muddy track, and Bauman's twenty-spot went down the drain. From that moment on, he knew he was sunk unless he forgot about the race track and took some more positive way of dealing with his blackmail problem.

It was getting tougher and tougher to find the weekly hundred.

Before long, he'd be embezzling or holding people up or else coming right out and breaking the truth to Ethel and facing the consequences, which would not be pretty. And the cold suspicion was dawning on Bauman that perhaps his obligation to Joanne would not end with the final payment at the end of the year. Why should she stop there? Perhaps she would go on, bleeding him dry for the rest of his life, extorting new payment after new payment and never being satisfied with what he gave her.

Bauman knew that he would never last out the year this way. If the strain didn't break him, it would be a sheer miracle. He had to do something.

He made up his mind at the end of the sixth week.

He was going to have to kill Joanne Harris.

CHAPTER TEN

Ethel Bauman was getting the adultery habit. That wasn't really a hard habit to get, once you were in the swing. And Ethel was very much in the swing by now. Weeks had passed since her first wild session of love making with Charlie Hawkins, and what puzzled her now was how she had been able to get along any other way for so long.

They had things down to a routine, by now. Every day, as soon as her husband headed for work and her daughter went off to school, Ethel would throw herself into her household chores with fierce energy, so as to have them out of the way by noon at the latest. Then—maybe three days a week—Hawkins would come to visit her.

That was easy for him. His wife was a schoolteacher and she was away during the day. His kids were away, too. So they were both alone, he one floor below her. Of course, he couldn't come upstairs to make love to her every day. Ethel would have preferred things that way, but she had to recognize that there were certain human limitations on the man. He had to sleep with his wife at least *some* of the time, or she'd get suspicious.

Weekends, of course, were out. But that left five days a week. Some weeks, Hawkins came up on Monday, Tuesday and Thursday. She timed her trips outdoors, to the market and such, for the days when he wasn't around to give her pleasure.

She felt very strange about her new career as an adulteress. She had lived such a conventional, prosaic life up to now. True, she had lost her virginity before her marriage, but that had been the only daring thing she had ever done in her life. And the man she had lost her virginity to had been the one she ultimately married, so even that hadn't really been particularly wicked.

And now—

Now she had been unfaithful to her husband a few dozen times. She had learned things about the act of love, and about her own responses, that she had never suspected before. Hawkins was an active, virile man, pretty bored with his wife, who was willing to put all his strength to work to make Ethel happy. So she was blossoming. She was radiant. Five years had dropped off her, it seemed; she had lost a little weight, and she looked fresh and glowing, with that special glow that a woman casts when her physical needs are being taken care of properly.

It was strange. As Ethel glowed ever more radiantly, her husband seemed to be aging in the same proportion. Ethel didn't know what was the matter with him anymore. Fred seemed so tired, so discouraged, so elderly all of a sudden. He had lost weight, too, but it didn't look good on him; he had started getting gray very fast; his face was wrinkled and weary. Ethel didn't understand it. He hardly even tried to sleep with her anymore. He seemed to have gained fifteen years in the last month and a half.

She wondered about it, sometimes. Maybe he was sick—maybe he had some kind of tumor that was sapping his strength from within. "You ought to see a doctor," she suggested, but he shrugged the suggestion off. Maybe it was nothing but a bad case of overwork, Ethel decided.

She didn't really care too deeply. Right now she was much too wrapped up in herself—in her love affair.

My love affair. The three words made her tingle with excitement. To rise above the drab boredom of daily life, to know thrills and ecstasies— well, sure, that was wicked, but wasn't she entitled to a little wickedness once in her life? She had been good so very long. Besides, she was still young, still passionate, and her husband seemed to have lost all interest in her. It was hardly all her fault if she turned to infidelity, was it? She had to do something to keep from withering away from boredom and frustration.

Charlie Hawkins was the answer.

She waited for him now. It was ten after twelve on a hot May day, a Monday. Ethel had already made her daily telephone call to her husband's office, and had had her usual vague and unsatisfying conversation with him. He didn't have much to say these days.

Ethel was wearing a bathrobe over nothing at all. She liked being naked for Charlie. Her body, alive now with a voluptuous eagerness it had not known for a long time, pulsed with anticipation and yearning. She was aware of the pounding of her heart, the pulsing of the nipples of her breasts. Soon he would be here, she thought. Soon she would run to him, and throw off her robe, and stand nude before him, and—

She busied herself preparing the drinks. Charlie Hawkins liked vodka and orange juice too. He, too, appreciated its lack of a telltale flavor.

Ethel wasn't drinking as much now as she had been a few months before. Love, not alcohol, was her favorite boredom remedy these days. Her drinking—with Charlie—was purely sociable, and they generally had just a single drink, maybe two, before they got down to the business of love. So she was buying a lot less vodka than before, and drinking a lot less. She felt better for it.

Now she opened a fresh can of orange juice, got everything ready. Her body was tense with need. She hadn't seen him since last Thursday, and since Fred hadn't wanted her all weekend, Ethel was aching with desire. Friday, Saturday, Sunday—this was the fourth day. That was a long time to go without a man, when your needs are awakened this way.

She heard him in the hall. A moment later, the bell rang. Ethel scampered to the door, her breasts bobbing under her loose robe. She opened it, and let him in to the apartment.

"Charlie—"

"Hi," he said. "How's my baby?"

"Hungry for you, Charlie."

Hawkins grinned. At the outset of their relationship, he had been hesitant, uncertain, troubled about everything. When they were actually loving, he was self-confident and capable, but the rest of the time he had been worried about the risks they were running and the possible consequences. Now, that was wearing off. They had been getting away with this for six weeks now, and he was beginning to get assured. When he walked into the apartment, it was with a swagger of bold triumph.

Ethel closed the door. Then she went to him. She pushed against him, giving him plenty of action. His arms went around her, his fingers digging at the soft flesh of her shoulders. Their lips met. His kiss grew demanding. Ethel trembled with passion.

She pulled away from him after a moment. "Let's have a drink, huh?" she said.

"Sure thing. God, what a hot day this is! It must be above ninety."

"Make yourself comfortable," Ethel said.

She walked toward the kitchen to get the orange juice out of the refrigerator. Pausing for a moment at the door of the living room, Ethel shrugged her bathrobe off and draped it across the back of the chair. Completely nude now, with her back turned to him, Ethel could feel the tingle of his eyes as they passed down her body toward her buttocks.

When she returned a moment later, carrying the tray with the drinks,

Hawkins had undressed, too. Ethel smiled at him. She came toward him, her body eager, her breast tips going rigid as he looked at her. Even now, weeks after the beginning of their affair, Ethel had never lost that sense of thrill as she stripped for him. She loved to have him look at her. He had a way of caressing her with his eyes alone that practically drove her wild.

"Here," she said, handing him his drink. "Drink hearty."

Hawkins grinned. He reached with one hand to take the glass, and with the other to cup briefly the jutting globe of her left breast. He pinched the lust-rigid nipple playfully, put the glass to his lips, and said, "Cheers." They both drank.

Ethel shook with need. She got her drink down the hatch fast. Hawkins seemed more relaxed. He sat there, as she looked at him.

She moved toward him, putting her empty glass down. Dropping to her knees on the bare floor, she crawled up to him. She gazed with rapture at his face which glowed with anticipation. She caressed him lightly, teasingly, and then kissed him, tantalizing.

He sighed deeply. He was impatient, wanting more, but thrilled by her fleeting caress.

She tired of teasing and grew passionate. This was something that disgusted Fred, but Hawkins was different—she knew from his hoarse breathing how much pleasure she was giving him. Her own body tingled ecstatically. At times like this, she was aware of the strength of him, in the most direct way. Once, a few weeks ago, she had finished him this way. That had left her unsatisfied, of course, but she had been pleased simply to be able to gratify him. And then, after resting half an hour, he had pleased her the usual way, anyhow.

Now, Ethel paused when she knew that he was growing excited. Her own need was too great today to permit any one-sided pleasures. Breathing hard, Hawkins put down his glass and said, "Now, my turn."

He got down on the floor with her. Ethel lay back, closing her eyes, knowing that delicious sensations of pleasure soon would be hers. She loved Hawkins' hand running over her body, from her breasts to her knees. He held her legs a moment, and then Ethel began to gasp in pleasure as his kisses began.

She went wild with ecstasy. He knew how best to thrill her completely, cupping her breasts with gentle hands as he pleased her. Soon, Ethel was shivering with delight.

"Now both of us,'" Hawkins said.

That was something he had shown her last week—a simple and obvious way that they could both offer pleasure at once. She didn't know why that had never occurred to her, except that her mind wasn't really trained for thinking that way yet. But he guided her into position, pressing his hands on her buttocks and swinging her. Her anticipation was so great she could hardly control herself. A moment later, she trembled as he returned to her and busily renewed the pleasure.

For long moments they continued. Her hands touched him tenderly, and he grasped the heavy hills of her breasts. They moved eagerly. Ecstasy rippled through Ethel's entire body, and she trembled, feeling chills of delight.

At last she could wait no longer. "Hurry!" she cried hoarsely. "Now, Charlie! Now!"

They separated hastily, then found one another again. Their mouths met in a frenzied kiss, their hands groped and caught each other, then tore apart as their arms tangled in a tight embrace. Her body was out of control, screaming for him.

He took her.

"Oh, yes!" Ethel half-shrieked. "That's good, that's so good yes, yes!"

He laughed, a deep, booming, confident laugh. He drove her to the heights of passion immediately. Ethel clung to him, reeling dizzily, stunned by the power of the sensations she was experiencing. Had anything ever been like this with Fred? Ever, even in the beginning when she had been young and wonder-smitten by love? She didn't think so. She didn't think anything had ever been so powerful.

Hawkins continued. Her heavy breasts flattened. Her tall nipples drilled like little pebbles. Ethel flung her arms out, then tightened them high around his shoulders. She twined them around him, hammering her nails against the skin of his back.

He worked in a mild rhythmic tattoo. Ethel met him with eager counterassaults of her own. Her whole body shook.

Then the full fury of her culmination arrived. Higher she soared, higher and yet higher, into wild, unknown regions of ecstasy. Every nerve in her body trembled like a taut bowstring. Her body itself seemed to dissolve and drop away, leaving nothing but pure sensation behind. Her eyes were closed, her arms were locked around Charlie Hawkins' broad back, she was working furiously. She was aware that he had achieved his fulfillment. She experienced the blaze of her own.

Then everything ended.

Slowly, artfully, Hawkins brought her down from the heights of her passion, until they both lay quietly on the floor, breathing hoarsely, their bodies stippled with sweat. His hand rested on her breasts, cupping both the big mounds together. Ethel did not open her eyes. She listened to the fading thunder of her heart.

As always, in the moments after the greatest joy, there came the doubts and the inner questions. She did not voice them. Why ruin his pleasure? Why insert a note of uncertainty and fear?

Yet she could not help but feel apprehensive. The very intensity of her ecstasy, the dynamic, triumphant surge of sheer pleasure, had made her feel troubled. For she knew that in this world you never got any pleasure without paying a price. What she was doing was shameless, wicked, immoral. No matter what rationalization she offered, there was no getting away from the fact that Ethel Bauman was breaking her marriage vow. She lay there naked on the floor of her own apartment in wantonness, and she could pretend that she was doing so out of boredom or because her husband was neglecting her, but the fact still remained that she was doing something wrong.

She knew she was doing wrong.

And she knew that fate was going to exact a price, it had to. Pleasure wasn't free, Ethel knew. There was always some sort of price.

It was Monday of the seventh week, and Fred Bauman knew he was near the end of his rope. He couldn't go on paying Joanne Harris her blackmail money much longer, and he couldn't afford to let her expose him. The time had come to take the step that he had been planning in a hesitant way for some days now.

He wasn't sure quite how to begin. The first thing he tried was, he knew, doomed to failure, but he tried it anyway—hoping it might work. If some new Post Office clerk, who didn't know all the rules and regulations, happened to be on duty—

What he did was to telephone the Times Square Station Post Office and say, "Is it possible for you to give me the home address of somebody who rents one of your Post Office boxes?"

"I'm sorry, sir, we can't do that," was the firm reply. "It's strictly against our policy to divulge such information to anyone."

Protesting, Bauman said, "It's extremely important that I get in touch face-to-face with a certain boxholder this afternoon. It's a matter of great importance to her. I know it's a little irregular, but couldn't I possibly have her home address?"

It was like arguing with a machine. "I'm afraid not, sir," Bauman was told. "Boxholders pay for the privilege of privacy, and we cannot release personal information concerning them."

"I see," Bauman said unhappily.

Then came an unexpected statement: "If you wish, sir, you could give me your message and I would phone the person in question—strictly as a favor, you understand. The Post Office Department doesn't prescribe such services. You say it's urgent?"

"Not that urgent," Bauman said. There was no sense sending any messages via a third party. That would only get Joanne scared. He thanked the Post Office man for the offer, and hung up.

So they wouldn't let him have the home address. Well, that wasn't really a surprise, Bauman thought. There was another way of making contact with her.

He pondered it all evening. His mood was tense and edgy. It was a direct contrast with Ethel's. She was buoyant and cheerful, whistling and grinning. Bauman didn't understand why his wife was in such a bubbly mood these days. Always waltzing around the apartment, always gay and merry. She had taken off some weight too, and she looked livelier and healthier than he could remember her being in ages. What was the story?

He didn't know. Certainly it couldn't be anything he had done, because he knew that during this time of stress he had been little but a grouch. Even when he slept with her, once or twice a week, he didn't sense that she enjoyed him in any way. But the rest of the time she was as happy as a vagabond.

Was she ill, he wondered?

But he doubted that. Maybe it was simply springtime, Bauman thought, that was making Ethel so cheerful all of a sudden. He put the matter out of his mind. He had more serious things to think about.

The next day was Tuesday. At lunchtime, Bauman stopped into the bank and bought his usual hundred-dollar money order. It took his last remaining supply of free cash to do it, but he didn't let that trouble him, because he knew that this was going to be the last one.

He did not put the money order into the mails, as he had done with the previous six. Instead he put it in an envelope, slipped it into his desk drawer, and left it there overnight.

Reaching his office at ten minutes to nine the next day, Bauman took the envelope from his drawer and crossed the room to his superior's desk.

Bauman said, "Tom, I've got to go out on some errands this morning. A little shopping for the home—I'd like to get it done before the afternoon rush starts. I'll put in the time after five o'clock today. Will that be okay with you?"

"Sure, Fred. Anything you like. You know it doesn't matter, as long as the work gets done."

Bauman smiled. "Thanks, Tom. I appreciate that."

He left the office and walked briskly across town to the Times Square Post Office station. It was a warm morning at the end of May, with a balmy breeze blowing down the crosstown streets.

He reached the Post Office at quarter after nine. *I hope she hasn't been here yet to pick up her mail,* Bauman thought anxiously.

Somehow he doubted it. He didn't think Joanne Harris was the type to get up this early in the morning, even for the sake of collecting a hundred dollars.

Strolling into the lobby, Bauman looked around for the rooms of Post Office boxes. He found them after a moment or two of searching, and casually sauntered toward them, watching for the girl lest she come up on his unawares. He looked up and down the rooms of boxes for the right one. Ah. Number 356. There it was.

Through the smoked glass window of the box, Bauman could see an envelope lying within. Good, he thought. That meant she hadn't been here yet to pick up her mail.

He walked over to the stamp window, keeping an eye on the boxes, and joined the line. He edged up step by step to the counter, continually glancing over his shoulder to make sure he didn't miss the girl.

The clerk had to ask him twice what he wanted, before Bauman realized he was being spoken to. Shamefacedly, he swung around and peered through the window. "Uh, give me two five-cent stamps," Bauman blurted.

He put down his dime, took the stamps, jammed them in his pocket. Still no Joanne. Plenty of people were showing up at the boxes to get their morning mail, but nobody that he recognized as the girl. He hoped he would recognize her. After all, he had seen her for only a short time, at night, nearly two months before. Naked he would certainly spot her. The memory of those bare breasts blazed in his brain. But he wasn't so sure about her face. The details of her features were beginning to fade.

He waited. He knew that loitering in the Post Office all day would simply not be allowed. Sooner or later some Post Office guard would decide that he was casing the joint, and would ask him what he wanted. And then Bauman would have to leave.

He also knew that the girl might wait all day before she decided to go down to the Post Office and pick up her mail. Could he wait here all day for her? That would be abusing the privilege he'd been granted at the office. They were expecting him to be out an hour or so at most, not the whole day. Besides, she might not even come at all.

Still, he had to find her.

Without taking his eye from the boxes, Bauman went to another stamp window and shuffled along the line until he reached the front.

"Give me an air letter sheet," he said, because it was the first thing that came to his mind.

He paid his eleven cents and got the air letter. Then going to the table that faced the wall in which the postal boxes were mounted, Bauman picked up the cheap ballpoint pen that was chained there and started to write a letter, pausing every few moments as if to think of a phrase, but actually simply looking up to see if the girl had arrived. She hadn't. Well, no one would accuse him of loitering, if he seemed to be writing a letter. Nor had he missed her, he knew, because the letter that had been in her box was still there.

Bauman had no idea of what to write, so he slowly and gravely covered the blue air letter sheet with the words, "Having wonderful time, wish you were here," over and over again. By ten o'clock he could no longer stall over the letter anymore. He put down the pen, folded the air letter sheet as instructed, and sealed it. Addressing it to *Santa Claus, The North Pole*, Bauman slowly carried it across the floor and dropped it in the airmail chute.

Ten-fifteen, now.

Bauman went outside and paced up and down in front of the main entrance of the Post Office. Every few minutes he darted a glance inside to see if she had come in through some other door. The day was getting very hot, now, and Bauman was roasting in his jacket and tie.

Ten-thirty.

Ten-forty-five. They were going to be wondering, at the office, what had happened to him.

At eleven o'clock Bauman went back inside the Post Office and checked her box. The letter still sat there. He went to the stamp window, and bought a second air letter sheet. If necessary, he was ready to kill the whole day this way.

As he started to go to the writing table, he looked up and saw her—at last.

She was opening Box 356 and reaching in for her mail.

CHAPTER ELEVEN

Karen didn't know how much longer she was going to be able to stay sane. The weeks were sliding by. The weather was turning hotter. She was getting closer and closer to final exams, and she knew she was heading for a really catastrophic blowup in two or three of her courses. She couldn't help that. She was going out of her mind with the need for a man, and she didn't know what to do about that.

This was a funny business. Karen had always thought that in our society men are forever chasing after women, looking for love, and women are forever fending them off. Not so. At least not where she was concerned. Down on the level of Karen Bauman, age fifteen plus, it worked just the opposite way. She wanted love—and the boys were scared stiff of her. What was the matter, she wondered?

She wasn't ugly. That she was sure of. She was a provocative girl if she was anything. She didn't have two heads. Her personality didn't repel people.

So why wouldn't anyone sleep with her?

Karen knew the answer to that. It was because she went out with the wrong type of boys. She went out with the nice clean-cut middle-class sixteen- and seventeen-year-old boys who Simply Didn't Do That Sort Of Thing. They were too polite, too well-behaved, to perform a dirty act like that with a girl of their own background.

They were scared, Karen knew.

Scared of getting into trouble, for one thing, because there was a law about going to bed with a girl under the age of eighteen. Scared of other things too, though. Scared of maybe having to marry her, which could louse up their own plans for an Ivy League future. Scared of catching something—for how did they know they would not? Most of all, scared of being shown up like the immature kids they were, kids who didn't have any idea what to do with a girl.

Karen knew where she could go if she wanted an initiation into love. Go across town, into one of the tough sections. All she had to do was stand around for ten minutes wearing a tight sweater, and she'd get picked up and taken care of. That was for sure.

But she hesitated.

Now *she* was the scared one. She was afraid of rough treatment; she was afraid of the whole slum setup. She preferred to get her first loving from a boy in her own background group, somebody she went to school with. But that didn't seem too easy to arrange.

She had tried. She had tried with Dick Stearns, in the most obvious way, and the net result had been that now he shunned her in school as though she were carrying the Black Death. He wouldn't even look at her when they passed in the halls, and he would have resigned from the United Nations Club except that Karen's academic difficulties had forced her to drop out instead.

Naturally, she wasn't dating him anymore. But it was just as bad with the boys that she did date. Karen would ever so discreetly let them know that she could be had, but either they didn't get the message or else they chose to ignore the message.

All her passionate wriggling, all her gasping and sighing, all her lustful kisses, all her little hints, failed to produce the desired effect. Karen was chaste but not chased. What did you have to do, she wondered, to get made in this world?

She knew the answer: you had to grow up. A fifteen-year-old who didn't live in the slums simply didn't have the opportunities of immorality that a more ragged girl did. She was bound by the rules of her own society, and she would just have to wait until she was a few years older and a different set of rules applied to her. A time would come when it would be unfashionable for a girl in Karen's group to be a virgin—but right now, virginity was in and sin was out.

Karen didn't know how she could manage to hold out until she was eighteen or thereabouts. But, as things turned out, she didn't have to wait after all.

It happened about quarter to five on a Wednesday afternoon in May. Karen had stayed late at school, not to serve in one of the extracurricular clubs, but for the more humiliating purpose of attending an after-hours cram course in Spanish held for the benefit of flunking students. Now she was on her way home. She had to walk four blocks from the school to the bus stop.

As it happened, the route she travelled took her through a safely middle-class neighborhood. But just to the south was a broiling, roistering slum zone, which luckily had a high school all its own.

Karen stared into the rundown area as she skirted along the north edge of a slum district. The school itself, and the homes of everyone who went to it, lay in it. Out there, she knew, a girl stopped being a virgin when she was eleven or twelve, and usually had had many men by the time she was fifteen. Karen wasn't all that eager to find out about love. But she envied the slum people the freedom of morality that they had. That was about all you could envy them for, after all.

She was still a block from the bus stop when the boy came up to her.

It was hard to tell his age. He was small and thin and wiry, and stood no more than inch or two taller than Karen. From his height and from the slightness of his build, he might have been fourteen. But his face was no fourteen-year-old face; his eyes were cold and hard, his lips thin and predatory, his forehead creased with lines. It was the face of somebody who knew what hunger was and how it felt to have rainwater dripping through the ceiling onto your bed. His face was smudged and his dirty white T-shirt was torn in a couple of places. He was sweaty.

He crossed Karen's path and said, "Hello, good-lookin'."

"Hello."

"Where you goin'?"

"Home," she said. Her heart picked up a beat or two. He was blocking her.

"Let's go take a little walk," he suggested.

"Where to?"

"You come visit me."

Karen shook her head. "Some other time," she said, and started to walk around him. He promised adventure and mystery—but also danger. She wasn't all that sure she wanted the kind of adventure he offered.

But she didn't have any choice. She took two steps, and then he moved against her. His face was inches from hers. He reached into his pocket and came up with something, holding it between them, not far from the rising thrust of Karen's breasts. Karen saw what it was. It was a switchblade knife. His finger was on the button.

He said in a low, ugly voice, "You raise a squawk and I gonna cut you good. Come on with me and make like you want to."

Karen's pulse raced, "What are you going to do?" she asked.

"You'll find out when soon enough," he told her. "Come on and keep quiet."

He slipped his arm through hers, and they walked off—crossing the street that divided one neighborhood from the other. It all seemed somehow dreamlike to Karen, that she should be kidnapped on the public street in broad daylight by this dirty little slum boy. She was afraid—and yet intrigued at the same time. Maybe the thing for which she had been searching so hard had found her, she thought, when she wasn't even looking.

He was very close to her. One of her breasts was pressing his side. The contact excited her. They walked a block and a half, until they were on a street of old, dilapidated apartment houses.

"In here," he said.

He guided her into the basement door of one of the houses. Karen felt herself moving through a dark passageway, then through an inner courtyard, finally into another passage with what were probably storage rooms opening off it. He opened a door.

"Look what I got," he announced.

By the dim light, Karen saw five or six boys, ranging in age, she guessed, from about thirteen to sixteen. They were sitting around on the floor in a dismal, cob-webbed room. The strong smell of beer was in the room. The boy who had brought her pushed her in.

He closed the door. And locked it.

He turned to her and said, "It won't do you any good to yell down here. But just in case, one peep out of you and I'll knock all your teeth right down your throat."

"Hey, looka the boobs!" somebody said in a high, piping voice.

"Get her shirt off?" said somebody else.

"Give her some beer first."

Karen began to feel frightened. There were too many of them, and this place was too sinister. She wouldn't have minded one of them, losing the virginity that plagued her so much, and going home at last released from the demon of her innocence. But half a dozen of them, in this steamy, foul-looking basement room—

"Here," one of them muttered. "Have some beer, sister."

He thrust a can almost into her mouth. Karen took it—her hand was shaking, she realized—and drank it down. She didn't like beer much. The first taste was bitter, and made her want to gag. But it was cool, and she was thirsty and afraid, and drinking the beer calmed her. She swallowed gulp after gulp.

Then she looked around. "What's going on here?"

"We gonna have some fun," they told her. "Take your clothes off!"

"Sure," Karen said. "Be glad to."

They looked startled at that. Obviously they were expecting her to put up a tough resistance. They were all ready to jump her and hold her down. But they were in for a surprise, Karen thought. She grinned at them.

Then she began to unbutton her blouse.

They were awed. She opened it, button by button, and took it off and carefully draped it over her school-books on the floor to keep it from getting dirty. She stood there facing them in her bra and skirt, and said, "You want more? Let's have more beer."

"Give her a beer, Joey," someone said.

She took the can and put it to her lips. The beer gave her courage. She drained the can as though it contained ice water. Funny how beer began to taste better after the first few sips, she thought. She felt woozy and excited. This was one fantasy she had never had, but she had the feeling she was going to enjoy this—if she didn't panic.

Karen tossed the empty can to one of her audience.

Then she unhooked the bra and peeled it off.

She heard them gasp in pleasure as she bared her breasts, letting them see the two big, firm, red-tipped mounds. Did the slum girls they made have breasts like that, Karen wondered? The skinny, badly-proportioned girls with the poor diets?

Her breasts ached. The tips seemed to blaze. The idea of baring them like this to half a dozen boys at once made her feel almost dizzy.

"More beer," she said.

Another can was produced. Karen was still thirsty, but she was closer to her capacity than she thought, because after only a few sips she realized that she had had enough beer. The first two cans had gone to her bead. She felt very dizzy all of a sudden.

"Take it off, take it off!" they were yelling. Karen took it off.

She gave them a free show that was most likely infinitely more than they had been expecting. Down came her skirt, and then off went her half-slip, and her panties, and her socks, and that was all. She was completely naked in front of them. She stood there, letting their hard, beady eyes stalk the sloping contours of her breasts and the firm flesh of her legs and the lushness of her waist and hips and the firm globes of her buttocks, and she knew that this was the time, that something was going to happen right here and now in the weirdest of all possible ways, that the drive of her flesh was finally going to be satisfied.

"All right," she said. "Who's first?"

They looked at each other in complete bewilderment. Then the kid who had brought Karen here stepped forward and eyed her arrogantly, his nostrils flaring in lust as he looked her over.

"Me," he said.

She looked at the cold stone floor. "Get me something to lie on," she commanded.

He turned, snapped his fingers. "Get your shirts off, guys! She wants a mattress!"

They hopped to. In a moment, a pile of T-shirts lay spread out on the floor. It wasn't much, Karen thought, but it would keep her from getting dirty or chilled. She moved forward. She lay down.

She felt like a sleepwalker. Could this really be happening, she wondered, as she lay there feeling the cold stone through the shirts against her bare buttocks? Her soft hard-tipped breasts rose in excitement. The tough-looking kid was standing beside her, all but drooling.

Now for the first time Karen felt real terror. There he was, ready to take her, and suddenly the almost dreamlike nature of her acceptance gave way to panic. She didn't want to do this, not here in this strange filthy place, not with that lean boy, not with a crowd of others looking on. She had never meant things to be like this. This was going to hurt, this was going to be agony. Who had ever dreamed boys were so big? How could he possibly—?

"No," Karen said, suddenly sober. "No, don't—my clothes—"

He laughed. And then he grabbed her.

She struggled, but it was too late. He held her with a grasp of iron. She was caught, she could not free her limbs to fight him. His hands gripped the fleshy part of her arms. His sweaty T-shirt was against her bare breasts. She was trapped by him, and there was no escape.

"No," she whimpered. "*No!*"

"This is a hell of a time to change your mind, sister," he said thinly.

Then his body moved. And Karen was terrified. Was loving supposed to be like this? She gasped in pain. He was brutal, and her outraged body sent silent screams of pain through her mind. She closed her eyes and sobbed. He was her first lover, he was hurting her, he was—

He had.

The last painful rush. Stunned, unbelieving, Karen knew what had happened, knew that she had been transformed into a woman in that last violent moment.

She was a virgin no longer.

"Damn," he was muttering. "She never had anybody before! Can you beat that?"

"How about that?" a voice said.

Karen's mind swirled and whirled. He was working, in ceaseless energetic motion, and she experienced the strange new sensations. There was pain—oh, God, was there pain!—but along with the blaze of agony there began to come a different feeling, a thrill of excitement, a sensation of gratification, as nerves that had never been used before came into play.

This was no feverish fantasy of a lonely girl's bedroom now. This was the real thing.

Passion rose for her. She forgot the pain. She was aware only of the ecstasy. She began to gasp in wild excitement. She was vaguely aware that the boy was gasping, too, making hoarse animal-like sounds, faster and faster, and suddenly his hands grabbed for her breasts and held them tight, painfully tight, and he surged and shuddered, and she knew that, while she was still ascending, he had reached the peak of ecstasy.

And then he was moving away from her.

"No," she murmured dreamily. "Don't go—don't leave me—"

She tried to hold him back. How could he go away from her just when she was at the highest moment of ecstasy? But he did, and for a terrible moment Karen was alone and chilled, then a new one was with her, dropping to touch her nakedness with his strong hands, and she sighed thankfully and grasped him and continued her soaring arc toward bliss.

That went on and on.

Karen had no idea who was which. She went into a kind of fever of lust, lying there in a half-conscious state, sweat-dappled and busy, and boy after boy took her and moved away, giving his place to the next, and probably taking another turn later on. She did not know, and she wanted to try hundreds of boys tonight, the whole city if she could.

Her body was blazing. There was still some pain, and she knew that. She knew, too, that hours must be passing, that it might be eight, or nine, or even ten o'clock, that they were worrying about her at home, that she was late for dinner. Somehow that didn't matter either. She let them continue.

Endlessly.

She was lost in a frenzy of lust. Her mind, hazy with an overdose of passion, did not stop to make rational decisions. She lay there, ignoring all sanity. She suspected that there were more than the original six of them by now. They must be bringing the whole neighborhood in, she thought. Brothers and cousins and uncles and all the rest. Everybody, take a free turn.

And then, abruptly, there came an interruption.

Karen was the last to react. She was deep in her hypnosis of passion, in seemingly perpetual desire, and there was somebody working right along with her, and then he was no longer there. Karen waited, naked and eager for the next one, but the next did not come. She heard sounds as of people leaving the room in a hurry. What was happening?

A flashlight blared in her face.

"Come on, girlie, open your eyes," a harsh voice said.

She blinked. "I can't—the light—"

The light winked out. Karen opened her eyes. A policeman stood near her. He looked young and handsome, his stubble-chinned face somber.

"Are you next?" Karen asked.

"Not quite," he said. He was staring at her nakedness. Suddenly Karen felt pain. Her body was afire. Her breasts were aching.

"Get up," the policeman said. "The party's all over, girlie."

She tried to sit up, but she was dizzy, and she had to steady herself. She half-sat a moment, then tried to get up the rest of the way. She couldn't. The muscles of her legs were cramped. She was stiff and sore.

"What time is it?" she asked blurrily.

"Half past eleven," he said. "You had quite a party, huh, girlie? How old are you?"

"F-fifteen."

The cop gaped. "God," he said. He grabbed her by the arm. "Get up, will you?"

"I—I can't. I'm hurt and sore—"

"You ought to be. Everybody in the neighborhood standing on line for his turn. Where do you live, anyway?"

"Forest Hills," Karen murmured. She was starting to come out of her daze now. What had she done? She felt soiled, filthy, polluted. She had given herself to dozens of them, strangers, bums, who-knew-what. She began to tremble and shake.

"Forest Hills?" the cop said, "What the hell are you doing here, then?"

"I don't know," Karen whimpered.

"You don't know? Come on, kiddo. Put your clothes on and I'm taking you in. I don't know when I ever saw anything like this before. What kind of a filthy tramp are you, anyway?"

"I'm—not a tramp," Karen said. "I'm—I was—I never did this before!" She looked at him wildly. "I was a virgin this afternoon."

The cop shook his head slowly. "You know something, girlie? You're crazy!"

He tossed her clothing at her. With trembling fingers Karen pulled her bra on and tried to fasten it. She was dizzy with fear and confusion. Her brain was sizzling. She was starting to realize, now, the immensity of what she had done, and as that realization came home to her, she felt her sanity starting to give way. She was soiled forever. She would never be the same again. She had not simply lost her virginity today, she had lost her soul, her identity.

She tossed the bra away. "Let me go!" she yelled. "Don't come near me!"

Naked, she started to run from the room. The cop caught her, slinging his arms around her breasts and clamping her tight. She could hear him talking to some other person beyond the room. "Get the wagon," he said. "And a straitjacket. We got a real kook here. I think she's buggy."

Karen felt hysteria close in.

She began to scream, and the scream went echoing down the corridors of her tortured brain, and she went on screaming until they carried her, kicking and thrashing in the straitjacket, out of the building and into the police wagon.

CHAPTER TWELVE

Fred Bauman caught his breath as he stared at the girl by the Post Office box. Because of the heat, Joanne was wearing only a blouse and a light skirt; her slim, lovely figure was breathtaking, with those high breasts thrusting the front of the blouse out, and for a moment Bauman almost forgot that this was the girl who was cold-bloodedly blackmailing him and ruining his life.

Safely out of sight back of the writing table, Bauman watched her open the box and take out the letter. He could see it was some kind of circular. She scanned it quickly and then dropped it in the nearby waste paper barrel. She seemed disappointed that that was all, and no wonder; this was the first Wednesday in weeks that there hadn't been a nice little money order for a hundred dollars waiting in her box!

She started to leave the building. As she neared the door, Bauman stepped out from behind the table and said, "Hello, there."

She whirled, surprise brightening her eyes, and glared at him.

"You!"

"Me." Bauman's heart throbbed fiercely. He hoped that this plan of his was going to work out all right. "I want to see you. That's why I came."

"What do you want?"

"Outside," he said.

They stepped out, into the warm morning sunlight. Bauman saw the peaks of her breasts through her blouse, and desire formed a lump in his throat.

She said, "I didn't get my check this morning. I warned you about what would happen if you missed a payment."

Bauman shook his head. "I didn't mail it because I decided to bring it in person. I have it right here with me. In my jacket pocket."

"Well, let's have it, then," she snapped impatiently. "And from now on don't pay me any visits, you hear? Go back to mailing it the way you used to."

Bauman took the envelope from his pocket, ripped it open, and let her see the filled-out money order that was inside. She reached out for it, but he grinned at her, snatched it out of her reach, and put it back in his inside pocket. She stared at him.

"You playing games?" she asked.

"I'll give you the money later. Take me to your apartment and I'll give it to you there."

"My apartment? You dumb clown, you think I'm going to bring you up there?"

He winced at her words. "Joanne—"

"Give it to me."

"Joanne, look, I can't get you out of my mind. I wake up nights thinking about you."

"That's damn sweet of you."

"I want you," he told her, and there was truth in that as well as scheming. "Once more, Joanne—and not just in an automobile, either. Some place where I can appreciate you. Will you do that for me?"

"You got a good case," she said.

He ignored her coldness and leaned close to her, letting her see the intensity of his passion. In a low voice he said, "Listen to me, Joanne. Take me to your apartment now—and I'll give you all the rest of the money tomorrow! A check for three thousand. Payment in full."

"You mean that?"

"Of course I do," he said, meeting her appraising gaze and hoping she didn't see through him. "That's why I waited around all morning for you to come and pick up your mail. The check's all ready for you. I could even give it to you this afternoon."

The gleam of greed danced in her eyes. "How about letting me have it now?"

He shook his head. "Uh-uh. You're too shrewd, Joanie, but I'm not falling for it. No payment in advance. But I promise you, you'll have it by this afternoon. Just once more in your arms—"

Her apartment was on West Forty-fifth Street, near Ninth Avenue—a rundown neighborhood, with kids yelling in the streets and women hanging out the windows talking to each other. She had given in to his proposition readily enough, after Bauman had waved the promise of full payment under her nose.

Moneygrubbing little witch, he thought, as he walked along the midtown streets with her.

In half an hour you'll be dead, he thought at her as they walked. And I'll be free of you.

It was a walk-up apartment. She went first, he following her, up the creaking stairs. Nobody saw him as he entered. That was good. Nobody would see him when he left either, if his luck held out.

She threw open the door of the place. Two rooms, and messy. Dirty clothing all over the place, an unmade bed, drapery hanging askew on the windows. Cheap furniture that probably came with the room. There was a stale and musty smell about the place.

He felt perfectly calm now.

She said to him, "Come on, let's get this over with, buster. And then you go get the three thousand you were talking about."

"Sure," he said. "Sure. Come here."

She moved toward him, and there was a light in her eyes—a money-loving light, Bauman thought. And she was so young, too. She couldn't have been more than twenty-four. She was just a kid, a pretty kid with a good complexion and a pretty face, the kind of kid college boys liked to date, wholesome and good fun, the kind of kid his daughter Karen might grow up to be—

She was wearing a man's white shirt, open at the throat. The lovely globes of her breasts thrust against the shirt. Bauman made sure the door was shut and the window curtains were drawn.

She glided toward him, took his hands, put them to her breasts. Desire coursed through him as he touched the firm flesh through her clothes. He caressed her for a moment as they stood together, and she made small purring noises. Then he began to unbutton her blouse. It dropped away. Today she was wearing a bra, and he took that off, too. Her bare breasts were splendid, full and pale and dark-tipped.

"So soft," he murmured. "So nice—"

In another moment he had her completely naked, and then so was he. They moved toward the rumpled bed. Bauman wondered whom she had entertained on that bed last night.

He ran his hand down the silken smoothness of her. She was so very good, he thought. He lingered over the hard ridges of her nipples, and then slid his hand down the smooth front of her waist, slowly, delightedly. He held her, and then he put his mouth to hers, and kissed her, hard and passionately.

She wanted him now, he thought, gloating. He took her.

All his pent-up tension of the last month and a half freed itself in the wild headlong frenzy of that moment. He did not hold himself back. He had nothing to gain from giving her pleasure, and he was out for himself alone now, so his twisting, punishing body moved in eager motions.

He sobbed in ecstasy. His body jolted, shoved.

"Wait a second—" she said "Hold on—"

"No," he said.

He took his pleasure from her in fast, blazing ecstasy. Sweat burst from his pores. His body shook. This was the most expensive pleasure he had ever had in his life, but almost worth the price.

"Hey," she said. "You could have waited. Another minute and—"

Bauman laughed. "I wasn't interested," he said.

He took a deep breath. He reached down and put his hands to the ripe, lush globes of her breasts. Then, suddenly, brutally, he slid his hands upward and locked them around her throat.

In that moment, all his thirty-eight years flashed before him. They say that that happens to you in the moment when you die; but Bauman had never expected it to happen while he was killing someone else.

For that matter, he had never expected to be killing someone else, either. He saw himself as a schoolboy, and as a night student at business school, too busy for dates, and then getting his first job as a bookkeeper, and meeting Ethel when he was twenty, and falling in love with her, and thinking that she was the most wonderfully lovely girl in the world.

And here he was, eighteen years later, with his hands on the throat of a girl who had lured him into raping her and then had blackmailed him for nearly two thousand dollars so far. A girl who had been no more than three or four years old when he had married Ethel, a girl who had been playing hopscotch then and now was about to die.

His hands tightened.

Bauman held her away from him at arm's length, just in case she decided to claw at his eyes, but she didn't try that. She tugged at his hands, but the fury that rippled through him doubled his strength, and she could not budge him. From her came thick gurgling noises. Bauman almost felt like letting her go, but it was as if his hands were glued to her throat and he could not let her go. Her face was turning a mottled purplish color and her eyes, bulging, were frightful to see.

Bauman kept up the pressure and felt her beginning to go limp. He didn't dare release her yet—not while she was only half-dead. He gripped her throat, one minute, two minutes, days perhaps. Her eyes were closed and her head was sagging, lolling backward floppily.

She was blue in the face, now. She had stopped making noises. Bauman let go of her throat and she slipped back against the pillow. Picking up her wrist, he searched for a pulse and found none. He looked at her. He put his ear against her breasts. He heard nothing.

A mirror lay in an open handbag on the cheap dresser. He seized it, held it to her lips, looked at it. It did not cloud.

She was dead.

He was free.

She lay in a rumpled naked heap, her body loose-limbed, all her beauty gone from her. A little while before she had been passionate, exciting; now she was not. Bauman looked at her and wondered if this were just a dream.

No, no dream. She was dead, and he had killed her.

Bauman knew that he had to get out of here, now. Fast. Women got killed in cheap rooming houses all the time, and the police never worried much about it. He had taken care not to leave fingerprints on anything. Nothing except her throat anyway, and he didn't think they would be able to trace him from the purplish blotches on her throat.

He quickly got back into his clothing, looked around the apartment and turned to leave.

The door opened suddenly and somebody came in.

He was a tall man, over six feet tall, it seemed, and he dressed well. In the first shocked moment Bauman thought that this might be another victim of the dead girl but then he saw the man's eyes and knew that this was her confederate, the friend that she had once mentioned.

He looked surprised. And he was holding a gun.

Bauman backed away, mouthing something wordless and soundless that refused to leave his throat. He stood with his back against the dresser, with the dead girl sprawled naked on the bed in front of him.

The tall man said "So you killed her, eh?"

"I—I—"

"Go easy, chum. Calm down. I'm not going to use this rod unless you make me do it. What's your name anyway? Miller? No he's dead too. Bauman, then. Yeah, you must be Bauman. Joanne told me about you. The one from Forest Hills."

Bauman moistened his lips and looked from the nude body on the bed to the man with the gun.

"Are you Bauman?" he repeated.

Bauman nodded weakly. "Yes, Yes, I am. Who—who are you?"

The other shrugged. "I was a sort of a friend of your late playmate. You seem to have ended my friendship for me. Well, if you didn't do it somebody else would have, I guess."

"She was blackmailing me," Bauman said.

"Of course she was. I showed her how to work the dodge. I showed her lots of things she didn't know before. And then you came along and killed her." He didn't sound very disturbed. "Well, I was going to pull out of town anyway, without her. Now you saved me the trouble of explaining things to her."

"I don't understand," Bauman said.

"You will," the other said. He slipped the gun into his pocket as if to show that he was contemptuous of Bauman. "My name's Buddy. I was sort of Joanne's manager, you might say. But she was always yapping about the women I was seeing. It was okay for her to pick up guys and go to bed with them whenever she wanted to, but I had to walk the narrow path." He chuckled. "Poor Joanne. Well, the blackmail gimmick was a good one, but I knew one of these days she'd hit a sucker who wouldn't come across."

"What are you going to do with me?"

"With you? Nothing, chum. I'm going to hightail it out of New York City tonight and get me back to Chicago where I belong."

Bauman glanced at the naked dead girl on the bed. "You won't say anything about—about this?"

Buddy grinned cheerfully. "Sure, I won't say anything about it. Why should I? But you're going to meet me tonight and give me ten thousand as a going-away present, or else I phone the cops and tip them off."

A wave of dizziness rocked Bauman at the quiet words.

Not again, he thought.

Freeing himself from one blackmailer, he had only made things twice as bad for himself. Now he was a murderer—and he was being asked for ten thousand dollars!

He sat down heavily in a rickety chair.

"I don't have ten thousand," Bauman said in a dull voice, looking away from the huddled naked thing on the bed.

Buddy grinned. "Get it. Borrow it. Steal it. But come up with it by tonight or I call the cops. It won't be too hard for them to trace the money orders you were giving her and find a lead back to you. Of course if I keep my mouth shut you'll squeak through."

"Ten thousand," Bauman said.

"Yeah. In cash, certified check or money order. I'll meet you at half past eight tonight at a roadhouse called Marty's, across the river near Fort Lee on Route 4. You know how to get there?"

"Yes."

"Okay. Be there and make sure you have the dough. I'm gonna leave here now. You wait five minutes and then you leave too."

"Wait a minute," Bauman said. His business sense still functioned in his numbed mind. "How am I going to write a check? Who do I make it payable to?"

"Payable to cash," Buddy said. "You don't need to know my name. So long, fathead."

He turned and left.

Bauman stared at the dead girl on the bed, at the lush full breasts, the tender legs. He waited, counting out the minutes as they passed. When five minutes were up, he, too, left.

No one saw him as he slipped down the stairs into the open. It was a little past noon now. Kids were coming home from school and the sun was fearfully hot. And he had to produce ten thousand dollars—more than he had in his entire savings account—by half past eight this evening, or he'd be turned into the police as a murderer by a man whose name he didn't know, for the slaying of a lustful, immoral blackmailing witch.

It was incredible, Bauman thought.

But this time he knew exactly what his course of action was to be.

Raising the ten thousand dollars he knew, was impossible. It would plunge him so deep into debt that he would never get out again—and in any event he would have to make explanations to Ethel, and that way she would grow suspicious, and sooner or later she would drag the whole horrible story from him.

No. No money.

But there was another way out.

He had killed once, and his life was thus forfeit to the law. He could kill again without making matters much worse. They couldn't send a man to the electric chair twice. He had everything to gain and nothing whatever to lose by killing a second time.

First he stopped in a candy store and phoned Ethel. In a voice that amazed him by its steadiness he told her, "I'm going to have to work late tonight, Ethel. Maybe till nine or ten o'clock."

She didn't seem to mind. "All right, if you have to. Everything okay at the office today?"

"Yeah, sure," he said. "Sure. See you tonight—by nine-thirty or ten, no later."

"So long, Fred."

With that chore out of the way, Bauman stopped at a bank and cashed in the money order he had brought along as bait for the girl. Then he walked downtown to Macy's and visited the sporting-goods department.

He bought himself a hunting knife, five inches long and razor-sharp. It came in a scabbard that he could attach to the inside of his jacket. He paid for it in cash and left. The knife was the only way. He didn't know where he could get a gun without a permit, and besides he didn't know how to use one. And guns were noisy. Poison was strictly for the horror movies. And though he hadn't hesitated to strangle the girl, Bauman knew that force would be impossible with the man. Buddy was much too big.

Crossing over to Gimbel's, Bauman bought himself a pair of solid black gloves. Then, hungry, he stopped off for lunch at the Automat. He spent ninety cents for his meal. He had to remind himself that after today he would have no more hundred-dollar payments to make every Wednesday, no more scurrying around and cutting corners to find the cash. His only problem was the bank loan falling due in the autumn, and Bauman figured he'd cross that bridge when he came to it.

He was too tensed-up even to consider going back to the office at all. Instead, he killed the afternoon at a movie house on 42nd Street near Eighth Avenue, watching a couple of old films. One was a western and the other was a detective story. Halfway through the first film, he realized he had already seen it, five years before. He had taken Ethel.

He left the theater after seeing the western a second time—not really seeing it, just letting it slide past his eyes. The time was twenty past six. Rush hour was at its peak now; people were still flocking into the subways at Times Square, heading home to their wives and kid and their nice, quiet lives.

He would have been heading home now, too. Except that one rainy night he had decided to take the bridge instead of the tunnel, and had set off a chain of nightmare happenings that still hadn't reached its end.

Walking over to Sixth Avenue, he ate once again in the Automat. This time he wasn't very hungry. He left the Automat a little after seven and stopped in a stationery store. He bought a single envelope, took a blank check from his checkbook, put it in the envelope and sealed it. Then he slipped the envelope into his inside breast pocket, in the same pocket where the hunting knife was clipped.

He walked over to Bryant Park and sat down for a while. He closed his eyes, thought about Joanne alive and naked and passionate, thought about Joanne dead. She had asked for it, he thought.

At quarter to eight Bauman got up, walked north to 48th Street where he had left the car, and got in. He drove uptown on the West Side Highway to the George Washington Bridge, crossed over into New Jersey, found Route 4, and drove into Fort Lee.

It was eight-thirty on the nose when he pulled up outside the roadhouse whose garish neon sign proclaimed its name to be MARTY'S.

The thin sound of a jukebox whined in his ears as he walked in. The big man was waiting at a table in the back, nursing a beer. He looked at his watch as Bauman entered.

"Right on time," he muttered. "You bring the dough?"

"Sure," Bauman said. "You don't think I would have come out here just for a glass of beer."

"I don't think anything."

A waiter came by and looked inquiringly at Bauman. He shook his head and said, "No thanks. Nothing to drink right now." The waiter vanished.

The big man said, "Come on with me."

"Where?"

"Outside. In back. I don't want you to hand me the money in here."

Bauman shrugged and followed him through a back door that led outside. The back of the roadhouse was shabbily painted and dreary. Stacks of soda bottle cases stood heaped up everywhere, and empty beer barrels. It was dark out there. There was no moon. Bauman thought of another night when it had rained. He thought of bare, soft hard-tipped breasts and velvet arms.

This is going to be easy, he thought.

The big man said, "Okay. Let's have the dough."

Bauman took the envelope from his pocket and handed it over. The big man grabbed it and ripped it open with a quick swipe of his thumb. He reached in, pulled out the check, frowned—

"Hey, this a gag? The check's blank!"

"Oh, dreadfully sorry," Bauman said. "Wrong envelope. Heh-heh. Little mistake."

He reached into the pocket again and his hand closed on the hilt of the knife. It felt good to the touch. He brought it out casually, and before the big man could do anything Bauman leaned up and rammed the hunting knife into his throat. Buddy sputtered once, blinked in amazement and toppled as Bauman yanked out the knife. He landed heavily behind a pile of cases of soda bottles, out of sight and dead.

"Hey, mister," a thin voice said.

Bauman whirled in panic. The door of the roadhouse had opened, and the waiter was standing there, staring at him. "Mister," he said again.

No, no! Bauman thought wildly. *He saw too! There's always someone watching.* Every misdeed was part of a chain that led to another. *And now he thinks he'll blackmail me too. Everyone in the world is a blackmailer. But I'll escape this time.*

Bauman let out an agonized sob and thought of Ethel and Karen and the dead, naked Joanne. Then he plunged the knife into his own throat. There was a moment of blinding pain and that was all.

The waiter, standing framed in the back door of the roadhouse, went bug-eyed with shock.

"Damn," he muttered. "Stuck the knife right in himself. And I only wanted to tell him he left his car lights on! You'd think I caught him killing someone, or something!"

He didn't stay to see the other body behind the case. He had seen enough. He turned and hollered inside, "Hey, Marty, come on out here! Some guy went buggy and killed himself!"

THE END

You Can't Stop Me

ROBERT SILVERBERG

CHAPTER ONE

Half an hour after he got to Cleveland, Lou Andreas stopped at a big out-of-town newspaper stand on Euclid Avenue and bought all the New York papers he could find. It was a thick stack—the *Post*, the *Journal-American*, the *Mirror*, the *News* and the *World-Telegram*.

He hadn't been able to find copies of the *Times* or the *Herald-Tribune*. They were sold out. But that was quite all right, Andreas figured. The *Times* and the *Trib* were interested in politics and the stock market and subjects like that. They didn't devote much space to rapes or murders.

Or rape-murders.

Andreas slung the stack of papers under his arm and took them up to his hotel room, and started to riffle through them page by page by page, looking for the one particular story he hoped to find.

It was slow work. He had to read up and down every column, carefully. He didn't want to miss it.

He lit a cigarette. And another, a while later. And a third.

He was on his fourth cigarette before he found the story he was looking for. It was on an inside page in the *Journal-American*. It hadn't made the morning papers at all, and the other afternoon sheets had missed it.

He read it with loving attention.

The nude body of Marie Raimondi, 32, was found late last night in her hotel room at 609 West 114th Street. Detectives said she had been sexually assaulted and strangled to death. According to neighbors, Miss Raimondi was unemployed and had frequent male visitors. Police are investigating ...

Andreas had a good laugh over the prissy way they had put it: *Unemployed and had frequent male visitors.*

What the hell did they think they were, a family newspaper?

Why didn't they just come right out and call a spade a spade, for God's sake?

Unemployed. Frequent male visitors.

Sure. Marie Raimondi had been a chippie, a floozie, a trollop, a tart. A tramp. A pay-for-play girl.

Come right out and say it: *a harlot.*

And now she was a dead one, Lou Andreas thought pleasantly. She had taken one customer too many, that night, and it had been a very serious mistake for her, the most serious kind of mistake a girl can make—a fatal one.

"*Police are investigating ...*"

Sure. Andreas knew exactly how the investigation would go. The cops would look around the girl's cheap hotel room for obvious clues—the murderer's shirt, maybe, or his wallet—and, finding nothing useful, they'd shrug their shoulders and write the case off as unsolved.

The cops wouldn't break their humps over it. Chippies get murdered in cheap hotel rooms all the time. The police don't care. The girls are nuisances anyway, and it saves the taxpayers some money to get rid of them this easy way. There never was any big investigation after a murder like that. The criminal could get away without any trouble at all, just like that.

Lou Andreas knew.

Because Marie Raimondi had been his fifty-eighth victim in the last ten years.

Carefully, he folded up the discarded New York newspapers. He had found what he wanted, and he had no further use for the papers now. One by one he stuffed them into the hotel room wastebasket.

He did not remove the clipping about the murder. It was a great temptation to him to keep a scrapbook, but he knew it was a stupid idea. It would have been the height of foolishness to keep a clipping file, thus tempting fate by an accidental exposure. He only needed to remember the number.

Number fifty-eight.

He rose and went to the rickety dresser, and opened the bottle of Scotch he had picked up earlier in the day, after leaving the airport. He poured an inch and a half of whiskey into a water glass, and filled the glass at the bathroom tap.

Gravely, he held the glass up in a toast.

To me, he thought.

He downed the drink and grinned at himself in the bathroom mirror. What he saw there wasn't bad. A slim, hard-faced man of twenty-seven. He was tall and thin, so thin that he gave the appearance of fragility, but there was great strength in the slender frame, in the long, flat muscles. His face was wide, with jutting cheekbones, a broad nose, thin wide lips, dark eyes set far apart from one another. It was a faintly ominous face, which was exactly the impression Andreas wanted to create. He was far from handsome, but there was something magnetically appealing about his brooding ugliness.

It was the kind of face that attracted a certain type of woman.

The type of woman it attracted was precisely the type that Lou Andreas loved to kill.

He poured a second drink for himself, and thought about the death of

Marie Raimondi.

He had picked her up, two nights before, in a bar on Broadway near 103rd Street. He had been in New York for three days without a score, and the time was ripe with something to spare.

She was standing at the bar, joking with the bartender. She was a girl of middle height, with long black hair, coarse hair, almost kinky, shining with highlights. Her face was good, her figure more than good, with two firm-looking breasts jutting like melons against the front of her blue cashmere sweater. Her ankles were a little thick, Andreas noted. But she wasn't bad-looking. Too much makeup, but that was a kind of professional trademark.

She looked young. Under twenty-five, for sure. There was a shopworn look to her, but he could still detect signs of the innocent girl that she once had been, not so very many years ago.

He walked over to her. She looked up at him, and there was a sparkle in her eyes as she surveyed his height and the strangely attractive ugliness of his face. The cheekbones, Andreas had long thought, seemed to hold some magic.

He grinned at her.

She grinned back. "Hi," she said. "All alone?"

"Afraid so."

"Buy me a drink and I'll keep you company."

"Okay," he said. She wasn't very subtle. But he wasn't looking for subtlety.

He bought her a drink, inching his long legs down onto the bar stool alongside her. She sidled against him, rubbing her thigh along his. He felt the warmth of her, smelled her cheap perfume. The heavy cone of her breast dug invitingly into his side.

He bought her a second drink, too.

Then she said, "Suppose we go where we can have some privacy, huh?"

"Sure," he said. "Where?"

"My place. It isn't far."

He paid for his drinks and they left the bar. It was a nice April night, still a little cool, but with the early tingle of spring in the air. The moon was practically full, a great glowing orb. The night was made for romance, Andreas thought pleasantly.

Or murder.

"Where do you live?" he asked.

"114th. It's a short walk. Eleven blocks. You want to take a cab or something?"

"No. No. Let's walk. It's a nice night."

They walked. After a block or so, Andreas asked her, "What were you doing so far downtown?"

"I had to. You can't get anywhere up by where I live. That's Columbia University, up there. The bars are all full of the college girls. They *give* the stuff away. Believe me, the competition's murder for a girl who's trying to sell it."

Andreas grinned. "Yeah. Yeah, I see what you mean. What's your name, anyway?"

"Marie."

"I'm Lou," he said.

"What line of work are you in, Lou?"

"Salesman. Traveling salesman."

Marie guffawed. "No kidding! How do you make out with the farmers' daughters?"

"Lousy," he said. "I do my selling in the cities. You got to look hard to find a farmer's daughter in Manhattan, you know that?"

"Yeah," she said, laughing gaily. "Yeah, we don't have so many farms around here these days."

They came to the building where she lived, finally. It was a blocky gray six-story place that once had been a rich man's apartment house, back thirty and forty years ago when the Upper West Side had been Manhattan's most fashionable residential neighborhood. But the roomy old seven and eight room apartments had long ago been carved up into single units, and the place was inhabited now by college students, elderly widows, and a sprinkling of prostitutes.

It was close to midnight. Nobody saw Andreas enter the building with her. That was always the ticklish part, and more than once he had had to pass up a kill because someone sharp-eyed had had time to observe and remember him as he brought a girl home. This time all was clear.

Her room had a run-down look and a stale smell. It was no bigger than 12 x 14, with a single small dirty window. The flaking green paint hadn't been renewed in at least a dozen years. There was no lighting fixture, only a pair of small dim floor lamps. The ugly metal spiderweb of a sprinkler system crawled across the cracked ceiling.

She locked the door and smiled at him with her painted lips, and gave him the professional smile, and pulled the cashmere sweater over her head. Underneath, she was wearing a thin rayon blouse. She began to unbutton it.

Andreas stood leaning against the wall, hands in his pockets, watching her strip.

The blouse was off, now. "Come here," she said. "Help me with my bra."

"Sure," he said.

He sauntered over to her and casually unhooked the bra. The cups tumbled away, revealing the bare hillocks of her pale young breasts.

They were good breasts, he saw. High up on her chest, and round and close together. The skin was clear and white, no ugly veins showing beneath the surface. Small nipples, very dark red in color. They were breasts that would fit sweetly into a man's hands, and nestle there, soft and resilient, like two big rubber apples.

Andreas wondered how many men had handled those breasts. Plenty, probably. But now they were due to go into retirement, he thought.

"You like them?" she asked.

"They're swell."

"You can touch, if you want."

"Yeah. Yeah."

He put his hands on her boobs, felt their warmth, their firmness. The nipples were already hard, like little rocks jabbing into the skin of his palms. He gripped the breasts, digging his fingertips into the rosy flesh. He rotated them, moving around, pressing them together. Marie grinned. A little hiss of desire escaped her moist, full lips. She rubbed her thighs together in anticipation.

"Undress me!" she whispered.

Andreas undressed her. He peeled away the skirt, and the half-slip, and the stockings, and the panty-girdle, and there she was naked.

He looked at her.

He could see now why she had gone into streetwalking instead of into modelling or something like that. She just didn't have it, below the hips. She wasn't bad, but she wasn't terribly good, either. She was thick through the waist. Her thighs were flabby. Her buttocks were too full, so that they jiggled, and there were little puckered dimples in the flesh. And her ankles were thick, too. Above the waist, she was terrific. Below, ordinary. She had probably tried all sorts of slimming exercises, Andreas figured. But none of them had ever worked.

And now it wouldn't matter.

"Now I'll undress you," she said.

He shook his head. "No. I like to keep my clothes on when I do it."

"Okay. Any way you like." Naked, jaunty, she smiled at him and said, "You want to pay me now or later?"

"Later. How much is it?"

"Fifteen."

"Okay," he said.

They moved together toward the bed. He opened his clothing. He was ready, this time, unlike that other time so many years ago. He felt her hands on him, stroking him, squeezing, rubbing. He didn't bother to take precautions. She looked clean. His eyes roved her body, saw the red-tipped breasts, the beckoning softness of her white, smooth, just-too-thick thighs.

She lay down. She moved her thighs for him. He stared at her for a moment.

Then he lay down with her.

Her body was warm and soft. Her arms went around him, and her lips sought his. He met her mouth. A tramp's kiss he thought. You didn't often get that. Tramps like to keep their mouths shut. Other parts could be wide open, but they closed their mouths.

She opened wide.

He took her. It was good to glide into the warm, soft harbor of her, but he knew that there were greater pleasures awaiting him. Their bodies moved. She was a pro through and through; she matched rhythms with him as effortlessly as though they bad been lovers for years, and body pistoned against body, thrust and counterthrust, jab and answering jab.

Deeper, deeper he probed into the passion-heated recesses of her body. He worked his hands underneath her, dug his fingers into the ample flesh of her buttocks, pulled her upward toward him, and thrust deep.

She gasped. Real or phony, he wondered? Genuine excitement, or trampish fakery?

No matter.

Nothing mattered anymore.

He felt the onset of pleasure, the tingling sensations, the throbbing pulsations of fulfillment. She sensed what was happening, and suddenly her whole body was trembling, and she was moving with renewed energy now, thrusting against him, pounding her body against his, hitting him hard, giving him his money's worth.

He froze.

He held tight to her, one hand gripping fleshy buttocks, the other holding a firm round breast, and the culmination rocked through him. There was the shudder, the sudden burst of ecstasy, and then the finish.

Drenched with sweat within his clothes, he lay resting, gathering his strength for what would now take place.

She said, "You okay?"

"Sure," he said. His voice was hoarse. "It was great, Marie. Really great."

"You want to let me up now?" she asked.

He smiled. "You in a hurry to get back on the street?" he asked.

"Well, you know how it is. A business is a business, Lou."

"Yeah. Yeah, I understand. Okay, just a second, will you? Let me get my strength again."

"All right. You rest. But just a minute or so, huh?"

He nodded. Then he withdrew from her, and sat up, and looked down at her full-breasted nakedness. He smiled, and put his hands on her full, ripe young breasts, gripping them, letting the coral tips show through between his spread fingers. He held her breasts for a moment, savoring their warmth. Then he slid his hands higher up her body, to her smooth shoulders, and he caressed the velvety flesh for a moment.

And then he brought his hands to her throat.

He let the fingers rest lightly over her Adam's apple for an instant. She was smiling, but the smile gave way to a puzzled frown a moment later.

He tightened his grip ever so slightly.

The frown deepened. Puzzlement turned to terror, and then to awareness. Andreas was a connoisseur of such moments. Studying her face as he had studied so many other faces in the past, he knew just when her facial muscles began to bunch for a scream, and suddenly, with steely power, the fingers dug in, cutting off her breath before she could launch the scream past her teeth.

He was an expert by now.

His tightening fingers choked the scream down into a little whimpering gargle. She thrashed about on the bed, kicking her legs helplessly like a pithed frog. Her breasts bounced and quivered, but he held her down.

His fingers continued to press inward.

Her eyes began to protrude. Her face purpled. Her body went limp, her head sinking back against the pillow as though he had snapped her spine.

She looked dead, but he did not release her. In his long experience, he had come to understand that strangulation was a funny business, that sometimes what looked like death was not really death. Once he had thought he had killed a girl, only to hear her cry out as he slipped away, and he had had to return to finish the job. After that, he took no chances.

He held onto her now. Her color deepened. Her swollen tongue lagged from her lips, and a trail of spittle fell to the motionless rounds of her breasts.

Finally Andreas released her. He gave her a shove, and she tumbled to the floor like a sack of books, and lay there, twisted over, her face down, her long black hair half hiding her breasts. He looked at her. He pushed her over, touched the flesh of her buttocks.

She felt cool. Life had left her.

Andreas felt the flood of ecstasy sweep through his being. Mere sex wasn't the greatest thrill, he had discovered long ago. *This* was.

The taking of a life.

The avenging of an old wrong.

Number fifty-eight, he thought.

Smiling, with shivers of pleasure dancing along his backbone, Andreas knelt over her, checked her, felt between her breasts for some flicker of heartbeat, found none, wet his hand and held it over her nostrils to detect breathing, and then, satisfied, rose again.

He stood for a long time, listening to the thunder of his heart. When he was calm again, he took a last look at the crumpled naked corpse on the floor. The breasts that had seemed so sensuous, so full of life a short while ago, were now nothing but lumps of dead meat. Her skin seemed to have turned gray all over, except where it was a deeper purplish.

He turned away.

He let himself out of the room without leaving any fingerprints on the doorknob, and quietly went down the back stairs of the building. No one saw him leave. On the third floor, he heard a wild giggle, and he turned and look down the corridor and saw a young couple embracing. The girl's skirt was up in the air, and her body was pressed tight against the boy, and from the motions of their hips it was easy to see that he was making love to her standing up. Andreas smiled. They were too busy to notice anything. He kept on going, down to the ground floor and out of the building.

He took the subway home. It was a long wait for a train. Half an hour later, he was in his own hotel room. He took a meticulous shower, clambered into bed, and slept the soundest sleep in weeks.

The next morning he packed. He bought a plane ticket for Cleveland and was at the airport at noon.

No one could ever know the truth about him. He drifted from city to city, a salesman of furnace appliances, a man with no family, no friends, no one who might recognize him and start trouble. He had no entanglements. He lived in cheap hotels, traveled constantly, never stayed in one place for long. And when he felt the overpowering need build up inside him to fever pitch—

Then, when the ache seemed to twist his bones and the face in his mirror was the lace of an oddly mortified stranger—

He killed.

CHAPTER TWO

It had started ten years earlier, in the same city of Cleveland to which Lou Andreas had come after killing Marie Raimondi. He had been seventeen, then, a tall, skinny, painfully shy boy, with the usual quota of adolescent pimples and somewhat more than the usual quota of adolescent inhibitions and confusions.

He was a junior in high school.

He was in love.

Her name was Rosalie, and she was in his chemistry class, and she was the most beautiful girl Lou Andreas had ever set eyes on. She was Swedish, with blonde hair and blue eyes and a wondrously milky complexion. She was a radiant girl, full-breasted and lovely, who seemed to give off an aura of beauty and charm and innocence.

She was a virgin, of course, Lou Andreas had no doubt of that.

He was a virgin too.

In his adolescent fantasies, he dreamed of putting an end to both such situations with one mighty stroke. He would take Rosalie on a date, and then, late some Saturday night, they would return to her home, and they would sit in her parlor while her parents slept unsuspecting upstairs. They would sit close together on the couch, Lou Andreas told himself, and he would look at her and see the smoky excitement beginning to rise in her wide blue Scandinavian eyes.

And then he would put his hands on the front of her silk blouse, and he would feel the magnificent rounded hills of her breasts within. He would squeeze them, ever so gently—for the books said a girl's breasts were highly sensitive areas of her body—and she would begin to throb and moan a little bit as she warmed up.

Next they would kiss. It would begin chastely, of course. Lips to lips. But then her mouth would open to him, and his tongue would slip slyly inward, all the while his hands working on her boobs, and her body would start to writhe a little, and his tongue would touch hers, and then would explore the soft warm darkness of her mouth.

Now she would be practically begging for it.

He would start to undress her.

He would unbutton her blouse and slip it from her shoulders, laying bare the beautiful arms, the marvelous throat. Then, before she could find time to object, he would unhook her bra— Was it hard to maneuver the catch, he wondered?—and he would pull it away from her, exposing the proud young hillocks of her bare breasts.

He had seen breasts before, at girlie shows, but there had always been a haze of cigarette smoke and a distance of at least a dozen rows, and he had never had a really good look. But now Rosalie's breasts would be naked right in front of him, and he could stare at them close up, and see the way they curved out from her chest, and how the puckered little nipples sprouted, and how the mounds of firm flesh were shaped and contoured.

And when he got through looking, he could touch.

He could put his hands right on them, and feel their warmth and their softness. He would play with the little nipples, rubbing them between his fingers until they grew hard. The books said a girl's nipples turned hard when she was sexually excited. Lou Andreas believed the books. At seventeen, he didn't have any empirical evidence to go by, but what the books said was good enough for him.

So he would play with her nipples. Then he would put his face to her breasts. Right up between them, so he could inhale the perfume of her body. He would take her breasts in his hands, and push them close together so the sides of them pressed against his cheeks as he burrowed between.

Then he would kiss her nipples. One at a time, taking them to his lips, caressing them, drawing on them. Rimming them between his lips and biting down, of course not hurting her, just stirring her up.

He could picture her at this stage. Her face flushed, her delicate golden hair rumpled and disheveled, her bare breasts heaving with excitement.

Now he would complete the job of undressing her.

There would be nothing to it. She would be almost groggy now, doped up with passion, and he would simply peel the clothes away from her, remove every stitch, skirt and slip and stockings and panties and whatever else she had on underneath there, until she was sprawled out naked on the couch, and he could look at every inch of her.

He'd give her a good inspection. He'd survey the pink ripeness of her, the flatness of the belly, the tender beauty of her thighs.

Then he would undress himself.

In a moment he would be naked in front of her, and the sight of his nakedness would inflame her all the more, would push her clear to the brink of ecstasy. Her arms would reach out for him, hungrily pulling him down on top of her,

"Lou," she would whisper passionately. "Lou, I want you so very much…"

His hands would stroke the insides of her thighs, and then the softness of her waist, working round and round the goal but never coming to it, while she churned in impatient desire. And then he would approach and caress, and feel the warmth, and listen to the harsh panting of her breath.

"Take me!" she would cry.

He would press his body down against hers. Her body would welcome him.

With a single eager motion he would make a woman of her and a man of himself.

He would keep his eyes open while he was doing it, so he could see the expression on her face as the rod of his virility obliterated her golden innocence. He would sink deep, wiping out her virginity forever, staking a perpetual claim to her body, and as he thrust and thrust again he would send her to unforgettable heights of passion, and then as she trembled with delight he would attain his own fulfillment, both climaxes coming in the same split second, and then, afterward, they would hold each other tight and vow eternal love, and after a while he would rise from her and they would dress and he would kiss her tenderly good night, and she would see him to the door and he would step out into the star-flecked silence of the night, walking on air all the way home, full of the joy of being a man and having given his own woman pleasure.

It was a very satisfying fantasy.

The only trouble was, it never got past the fantasy stage.

Lou Andreas dated Rosalie four times over a period of ten weeks, the autumn he turned seventeen. There were no spectacular seductions. He did not lay bare the rosy-tipped beauty of her breasts. It did not fall to his lot in life to part her virgin thighs. Nor was he lucky enough to find himself looking down on her passion-flushed face as he deftly and powerfully took her innocence.

No.

What really happened was this:

On their first date, he took her to the movies, and they held hands all through the show. Handholding was part of the normal routine of having a date, and there was nothing particularly sexual about it. On the way home, Lou wondered what his chances were of getting a kiss out of her. He decided that Rosalie wasn't the sort of girl who kissed on the first date. He dropped her at her door, grinned awkwardly at her, and left unkissed.

So much for the first date.

There was no problem making a second date with her. And she was a great deal warmer, on this date. That is to say, not only did she hold hands with him in the movies, but she made no objection when he slipped his arm around her shoulders. She snuggled up close to him.

He spent most of the movie debating whether or not to snake his long arm so far around her that he would be able to touch the side of her breast. His final conclusion was that it was risky, and might undo all the progress he was making with her. He kept his hand on her shoulder.

When he took her home, he was bolder than before. He kissed her. She let him do it. The only trouble was that as he brought his face down toward hers, she turned in what was obviously a well-rehearsed maneuver, so that his kiss landed in chaste and brotherly fashion on her satin-smooth cheek.

So much for the second date.

On the third date, Lou scored, mouth-wise. They had gone dancing, and he managed to get in a certain amount of intimacy in the clinches, pressing his body tight up against hers so he could feel the globes of her breasts on his chest. She didn't seem offended by the closeness. And when he took her home, she let him kiss her. Square on the lips. It was a long, warm kiss, but just as Lou was pondering the chances of getting his tongue into her mouth, she deftly broke away from him and that was that.

So much for the third date.

On the fourth—and, as it proved, final—date, Lou tried to advance another step toward his goal of getting inside her house and fulfilling his dream of stripping her and taking her on the parlor sofa. As they were kissing good night, and it was a tongue kiss this time, he hesitantly and cautiously brought his hand up and put it firmly over her left breast.

It stayed there about three seconds.

That was long enough for Lou to savor the heft of the breast, to feel its fullness and its firmness beneath the sweater and the flimsy bra. Then Rosalie pivoted out of his embrace. Her face was flaming.

He thought she was going to slap him. She didn't. She simply said, "Don't you ever do a thing like that to me again, Lou Andreas!"

And then she was gone, into the house, *slam!*

Naturally, he never did get an opportunity to do a thing like that to her again. For one thing, it was weeks before he had the nerve even to look in her direction, let alone to ask her for a date. He felt as though he had done something unbearably vulgar.

Toward the end of the term, he began to work up courage to approach her again, but a startling bit of news put a quick finish to that.

A classmate and friend of his said, "Hey, you hear that Rosalie's getting married?"

It was a bombshell. "*Married?*"

"Yep!"

"She can't. You're not allowed to be married in high school."

"She's quitting school. She's got her parents' consent, and anyway she's over seventeen. She doesn't have to stay in school if she doesn't want to."

Lou shook with amazement. "For God's sake," he muttered. "Who's she marrying?"

"Bob Anders."

"You're joking."

"Nope. I got the word just now from Rosalie's pal, Janet. She's quitting school at the end of the semester and marrying Anders."

Andreas was in a daze all the rest of the day. Bob Anders had been a star of the school's basketball team a few years back. The year Lou had entered the school, Bob Anders had been the captain of the team, and made All-City with a 22-point average. He was a husky blond, about six feet four. He had graduated two years ago, and now was on the varsity at Ohio State. When Lou had tried out for the freshman basketball team, there had been a lot of joking about the similarity of the names—Anders and Andreas—and the total dissimilarity in their playing abilities. Anders was a star. Andreas could just barely dribble without getting tangled up in his own legs.

And now Bob Anders was marrying Rosalie.

The wedding took place February the first. It was a big social event, and everybody important in town was there. Lou Andreas wasn't. He stayed home, uninvited, brooding about the fact that in some hotel room this evening Bob Anders would strip away Rosalie's wedding finery, would lay bare her pink-and-gold nudity, and with masterful ability would take her virginity.

It was a bad night for Lou Andreas. He hardly slept. In the morning he stared at his haggard, bloodshot face and told himself that he had to forget Rosalie forever, forget all his fantasies of laying her. She was someone else's wife, and he would never again be able to dream about her.

He had to do something.

Pressure was building up in him to the boiling point. He was past seventeen, and still a virgin, and most of his friends had scored already—or said they had—and now the Rosalie business made him feel like dirt.

He knew what he had to do.

I'll go out and get it, he thought. *I'll pick up a tramp and do it with her.*

It sounded very easy. He knew that there were places in town where all you had to do was walk down the street, and girls would pick you up. You paid them ten bucks and went to their rooms, and they laid down and let you do it to them. There was nothing to it.

One Saturday night he decided that the time had come. He would shed his boyhood.

He got into his father's liquor supply, and put away three shots of rye. He was too tense to get drunk, but the liquor gave him enough Dutch courage to see him through what he had resolved to do.

He headed downtown.

He sauntered down the street, wondering what would happen if nobody tried to pick him up.

He didn't have to wonder long. As he stood around in front of a movie house that was showing a burlesque film, staring at the stills of nearly-naked girls on the posters out front, a girl came up to him.

"Hi," she said. "You waiting for anybody?"

"Nope."

"Want a good time?"

He looked at her. She was only a little older than he was, he thought. She was a full-blown brunette whose heavy breasts seemed about to burst through her tight yellow sweater. He could see the little round buttons of her nipples through the sweater, as though she had no bra on underneath.

He said, "You bet I do."

Her eyes sparkled. "Come on with me," she said. "I got a room near here."

There was a tremendous pounding in his chest. He thought his rib cage would burst. This was it, he thought. This was the moment he had dreamed of almost since the time he knew what sex was. This girl had been walking around all her life, destined to be the taker of his virginity, and now he had found her, and this was the moment.

He went to her room.

It was small and dingy and mangy. But he didn't mind that. It was as he expected it to be. He didn't mind the fact that the girl looked coarse and vulgar, either. That was par for the course. Her lipstick was thick and smeary, and it was orange—he hated orange lipstick and her eyes were heavily shadowed, and she wore false eyelashes so phony-looking that they were grotesque.

He didn't mind.

She closed the door of her room and said, "You got ten bucks?"

"S-sure."

He clawed the money from his wallet and handed it to her. She took it carelessly, dropping the bill into an open dresser drawer.

Then she undressed.

Undressing was quick for her. Up went the sweater, over her head, and her breasts were bare. No bra, as he had guessed. Down came her jeans.

No panties, either.

She was naked except for her socks.

Andreas stared at her, and the tension grew in him, and there was a lump in his throat so big he was afraid it would choke him. At last he was in a room with a naked girl. At last. Nothing to stop him from looking and touching.

He came forward. He stared at her, at the big round breasts, like swollen melons, with the little dark tips that were her nipples. At the fleshy belly, at the firm thighs. She couldn't have been much past eighteen, but she looked like she had been around.

He was scared.

Scared green.

He watched her take a towel and spread it out on the bed. Then she plumped her buttocks down against the towel and lay back, bringing her knees up and opening them wide.

"Come on," she said. "I ain't got all day."

He nodded. He took his shoes off, but kept the rest of his clothes on, and moved toward the bed.

She said, "You got protection?"

"N-no."

"What's the matter, you aren't scared of getting a disease?"

He shrugged diffidently. "I—I guess I never thought much about it."

"He never thought much about it!" she repeated acidly. "Well, I'm clean. You won't catch nothing from me. But I might catch something from you, know what I mean? Not just a disease. I don't want you making no babies in me." She leaned over, her heavy breasts swaying as they dangled forward, and she took something from a nightstand drawer at her bedside. "Here. Put this on. It's on the house. My compliments."

She tossed it to him. He was so frozen with tension that he made an awkward stab at it and missed. He had to bend to pick it up.

His hand shook as he opened his clothes. This was the moment of truth, when he showed himself to her. He removed the paper wrapper of the thing she had given him, and unrolled it. But he had trouble putting it on.

"Come here," she said sarcastically. "I'll do it for you."

He felt her hands on him. Then she looked up, startled, as she felt the softness. "What's the matter with you?"

"Please—please, this is my first time—"

"Okay. Let's see what we can do."

Her hands touched him skillfully, expertly. No use.

He was too nervous, too frightened to be able to do anything. Never before had this happened, to him. Of course, he had never tried to have actual love, but he had always felt the tensing of his body, as he embraced a girl, kissed her, dreamed of taking her. Now that he had the actual opportunity—

Nothing.

Cursing, the girl was busy over him. She tried several different things. None of them worked. Finally she leaned forward. He felt her kiss. Tingles of thrill ran through him.

But no burst of virility.

He was afraid, afraid of her, afraid of sex, afraid of everything. And the fear killed his desire.

She looked up. Her eyes were scornful. "Okay, get outta here. You've wasted a lotta my time."

"No—please—"

"Clear out, you damn faggot! You think I need you? You think I'm gonna play games with you? You come here, you gotta be able to get with it!"

He stepped back, his face blazing. She hopped up from the bed. Her great globular breasts bounced and jiggled as she rushed to the dresser drawer. She was in a fury now over his impotence.

She grabbed his ten-dollar bill and hurled it at him. "Go on!" she shrilled. "Get out, fairy! Get out!"

He felt dazed. Numbly, he picked up the crumpled bill. He searched for his shoes and slipped into them. The naked girl raged at him, scalding his ears with acid obscenities, describing him in savagely humiliating terms.

As he looked at her—as he eyed her big bouncing breasts, her firm belly—he felt the first belated quickening of desire.

But it was too late.

She practically threw him out of her room, bubbling over with anger. The door slammed.

Lou Andreas stood there, tears in his eyes and a dull throb of unsatisfied lust in his body. And then, still a virgin, he crept away. He didn't know it, but he was going to bear the scars of that incident for the rest of his life.

CHAPTER THREE

Crushed, he headed for home. It was still early, only nine o'clock. Saturday night was just beginning.

There was no one at home. He stared in the mirror, broodingly squeezed a pimple. He closed his eyes and saw the naked harlot prancing and shouting. Then the image faded and became Rosalie, slim and chaste-looking, but a virgin no more.

For a while, he thought of killing himself. Then he shut the bathroom door, accomplished himself, and, with some of the tension diminished, the suicidal thoughts left him. But he felt shattered and humbled. His ears still rang with the unprintable insults of the angry whore.

He had another couple of drinks.

She had no business calling me those names, he told himself consolingly. She knew I was a virgin. She could have been sympathetic. She could have helped me. Another couple of minutes and it would have been okay.

His mistake, as he saw it now, was to have gone to a young tramp. She was still pretty new in her trade, and probably had all kinds of guilt complexes. Her temper was short and she had flown off the handle when he failed to come across. If he picked a wise old harlot, he figured, she would have taken a more maternal approach, would have helped him over this difficult crisis in his life.

Too late now.

What was done was done.

But there was a way to undo it, Lou Andreas thought. He began to see clearly how he could assert his own masculinity, how he could redeem himself for the horrendous bungles that had marked his attempts at being a man so far.

I'll kill her, he thought.

His spirits rose. He felt angry with himself for having made such a fool out of himself. And for the girl he felt nothing but hatred—vivid, uncontrollable hatred.

Killing hatred.

It was almost ten o'clock, now. Getting late, but not all that late. For the second time that night, he got his jacket and left the house and went downtown. Back to the tramp's room. He was determined to punish her for having scorned him. She'd regret that spew of gutter filth, he thought.

He knocked at her door.

No answer.

He knocked again, louder.

No answer.

He put his ear against the door, wondering if he'd hear the sounds of passion, thick grunts and sighing moans. But there was no sound. Nothing.

I'll wait, he thought.

He moved off into the shadows of a nearby staircase. A few minutes passed. Then it occurred to him to try her door. It was open. He looked in.

The room was empty. He closed the door again.

Obviously she was out, hunting up some new customer. Well, if she had any luck, she'd be back here with her client in a little while. Andreas decided to wait, hidden in the stairwell. Then, when the customer left, he would enter the tramp's room before she had a chance to leave, and he would kill her.

He waited.

An hour ticked by.

A second hour. Midnight came and went.

Where was she?

Still walking the streets, looking for a customer? No, he thought. That was impossible. With those big round breasts jutting out of her sweater, and with her aggressive way of making a pickup, she couldn't possibly be having this much trouble. What had happened, Andreas decided, was that someone had taken *her* home for the night. If that were the case, she wouldn't be back till morning.

He couldn't wait till morning. His parents would worry about him.

It was half past twelve, now. One o'clock. Getting later all the time. No sign of the girl. He bit his lip, dreamed of what he would do to her when she finally showed up.

If she showed up.

She didn't. At quarter to two, he decided he had spent enough time huddled there in the shadows, and he left, his murderous dream unfulfilled, his quest for manhood still not at an end.

But the idea of revenge grew inside him—revenge not only against her, but against that whole tribe of women who sold their bodies to men.

Three nights passed before he was able to find the time to go back to the disreputable boarding house. He hesitated for a moment outside the door, and heard the sound of a radio playing within.

She was home!

Murder surged within him. He hammered on the door.

It opened. A man in his fifties, bald, wearing an undershirt, thrust his head out.

"Yeah?"

"I'm looking for—for the girl who lives here—" Andreas blurted.

The man scowled. "Good God, she musta been the biggest tramp in Ohio! You're the thirtieth guy who's been here! Well, she don't live here anymore."

"She—doesn't—?"

"She moved a couple days ago. I moved in last night and there been nothing but guys banging on the door looking for her. She ain't here. I wish she was. I could use her myself. I oughta put a sign on the door to keep you guys from bothering me, that's what."

Andreas managed a faint smile. "I'm—sorry I disturbed you. You don't know where she moved to?"

"No."

The door slammed. Andreas turned away, his shoulders slumping, his dreams of revenge popping into oblivion like pricked soap bubbles.

Gone. Left no address.

He didn't even know her full name. There was no way he could find her.

It doesn't matter, he told himself. *One tramp's just the same as another. If I can't get even with this one, I'll take care of someone else.*

His mind was made up, now. His way was clear. All he needed was a victim.

A couple of days went by before he found one. He went back to the same neighborhood where the girl had picked him up, and after spending half an hour loitering around in the streets, he went into a seedy bar and grill.

He felt nervous. He hadn't had much experience in bars. He was four years underage, but maybe because of his height they wouldn't make any trouble for him. He hoped not. He had had enough embarrassment and shame at the hands of the adult world, for a while. Getting tossed out of a bar would be too much.

There was a girl in the bar. No, a woman. She was sitting by herself, on a high stool at the bar. Everyone else in the bar was watching television, but she was watching the door.

Watching for potential customers, of course.

Andreas grinned at her. He felt gawky and awkward, but a burning purpose drove him on.

She grinned at him. With an easy gesture of her head, she beckoned him to come sit down next to her. Andreas went over.

"Hi," she said. "I'm Jill."

Her voice was deep and husky, almost a man's voice, a baritone. Andreas eyed her carefully. She was about thirty, at the very least, maybe even more. Her hair was reddish-brown, but there were streaks of gray in it that she hadn't bothered to hide. She wasn't bad-looking. She was a little heavyset, but not much. She filled her sweater well.

She looked shabby, though. Worn. Frayed around the edges.

It was a trampish look. The look of an aging harlot, of a tired woman who had offered her legs a couple of thousand times too often over the last decade and a half. There were fatigue lines around her eyes, loose flesh starting to gather at her throat.

"Hi," he said, and sat down next to her.

I'm going to put you out of your misery, he thought quietly, and was astonished at how calm he felt about what he was going to do. There was no tension in him. For once, he felt perfectly the master of his actions.

"Let's have a drink, sweet."

"Sure, Jill," he said, a touch of bravado creeping into his voice. "What are you drinking?"

"Gin and tonic."

"Okay," he said. He beckoned to the bartender. The man looked bored and seedy, and he didn't even begin to question Andreas' age. "Two gin and tonic," Andreas said, and the man brought the drinks. Lou slipped two dollar bills onto the counter, pocketed his change.

By now he knew the pattern that would be followed. They sipped their drinks, and then the woman said, "You know, there's no sense you tossing your money away paying Jimmy's prices here. Eighty cents for a gin and tonic! Hell, for four bucks you can get yourself a whole fifth."

"Yeah," Andreas said. "You're right."

"Tell you what," she said, managing to grin brightly. "Let's you and me pick up a fifth and go over to my place for a party, huh? I got a room right around the corner." She ran her tongue over her lips provocatively. "We can have ourselves a little fun, you and me." She nudged him.

"Good idea," he said.

They left the bar. There was a package store right across the street. He left her outside, and went in alone.

The proprietor was short and fat, and wrinkled up his face in immediate suspicion of Andreas' age. But he made no requests for an ID card.

"Yeah?"

"Fifth of gin," Andreas said, keeping his voice as deep as he could make it.

"What kind?"

A shrug. "I don't know. What can I get for four bucks a fifth?"

"Try the house brand," the man suggested. "Three-seventy-nine. It isn't bad."

He put the bottle in front of Andreas. It was a frosted bottle with square corners. Andreas handed the man a five-dollar bill, solemnly took his change and the brown paper bag containing the bottle, and left.

"I got it," he told the waiting Jill.

"Good. I got some tonic upstairs. And ice. We'll have us a ball."

He stared at her. The plan was forming in his mind. He was still in the sway of that icy, amazing calmness.

They walked to the corner, rounded it, came to a four-story brownstone. As they climbed the stairs, Andreas wondered whether he would take her or simply kill her. He wanted badly to lose his virginity. But on the other hand, this business of murder was a tricky one, and he was afraid that if he delayed the blow, he'd chicken out altogether. He had to strike while the kill-fever was on him.

All the way up the stairs, he turned the problem over in his mind.

But then it solved itself just as they entered her little apartment.

She unlocked the door and stepped inside. As she reached for the light, she said, "Well, here we are, pal. Be it ever so humble, there's—"

Andreas moved automatically, like a mechanical puppet. He withdrew the gin bottle from the paper bag as though drawing a sword from its sheath. He grasped the bottle firmly by its neck.

He drew himself up to his full height and lifted the bottle high above his head.

He brought it down in a smooth arc against the back of the woman's skull.

It was a moment he never forgot. There was the sudden delicious shock wave that came rippling up his arm as the first heavy blow crashed into her head, and here was the immediate thud of her body hitting the floor. The bottle did not break. But her skull did. A little surprised at the strength he had put into the blow, Andreas stared down at her and saw the blood come seeping out into her hair, matting it and staining it bright red.

He knelt.

He lifted the bottle again.

He had to be certain she was really dead.

He brought the bottle down, clublike, a second time, a third, a fourth. He hit her again and again, until her head was only so much soggy pulp. It had split like an eggshell, and fragments of brain oozed out. He took care not to let any of it get on his clothing.

After a long while, he stopped. There could be no doubt, now. No living creature could survive that kind of treatment. His eyes were fixed and glassy as he looked down at the ruin of her skull.

He was bathed in perspiration. And a strange tranquility stole over him, almost like the aftermath of a sexual orgy, now that it was done.

Revenge!

He had had his revenge!

But, of course, he was not finished. He straightened up, found the discarded paper bag, and used it to wipe the blood and brains from the end of the still unbroken gin bottle. Then, setting the gin bottle down, he carried the paper bag into the bathroom, ripped it up, and flushed it down the toilet. He was careful not to touch any surface that might retain his fingerprints. He was not too worried—Even if they found his prints, how would they identify them as his, since he had never been printed for anything?—but he wanted to be cautious about it all the same.

He realized that he could not leave the murder weapon behind. The gin bottle bore the house label of a local liquor store. The police would certainly go to the store first off, and ask who had bought gin lately.

"Well, there was this tall kid with pimples," the proprietor would say, and the search would be on.

No. He had to take the bottle.

He found another paper bag in the dead tart's kitchen. He put the gin bottle in it. Then, cautiously opening the door, he peered into the hall. No one there. The coast was clear. He tiptoed out, and downstairs.

Safe!

As he walked through the dark streets, a wonderful exhilaration came over him. It seemed that he was eleven feet tall, a giant striding through the night, heedless of the puny mortals about him.

He had killed.

He had killed a harlot.

He had avenged himself for the shame of his impotence of the other night. The slate was clean, now. He could begin afresh. A man who had taken a life was a man, not a boy, and he could go on from that point.

He strode through the streets. The blocks melted away. Eight blocks, ten, twelve. He came to a quiet park, a little island of shrubs and benches in the middle of the city, and he sat down and wrenched the cap off the bottle of gin and put it to his lips.

He drank deep.

It was cheap gin, rotgut, and it burned his lips and throat as it went down, but he let it gurgle down the hatch as though it were water. He was high already, high from the excitement on him. Before he quite knew what he was doing, he had put away almost a quarter of the bottle.

He came up for air. He capped the bottle again.

He sat there, quietly enjoying life.

I should have laid her first, he thought. *I didn't need to rush like that. It wouldn't have cost anything. I could have had her first, and then bashed her skull in.*

He closed his eyes and dreamed of what it would have been like. The soft warm breasts filling his hands the firm thighs locked to his body. The thrusting of her hips, the urgent savage motions, then the wild moment of fulfillment—

Too late now.

He had been impatient. There he was, alone with the woman in her room, and all he could think of was clubbing her brains out. Well, he regretted it, but there were other tramps in Cleveland. He'd get another chance to lose his virginity, sooner or later. Preferably sooner. In the meantime, he could console himself with the thought that he had risen above the clods, that he had made something special out of himself.

It had been an execution, he thought.

An execution of a sinful woman.

He uncapped the bottle again. He took another swig. A cold wind was blowing in off the lake, now, but he didn't mind it much, not with all that gin rattling around inside him.

He looked at his watch. Ten past eleven. Time to be getting on home.

But there was all this gin, he thought. He couldn't waste it by tossing it into the bushes. And he couldn't bring the bottle home with him. And he certainly couldn't drink any more gin himself.

He saw someone strolling through the park. A middle-aged man, shabbily dressed, a drifter, a bum. Andreas hurried up to him.

"Hey! Hey, mister!"

Bleary eyes peered uncertainly at him. "Yeah. You want me for something?"

"Here," Andreas said. "Merry Christmas. Go have yourself a party."

He thrust the bottle of gin at him. The derelict stared at it in bewilderment.

"For me?"

"No, for your Aunt Sally!"

The man didn't waste any more time in discussing the situation. He took the bottle quickly from Andreas, stared at it, shook it, heard the gin slosh up and down inside, and with a bemused grin wandered away, clutching the bottle tightly to his chest.

Andreas smiled. He had thereby disposed of the murder weapon, he realized.

Time to head for home, now.

He retraced his steps, found a bus stop, waited. A bus came along. He got aboard, lurching a little, trying hard to hide his drunkenness.

The bus was practically empty. An old man sat up front. Then a couple of middle-aged women sat together, and finally a pair of teenagers. Andreas went to the back of the bus and sat down and watched the teenagers. They were snuggling together, necking and kissing. The boy had his hand in the girl's sweater, and was trying to get into her bra as well, judging from the way he was wiggling around in there. He looked about sixteen or so, the girl a little younger.

A surge of jealousy ran through Andreas. *Why does that kid have a girl and I don't? I bet he's made her. He's younger than I am and he's made her.*

But then he consoled himself with the thought that he could make a claim that few others could make: he had taken life. He was something special. He was almost godlike, in a certain sense.

He was home by midnight. His parents were still up, but in bed. As he passed their bedroom, his mother called out to him. "Where'd you go tonight, Lou?"

"The movies," he said.

"You have a date?"

"Nah. I just went by myself."

"You have a good time?"

"Sure, Mom. A real good time. Good night, Mom."

"Good night."

He went into his room and got his pajamas on. He felt a little woozy from the gin, now. It was hitting him in a delayed reaction. He brushed his teeth, washed his face, rubbed some ointment onto the pimples.

He looked in the mirror. His face seemed to have taken on a more sinister look, now that it had become the face of a murderer.

Sudden desire hit him. His belly churned wildly. He gripped the edge of the sink, biting down hard on his lower lip as the spasms of lust rocked him. It was worse now than it had ever been before.

He was in a cold sweat. But there was a time-tested remedy for situations like this. It was not very gratifying, but it would do as emergency first aid. He closed the bathroom door and relieved himself, and calmness returned.

That was a bad one, he thought. *The worst yet.*

So even killing wasn't the full answer, he realized. It was part of it. But not all.

As he got into bed and waited for sleep, he knew that he would have to see to the rest of it before much more time slipped by.

CHAPTER FOUR

In the morning he began to feel worried.

It had all seemed too simple. Pick up a girl, bash her brains out with a bottle of gin, walk away and never be traced. Was murder as easy as that?

If it was, how come they had so many executions every year? Why were the death houses full all the time?

As he went through his morning routine, as he brushed his teeth and shaved and had his breakfast and got together his schoolbooks, as he did all the normal things a high school junior does every morning, it seemed incredible to him that he had done the thing he remembered doing last night, and even more incredible that he would get away with it.

All that morning, as he went from class to class, he kept expecting to be called out of the classroom, down to the principal's office.

"There's a policeman here to talk to you," they would tell him. And click would go the handcuffs around his wrists.

No one came for him.

He was sure they would, but no one did. He was positive they would be investigating the murder by now, asking questions, being told by the bartender that the last one seen with the dead woman was a tall, pimply-faced kid, and maybe he had left some terribly revealing clue at the scene of the crime, and—

No.

His fears were groundless.

The day passed, and gradually his confidence returned, and he looked at his classmates as though they were mere children. He was on a different level, now. He had passed out of the world of childhood.

On his way home from school, he picked up the afternoon newspapers and leafed tensely through them. No report on the murder. He wasn't really surprised. Probably nobody would find the dead woman for a couple of days, and he couldn't expect to see a story in the paper for a while after that.

For the next couple of days, he watched all the papers diligently, going through every story on every page. It even surprised his parents. "Since when are you such a newspaper bug?" his father asked him.

He just smiled and said, "It's for an assignment in school."

But he found nothing.

Evidently the newspapers didn't deem it of any importance to write up the bludgeoning of a local prostitute. Probably it happened all the time, two three times a week, and they just didn't bother to devote precious space to such trivia. Andreas kept watch on the newspapers for ten days. He didn't miss a line, so he knew he hadn't overlooked the story. And it was unthinkable that they wouldn't have discovered her rotting body by now. So the story simply didn't make the papers.

Andreas was disappointed.

He had looked forward to seeing the details in the paper. Somehow the absence of a news report on the murder made the whole incident seem unreal to him, something hazy and dreamlike that might not actually have happened. Sure, he could remember the crunch of bottle on skull, the thud of body against floor, but something in black and white would have made the experience all the more authentic.

But they never wrote it up.

It was one of the reasons why he had to commit his second murder. It was because he had stopped really believing that he had ever committed the first.

There was a girl named Marian Peterson. She was in Andreas' class in high school. Andreas did not murder her, though he toyed with the idea. But she was very important in the story of his life, all the same. She stole his virginity.

It was not exactly a difficult achievement to get with Marian Peterson. The fact was well known around Andreas' high school that she was a girl who could be had. There were several girls in the class who had sluttish reputations, but Marian Peterson was the one whose name was most repeatedly blackened in lunchroom gossip.

Andreas had known that for a long time—more than a year, now.

"All you have to do is touch her boobs," someone had told him. "She goes wild."

For a whole year, the fact of his virginity had been festering in him, and he had been all too thoroughly aware that a single date with Marian Peterson would put an end to that troublesome condition of innocence, and yet he had not allowed himself to ask her out.

He knew why.

Lack of guts, that was the reason.

He was shy and unsure of himself. He had never made it with a girl. Here was Marian, an alleged nympho. Suppose he asked her out and failed to score? His ego would be damaged forever. Why, it might turn out that he was the only boy in the whole damned city that she would say no to. He didn't want to take the risk of being refused. Nothing ventured, nothing lost, was the way he reasoned it.

But now he had changed. He had not been afraid of committing a murder; why should he be afraid of asking Marian Peterson for a date? He was a different person, now, bold and aggressive and self-confident. It was ridiculous for him to hang back in soggy cowardice.

About two weeks after his criminal act, he met Marian in the hallway, and said, "Hey, what are you doing tomorrow night, huh?"

"Nothing much."

"Feel like taking in a movie with me?"

"Sure, Lou. I'd love to."

So it was as easy as that. All he had to do was ask and she would agree.

He was in a fever of lust all that night. He hardly slept. Tossing and turning from midnight to dawn he thought many times of resorting to his furtive method of self-pleasuring, but he steadfastly resisted temptation. He remembered only too well his fiasco with the saucy, big-boobed tramp three weeks earlier. He didn't want a repetition of that, and so he wanted to be right at the peak of his need when he turned to Marian Peterson.

The long day crawled away. Evening came. He had arranged to borrow the family car. At half past seven, he drove over to Marian's place. He was wearing his best suit. He had shaved twice that day. He was thoroughly deodorized.

He was all set for the big night.

Marian was ready when he honked his horn out front. She appeared, grinned hello at him, and slipped in alongside him. Andreas gunned the engine and away they went.

It was a funny thing about Marian, he thought. The other two girls who were reported to be nymphos were both dogs—Ruth Cloud and Billie Morris. Ruth was dumpy and pasty-faced, and Billie was big and gawky, and you could look at either girl and know that they put out simply because if they didn't nobody would ever want to date them.

But Marian was different.

Marian was a good-looking girl. Not beautiful, maybe, the way blonde Rosalie was beautiful, but she was easy enough on the eyes. She was a short girl, about five feet three, but well built, in perfect proportions. Her breasts were high and firm, not terribly big, but placed nicely, and her legs were trim, and she had wide, intelligent eyes and a good face and attractive brown hair.

Why would a good-looking girl like that be such a rabbit, Andreas wondered?

Maybe she was mixed up in the head, he figured. Or maybe it was some kind of glandular thing. He had heard about cases like that. Girls who were so eager in the glands that they just had to get loved every few days or go out of their minds. It had to be something like that with Marian, he decided.

They went to the movies. He held her hand, and then he put his arm around her shoulder. But he didn't go any further. It wasn't out of shyness, this time. It was out of fear that if he did something provocative, if he touched her breasts in the movie or did anything like that, it would heat her up and she would try to rape him in the theater. "All you have to do is touch her boobs," he had been told. "Then she goes wild." Well, he didn't want her going wild in here.

After the movie, they stopped off for ice cream in a local parlor. Then they got into the car, and he drove off, toward Marian's house.

There was a bulldozed housing development a few blocks from her place. The shells of the houses were up, nothing more. They hadn't even put up the street lights yet. It was black as a cave there.

Andreas pulled the car up next to a mound of dirt and said, "Let's stop here for a little while, okay?"

"Okay," she said.

He turned to her. A faint flicker of moonlight was the only illumination. But that was enough. He had always had good night vision. He could see her clearly, now. There was a smile on her lips, a smile of anticipation.

He reached for her.

He slipped one arm around her shoulders, and drew her toward him, and he brought the other hand down firmly over her right breast, and held it there, cupping, squeezing.

She gasped.

There was no mistaking the sound. He had touched her breast and she had sucked in her breath as though he had just branded her with a white-hot iron.

Touch her boobs and she goes wild, they said.

It looked like everything they said about Marian Peterson was gospel.

For a long while, maybe three or four minutes—and that seemed like an eternity to Lou Andreas—he sat there in the car massaging the front of Marian's blouse. She got hotter and hotter. She could hear her panting, could feel her breasts rising and falling rapidly, agitatedly.

She pressed close to him. Her warm, wet lips found his earlobe. She nibbled. He squeezed her breasts harder. He felt her poking the hot tip of her tongue deep into his ear. It was a maddeningly exciting sensation.

He began to unbutton her blouse.

It was all happening so smoothly, he thought, feeling good about things. Button after button after button he opened, until he had accounted for all of them.

His hands slipped inside.

He operated with the greatest of ease, as though he were a playboy from way back. His big awkward fingers went sliding around to Marian's shoulder blades, and he found the straps of her bra, and nudged them inward.

The hooks gave.

The cups dropped away from her breasts.

He didn't remove her blouse, but he slipped her bra down and away, so that he had a clear shot at her bare breasts. They were high and firm and round. Smallish, nowhere near the melon-sized things that the tramp with the sarcastic tongue had had. But they filled his hands.

He held them.

Marian squirmed with desire.

He cupped both her breasts, gripping them tightly, enjoying the way the soft warm flesh yielded to his fingers. The nipples were like little wrinkled pebbles sprouting from the tender cones of flesh.

Marian edged up against him. She was pulling up her skirt, yanking her underclothes off—not even waiting for him to get around to the job. Out of the corner of his eye, he saw something pink go sliding to the floor of the car. Marian's panties, he realized.

He leaned forward and put his face against her breasts. He opened his lips wide and a nipple popped into them, and a couple of inches of warm firm flesh. He drew as much of the breast into his mouth as he could. His tongue lolled back and forth over the rock-hard swelling of Marian's nipple. He caressed away, and from her moans of passion he knew he was getting through to her.

While busy with her breasts, he put his left hand on one of her calves, just above her bobby-sox, and drew it speedily northward up her bare, cool calf. She had shaved her legs today, and her skin was smooth and shiny.

Up, up, up!

He got to her knee quickly, and hardly hesitated there, but kept on going, up into the soft fleshy warmth of her thigh. It seemed like a good place to pause, and he did so, gripping the thigh in his outspread hands, digging the tips of his fingers into the warm, fantastically smooth skin.

Then he moved higher.

Inch by inch by inch—not because he wasn't in a hurry, but because he wanted to work the girl into a real gyrating frenzy. Suddenly he felt warmth.

Marian stiffened as though stabbed.

Her body was trembling with need. It was almost frightening to feel the forces churning within her, to sense the power of her desires.

Her hands stole to his body.

He caught his breath as her small cool fingers touched him. There was no fear now that his first fiasco would be repeated. He was proudly ready now, overpoweringly so. His inhibitions were gone.

"Come on," she panted. "Now!"

She squirreled her body around on the seat, pulling one leg up, twisting the other down, making room for Andreas between them. In the semi-darkness, he looked down at her, saw her thighs and breasts as she pulled her skirt up.

He settled into place.

He felt her eager hands guiding him to the seat of warmth. He closed his eyes and drew in his breath, and told himself that this was the moment, that long-awaited instant in which he said good-bye to innocence.

He could feel himself approaching the gate now.

He felt warmth, and soft smoothness.

He thrust forward. She answered with an upward motion of her hips, and her body engulfed him, and he slid easily and smoothly to her, down to the depths, and he smiled and buried his face in the hollow between her cheek and her shoulder, and thrust and thrust again, and realized that he was a virgin no longer, that as of that last moment when he entered her he had cast away his innocence, that in blending his body with hers he had crossed the divide into manhood.

It felt good.

It was a wonderful sensation, so relaxing, so marvelously agreeable. He moved, and she moved with him. and he went deep and withdrew, went deep and withdrew, and he felt the first tickling, prickling, tingling throbs of the ecstasy that was waiting for him, and he bit down hard on his lips, trying to hold it back, waiting for Marian to catch up with him.

Another moment and she was there.

She was blazing beneath him. Her body rotated hips churning, moving with such violence that she nearly threw him free of her body, which was the last thing either of them would have wanted to happen at that moment. He rode along with her.

It was astonishing how she was gasping and thrashing around. She was a wild one, all right. He worked one hand between their bodies and caught hold of one round perfect breast, and gripped it tight. He managed to get the other hand under her, drawing it along the upholstery of the car seat until he had it securely wrapped around her taut, firm, globular right buttock.

He held her tight.

He lifted his mouth from hers for a moment, coming up for air, and he heard her gasp, "Baby, I'm going crazy—"

"So am I," he wanted to say. But he was abruptly unable to say anything, because her lips were glued against his again and her tongue was rammed almost as deep into his mouth as his body was to hers, and then fireworks were going off in his brain and it was all he could do to go on thinking, let alone frame intelligible and coherent sentences.

It happened.

Not with a whimper but a bang.

There was a fiery explosion somewhere within him, an up-welling jet of burning intense heat, and his whole body convulsed in spasming ecstasy, and he was dimly aware that something similar was happening to her, and it was absolutely overwhelming, the most wonderful sensation he had experienced since—

Since he had killed the tramp named Jill.

In the startling moment of clarity that followed the final wild burst of pleasure, he was able to compare the two sensations, and to find that they were not really very different. When he had brought the bottle down to deliver the fatal blow, he had felt a powerful surge of pure pleasure. And, just now, at the moment of climax, he had had another such jolt. One had been emotional, psychological. The other had been physical.

He was not at all sure which he preferred.

Sex was great, he decided. It lived up to all its advance billing.

But yet—

There was a terrific kick in murder, too. And, what's more, it had the advantage of novelty. Everybody got loved, sooner or later. But how many people combined sex with murder? Damned few. If he wanted to rise above the common clods, he could do it by taking life.

The thought flickered through his mind:

Why not kill Marian?

It wouldn't be hard. She was a short girl, not the athletic type. She wouldn't put up much of a fight. Besides, he had her body trapped beneath his. She couldn't wiggle if he didn't want her to. All he had to do was slip his hands around her throat, and squeeze, and squeeze a little harder, and before long she would be dead. She would die right while the afterglow of sex was still on her.

No, he thought.

He weighed the situation and decided to spare her, and even the negative act of deciding *not* to commit a murder gave him great pleasure, gave him at least a taste of the godlike ecstasy that had been his as he crushed that aging tramp's skull.

He couldn't kill Marian.

It wasn't that he was afraid of getting caught. Sure, it was known that he had dated her tonight, but he could always claim that someone had raped and strangled her after he had left her, and if they didn't break down his story he would get away with it. But he had a different reason for not wanting to murder her.

Marian was a person.

The tramp that he had killed was a nobody. He didn't even know her last name. She had no real existence as a human being. She was just a body for sale, and a pair of breasts, not an individual. So he could snuff her out like a stepped-on bug.

Besides Marian had not done anything unkind to him. She had been good to him. She had opened her body to him. True, not because she loved him, but simply because she was a nympho who obeyed her reflexes. Still, she had given in to him.

It was a tart who had mocked him. Marian was a tramp, but no tart. She gave it away.

Death to all tarts, he thought. *But Marian can live.*

He lifted his head and looked down at her. He kissed her breasts, one at a time, caressing the rosy nipples playfully. Marian would never know how close she had come to death just now.

They sat up. He adjusted his clothes. She snapped her bra, buttoned her blouse. She found her panties, down by the floorboards, and he watched as she pulled them on, enjoying the little flicker of bare thigh that he saw before she got them into place.

She smiled at him. "That was fun."

"Yeah."

"You're pretty good, Lou. You must have had a lot of experience."

He shrugged. "Oh, not that much."

"Don't kid me. I've been around plenty, and I can tell. You really know how to please a girl."

He beamed at her. She snuggled up next to him, and he started the car and drove her home, with a warm feeling of accomplishment growing in his bosom. He was a man at last. He was on his way!

CHAPTER FIVE

Spring moved along. And as the weeks passed, Andreas almost came to wonder if he really had killed an old harlot named Jill, or if the whole thing had simply been a fantasy of his feverish, sex-hungry brain.

He couldn't be sure. There hadn't been any newspaper story, no tangible proof at all that he had really done it. He began to doubt it.

He began to think that perhaps he ought to strike again.

He had certain theories, now, that he wanted to check. He had been doing a lot of thinking about the relationship between murder and sexual pleasure, and there were certain experiments he wanted to carry out. It was no longer a matter of sexual need. He was quite well taken care of, now. He saw Marian Peterson every couple of weeks, and she was always good for a torrid session. He had dated a couple of other girls, too, and one of them, Joanie Mason, had turned out to be seducible, while the other one, Liz Hagerty, insisted on keeping her panties on but wasn't averse to pleasant games of other sorts.

So he was making out all right.

It was purely for experimental purposes that he ventured into the burlesque strip to pick up another girl.

This one was a blonde. At least, that was the flag she was currently flying. There was a phony platinum sheen to her hair. She wore it flounced out, in a puffy mound that was an ancestor of the bouffant look that everybody would be wearing a few years in the future.

She had style, this one. She was about twenty-five, Andreas figured, and she walked with a mincing, exaggerated, hip-swishing gait that was at once rather silly and also rather attractive.

She was good to look at, too. She had plucked her eyebrows into two pencil-thin arcs. Her face was lean, a little long-nosed but she had a sexy look about her. And big breasts, high and pointy.

Andreas picked her up outside a cafeteria. He had watched her through the plate glass window, and she saw him, and came out, and stood by the door, and took out a cigarette and popped it in her mouth, and then went fumbling through her handbag looking for matches.

It was a good come-on. Andreas walked over and said, "Want a light?"

"Thanks a million." She looked up at him and winked. "You're a friend in need, good-looking."

He struck a match and leaned close to light her cigarette for her. She puffed it into a blaze. He could smell a musky perfume on her.

He said, "You busy now?"

"Nope."

He went home with her. Making a pickup was an easy matter for him, now. He had a kind of sixth sense about finding girls who could be had, and once he found one, it was simple enough to get the point across.

She had a neat little apartment. It mirrored her own appearance: stylish, but a little flashy. As they came in, she said, "I don't want to seem impatient or anything, but I'd sort of prefer it if you paid me in advance."

"Sure," he said.

"You know how it is. You give a guy what he wants, and some of them, they don't feel like paying after they've had it. It's a raw deal. What can I do, go call a cop on them?"

"I understand," Andreas said. "How much?"

"Well, I usually get twenty-five. Let's say twenty because you look like a nice kid."

Andreas frowned. He didn't want anyone calling him a kid, nice or otherwise. Maybe he wasn't quite eighteen yet, but he was six feet two and he looked older than his age, and for a tramp to be calling him a kid was in a way to revive the insults that still rang in his ears.

He said, "Twenty's still a lot."

She smiled sizzlingly. "I'll give you your money's worth," she whispered, her voice husky.

He shrugged. She'd give him more than his money's worth, he thought. But she didn't know that now. He took out his wallet and peeled off two bills. She took them and slipped them into a book by the side of her bed.

Then she said "Make yourself comfortable. You want a drink?"

"No," he said. "You know what I want."

"Yeah. I can guess. You got any preferences?"

"Strip for me," he said. "Put some music on and do a strip act."

She giggled. "Okay. Whatever you like."

Andreas turned on the radio and twiddled the dials until he found some music with a lively beat. The girl moved out into the middle of the floor. He didn't even know her first name, he realized suddenly. Well, it didn't make much of a difference in the long run.

She began to dance.

She was pretty good at it, he saw. She didn't have a professional stripper's timing, but she had a good natural sense of rhythm. She knew how to bump and grind. She moved gracefully and seductively.

Andreas settled back comfortably on the bed to watch her strip.

She moved back and forth in the middle of the room, her eyes slitted with lust, her hips moving, her shoulders undulating, her breasts now thrusting forward, now retreating. She made a complete circuit of the room, then hauled her skirt up on one side, showed him her stockinged leg almost to the hip, and kicked off a shoe.

She slid the stocking off.

She danced toward him, waved her breasts in his face, then retreated. Slowly, voluptuously, she peeled off her sweater. She had on a yellow bra underneath. She put her hands over the cups and squeezed them, made a little moaning sound of soft passion.

Andreas continued to watch. And as he watched, he thought about how he was going to kill her.

Not like the other one. That was too crude a method. He hadn't really liked the blood and brains spattering everywhere, the ugly sounds of breaking bone, the need for repeatedly bashing the bottle down. No, he wanted something subtler, something a little more suave and gentlemanly.

Like strangling.

That would be fine, he thought. For one thing, the girl would suffer more. That other one had been knocked cold by the first blow, and the rest of the time had been spent simply smashing life from an unconscious hulk. Strangling, though that meant awareness almost to

the very end, didn't it?
So it would be strangling.
And when?
Before, like the other time? No, that was silly. So long as he was here, he might as well take the one pleasure from her before taking the other.
After, then?
Well, why not during?
It was an interesting idea. It was an experiment he wanted to try, one of several. He decided that would be how he would do it.

She had slithered out of her skirt now. Flaring hips and firm thighs confronted him. Her panties were green and gauzy.
Off came the bra.
Her breasts were firm and full. Now they were gleaming with sweat. The nipples were very small, set in tiny dark aureoles no larger in diameter than a twenty-five-cent piece. She pressed her hands over her breasts, squeezing them, pushing them up and together. The nipples protruded between her fingers like two blind, staring red eyes.
She rolled her panties down, now. Slowly, inch by inch, over the breadth of her hips, over the solid columns of her thighs. Down they dropped, to the knees, the ankles, and off.
Nothing cloaked her nudity now but her garter belt and a single stocking.
She approached the bed. She lifted her leg, indicating that she wanted Andreas to remove the stocking for her.
He grinned. He unclipped the garters, and rolled the nylon down. Her leg was satin-smooth, the flesh cool and sweet-smelling.
Standing before him, hands on her hips, she let him inspect her nudity. Only the garter belt hid her now, a single line of elastic around her waist, cutting into the fleshy mounds of her buttocks just above the little dimples. With a happy cry she whisked the belt off.
Now she was nude.
"How did I do?" she asked. "Am I good as a stripper?"
"You're great," he said.
"Wait," she said. "I got other talents too. You wait and see."
She advanced toward the bed and threw herself down next to him. She started to unbutton his shirt.
"No," he said "I want to keep my clothes on."
It would be easier to make a quick getaway that way, he thought. In case something went wrong and he had to flee. He didn't want to have to stop to scramble into his clothes in that event.
"Any way you like," she said.

He cupped her breasts. They were hard and round, filling his hands. Her body squirmed against him. She smelled clean and good. She didn't really seem trampish at all— she was definitely a higher-class girl than the two he had picked up previously.

But that wouldn't save her.

He stroked her body, enjoying the sleekness of her, the way she wriggled and shivered as he heated her up. Some whores, he knew, were frigid and just went through the paces mechanically, but not this one. She was giving him the old college try. You had to give her credit for that.

She rolled over onto her back. She drew her knees up, and spread-eagled out, waiting for him.

"You ready?" she whispered.

"You bet!"

He lowered himself on top of her. Her body was warm and willing to receive him. With an ease born of plenty of experience, Andreas took her.

He drove deep. Her body quivered, and she arched her back high away from the mattress, and he took advantage of it, his hips pistoning with repeated energetic thrusts.

This was going to take timing, he thought.

He played it cautiously. He could all too easily let himself be carried away by the passionate plunging of her body, and surrender in one grand cataclysm of ecstasy. But he didn't want it that way. He wanted to stay in control, all the way right up to the final moment.

Their bodies moved. Faster, now.

Faster.

She was giving him his money's worth. Her hips wriggled, her body rolled. Her fingers dug into the muscles of his back, pressing tight against him. He rose away from her for a moment, then lowered himself again, filling his hands with the round fleshy balls of her breasts. With slow pumping motions he brought himself closer to the moment of fulfillment. It drew near.

His hands slid upward from her breasts, lingered for a moment at her collarbone, then moved upward still farther. He let them rest lightly, almost playfully, on her throat. His fingertips caressed the soft skin. He stroked her lovingly, and all the while his bucking, thrusting body continued to move inexorably toward the culmination.

It was very close, now.

His fingers tightened, automatically.

"Hey," she said. "Don't do that! You're hurting me."

He smiled. He could feel the churning frenzy building up in him, now.

Another second or two—

It arrived.

It hit him with terrific impact, and in the same instant that the full force of his passionate ecstasy rocked through him, he brought his hands closed like a vise round the girl's throat. He had big hands, and they completely engulfed her, and the strong fingers dug inward, thumbs pressing down on the little hard Adam's apple, and there was a moment when he felt it resisting the downward pressure, and he heard her making a hoarse, gargling sound. And then he felt the wall of cartilage collapse inward under his pressure.

Even as he was strangling her, her body continued to move automatically in the rhythm of love. Her hips still rose and dropped back, even while he was in the process of taking her life.

The only trouble was that the double excitement left him unable to follow the sequence of events. He was drowning in his own pleasures. He clung to her throat, squeezing inward, his thumbs nearly touching her spine now, and as he crushed the breath from her, he felt the electric surge of ecstasy, and for one dazzling moment he thought he would go insane from sheer delight.

Then it was over.

Both at once.

There came the searing spurt of physical release, and in the same instant the awareness that he had slain the girl at the height of his spasm.

Or was she dead?

Her body still moved. Unbelievably, she seemed to be having a climax. He stared at her. Her face was a hideous mottled purple, and her eyes were bulging from her sockets. But down below—what was that quivering, that sudden convulsive spasming, that familiar quiver?

Could she really be reacting sexually—after she was dead?

He clung to her, dazed by it all. His body still moved, in the final afterthrusts, and there was no denying the trembling spasms of her muscles. And yet his fingers were buried in her throat, and her head lolled limply, and there was no life in her eyes.

After a long moment, Andreas withdrew from her body and stood up. There was a feeling of warmth in his body, of satisfaction. He zipped up his trousers and looked down at the crumpled body on the bed.

It wasn't a pretty sight. It was an improvement over that other corpse, with the spattered blood and brains, but it still wasn't anything very decorative. She had turned a ghastly color. And her eyes—popping out of their sockets that way, practically about to roll down her cheeks—

For a moment Andreas thought he was going to be violently sick. But he got control of himself.

"Hey," he said in a quiet, soft voice. "Hey, you! Are you alive?"

No answer.

"What's the matter?" he asked. "Cat got your tongue or something, girlie?"

Silence.

"I guess you're dead," he said. "Is that your trouble? That you're dead? Jeez, you got big trouble, you know that, girlie? You got the biggest trouble somebody can possibly have."

He giggled. He felt a little high, almost on the edge of hysteria. He stared down at her, at the firm, pointy-tipped breasts. Her breasts were turning a strange color, now. Blobs of congealed blood were making them dark. She had been such a pretty girl, he thought. With her plucked eyebrows and her blonde hair and her round little boobs and her tight little curvy butt. And now she was just so much dead meat, ready for the hopper.

She lay there with her thighs apart and her body posed in grotesque invitation.

A sudden surge of desire grew in Andreas.

For a moment, he was tempted to throw himself on her dead body and ravish her all over again. But he had not yet come to that. The idea had a strange appeal to it, but he told himself he had lingered long enough, that it was time to clear out before someone found him here.

He checked the room, searching for evidence that could be used to track him down. He found none. He took one last look at the strangled girl on the bed, trying not to see her face and throat. Her slim nudity seemed pathetic now that life had left it.

I wonder what your name was, Andreas thought.

He tiptoed out.

Moments later, he was in the street. No one had seen him leave. His luck had held. A second tramp had perished, and so far as he could see there was no way he could be accused of having committed the crime.

He felt good.

He felt a little hit like an angel of extermination. He was ridding the world of the female trash that preyed on men. Why, he was certain that if he ever got arrested for his crimes, no jury would convict him. He was performing an act of justice each time he destroyed some miserable prostitute.

He headed down the street, walking with a proud and regal stride.

"Hey! Hey, Lou!"

Andreas turned. He saw someone waving at him in the darkness. For a moment, in his self-intoxicated mood, Andreas was unable to concentrate on recognizing the other. Then he came down to earth. It was a classmate of his, a fellow named Sid Burch.

Burch was short and beak-nosed, an aggressive little piledriver of a guy. He and Andreas were acquaintances more than real friends. Andreas didn't go in much for making really close friends.

Burch said, "Hey, man! Where you going?"

"Home, I guess."

"Too early to go home. Want some action?"

"What kind?"

Burch's eyes glittered. "I got this tramp lined up," he said. "Ten bucks for the works, and I mean the works! She told me she got a friend, so if I brought a friend along we could double up, you get what I mean?"

"Yeah," Andreas said.

"You interested?"

"I don't think so."

"Ah, come on! They're clean. They won't give you a dose or anything."

"That's not it," Andreas said. "It happens that I just got made myself. I'm on my way home. I'm not looking for any more action right now."

Skepticism showed in Burch's eyes. "Yeah. I bet."

"It's the truth."

"Who were you with?"

"A girl," Andreas said. "Look, you run along or you'll be late for your action, Sid."

"Come on along with me," Burch repeated.

"Why you so hot for company?" Andreas laughed. "No, I got mine for tonight. You go have yourself a good time without me."

He walked away.

He wondered if the tramp Sid Burch was going to meet happened to be one with puffy blonde hair and plucked eyebrows. Sid was going to be in for a nasty surprise, if that was his date for the evening. But Andreas doubted it. The late Miss Plucked Eyebrows hadn't been a ten-buck lay. Probably Sid was going to make some old bag who'd been in the business since the Spanish-American War.

Lou Andreas shrugged. He began to whistle as he walked. There was a big orange full moon overhead. A lover's moon. He was really relaxed, easy now. There was nothing like a murder to relax you.

He whistled merrily all the way home. And he slept the sound sleep of someone who has done a good day's work and has earned his rest.

CHAPTER SIX

This time, the story got in to the newspapers.

Andreas found the bit the next day, and it made his blood run cold to see it. He had been disappointed when the first killing failed to break into print, but now that this one had, he felt tremors of fear.

The girl had been found by a client who had come calling. He had knocked, and hearing nothing, had gone in. There was the nude, strangled corpse. The client, whose name was not known, had skedaddled, but not before waking up the superintendent of the building and telling him to get the hell upstairs to Apartment Such-and-Such.

The super had gone upstairs. There had been Miss Plucked Eyebrows. The super had called the police. The police had come to investigate. That was all the story said. There was no mention of a possible lead.

"Miss Valentinetti was unemployed," the article declared.

Valentinetti. Doris Valentinetti. So he knew her name, at least. He wondered if she had been a religious tramp.

No matter now. Her blackened soul rotted in hell, Andreas thought pleasantly. All the sins were being burned out of her down there. He pictured her strung up by her thumbs over a blazing fire. Her legs were stretched wide apart by two ropes, and the fire was burning away the lustful ecstasies that had taken place there.

He carefully snipped the clipping out of the newspaper and put it in his wallet, and carried it around for a couple of days. Then it struck him that he was doing a stupid thing. It was like carrying a loaded gun around with him. Suppose he got hit by a car? Not seriously, just enough to knock him out. And they went searching through his wallet for some identification, and found the clipping.

Why would a teenage boy carry a murder clipping? Obviously because he had committed the murder and was proud of the fact. So he would wake up in the hospital under police guard, and a beefy lieutenant would glower at him and say, "We'd just like to ask you a few questions, son—"

No, he thought. Carrying the clipping was much too risky. He took one last look at it, then lit a match to it and watched it burn, and thought once again of Doris Valentinetti burning in hell with her legs spread over a raging fire, and smiled.

A long time passed before Andreas committed his next murder.

He was uneasy about trying again too soon. There had already been two murders within a space of a few weeks. The first one had gone all but unnoticed. The second one had made the newspapers. Let there be a third one, and there would be mutterings about a crime wave. Extra police would be put on duty. The city's population of prostitutes would be particularly wary. The slightest menacing gesture a client made would touch off wild screams that were sure to bring a cop. So he took a vacation from murder.

He let the months go by, and gradually the city of Cleveland began to return to normal, if it had ever really left there, and spring turned to summer, and summer came round to fall, and Lou Andreas turned eighteen and entered his senior year in high school, and all that time he remained chaste so far as the act of murder went, though certainly not chaste in the usual sense of the word.

As a matter of fact, he was quite well fixed so far as sex went. Now that he had outgrown his adolescent gawkiness, he was discovering that he had no trouble getting girls to open up for him. He had a smooth line and the unshakeable self-confidence that a person tends to get after he's committed two murders and gotten away with both of them.

A funny thing happened to him on his way to graduation, too.

A girl fell in love with him.

Her name was Tony. Antonia, really, but nobody likes to be called Antonia. Her name was Tony, Tony Neale. She was in the senior class at his high school, just as he was, but there were 850 students in the senior class, and even in four years one doesn't get to know all of them. So it happened that he didn't meet her until midway through their senior year.

She was cute. She was a lithe brunette, five four and a half, shiny black hair and shiny brown eyes, pearly teeth, a ready smile, and a lovely bosom. She was also smart. She was way up near the top of the class academically, with a 98 plus average, and she was leader of the academic honor society, and she had already been accepted by Radcliffe, Wellesley, Bryn Mawr, and half a dozen of the other best women's colleges, and the schools were fighting among themselves to see which one would give her the biggest scholarship and land her.

Under the circumstances, it was a little odd that she would fall in love with Lou Andreas. Call it attraction of opposites. She had a reputation for being something of a grind, and she was college bound. While Andreas just about managed to pull through with a 71 average, had no plans for going on to college, and was regarded around the school as something of a lady killer—though no one knew how accurate the designation really was.

They didn't have much in common. But they hit it off pretty well. For Andreas, it was just a matter of sex. For Tony, though, it rapidly became love.

Which led to complications, and taught Andreas a thing or two about getting involved with other people.

Their romance started simply and innocently enough the week before Christmas. They were in the same American History class, and Andreas was having trouble. He had fallen behind in the reading, and he was hopelessly bogged down in the year 1776, while the rest of the class was along to 1812 already and heading merrily on to the Civil War.

He needed help badly. And, as it turned out, one day after he had made a particularly horrible botch in class, he found himself walking across the Quad with Tony Neale, and she said to him, "Do you think it would help if I studied with you during the Christmas vacation?"

"Probably would."

"You've got to start catching up," she said seriously. "It'll be January before you know it, and those final exams will be here."

Andreas didn't really give a damn about the final exams, though he didn't tell her that. Unlike Tony, unlike most of his classmates, he wasn't going on to college. The academic life held no interest for him. That being the case, it didn't matter much to him whether he flunked all his classes or not. He didn't need marks, didn't even need the high school diploma. The only reason he had stayed in school was that he had nothing much to do outside except go to work, and that idea didn't terribly much appeal to him.

He kept all these thoughts to himself. Somewhere the back of his mind was the thought that it would be fun to lay Tony Neale, and if he had to submit to a certain amount of history coaching in order to score, well, it was a light enough price.

So they began to study together during the holidays—sometimes at his place, sometimes at hers.

It was always very chaste, at the start. They would sit down with textbooks and notebooks, and they would go over the work very seriously and diligently. Andreas didn't want to make any passes while they were studying. It might give Tony the idea that he was a frivolous person.

So he plugged away. From time to time, he caught her looking at him in what might be interpreted as a frivolous way, but he forced himself not to capitalize on the opportunity. She seemed to be interested in him. Good. He'd take care of that soon enough.

He was convinced that she was a virgin. Somehow, girls with 98 averages always were virgins. There was something about academic success that made a girl prudish. Pretty as Tony Neale was, and she was undeniably a dish, Andreas was positive that she knew nothing about sex at first hand. He was more than willing to teach her, though. It was the least he could do, he figured, in return for the history coaching.

A day before Christmas he said, "Tony, do you happen to be free New Year's Eve?"

If a girl of eighteen does not have a date for New Year's Eve by the middle of December, there are several possible explanations. One is that she is so abysmally ugly that nobody cares to ask her out. Tony Neale clearly did not fall into that category. The second explanation is that she is such a retiring and scholarly type that she is not interested in partaking in revelry. For all her studiousness, Tony did not seem to fall into that category either.

The third possible reason is that she is keeping the date open, hoping that somebody special will ask her.

When Lou Andreas asked her, she looked at him with glittering eyes and said, "Yes, Lou. I'm still free."

Lou Andreas knew that he was in like Flynn with Tony Neale.

They arranged a date forthwith. One of their classmates, a Jerry Braun, was giving a party, and Andreas had been invited. He brought Tony.

Jerry Braun lived in a well-to-do suburb about half a mile on the other side of the high school district, a longish way from the second-rate area Andreas lived in. The house was a three-story brick affair standing in the center of a handsome landscaped plot. It had snowed the day before, and the towering spruces and pines adjoining the Braun house looked like giant Christmas trees, an effect helped along by the hundreds of colored lights that had been wired into them.

There were about fifteen couples at the party. It took place in an enormous game room in the Braun cellar, and the Brauns had hired a four-piece combo to provide the music for their son's party. The cream of the senior class was there—the academic leaders and the athletic stars as well. Andreas had been puzzled by the invitation, since he didn't rate as one of the class leaders.

But Tony did. Had Braun—who was no special friend of Andreas invited him because he wanted Tony at the party? It seemed that way. These were Tony's friends. Andreas felt a little out of place at first.

Not for long, though. There was a well-stocked bar, and Jerry Braun certainly knew how to make the booze flow in the best suburban tradition. Two cases of champagne occupied the refrigerator back of the bar—no domestic stuff, but good imported bubbly. And every now and then, the joyous sound of a popping cork told that another bottle had been opened and was making the rounds.

Andreas drank his share, and maybe a little over. And Tony was guzzling heavily too, he noticed.

She's trying to drown her inhibitions, Andreas told himself in happy anticipation.

Certainly Tony did not look much like a prudish honor student tonight. She was wearing a green party dress, dazzlingly low-cut. The white cones of her breasts were all but spilling over her scoop neckline. When he stood behind her, he could see practically all the way down to her nipples. The nipples themselves were out of sight, but when she pivoted and put stress on her bra, it was possible to see the faint reddening where the aureoles began. Her breasts looked firm and round and lovely, just the right size for breasts to be. Andreas wondered if he'd get his hands on them before the night was out.

He did not have to wonder long. Not only Tony's dress but her behavior were on the distinctly non-prudish side that night.

He kissed her for the first time about half past ten that night. They were dancing, to some slow, dreamy melody, and they would have been cheek to cheek if he had not been eight inches taller than she was. As it was her high heels cut the difference somewhat. The sweet fragrance of her black hair was in his nostrils, and as they danced toward a dim corner of the big basement he drew her tight, and felt the rounds of her breasts flattening against his chest, and let her feel the urgency of his body, and he drew his lips across her cheeks until they reached her mouth, and they kissed.

It was a tentative kind of kiss. She seemed unprepared for it, even a little shy. He started to slip his tongue into her mouth, but she kept her jaws closed, extending only the tip of her own tongue a fraction of an inch between her teeth to meet him. For a sinking moment Andreas felt that he had been right about her, that she was far too prudish for him to hope to get anywhere with her.

But a first kiss is not always indicative. A few moments later they were kissing again, and this time it was a torrid one indeed. Her teeth parted to admit his questing tongue, and he slipped in, exploring the warm, moist, champagne-tasting interior of her mouth. Her tongue played games with his, and their bodies came flat together, and she moved her hips from side to side, in a frankly suggestive manner that smacked more of the trollop than of the honor student, and he locked his arms around her and held her tight.

Then they were making their way to a love seat in the dark corner of the room, and, with their backs to the laughing partiers and the perspiring combo, they kissed once again. Andreas' arms were so long that he could snake one around her shoulders and bring his hand down past her clavicle and into the front of her dress. He did it. His nimble fingers probed downward around the crest of her bust, capturing one firm breast and pulling it free of the bra so he could cup it entirely.

It was a sweet little breast. And not so little either. It seemed about softball-size to him, but without seams. It was round and resilient to the touch, and the nipple was like a hard little nut as he caught it between two fingers.

She was panting. She was excited. As they clinched, her hand strayed across the front of him, and moved as though she were taking the measure of him.

But that was as far as they could go here, in public. Even in a darkened corner of the room, they had to remember that this was a high school party, not an orgy. So they restrained themselves. They petted for a while, until the heat got too strong for them, and then they forced themselves to break off and rejoin the party.

The evening crawled along in a slosh of champagne.

Midnight came. Noisemakers were duly shaken, tin horns were properly blown. Balloons were burst galore. Fifteen young men turned to fifteen young ladies and kissed them passionately while the combo played raucous sounds to greet the new year.

When he came up for air, Andreas looked at Tony, and saw her eyes glowing with love and desire. A surge of triumph welled up inside him. She was his! Only a fluke could block him from scoring now!

But long hours remained before he could collect his victory. When one is invited to a New Year's Eve Party, one is expected to stick around until a decent hour—three in the morning at the very least. Andreas would have been happy to skip out at midnight and head for the privacy of his car. But such things were simply not done.

"Do you want to leave?" he asked her, about two in the morning, when the combo had left and the atmosphere in the cellar was getting heavy with cigarette smoke and the fumes of stale whiskey.

"Not yet," she said. "It isn't right."

"It's after two."

"A little while longer," she said. She leaned close to him. "We mustn't seem too eager, darling!"

The words were like a gleaming promise. Grimly, he waited out the time.

At quarter to three one couple left. That was a signal, and in the next ten minutes half a dozen other couples headed for the cloakroom, Andreas and Tony among them. A hard core of night-owls remained. "We can't waste all this champagne," someone said. Andreas grinned. He had better things to do than pop corks now.

They emerged into the night. It was fiercely cold; the mercury was hovering around the zero mark, and the stars blazed against an incredibly black sky. Quickly, they hustled into Andreas' father's car.

Tony lived only six blocks from Jerry Braun's. Andreas hoped she would invite him in. It was so cold that it was inconceivable to make love in a parked car. If they turned the heater on, they'd probably be found asphyxiated in the morning, maybe with their bodies still joined. That would be quaint, he thought, but he didn't really go for the idea.

He was drunker than he thought. He had trouble starting the car, because it was a problem to coordinate his thumb on the starter with his foot on the accelerator, and the car kept stalling out. On the tenth try he got it going. He started to move, felt the car lurch alarmingly three feet to the left as it slid on the ice, and just managed to get it under control before he mounted the curb and sideswiped a massive tree.

He drove with exaggerated care to Tony's house. A light was on inside.

"Are your parents up?" he asked.

"I doubt it. That's just a light so I don't break my neck going in. Come on. I'll fix some hot chocolate for you. I wouldn't want you to freeze on the way home."

He followed her into the house, wondering whether or not her early ardor had cooled. It was hard to tell. She led him into the living room, and left him there while she put up the hot chocolate. It was all so very domestic that he began to think he had missed his chance.

I should have taken her at the party while she was ready, he thought.

It wouldn't have been all that hard to do. While they were on that loveseat with their backs to the crowd, he could have worked her panties off and arranged his clothing. And then he could have casually arranged one of her legs across his lap and drawn her close as they sat there.

The thought of sitting between Tony Neale's cool, firm thighs hit him like a dagger's blow. He bit his lip as desire flooded through him. *What an idiot I was not to do that when she was wined up! Now she's calmed down. Hot chocolate, for God's sake!*

Tony came back into the room. She was carrying a little tray that contained a teakettle and two coffee cups. She set the tray down and poured the hot chocolate for them. Then she carefully closed the living room doors.

She joined him on the couch.

For a few moments, nothing more torrid than the consuming of hot chocolate went on. Then she set down her half-empty cup and nestled against him.

Her hand went to his thighs, and a moment later, Andreas realized that her emotions hadn't cooled off at all. She was as ready as she had been at the party. Maybe even more so.

She pulled his clothes open.

She lowered her head, and Andreas gasped as he felt the warmth of her lips. He had never dreamed he would get this far with Tony Neale, certainly not on what was actually their first date. She didn't seem to be the type to go in for such intimacies.

He ran his hands through her glossy black hair, then slipped his fingers into the front of her dress to cup the round firm globes of her breasts. He could feel her nipples, hard as rocks.

The sensations that were running through him were fabulous. No girl had ever done this to him before. He had wanted it, but he had never asked, and nobody had suggested. It was a wonderful feeling. And Tony seemed like an expert.

Andreas closed his eyes. He was panting hard, now. Another couple of moments and he wouldn't be able to hold back the surging rush of pleasure.

Was that what she wanted?

Was this her way of preserving her virginity?

No. He was as wrong about that as he had been about her overall prudishness. For, as though realizing that she was pushing him to the brink of fulfillment, Tony lifted her head. Her lips were moist and shiny, and there was a look of star-spangled desire in her eyes.

He sat there inflamed with desire, and reached for her.

"Wait," she said.

She stood up, lifted her dress. Andreas caught a dazzling glimpse of nyloned legs, of pale thighs, of pink garter straps against pink flesh, of white lacy panties. Then she was pulling the panties off.

She tossed the panties aside.

Then she sat down across him, her legs dangling off to the sides. She lowered herself carefully, embracing him as she settled into place.

Her eyes sparkled.

"Happy New Year, darling!" she whispered, and began to move in a casual rocking motion.

CHAPTER SEVEN

It was just terrific, Andreas thought.

He sat there with the soft upholstery underneath him, and this beautiful and brainy girl above him, and he didn't have to do a thing except enjoy it. Tony did all the work. She moved from side to side and round and round and up and down, lifting herself and lowering, lifting and lowering.

He had heard about this way of making love. But he had never tried it. In the little more than a year of his adult love life, he had been to bed with a number of different girls, but he had always stayed close to the standard positions. Trust a brain like Tony to want to try experiments, though.

This was pretty good. The only disadvantage was that he couldn't feel much of her body except in one particular place. The other ways, he could at least feel the girls' warmth pressed against him. And he could see them naked. Here, he couldn't see much.

But that was mostly because Andreas hadn't taken her clothes off. It was too risky, with her parents upstairs and all, to actually strip her. And anyway he could undress her part way. It was no trick at all to reach into the front of her low-cut dress and pull out her boobs. They came free of the bra easily, and rested out in the open, round and pink and sweet, with the nipples jutting up swollenly. He put his hands over them, and cupped and kneaded them.

The action was getting pretty furious now. His face felt hot, and hers was flushed too. Another advantage of making it this way, he discovered: he could watch the girl's face. He could tell pretty much what was going on inside her.

And right now, what was going on seemed to be plenty. Tony's eyes were just slits. Her mouth was all pulled out of shape by the tensions unfolding within her. Her nostrils were flared wide. Her entire expression had taken on a passionate, half-crazed look that distorted her face completely. She just wasn't the Tony he knew, the calmly pretty girl who always had the right answer to the teacher's questions.

Now she was a wildcat.

Andreas gripped her breasts tightly, squeezing them until it must have hurt her. His body began to rock in ever-increasing tempo. His breath came in ragged snorts.

"Now!" she hissed.

He nodded and let himself relax. He felt an inner spasm come from her, and it was the last straw, pushing him into the abyss of ecstasy. Powerful urges grasped him tightly, and he sighed and bucked upward and felt the aching, pounding pulsations of the climax, and at the same moment he was aware that her body was trembling and shaking in a slam-bang culmination.

And it was over.

She was draped on top of him, and his hands were on her bare breasts and her party gown was crumpled and creased, and she was saying, "Happy New Year, darling! Happy New Year! Happy New Year!"

He managed a tired smile. "Happy New Year, Tony," he whispered.

That was how it began. As he drove slowly home through the sub-zero cold of five in the morning, he felt dazed and bewildered by the show she had put on. A virgin? Hardly. She was a regular sexpot.

Funny, he thought. You never know about some people. A quiet, hard-studying kid like Tony Neale turns out to have a blazing furnace in her body. You just never know, he thought.

Once they had begun, of course, there was no reason to stop. He phoned her the next day, about three in the afternoon, and they talked quite calmly about the Monroe Doctrine and the Election of 1824, just as though nothing out of the ordinary had taken place the night before.

"I want to see you," he said.

"I want to see *you*."

"Okay, so let's see each other."

They got together. His parents had driven down to Columbus for the day to visit his mother's mother, and he had stayed home on the pretext that he had studying to do. Tony took a bus to his house.

She looked gorgeous. She wore a red sweater and a pair of green stretch pants, and the cold—ten degrees today—had turned her cheeks rosy and made her look the picture of healthy young girlhood. The mere sight of her rushing down the street probably gladdened the hearts of old folks, who could rejoice in her youth and prettiness and innocent freshness, without needing to know about the acts she had indulged in during the dark hours of the night.

He kissed her as she stepped inside. He drove his tongue deep into her mouth and slipped his hands up under her sweater to grasp the cups of her bra and dig for the warm flesh underneath.

But she broke away.

"Uh-uh," she said. "First we have to study. Your parents aren't coming home till late, are they?"

"Not till midnight, I guess."

"So we've got plenty of time."

They studied. Tony insisted on it. For the moment, she was her old prim self. She spread out their notebooks, and gave him a detailed quiz on the administration of Monroe, Madison, and John Quincy Adams. He was a little surprised at how well he did. She was a good teacher, on top of everything else.

He forced himself not to make any passes at her. They studied for more than an hour. Then at five o'clock, Tony said, "All right. That's enough history for now."

"Whew! It's about time."

"What's the matter?" she asked. "Are you in a hurry to do something else?"

"Who? Me?" he grinned.

She went over to the couch. "Come here," she said. "Come here and undress me."

He peeled the clothes away from her quickly. It was tremendously exciting to be undressing her. There was something far more appealing about seeing the complete nudity of a girl he knew than of viewing a stranger, a casual pickup. She had an identity for him. She was Tony Neale, girl brain. And now he was being privileged to view her body. In a way that was even a greater privilege to him than the liberties he had been allowed last night, though he knew that was a strange upside-down way of looking at things.

She was beautiful.

Her body was a lovely pink color, without blemish. Her breasts rose, full and firm, neither too big nor too small, with perfect little puckered nipples set in rosy aureoles. There was a softness about her, but not a slackness. Her body was taut of torso and of buttock. Her navel was deep set, her thighs slim and attractive.

She seemed to enjoy having him look at her. She lay there, nude, posing for him, and grinning.

"Now you," she said. "Hurry!"

He dropped his clothes helter-skelter and presented his lean nakedness for her. She seemed to approve. He recognized the glow of lust in her eyes.

"Come here," she commanded, in a husky erotic tone that would certainly have shocked any of the teachers who so consistently gave that nice hard-working Neale girl the highest marks in the class.

He went to her.

Her soft, warm body opened to him.

This time, it was even better than the night before. They were both sober and clear-minded, which helped. They were both completely nude, which helped even more. And there was no chance anyone else in the house might stumble upon them in the act, which helped still further.

So it was perfect. He filled his mouth with her tongue and his hands with her breasts, and she filled her arms with his body, and they spiraled on up to the summit of passion, and attained it, and then drifted down again like intertwining snowflakes, slowly, slowly, until they came to light and rested quietly.

A long while later, she said, "You know, this whole thing would never have happened if you had been doing your history homework."

He laughed. "You're right. You're so right." His hands caressed the satiny swells of her breasts. "It's a funny thing, Tony. I never dreamed you were this kind of girl."

"What kind of girl is that?"

He reddened, realizing he had blundered. "Well the kind of girl who enjoyed sex and all—"

"What sort of girl did you think I was?"

"A bluestocking," he said. "A grind."

"I am."

"But —"

"But what? Can't a girl get good marks and still like to get made, Lou?"

The coarse word seemed out of character for her—but, he knew, the "character" he had in mind was not very similar to the real Tony Neale. He said, "I don't know. It just seemed to me that you'd be an iron maiden. That you were above such physical things."

"You've got a lot to learn about me, then."

"I see that I do."

She let her hand trail provocatively down his body. It paused at his chest for a moment, plucked at the carpet of matted hair in a playful way, then wandered still lower. The small fingers reached their goal and lingered there.

She said, after a long silence, "Up till now I've been a city virgin and a country slut."

"Huh?"

"I mean I've compartmentalized my life. My sex life. Up till now I've never slept with a boy except between the end of June and the beginning of September. I always figured that during the school year I would keep my mind on my studies. I'd do some dating, sure, but I wouldn't go all the way. And then in the summer, anything goes."

"You go away for the summer?"

"To camp," she said.

"And you sleep around?"

"Yes. Ever since I was fifteen, I guess. Three summers ago. I had affairs each summer. Two or three weeks with each boy. I guess I've slept with about a dozen boys altogether. But never in the city. That's why you thought I was a virgin and a prude. You're my first city lover."

He was a little stunned by her revelations. "A dozen boys—"

"Does it shock you?"

He shrugged. "It—it sort of surprises me," he said. "I mean, it's not that I'm disapproving of you, or thinking of you as promiscuous or anything. After last night I knew you weren't any virgin when I met you. But—well, you know how it is when you have a friend, and he tells you his name is Joe Smith, and after a couple of years he comes along and says he was only kidding, his name is really Jack Jones? It's that kind of thing. You form a set of attitudes about a person, a way of looking at her, and then the person comes along and tips everything over. You've got to readjust all of a sudden. Sometimes it isn't so easy."

She laughed. "Poor Lou. I've confused you." Her hand tightened on him in sudden intimacy, and she said in a low murmur. "Would you like me to try to live up to the old image you had? I can try to pretend I'm a virgin and a prude if you'd like."

Grinning, he shook his head and cupped her breasts, rolling them around gently.

"No," he said. "I'll get used to the new image. I like it better. A hell of a lot better."

Desire surged in him. He shifted his position, and she accepted his weight. A moment later, he gave up to the pulsing warmth of her, and she took him, and he slammed down hard and they went dizzily away to bliss once again.

It was all a very ducky arrangement. As of the beginning of the year, they were steadies. Andreas had been dating two or three other girls, strictly for sex, but he dropped them right away. He didn't particularly need them, now that he had Tony, who was as smart as she was beautiful, and who was explosive as a firecracker in the rack.

They made a good couple. He was tall and leggy, she was medium tall and filled her sweater well, and it looked like the great American love story. Of course, the long-legged young man with the crewcut was not quite as clean-cut and normal as all that, since he had murdered two prostitutes only about a year ago, and that was not considered proper conduct for the American high school senior.

Andreas hardly thought about the murders, now. They had happened a long time ago, and they were both coming to seem hazy and dreamlike in his mind. It was almost as though they had never happened. Not quite, since he could quite plainly remember strangling the tramp with the plucked eyebrows, and he still could summon up a memory of how it had felt to bring the gin bottle down on the back of that other one's skull.

Even so, the murders had dwindled into insignificance now. They had taken on the aspect of ancient history, of small mischiefs committed in the remote past. Once he had let the air out of the tires of his teacher's car, when he was in the fifth grade, and once he had shot a squirrel with an air rifle, and once he had deliberately smashed the window of a neighbor he disliked, and once he had murdered two prostitutes.

Little peccadilloes. Nothing to trouble his conscience now, really.

So he kept company with Tony. They studied together, and they went to basketball games together, and they also slept together.

Often.

They did it at her house when they could, or at his house when the coast was clear, and when the weather got a little warmer they did it in his parked car. When the car was unavailable for his use, there were other methods. One Saturday night they went up onto the roof of the apartment house where he lived. There were benches up there, tucked away between the clotheslines and the incinerator stack, and nobody ever went up there. She was wearing jeans and a sweater. She kept the sweater on, but stripped away the jeans and her panties and climbed onto his lap.

He rubbed her bare buttocks to keep them warm while he was taking her.

Oh, there was plenty of fun and frolic for the two of them during those happy months. Of course, there were certain little problems. Certain gulfs that arose between them.

The biggest one was the matter of college. Come June, they would graduate from high school, and come September, she was going to go off east to college.

She wanted him to go to college too.

"It isn't too late," she said. "You couldn't get into the Ivy League schools, I guess, not with your marks, but you could try a state college—"

"Let's talk about it some other time," he said evasively.

"But it's important. You can't have any kind of career if you don't go to college."

"Sure I can. I could be a salesman, or a shopkeeper, or maybe a newspaper reporter—"

"I mean a real career," she said. "Like being a doctor or a lawyer. Or even a teacher. Something that gets you respect."

He shook his head. "I'm not cut out for college," he insisted. "Let's drop it."

It bothered her, of course. Here she was, college bound and he was only a slob with a 71 average whose highest ambition was being a shopkeeper. She loved him, so she kept company with him, but she didn't share any of his career values, and they both knew it.

Andreas didn't worry about that much. College wasn't for him, and Tony would come to see that soon enough. The real trouble was that Tony wanted to marry him. He realized that practically at the outset.

Tony had their future all planned. They would both go to college, and they would correspond for four years, and travel to see each other at vacation time, and then they would get married and have careers and children and a mortgage and all the rest.

That was what she wanted.

He didn't.

He couldn't see marriage for beans, not to Tony or anyone else. Marriage meant a kind of permanence he wasn't prepared to get involved in. Besides, he knew damned well he wasn't good enough for Tony. If she thought they could be happily married, she was fooling herself. He would grow up watching television and going bowling and drinking beer, and she would want an intellectual kind of life, and he simply couldn't give it to her. She deserved a college guy, a professor or a doctor. Not him.

He figured she'd wake up to that fact sooner or later. She'd see that what they had was no good on a long-term basis, and they would break up.

"It was fun," he would tell her. "We had a good time with each other. But it couldn't have lasted."

Andreas guessed that as they got closer to graduation, she would begin to think things through more clearly. It would become all too clear to her that there was no future in their romance, and one day she would tell him it was all over. They would have had six months together, six damned good months of fun and sex, and now their roads would part. She would go off to college and the intellectual life, and he would go his own way, and maybe they would send Christmas cards to each other in the years to come.

That was a nice simple way of ending it. After all, it wasn't as if they were star-crossed lovers. She had openly admitted that she had had affairs with a dozen guys before him. If he had been her first, well, he could see that the entanglement would be hard to break. But the twelfth or thirteenth—?

The only trouble was, she didn't seem to be getting the message.

April came and went.

May ebbed away.

Graduation day was only a few weeks away, June 15. And still she twined her body willingly about his, and whispered, "I love you, Lou" as she gave her soft warm self to him.

He accepted the sex. Gladly. But he was worried about the shape of things to come.

Late in May he said, "Well, I guess you'll be going off to summer camp soon, huh? First of July?"

"No," she said. "I'm not going this year."

"But you always go. I thought you've been going to this camp since you were six."

"Not this year. They offered me a job and I said no. I want to be near you," she said. "I can't go off and desert you for two whole months. Not when I'll have to leave for college in the fall anyway. I've taken a job in the city. We'll be able to see each other all summer. That'll make it easier for us to get from September to Christmas."

It was an ominous bit of news. Not going off for her summer of sex? Staying here with him?

Didn't she understand that this couldn't last, that he wasn't what she needed?

She didn't seem to be getting the idea. He had made it clear that he wasn't going to college, and she had seemed to accept that, finally. And still she wanted him. And still she said she loved him.

May ended. Sweet June arrived.

Graduation neared. Tony was second in the class, and the highest girl on the list. The only one with a higher average was a little myopic bookworm named Richard Felks, whose average was a smidgin higher than Tony's. Considering how active Tony's social life had been, her performance was amazing.

Andreas was higher on the list than he had expected, too. His average put him in the top three hundred, more than halfway up the ladder—though there were fifty right behind him. He was going to graduate, thanks to Tony. His marks had improved tremendously.

He wondered whether he should take the initiative and break off the affair. He decided not to. Why deprive himself of Tony's cuddly body during the summer? She was the best one he had ever had, after all.

He figured that the romance would come to its inevitable end and in the fall, Tony would go off to college, and she was bound to meet somebody there who was more fitting as a permanent consort to a girl of her talents. She would send him a "Dear Lou" letter, and that would be that. No need to be brutal and premature about breaking off. It would happen in the due course of events.

So he continued to take pleasure from her body. On the warm nights, they would frequently go up to the benches on his roof. He had found a way of bolting the door, in the unlikely event that anyone would want to come up there. Then they would both remove all their clothes, and would lie naked under the stars. He would fill his mouth with the sweet apples of her breasts, and would stroke her soft thighs, and they would open for him and he would plunge eagerly into the valley of delights.

It was great fun for them both. And, though Tony still had marriage on her mind (even if she never came right out and said it) he knew damned well that her ideas of wedlock with him would fade once she got to see what the Ivy League had to offer.

He was sure of it.

But a nasty shock was waiting for him. On the night before graduation, he drove over to Tony's place to pick her up. He honked the horn and she came out, looking delicious in a breasty polo shirt and a pair of tight black toreador pants that hugged the lush contours of her buttocks and thighs.

She got into the car. He reached for her, one hand heading for her breasts, but she shoved him away.

"What's wrong?" he asked, surprised at her brand-new coolness.

"Plenty," she said. He saw her lips trembling. She seemed pale. Then she spat it out: "Lou, I'm going to have a baby!"

CHAPTER EIGHT

It was just the news he least wanted to hear. If she had just kicked him in the gut, it wouldn't have given him more of a jolt.

She was going to have a baby.

A baby, for God's sake?

A *baby?*

He said, "Are you sure?"

"Positive."

"What does that mean?"

"My period was six weeks late. I took a rabbit test. It came out positive. There isn't any doubt about it, Lou. I'm definitely pregnant. The baby is due around the middle of January, I figure."

Andreas stared at her in disbelief. Somehow he had never dreamed this would happen. They hadn't bothered with taking precautions, because it was too much of a nuisance and interfered with pleasure, and in the first month or so they had both worried some about pregnancy. But nothing had happened, so he had developed a naive faith that nothing *would* happen.

And now this.

He started the car and drove off, heading for no place in particular. His hands gripped the wheel tightly. His knuckles whitened.

"So you're sure you're sure."

"Absolutely."

"Do your parents know?"

"Not yet," she said. "I had to talk to you first, before I could say anything to them."

"Yeah." He was silent for a moment. He drove mechanically, up one street and down the next. "Well, we got to find ourselves a doctor, I guess. I've got a little money saved up, but it ain't very much. A thing like this, I hear it costs maybe five, six hundred dollars."

"To have a baby?"

"To have a baby removed," he said bluntly.

"But you don't understand," she said. "I want to have the baby, Lou."

He hit the brake so hard they both nearly went slamming into the windshield. He pulled off alongside the curb and stared at her as though she had just uttered something unimaginably foul.

"What?"

"I said I want to have the baby." Her voice was calm, almost steely with determination.

"That's what I thought I heard you say." He ran his tongue over his lips. "But—but that doesn't make any sense, Tony!"

"Why not?"

"Because—because—" He fumbled for words. "Because you're starting college in September. You can't go to college and have a baby. What are you going to do, keep a bassinet in your dorm room?"

She smiled. "I've thought about that. I can have a full semester of college before the baby comes. Then I'll take a year and a half off. When the baby's old enough, I'll leave it with a nurse or maybe its grandparents during the day, and go back to college to get my degree. Of course, I won't be able to go to one of the fancy Eastern colleges. Some of them don't accept married women, and in any case we wouldn't be able to afford the tuition, even with a big scholarship, and I don't want to have to ask more help than is really necessary from my parents, so—"

Andreas stared at her through a growing haze of fear and confusion. *In any case we wouldn't be able to afford the tuition*, she had said. *We. We.*

So she was comfortably assuming he would make an honest woman out of her. She was so sure of it that she hadn't even taken the trouble to check things out with him. *We*, she had said, comfortably lumping him into the scheme of things.

He started the car again. Driving made him feel calmer, and calmness, coolness was what he needed right now.

"You won't consider getting rid of the baby?" he asked.

"No," she said. "I couldn't. You know I'm not religious, but even so, an abortion is just like murder. I couldn't do anything like that."

Why not? he asked silently. *What's so hard about murder, anyway?*

She went on, "Besides, I want to have babies, Lou, I've heard of cases where girls who have abortions become sterile permanently. I'd rather have a baby too soon in my life than never have any at all. And I don't mind leaving school for a while. All my life I've been studying like a demon. Maybe it'll be good to sit home and change diapers and look at television like a nice little housewife for a while. I can use the change of pace."

Andreas nibbled worriedly at his lip. Her level-headed words rolled over him like a sentence of death.

She wanted the baby.

She wouldn't dream of abortion.

And she expected him to marry her.

She had everything worked out pretty neatly, all things considered. Probably she had gone through hell for a while after she found out about the pregnancy, but finally she had come to terms with the situation and found a way of planning her future around it.

Her future and his too.

Well, he didn't want any part of it.

He was eighteen and a half years old, and if Tony had her way he would be a husband and a father before he was twenty. And then a long grind for the rest of his life. Yapping kids, and bills to pay, and someday Tony's college expenses, and he'd never get off the merry-go-round.

Not unless he refused to get on in the first place. How could he wiggle out?

The first thought that rose to his mind was murdering Tony. It slithered upward so easily that he felt a little chilled. Even after two murders, he still felt a certain queasiness about the act of taking life.

But the instant that he considered the idea of killing her, he saw how suicidally impossible it was.

Tony was no nameless, friendless tramp. She was a girl who came of good family, people of substance. And a great many people, including her family, knew of her romance with Lou Andreas.

Unless he chopped her body into hamburger, or weighted it down and tossed it into Lake Erie, someone would find it. There would be an autopsy and it would he discovered that she had been pregnant.

Who had made her pregnant?

Lou Andreas, of course.

Who had killed her, then?

Lou Andreas, of course.

Her parents would hire detectives. They'd track him down no matter where he went. And then he'd be tried and found guilty. They'd send him to the death house.

That was no good. Better to marry her and put up with all the jazz that followed, than to kill her and die a murderer's death before he was even old enough to vote.

He dropped the idea of killing her.

What then?

He'd think of something sooner or later, he figured. In the meanwhile, they had reached the park. He found a shady inlet and pulled up.

It was important for her to go on thinking he was with her, right up to the end. If he let her know he planned to back out, she might get her parents to put pressure on him. A shotgun wedding wasn't much to his way of thinking.

He turned to her. A shaft of moonlight lit up her face, and he was struck by the beauty of her. She was certainly a handsome girl. And passionate. And smart. Some guy would be damned lucky to be marrying her.

But not Lou Andreas.

She looked at him and said, "Do you love me, Lou? Really, I mean?"

"You know I do."

Her soft lips were against his. Her tongue slipped lightly into his mouth. He put his hands over her polo shirt, and felt the firm breasts within, and squeezed them, wondering how soon it would be before those breasts would start to fill with milk, and what her figure would look like when they did.

Her body squirmed against his. Her fingers stroked his cheeks, then dug into his shoulders.

"I love you, Lou," she whispered.

He didn't answer. Instead, he found the button of her toreador pants, flipped it open, drew the zipper down. He began to work the pants off her. It was a hard job. They clung to her hips like a skin graft.

She giggled. "I've gained two pounds already. Both of them on my hips."

She helped him tug her pants off. They came, finally, and the panties with them. She kicked them onto the floor of the car and sat there, naked below the waist.

Andreas looked at the nearly flat curve of her belly. It didn't seem any different.

"I don't see any babies in there," he said.

"It won't show for months. But it's in there, all right, even if it doesn't show. Right now it's practically microscopic. It's like a tiny fish. A guppy."

He put his hand over her belly, as though expecting to feel the guppy-like thing sprouting within her. He felt nothing but the warmth and the softness of her skin.

She began to pant a little as he touched her.

He felt her opening his clothes.

Their bodies came together, cramped up on the seat of the car. He took her roughly, almost brutally. He sent his body slamming to her with a violence that he hoped would jar free the creature she said he had spawned in her womb. Gripping her buttocks tightly, he slammed at her again and again.

He had no way of knowing what effect his roughness was having inside her. But it was certainly affecting her passions in a powerful way. Within moments, she was sobbing in near-ecstasy. Her teeth fastened themselves in his shoulder, and she bit down through his shirt. He winced in pain and dug his fingers deeper into the soft, yielding flesh of her velvet-smooth buttocks.

Their bodies moved in unison, faster and yet faster. The snorting sound of their breath must have been loud enough to hear fifty feet away.

The moment of fulfillment was coming. For him, for her. She got there first. Her entire body trembled and burst into cold sweat, and he felt her quiver inwardly, and she half-rose from the car seat, gripping him tightly, and as she reached the full frenzy, he closed his eyes and gave vent to the eddies of ecstasy that were rippling through his own frame, and passion came to him and spent itself, and he found himself hoping that somehow magically he had rendered her no longer pregnant, but he knew it was a futile hope, only a dream, no damned good at all.

The next day was graduation day.

The graduating class, eight hundred fifty strong, duly assembled in the main gymnasium of the high school, wearing the appropriate gowns and the appropriate mortarboard hats. Girls sat on the left side of the gymnasium, boys on the right, and in the balcony, where the crowds sat during the school basketball games, sat hundreds and hundreds of beaming, pride-swollen mothers and fathers and grandparents and friends and miscellaneous relatives.

The graduates stood. They sang a hymn. Then they sang the school song. Everything in four-part harmony. They had been rehearsing one period a week all term.

The principal read a passage from the Bible. The class's grade advisor came forward and made a little speech about what a remarkable class this class was. Another hymn was sung. Then the feature speaker of the day was announced. He was a local political figure, a state senator who wanted to become a member of Congress in November, and who was starting the traditional speechmaking circuit.

He delivered a long, resonant, and pompous oration, full of sound and fury and a good deal of wind. He spoke of the challenges of life, the great tasks that lay ahead for youth, the problems of career and marriage. It was High School Graduation Speech Stock Model B.

All through it, Andreas kept staring across the aisle at Tony. She grinned back at him. Every time the speaker made a reference to marriage or motherhood, Tony would wink at him. Andreas fidgeted. It seemed to him that her winks were announcing to the whole auditorium that she was pregnant, that Louis F. Andreas had possessed her pretty thighs and had deposited a baby in her belly.

The speech ended. Finally.

Mrs. Roth, the grade advisor, returned to the podium to hand out the class prizes. The History Award, the Science Award, the Latin Prize, the John G. Brewster Literature Award, the Jacob F. Macomber Award for Excellence in Mathematics, and so on, down a long list cunningly designed to give some sort of prize to almost everybody in the top rung of the class.

Again and again Tony ascended the podium to collect an award. Andreas kept count. She won nine awards, which was exactly as many as the next two top winners combined carried off. She got the History Award, and the Macomber Math medal, and the Citizenship Award, and six others, Some of them were just certificates, one was a gold medal, one was a bronze medal and a certificate, and three were $25 savings bonds.

He felt proud of her. There she was, going up front again and again in her shapeless black gown, the standard graduate garb. The gown hid the supple beauties of her thighs and buttocks, it cloaked her lovely legs, it obliterated the jutting fullness of her firm young breasts. The gown also cloaked the valley of her legs, and hid from sight the baby that was quietly growing in her womb.

How many people suspected that this much-honored girl, this good citizen, was carrying around an illegitimate baby?

Not very many, he thought. To most of them, to just about all, she was probably the prudish bluestocking he had once pegged her as. Little did they know what heights of passion the winner of the Jacob F. Macomber Award for Excellence in Mathematics was capable of attaining. A lot of people would be in for shocks around September or October, when that baby started to puff her belly up, and anybody who could count on his fingers could make the discovery that the chaste and intellectual Tony Neale had been getting made at least as far back as late spring, and maybe even before then.

Andreas smiled. Even though he was in a mess, it was good to feel one up on the world.

The final hymn rolled to the rafters. The long ceremony was over. The graduates filed out of the gymnasium, and off into the locker rooms to get out of their gowns. Bored-looking teachers stood by to take the gowns as the graduates removed them.

Then it was down into the gym again, to meet the proud parents. Andreas' parents had come, and so had Tony's and the arrangement was that everybody would meet and go out for dinner to toast the new alumni. Andreas didn't like that arrangement much. It was too much like a formal ceremony binding him to Tony, when the parents met. But he wasn't able to get out of it without hurting everyone's feelings.

The rest of them were all waiting for him by the time he finally handed in his own and returned to the gym. His parents were there, and Tony's, and Tony too, and Tony's nine-year-old sister. Everyone was standing around looking slightly self-conscious. His parents had never met Tony's before.

It was an awkward situation. Tony's father was a rich lawyer, and her mother was one of those well-groomed, strikingly handsome suburban women who have obviously never known a moment of need. Next to them, the Andreases looked shopworn and grimy, and they knew it. Andreas' mother as well as his father worked, had always worked, and between them they didn't make as much in a year as Neale did in three months. Andreas' mother had worn her Sunday best, but it looked faded and shabby, and so did she.

Andreas had never gotten along well with Tony's parents. Oh, they had treated him politely enough, but always with a distant reserve, a formal chill. Quite clearly they disapproved of him for not being academically minded, for not being headed toward some sort of professional career. They didn't understand why their brilliant and beautiful daughter would want to spend time with a workingman's son, and, of course, they were right about that. Andreas also suspected that they knew he was taking their daughter, and no parents ever take very kindly to that sort of thing.

Today, though, all coolness seemed forgotten. The seven of them went out to one of the best restaurants in town, and had a lavish dinner, steak all around, cocktails beforehand, wine with the meal.

It was more like a wedding feast than a graduation celebration, Andreas kept thinking. And every few minutes Tony would dart a warmly passionate glance across the table at him that nobody else could miss. He felt uncomfortable. He hated this young lover bit. He didn't want to play Romeo to a pregnant Juliet.

The wine made him drowsy. He closed his eyes, and a vision of Tony floated into his brain. She was naked, and the rosy tips of her breasts were stiff and swollen, and her lips were parted, and her soft thighs were waiting, and her arms were stretched out toward him.

But as he advanced toward her, himself naked and ready for love, a strange thing happened to the Tony in his vision. Her body began to change. Her belly started to swell. And her breasts filled with milk and grew bigger. Her breasts expanded until they were monstrous, the size of basketballs. And the rise in her belly grew and grew and grew, until it looked like she had a cow inside her.

Still she grew. She was tremendous. The rest of her, head and arms and legs, shrank to insignificance. There were only the giant breasts and the monstrous belly.

And then the belly exploded. Bits of flesh and entrails went spewing off in every direction. Blood fountained in a crimson jet. And when the debris had settled, Andreas was able to look into her now open womb, and see—

Himself.

Curled up naked in a fetal ball.

Milk was dripping down from the vast breasts, down into the shattered ruin of her belly, and he was drinking it. And now he was being squeezed downward, down through the birth canal.

He opened his eyes. He felt sick.

Nobody had noticed his lapse of awareness. He realized, from the conversation, that he had closed his eyes only for a matter of moments. He felt as though he had been dreaming for days.

Dessert came, and then coffee, and then the check. That produced a ticklish moment. Both fathers were clamoring for the right to pay the check. Andreas had had a glimpse at it; it was for more than fifty dollars.

If his father paid it all, it would mean a serious financial hardship. If Tony's father paid, it would seem insulting and patronizing to the poorer family.

There was only one way to avoid the problem, and Mr. Neale chose it. "Suppose we split the check," he suggested.

The check was duly split.

The two families left the restaurant, in a properly gay and festive mood. They separated, the Neales going off to their new Cadillac, the

Andreases going off to their old Chevrolet. Tony waved good-bye. There was love in her eyes. Andreas waved back. He thought of her beautiful nudity again, and then thought about the horrible vision he had had.

He went home.

At nine o'clock the next morning, his first morning of freedom, he went down to his local draft board and said, "I'd like to request induction."

CHAPTER NINE

They took him. Gladly. They had big quotas to fill, and they were having a hard time filling them, because everybody under twenty-six was either enrolled in college, or married and expecting a baby, or doing some kind of essential work. There was a real shortage of unattached, unimportant guys who could be turned into cannon fodder.

So they said, "We'll put you into our August quota."

"Nothing earlier?"

"Do you want to leave so soon?"

Andreas grinned. "I'd leave tomorrow, if you'd take me."

The registrar eyed him cautiously. "You aren't in any kind of trouble, are you?"

"With the law? Nah."

"Any kind of trouble."

Andreas shrugged. "Well, there's this girl who's hot to marry me. I'd kind of like to give her a chance to start forgetting me right away."

There was understanding. "I suppose she's pregnant?" the registrar said. He was a slim, white-haired man, who must have been as wise as he looked.

"She says she is," Andreas responded.

The registrar thumbed his cards. "Well, young man, we'll see what we can do for you."

They did the best they could, and that was fine. After a check of the records, they discovered they were one short on their July quota, and told him to report for his physical exam at half past seven the following morning, bringing along with him a three-day supply of clothing and whatever toilet equipment he wanted. If he passed, he'd be inducted and taken off for three days of registration. Then he'd have a couple of weeks at liberty, and on the first of July he'd leave for basic training.

He had no regrets about going into the army. Sooner or later, they were going to grab him. That much was definite. Usually they waited until a guy was about twenty-three or so, and just getting settled in his job. Then they yanked him out.

It was a lot better, Andreas figured, to go now and get it over with. He had no job waiting for him, anyway. Nobody liked to hire a guy who was 1-A. Two years from now, when he came out, he'd still be only twenty, and he'd have his military service behind and no uncertainties.

There was another reason for wanting to go in now, of course. The best reason of all. He would escape Tony and her baby. Tony's parents weren't the kind who would allow their daughter to have an unwanted child. They'd marry her off to somebody or other, he was certain, within a month or two, and her baby would have a name.

He went home whistling.

That evening he told his parents the news. They took it pretty well. His mother snuffled a little, but his father agreed that it was smart to get the draft out of the way right at the start. "This way when you come back, you'll have all the best jobs waiting for you," his father said. "A young man who's served already—that's the kind they like to hire."

His mother said, "Have you told your girlfriend yet?"

"I'm telling her tonight."

"Two years. Do you think she'll wait for you?"

"Wait for what?"

"To get married," his mother said.

Andreas smiled. "I wasn't planning on marrying her, Mom. She was just my girlfriend. That's all. Just a girlfriend, Mom."

Telling Tony was a rough bit. He wondered how he was going to manage it.

For half the evening he kept off the topic. They were alone at her place; her parents were out, and her young sister was asleep. He was sprawled out comfortably on the living room couch next to her. They had been necking a little, nothing very passionate. There was time for that later on, along about ten o'clock, which would give him a chance to get in and get out before her parents were likely to come home.

Finally he said, apropos of nothing at all, "I got some bad news for you, Tony. I got drafted."

"You're joking!"

"Uh-uh. I got the notice this morning. I report for my physical tomorrow, and if they like my looks I go in as of July first."

She looked pale. "My god! You're not joking, are you, Lou?"

"Wouldn't be a very funny joke."

"Drafted! They didn't waste any time, did they? One day after graduation."

He shrugged. "It's the breaks. Well, maybe it won't be so bad for me."

She eyed him uneasily. "And the baby?"

"I don't know."

"What do you mean, you don't know?"

Andreas knotted his fingers together elaborately. "What do you want to do, get married the day I go into the army and then not see me except Christmas for two years?"

"They'd let me live on the base with you, wouldn't they?"

"Maybe. Maybe not. It's a lousy life." He shook his head. "Listen, Tony. This don't make any sense. For us to jump right into marriage. We're still just kids, and I got to go into the service, now. Be smart, will you? Get rid of the baby. Go to college. I'll be out of the army in two years, and if we still love each other we can get married then, and have plenty more babies."

He saw the tears starting to well up in her eyes. He went on, "Marriage is a big thing, Tony. We jump in right now, we're likely to regret it forever. And think of the kid. Suppose we find out five years from now we weren't really in love, that it was all just physical. But by that time we're married, we got a kid. We can't just drop the kid down the toilet bowl. We got a responsibility. The time to stop the baby is now, before it's born."

"Do you really mean that?"

"Sure I do. It's the only smart thing. Otherwise the baby messes up your college, and I'm off in the army where I can't even support myself. Who needs it?"

It made a kind of brutal sense to him, and for a moment he thought he had gotten through to her. She didn't seem to suspect that he had engineered the draft call himself. She wasn't aware, apparently, that nobody under twenty-two was getting drafted unless he requested it. And, given the draft call, the rest of what he said made sense. An abortion was a lot more logical right now than a hasty marriage on the eve of his induction.

She was crying. He put his arms around her. She remained cold and distant.

He cupped her breasts. She pushed his hands away.

"Tony —"

"Let me alone."

He put his hands on her thighs. He worked them inward, trying to arouse her. He reached for her zipper, but she slapped his hand away.

"No," she said. "You've been in there often enough. Once too often. Not tonight."

"Please, baby!"

She glared at him out of tear-reddened eyes. "Don't you have any sense of decency? You sit there telling me to get an abortion, and then on top of it you try to make love to me! Well, I'm not your toy! I'm not a sex machine!"

He stared at her hungrily. He longed to possess her, to feel the ripeness of her breasts burning against his hands, to force his way between the tautness of her thighs. But she was denying him. For the first time since he had known her, she was saying no.

And she meant it.

Coldly, bitterly, she told him to leave. She refused to listen to any of his pleas.

"Go away," she said. "Go join the Army. Don't stay here bothering me."

He left.

He never saw or spoke to her again.

That night he killed for the third time.

He had not been planning to do it. He had all but forgotten the pleasures of taking life, and he had not been near a prostitute since he had begun sleeping with Tony. But he was washed up with Tony, now. And as he drove aimlessly through the city streets, he felt the powerful throb of desire in his body. He had grown aroused during his visit to Tony's, but she had not satisfied him. He would have to make a pickup, he thought.

He cruised through the downtown section until he spotted a girl, leaning against the window of a paperback bookshop. She was putting lipstick on, and there was something indefinably sluttish about the way she was doing it, out there in the middle of the street.

He pulled up at the curb and stuck his head out the car window. "Hey! Hey, girlie!"

"You calling me?"

"You bet. How'd you like to go for a drive?"

"Where to?"

"Through the park?"

"Sure," she said.

She came strolling toward him. She was young, he saw, no more than twenty tops. A redhead, this time. Not a carroty orange color hair, but a real fiery red. He noticed that she had reddish freckles, too. Her lips were thin, and her blue eyes had a greedy shine to them. She wore a loose white shirt, open at the throat, that did almost nothing for her figure. He could see breasts moving around underneath the blouse, and it struck him that she probably was doing without a bra in the late-June heat. It was fine for comfort, but didn't exactly enhance her sexual appeal.

He didn't worry about things like that. She got into the car next to him, and he went roaring away from the curb. No one had noticed her getting in, no one had seen the face of the fellow who had picked her up, and that was fine, because he didn't intend to bring her back from this ride.

He drove east along Euclid until they came to the park. She didn't talk much, but she didn't need to. She snuggled up against him, and lost no time at all in pulling at his clothing and getting her hand to him. He slipped one arm around her shoulders, and unbuttoned her blouse. His hand slid inside.

He was right. No bra. He cupped her right breast, and found it small and cool to the touch. He put one fingertip on the nipple and rolled it round and round.

They reached the park and got out of the car. The night was all but moonless, and in this darkness nobody was going to see them. They strolled up the walk together until they came to a clump of trees.

"Let's go in here," he said.

"Sure."

She hadn't said a word about money yet. Andreas figured that she was the kind that waited until it was over, then said, "How about a little something to remember you by?" and held out the hand.

They settled down in a cozy little nook completely ringed in by towering oaks and low-clustering rhododendrons. The night air was sweet and fresh, with her perfume of pink flowers drifting to them out of the rhodos.

He pulled her blouse open. Her bare breasts were small and pointy.

She grinned. "I'm pretty flat, I guess."

"You aren't any Bardot, that's for sure."

"Boobs never were my strong point. I got a nice backside, though. It's like they say, every girl's got to be good somewhere. With me it's my bottom."

"Prove it."

"You think I won't? Here. Take a look at this." She rolled over and hoisted her skirt. She hadn't bothered with panties, either, and by starlight Andreas peered at her buttocks.

She was right. She had a sweet little bottom. The cheeks were curved and tender, with dimples at the top where they sprang from her back. They were delicious-looking buttocks, easily her outstanding feature.

They reminded him of Tony's. The same pinkness, the same voluptuous fleshiness. He put his hands on them and they were smooth and cool to the touch, and the flesh yielded as he put his fingertips against them.

His hand stole down to the limit of her buttocks. The hand wandered and the girl began to pant. She started to make little purring sounds of pleasure as he caressed her.

He continued to caress her. She continued to gasp and wriggle in enjoyment.

And then, suddenly, he was bored with her wriggling, bored with her pants and gasps, bored with all her pleasure-sounds. He was so damned tired of fooling around with women. He wanted relief, simple relief.

Pleasure.

It occurred to him that he could take his pleasure from her in complete solitude, if he really wanted to. It was an idea he had toyed with a couple of times before, and had rejected for one reason or another. Now it struck him as a fun thing to do, a real gas.

He crawled toward her.

She lay face down on the soft grass, and he put his weight over her. Her skirt was hiked up around her waist, baring those matchless buttocks of hers, and her blouse dangled open so he could touch her bare breasts.

He reached underneath her. He slid his hands up her belly until he came to the little hillocks of her bosom. His hands closed over her breasts, containing them completely. He squeezed. She sighed. He kneaded. She moaned.

He played with her breasts for a little while. She wiggled her body from side to side beneath him, and he joyed the feel of her smooth buttocks moving against him.

"Is that how you like to do it?" she asked him.

"Yeah," he muttered.

"Okay. Any way you like."

They were all so obliging, these tramps. You wanted to come in from the servant's entrance, that was okay with them. You wanted it standing on your head, fine. Hanging by your heels in a doorway. You paid your money and you took your choice. They were there to serve.

This one, though, was going to serve in a way that Andreas didn't think she was going to like.

He continued to fondle her breasts, rotating them, pushing them together so the rock-hard nipples rubbed against one another. Then he moved his hands a little higher.

Higher.

Brought them into place around her throat.

Squeezed.

Lying on top of her like this, he couldn't watch her face as he strangled her. But the universe is full of such little imperfections, and he was willing to abide by them. In place of the sight of her dying face, he had other little amusements this time.

Such as the jolt that her body gave as the thought first penetrated to her that he was going to choke the life out of her as they lay here.

Such as the wild writhing beneath him.

Such as the sudden rigidity of her frame as the breath began to go out of her.

She didn't scream. She didn't even have a chance to. His steel-strong fingers had slid into place around her throat and had begun the inward tug in one fragment of a moment, cutting off her breath supply before she could even begin to react and let out a howl.

It takes air in the lungs to launch a scream.

All she could do was make little gagging sounds that couldn't carry six feet.

She scrabbled and husked and gargled for about thirty seconds. Then even those sounds ceased. Andreas held on, all the same. He wasn't sure she was dead. She was limp, but that didn't necessarily mean she was gone. He didn't want to let go of her throat and then have her suddenly come to life and start screaming for help.

He squeezed until his fingers were practically meeting in her flesh. Then, cautiously, he began to release her. She didn't move. He put his hands on her breasts. No heartbeat that he could feel, no trace of breathing. He felt for her pulse.

Nothing.

She was dead. Number Three. She lay face down, like a discarded doll. His weight still pressed down against her, but he didn't need to worry about hurting her now. She was beyond all pain.

Now for the moment of pleasure.

Smiling, Andreas leaned forward and pressed down hard.

He was a little surprised at how easy it was to take her this way. From what he had imagined, he thought there would be more resistance than this. But he told himself, the girl was a professional, and if she had Leo so proud of her backside she had probably sold it pretty often, and so the path had probably been opened for him by others.

There was a strange pleasure in taking her this way. Both the fact that he was taking a dead girl, and the fact that he was taking her in an unusual and abnormal manner, added to the intensity of his sensations.

His body scythed forward. The plumpness of her buttocks formed a soft cushion for him as he moved. He half wished that she were alive, so she could respond, press her buttocks upward against him, perhaps wriggle around a little from side to side.

But it was too late for that. He had been bored by her responses, and now he couldn't have them.

No matter. Every kind of pleasure involved giving up something else.

He bore down hard against her. Perhaps, if she had been alive, she would not have been able to stand this. He imagined it would be painful to be treated in such a manner. But she was beyond pain now as well as beyond pleasure.

He began to gasp. Sweat beaded his body. He closed his eyes, pressed his face against the nape of her neck. Her red hair smelled sweet, even now.

The moment of passion was on him. He drove hard, savoring the plump cushions of her buttocks, and then came the moment of release, the savage frenzied pounding of his fulfillment, and he caught his breath as the peak came over him and he debased her dead body.

It was over.

He rose, slowly, flushed and overheated, and adjusted his clothes. Then he knelt by her. With an unusual sense of feeling for her modesty, he drew her skirt down to hide the violated mounds of her buttocks. Then he tipped her half over, so he could look at her face.

It was the swollen, purpled face of death.

It was odd how her red freckles stood out against the mottled bluish-purple of her cheeks. He noticed too, for the first time, that the freckles continued down onto her scrawny breasts.

He let her drop back face down onto the grass. He stood up, feeling satisfied with himself. He had recorded his third kill, and in many ways it had been the most unusual and most pleasant.

He sauntered away, through the empty park. Returning to the car, he got in, drove quickly away.

CHAPTER TEN

At half past seven the next morning, after a sound and tranquil sleep, he showed up at the induction center for his examination. There were about two hundred other guys there, most of them looking pretty sullen and disturbed about the idea of getting drafted.

He marched along in line from station to station. He gave a couple of cubic centimeters of blood for his country, and patriotically contributed a urine sample as well. He was tapped, probed, X-rayed, and otherwise scrutinized in a variety of ways, a few of them highly intimate. He was given a long questionnaire to fill out, and he solemnly deposed that he was not in the habit of bed-wetting, that he had not had venereal disease, smallpox, diphtheria, and a number of other ailments, and that the general state of his health was good. He was unable to find any organizations on the list of subversive ones handed to him to which he had belonged.

He took a mental test. Part of it involved spatial perception, part of it verbal understanding. He did his best, and apparently his best was good enough.

By one o'clock, he had gone through the whole complicated rigmarole. Some of his fellow draftees had dropped by the wayside by this time. Half a dozen had been told off to talk to the psychiatrist, and one lad had proudly and loudly owned up to gonorrhea and had been plucked from line, and another came up with some mysterious manifestation when chemicals were dropped into his urine, and still another turned out to have a heart that made odd galumphing sounds when a stethoscope was pressed against his chest.

But there was nothing wrong with Lou Andreas that a team of bored Army medics could find. He went through the physical with flying colors, and not long after lunch he found himself swearing an oath of allegiance.

He was in.

"Congratulations, men," a tough-looking corporal rasped at them. "You've just taken the first step toward becoming one of Uncle Sam's trained killers."

Andreas had to grin at that.

He didn't figure he needed too much special training.

They bundled him off to camp for a few days, and then they sent him home, in his new uniform, to gather up the tangled threads of his existence. He had ten days of leave.

It was a pretty soft ten days. His family made a big fuss over him, as though he were going off to die, instead of to spend two years sitting on his can as a member of a peacetime army. His mother cooked all his special foods, the things he liked the most. His father gave him a hard-earned twenty bucks and told him to have a good time. He took the money to the pool room and ran it up to fifty in short order.

During those ten days he looked up a couple of his old girlfriends. They were glad to see him again, after the six months he had been out of circulation.

"What's the matter, you and Tony break up or something?"

"Yeah. Yeah."

"Jeez. I figured you two were real solid. I was sure you were gonna get married."

"Everybody figured that," Andreas said. "Everybody except me. That's why we broke up."

There was love galore during those ten days. He dated three girls, took each of them on three separate occasions, and took the remaining night for rest and recuperation. They had all come across for him before, but now they were more eager than ever, as though they wanted to get one last fling out of him before he disappeared into service.

He was impatient to disappear, though. For the first time since he had taken up murder as a hobby, he was in at least lukewarm danger of getting arrested.

Somebody had seen him walking through the park with the girl he had killed.

The story had made the newspapers. He had been away getting measured for his uniform when the story broke, but he looked up the papers he had missed when he got back. This time it was no squib on page sixty-eight. It was right on front page.

BODY FOUND IN PARK: GIRL RAPED, STRANGLED

The story went into more detail than was usual in such things. For one, the dead girl was unblushingly identified as a prostitute. Jean Sanders, that was the name they gave. Age twenty-two. Former night-club singer.

The story quoted the police medical investigator as saying, "There is no doubt that the girl was sexually abused. However, the rape was of an abnormal kind anatomically. And there is good reason to believe that she was strangled first and then sexually abused. The murderer is obviously seriously deranged."

The story was a sensation because of the grisly overtones of perversion. The mere strangling of a prostitute had hardly been worth printing. But this case had special angles that earned it a couple of days of notoriety.

And there was the matter of the witness.

She was a middle-aged woman whose name, naturally, was withheld by the police. She claimed to have seen the deceased and "a tall boy" get out of "a blue car, fairly old." They had walked toward a lover's lane. That was the last she had seen of them, and she had left the park soon after, too soon to see the boy come back alone. No, she could not identify the make of the car. No, she did not know its year. It wasn't a new car, though. Of that she was certain. Nor could she give any description of the boy other than that he was tall. It had been a dark night. She had happened to notice the girl's pretty red hair, that was all.

Now, there are several hundred thousand "tall boys" living in Cleveland, and a fair number of them can be expected to drive blue cars of elderly vintage. It would take the police a good long time to track down every blue car and question its owner. On the face of it, there wasn't enough evidence to lead the cops very far.

Of course, Andreas realized, there might have been more testimony by the witness than had gotten into the papers. Maybe there was a quite accurate description of the "tall boy," enough to narrow the search to a hundred or so possible suspects.

He felt queasy. But he had to sit tight and let time trickle out. The one thing he could not do was try to scram.

For all he knew, it was a trap. Maybe the police had already narrowed their net to a few dozen likely suspects, and then had let some news leak to the papers. Now they were watching to see if any of their suspects suddenly bolted from the city. They would move in fast.

Besides, he was the property of the United States Army. If he vanished abruptly, he would not only become a full-fledged murder suspect, but an AWOL as well. He'd be in a double mess. So he simply had to wait it out. If they hadn't caught him by July 1, he'd be safely ensconced in khaki far from Cleveland, and nobody would bother him again until the park murder case was completely forgotten.

So he waited. Uncomfortably.

The days passed. No one came around to arrest him.

And then it was July 1, and off he went to join the Army, and he let out a long sigh of relief at the awareness that for a third time he had gotten away with murder.

Being in the Army didn't pose any problems for him. It was an organization for idiots, run by idiots for an idiotic purpose, and as soon as Andreas caught on to that, he got the swing of things perfectly.

All you had to do was keep your head down and never volunteer for anything. Go through your two years day by day by day, telling yourself that nothing you do is of any damned use to the universe, and stay out of trouble. Don't look for extra responsibilities. Don't do an inch more than they tell you to do—but don't do less, either.

The months ticked off. Nobody noticed Private Andreas. Nobody clapped him on the shoulder and said, "You belong in Officer Candidate School." Nobody gave him the Distinguished Service Cross. Nobody made him a corporal. He got up to PFC, simply by staying around and keeping out of trouble, but that was the summit of his military career.

He didn't mind.

The government demanded that he throw away two years, and he was herewith contributing them. That was all. They wanted his physical presence inside a uniform. They weren't asking for his mind or his enthusiasm or even his interest, and they didn't get it. For reasons of public policy, it was necessary to keep a million men in uniform at all times, and Lou Andreas was serving his time as one of the chosen million, and that was that.

There was news from home, of course.

About a month after he had gone into service there came a letter from his mother. He was down in Georgia, sweating out Basic Training, and he was having a pretty rough time of it in those early days. But the letter more than made up for the fact that he had just spent twelve hours crawling on his belly through a muddy field.

"I think you will be interested to know that your former girlfriend Tony got married on Sunday," his mother wrote. "Her new husband is a boy named Thomas Oakes who goes to Harvard. The writeup on the wedding was in the newspapers yesterday. It was quite a big wedding. Did Tony drop you a line about it? I thought I would tell you anyway. You said you did not plan to marry her, so I guess you will not be terribly disappointed by the news, but maybe you will be surprised."

Andreas was surprised, all right. He didn't know any Thomas Oakeses, and he didn't think Tony did either. And less than six weeks had gone by since the night he had told her he was going into the army.

What had happened?

Andreas thought he could figure it out. Tony had probably gone to her parents and spilled the beans about being pregnant. And Mr. Neale had decided to do something fast. In that kind of educated, sophisticated, upper-bracket family, they didn't disinherit a girl for getting knocked up, and drum her out of the family. No, either they bought her an abortion in a hurry, or they bought her a husband. The main idea was to avoid a scandal, not to make speeches at the girl.

Well, Tony had been dead set against an abortion. So they had to find a husband. Andreas had a good idea of how it had been done. Tony's father was a Harvard man, and he probably got in touch with some of his Harvard friends. The problem was to find a young Ivy League kid who was not too ugly, not too dumb, had the right family background, and was short of cash. Maybe some kid whose father had just died, and who was going to have to drop out of school if he didn't get a windfall.

Next step was to introduce the kid to Tony. Then to push them into a whirlwind courtship. Without revealing she was pregnant, of course, Tony would have to steam the kid up toward marriage, subtly letting it be known that if they got married right away, her father would underwrite all the expenses of their next few years of schooling.

A quick razz-ma-tazz and the sucker was hooked. Engagement notices went out. A wedding was arranged. Tony Neale became Mrs. Thomas Oakes.

The young couple made plans to go back to Cambridge in the fall. Oakes would go to Harvard, Tony to Radcliffe. Oakes would feel pretty pleased with his deal. He had been handed an undeniably beautiful, sexy, and intelligent wife, whose father was not only wealthy but generous with his wealth. What more could a guy ask for, especially a guy who had been having financial troubles?

Andreas smiled. Along around September or October, Tony would make a sudden amazing discovery. "I'm going to have a baby, darling!"

Perhaps Thomas Oakes had been wondering a little. Possibly it had struck him as peculiar that between the wedding in August and the big announcement in October his wife had not had any periods. Perhaps he had noticed that her belly was getting rounder and rounder every day.

No matter. The news went out: the Oakeses were expecting an heir.

Did Tom Oakes know anything about pregnancy? Was he aware how long it took before a girl's belly should begin to bulge? Did it strike him as unusual that Tony should look so big when she was only in her second month?

Maybe Tom Oakes was coming to suspect that he had been sold a bill of goods, that Tony had been carrying something around in her belly as she stood squeezing his hand at the altar. Or maybe he had suspected that all along, and simply decided to take the bad with the good.

Who knew? Tony would get bigger and bigger, until, by the time she was in her fifth month, she looked strangely like a woman about to go into labor any day. Oddly, she would make her hospital arrangements in her fifth month too, which seemed a little hasty. And around the same time she would announce to her husband that she didn't think it was wise for them to practice marital relations for a while.

And by and by she would have a baby.

Andreas got another letter from his mother late in January that said, "I ran into a friend of the Neales the other day and she told me that your old friend Tony was now a mother. Yes, time does fly! She gave birth to a little baby girl several weeks ago. The child was almost three months premature, but I understand it was perfect in all respects and there will be none of the usual problems."

Andreas grinned broadly as he read the letter. Good old Mom! She didn't seem to understand a thing. She took the news at face value. A six-month baby that was perfectly formed? Who would believe that? And wasn't it funny that just about eight months ago, he had stopped seeing Tony and abruptly had joined the army? Wasn't there some connection, maybe?

Good old Mom. She was so thick-witted sometimes.

He put down the letter and let out a whoop that carried through the barracks. "Hey, guys! Guess what! I'm a daddy, for Christ's sake!"

"I didn't know you were married," somebody said.

"I'm not," Andreas laughed. "That's the great part I'm not, but *she* is!"

A little later in the evening, though, some of his elation died away, and he began to feel depressed. There was a baby girl. His child, and he would never ever lay eyes on her. That was too bad, in a way.

And Tony—the most beautiful girl he had ever known, and the most intelligent. He could have had her for keeps, and he had tossed away the chance. Now some other guy fondled Tony's rounded boobs at night. Some other guy lay between those soft thighs. Some other guy caressed the satiny buttocks, tasted the wet warmth of her mouth, listened to the soft panting sounds of her ecstasies.

He tried to shrug the thought away. If he had wanted her, he could have had her. He didn't want her. Nostalgia was silly. He had run away. He had made his choice freely, and there was no sense mooning about it now.

Still, he wished she'd send him a picture of the baby, at least. Just for old times' sake. Probably she hated him, but the least she could do was send along one stinking snapshot, couldn't she?

She didn't.

He never heard a word from her.

He decided he didn't really deserve to.

During the two years that he wore the uniform of his country, Lou Andreas added five more kills to his total, running the number up to eight.

It was easy to kill, when you were a soldier. They kept moving you around from place to place, and you lived the kind of rootless, drifting life that led to boredom and the itch of murder. Besides, you wore a uniform. That was camouflage. To a civilian, all soldiers look alike. They don't see past the uniform. They never can identify a face.

So it was easy.

Marvelously easy.

Andreas killed. It was his hobby. One soldier in the unit collected stamps, and another one carved statuettes out of wood, and another one read all the time, and another one always checked through everybody's pocket change for rare dates of coins. Those were their hobbies.

Andreas' hobby was killing.

He killed twice in Virginia, once in Chicago, and once each in Minneapolis and St. Paul. The kills were widely spaced, with three months between the two Virginia ones, then a six-month gap before he throttled a girl to death in an early-morning love tryst on the shore of Lake Michigan, and then four more months before he moved on to Minnesota. His Twin Cities kills came nine weeks apart.

All five girls were prostitutes. He took a special joy in eradicating tramps. Each time he killed he was taking another big step toward wiping out that stain on his manhood, that long-ago encounter with the slut who mocked a nervous virgin boy of seventeen.

The first one in Virginia was short and roly-poly, with big round breasts that jiggled and quivered like mounds of jelly. She had a southern drawl that made Andreas sick to listen to it. It took her five minutes to spit out a simple sentence that a Northerner could have managed in a couple of seconds. And when she finally got the words out, nobody could understand them, because of that accent of hers. She was from Mississippi, but she had come "no'th" to Virginia because that was where the big money was. At least, her idea of big money. She charged seven-fifty for her services.

Andreas took her twice in a filthy tar paper shack that had more in common with Mississippi squalor than with Virginian aristocracy. Then, when she was pleading for a third go-round, he let her have it. He cupped the enormous rounds of her breasts and squeezed them till she was foggy-eyed with passion, and then, when she didn't know whether she was coming or going, he grabbed her neck and pivoted her head around sharply until he heard the sound of a cracking spine.

It was a modification of his strangling method. The army had taught him several interesting ways of murdering without drawing blood, and he had decided to experiment with them in the pursuit of novel amusements.

The second Virginia girl was a mulatto. He picked her up in the slum section of town, and drove her around for a while. She was tall, almost six feet, and her skin was the color of fine mahogany, and her features were thin and elegant, with narrow lips and a high-bridged nose. But she was coarse and full of hate. She hated white men for having had her mammy, and she hated black men because they were downtrodden, and she hated any man who bought her body, because he was humiliating her.

So he put her out of her misery. They made love by the side of a country brook, and she lay there in the moonlight with her small hard breasts gleaming as though they were oiled, and he dug his fingers into her not-quite-kinky black hair and cracked her head against rock. It stunned her, nothing more. He carried her down to the brookside, and carefully arranged her so that her face hung into the water, and then he sat there, watching her, moonlight glinting on her brown back and bare taut buttocks. She never recovered consciousness. After she had been dangling into the water for half an hour, he pushed her out into the stream, and she floated away.

He felt a little queasy about that. There was always the remote possibility she *hadn't* drowned, and would wake up five miles downstream, naked and waterlogged and headachey, and would put the finger on him. But his unit was leaving Virginia at dawn anyway.

He was back by curfew time. And in the morning, he moved out as scheduled. So far as he ever found out, the girl had drowned. He counted her as number five.

He picked up number six in Chicago. A skinny tramp with a gutter tongue. He left her purple-faced on a beach in the middle of Chicago.

Number seven in Minneapolis. A Swede who had gone into prostitution after her husband deserted her. Andreas strangled her. Number eight across the bridge in St. Paul. A tired tramp of forty who was due for retirement anyway. The cunning fingers choked off her life.

It was a pleasant hobby, he thought. A lot more fun than collecting stamps. He had never understood how a guy could get any sort of kicks out of sticking little colored bits of paper into a book.

CHAPTER ELEVEN

The army spewed him out two years to the day after he had gone in. He had grown half an inch and had gained twenty pounds during his military tour of duty, and it was all muscle and bone. He was no longer thin and gawky now. He moved with strength and authority.

He didn't go back to Cleveland to live. There was no point in it. He had nobody left there. His father had died of a stroke, about a year and a half after Andreas had gone into the army. His mother had caught pneumonia at the funeral, which was held in the middle of a raging snowstorm, and she lasted about six weeks after that.

Which left him an orphan at the age of not-quite twenty-one. He inherited his parents' pitiful savings, about eleven hundred dollars after all the funeral expenses were taken care of, and he was on his own.

He lost no time getting a job. He became a traveling salesman dealing to wholesalers. It wasn't the most lucrative work in the world, but it paid him enough to cover his expenses and let him put aside a little besides.

And the job had its advantages.

It allowed him to travel all over the country. Since he was by nature a loner, a solitary man, he didn't mind. He rather liked the idea of living in hotel rooms and motels, moving on from city to city every few days. It provided a perfect form of protection for his career assassination, which now became the major interest his life.

He recorded kills around the country—wherever a girl willing to sell herself could be found. He killed them sometimes in cheap hotel rooms, sometimes on lonely country roads, sometimes in tumbledown shacks, sometimes in pleasant rolling farmland.

He got around.

He scored kills in New York, Des Moines, San Francisco, Cincinnati, Omaha, St. Louis.

He did his bit to reduce the population of fallen women in Detroit, Philadelphia, Atlanta, New Orleans, and puritan old Boston.

He played a little game with himself. He tried to knock off a girl in each of the major league baseball towns. His work took him all over the country, and he kept a careful mental tally. He finished the American League list first, picking up his eighth kill in Washington. Then the Athletics moved from Philadelphia to Kansas City and he had to go along to keep up to date.

The National League took a little longer. For some reason his sales route never took him to Milwaukee, and he had to go up there finally during his own vacation time to find a victim. Pittsburgh took him a while, too. But eventually he got all eight teams represented on his kill list, and that gave him the complete big league roster. He hadn't skimped, either. There were three New York teams in the major leagues, and he had seen to it that he had three kills for New York, two for Chicago's White Sox and Cubs. When the Dodgers and Giants moved West, he checked and found he had never scored in Los Angeles, so he flew out there and took care of that in a hurry.

In only a few cities did he fail to find a likely prospect for his hobby. In one or two places he had trouble making a pickup. Seattle gave him that kind of problem. There were plenty of easily made co-eds in Seattle, but he wasn't able to find any pros. In his book of rules, only pros counted as potential victims. So he had fun in Seattle, but didn't add to his list.

The tally mounted, all the same. He averaged five or six kills a year. 1957 saw him hit a peak, with eleven. He was in a murderous mood that year. But the year after, he slumped off to eight, and only nine the year after that.

The coming of new teams to the major leagues gave fresh impetus to his hobby. One year, he found it necessary to register new kills in Los Angeles and Washington. The year after that, Houston and New York had to be accounted for. He had no problems in any of the cases.

He had a strict rule that he would kill only once during each visit to a given city. He did not want to multiply the risks for himself. One killing could be overlooked by the police, or treated in a sloppy way; two killings the same month constituted a crime wave; the lives of innocent citizens might be in danger, and there would be a widespread manhunt.

That he could not risk. So he killed selectively.

Many times people asked him if he enjoyed his lonely life—no home, no family, never more than three or four days in the same place.

"Of course I enjoy life," Andreas would tell them. "I have my hobbies, after all."

Yes. It was a very fascinating hobby.

It gave him the deepest of personal satisfaction. Time and again, dozens of times now, some unsuspecting woman had atoned in full for the bitter mockery that had been showered on him when he was seventeen. His repeated revenge was a highly pleasant amusement.

Often at night he would lie awake, contemplating his hobby, and speculating on the appearance of the next victim. Blonde? Brunette? Busty? Flat-chested? Painted? Refined? Cool? Torrid?

There was an infinity of possibilities.

It was a fascinating hobby indeed.

Andreas had killed thirty-seven times before he varied the routine enough to include as his victim someone who was not a prostitute. It was the only time in his life that he deviated from his established and familiar pattern of slaying only those who sold their flesh to men.

The circumstances were special ones, though.

It happened in New York City. For business reasons it was necessary for him to spend an extended stay in New York, more than a month. It was the longest span of time he had spent in any one place since leaving the army, and he made up his mind in advance that he would not indulge in his hobby while he was in New York. A month-long stay would make him seem almost like a permanent resident, and that would increase the chances of getting nabbed.

Instead, he figured, he would find some girl and set up a temporary liaison with her. That would take care of his sexual needs for the month.

He had no trouble finding the girl. Her name was Avery, and she was a slim, good-looking brunette, about twenty-three, with short-cropped hair and smiling, sardonic eyes. There was an olive duskiness about her complexion that made her seem sultry and exotic, and the moment Andreas laid eyes on her—in a little Italian restaurant in Greenwich Village—he knew that he had to have her.

The project didn't seem to pose any problems. He looked across to her table, and saw that she was looking at him. Girls often looked at him. He had that kind of face and physique, rugged without being handsome, that attracted glances.

He grinned at her. She grinned back.

"Mind if I join you?" he asked quietly.

"Not at all."

He went to her table. The owner-waiter beamed in paternal delight. "Lou Andreas," he said. Since he had no plans for killing her, he had no intention of inventing an alias for himself to avoid trouble.

"Avery Donnell."

"That's a pretty name. Avery."

"Is it? Everybody else thinks it's horrible. It's a man's name."

"Does anyone mistake you for a man?" Andreas asked.

"Not often."

"So why worry about having a man's name?"

Avery shrugged prettily. "I don't worry about it. Other people do. It was my grandfather's name, you see. My father was hell bent on having a son to name after him. It was a big shock to him when he got his first look at me and saw I was missing some vital equipment. But that didn't stop him from naming me Avery anyway."

Andreas chuckled. "I once knew a girl named Tony," he said.

"Toni? That's pretty common. Short for Antonia."

"Right," he said. "But she spelled it with a Y ... She hated girls who spelled their names in fancy ways. Like Judi and Bobbi and Jayne-with-a-Y." Andreas stared off into nowhere for a moment. He hadn't thought of Tony in years. Her little girl—*his* little girl—was eight years old by now. Time moved along. "How would you like some wine?" he asked abruptly.

"Love it."

He beckoned to the waiter. "Get us some chianti, okay?"

Chianti appeared. They lifted their glasses. She smiled at him. She was a vibrant, alive-looking girl, full of life and vitality. And good-looking. Her close-cropped hair was a little too severe to suit her, but there was a supple softness to her, a fullness of breast, that made her look undeniably feminine all the same.

"What do you do?" she asked him.

"Go ahead and laugh. I'm a traveling salesman."

"You poor guy. You must know all the jokes."

"Eight million of them. Someday I'll write a book. Jokes That Have Bored Me. What kind of work are you in, Avery?"

"I'm a model."

"For artists?"

"Oh, no," she said. "I'm in advertising. You've probably seen me in the *New Yorker* a lot. I'm in this week's issue, for instance. The ad just in front of the center spread. A beer ad. There's this girl at a bowling alley —"

"I'm sorry. I don't read the *New Yorker*."

She looked at him in astonishment, as though he had just said he didn't breathe oxygen as a rule. "You *don't?*"

"No. Have I said something wrong?"

She flashed a brilliant smile. "No, of course not. It's just that well, I thought everybody read the *New Yorker*. I mean, whenever I have my pictures in a *New Yorker* ad, ten million people call me up and say they saw it. People stop me on the street. Strangers. So I kind of got the idea the whole world reads it. Like you and the farmer's daughter jokes, you know?"

"Well, maybe in New York the whole world reads it. But I travel around too much. I can't keep up with a weekly magazine, not when I'm in a different place each week. *You* try buying the *New Yorker* in Punk River, Idaho, sometimes."

She laughed. "I'd rather not."

"So you model for ads, huh? Does it pay well?"

"Oh, scads and scads!"

"If you're so rich, what are you doing in a cheap spaghetti joint like this?"

"Because the food's good," she said. "Do I need a better reason?"

"No. And how come you're eating alone?"

"You ask a lot of questions, Mr. Andreas."

"Lou."

"Lou. Okay. I'm eating alone because I feel like it. I'm an independent-minded girl and I don't necessarily mind appearing in public unescorted. Okay?"

"Sure," he said. "Okay."

He liked her. She had fire, she had dash, she had spirit. And looks. Already, in his mind's eye, he was peeling away her clothing. He liked what he saw underneath. He was eager to compare his imagined view of her with the genuine article.

They finished their dinner. They sat around for a while, dawdling over the last of the wine.

"Come on," he said finally, dropping a ten-dollar bill on the table. "Let's get out of here."

CHAPTER TWELVE

They walked around Greenwich Village for a while, talking and looking in store windows and holding hands. They stopped at a little two-by-four jewelry store and he bought her a pair of handsome ceramic earrings for four bucks. She didn't want him to spend the money on her, but he insisted, and she gave in gracefully enough.

A while later, they stopped in for drinks, and watched a Village poet reciting his epic work in the hopes of getting a handout, and then, about ten o'clock, they began aiming toward the finish of the evening. Which would be in bed. Of course.

There was no reason why not. They were both unattached adults. They liked each other. They had nothing else to do this evening.

Why not go to bed?

"Do you live far from here?" he asked her.

"About two blocks. But we can't go there. My roommate is home tonight."

"Roommate?"

"Her name's Elaine. She's a model too. She's got the sniffles tonight and I know she stayed in. I couldn't bring you there. I mean, unless you just wanted to sit in the living room and have a chaste cup of coffee with the two of us."

"That wasn't exactly what I had on my mind."

"I didn't think so. Well, we can go to your hotel, I guess. Where are you staying?"

"34th Street."

"That's not so far. We can grab a bus right on the corner here."

Half an hour later, they were in his room. It was a commercial hotel, nothing fancy, nine bucks a night, fifty-five per week. The company wasn't going to reimburse him for a month in the Waldorf-Astoria, after all. But this place would do. It was clean and quiet, and more than that can't be expected for nine bucks a night.

He had Room Service send up a bottle of bourbon and some mix. Even at a commercial hotel, it was an expensive thing, ordering liquor in the hotel. A five-buck fifth of bourbon and eighty cents' worth of soda set him back nine bucks, with a dollar more thrown in as a none too generous tip. What the hell, though; if he expected to have this girl as his regular mistress for the next four weeks or so, he'd have to spend some money on her, and in any event it was cheaper this way than paying for it when he needed it.

"Cheers," he said.

She grinned at him. "Down the hatch."

"I hope so."

They clinked glasses. Everything was on a cheerful, friendly, relaxed basis. They had a couple of drinks apiece, not even getting a third of the way into the bottle, and then she began to take off her clothes.

"Getting late," she said. "I'm supposed to be modeling lingerie at eleven in the morning tomorrow. Can't look all grumpy or it means a lot of silly makeup."

Andreas helped her out of her clothes. In a moment, she was nude. He liked her body. It had a slim elegance to it, a kind of steely tautness, like the mainspring of a fine Swiss watch. There was no excess flesh on her. She had breasts, nice round ones, that sprouted from her chest with a suddenness that was almost too abrupt. Her breasts were firm, full, youthful. They weren't maternal breasts. It was easy to see that she had never been through the strains of pregnancy. They were like the breasts of a seventeen-year-old virgin. Or like the breasts of a seventeen-year-old, anyway.

Good breasts. Good little nipples.

Good buttocks, too. Curved just right. A little too lean, perhaps. Almost mannishly hard. But good to look at and good to hold.

She looked athletic. Her hips were perhaps a shade narrower than Andreas preferred the hips of his women to be, but that was all right. Looking at her, surveying her litheness, he knew she was bound to be a sensation in the sack.

His mouth watered for her as he undressed.

"You model bathing suits?" he asked.

"Yes. Why?"

"Just wondering. I bet you're terrific in a bikini."

"I do a lot of bikini stuff," she said.

"You're terrific without a bikini too."

"You're just flattering me because you want to make me," she said.

"What gives you that idea?"

"I don't know. Call it women's intuition. I think you've got immoral ideas toward me."

"Just because I'm standing here naked, you mean?"

She laughed. She stretched her hands toward him, and he came to her, and the next moment her body was pressed tight up against his, and she was cool in some places and blazingly hot in others, and her nipples were drilling into his chest and her mouth was wide open against his and her tongue was deep in his mouth and the flatness of her torso was touching his, and his hands slid down her back and came to rest on the firm hard rounds of her buttocks, and held her close, and they moved toward the bed.

She let go of him and sprawled down, with her warmth open and welcoming to him.

He toppled down with her.

She laughed and gripped his shoulders, and dug her fingers in. Her eyes were wide open, and she seemed to be having the time of her life. Her breasts swayed a little as her body moved up to meet his.

He caressed her. His hands went down her body, down to where those luscious thighs began their swell, to the bowl in which his fire was to be extinguished. He touched her, and felt her throb and pant. Her own hands circled his body, teasingly, playfully, then came to rest with sudden determination on him.

They were expert fingers. They had been around, those fingers, and their owner knew exactly what to do to a man. Trembling, he returned the favors.

Her firm breasts were heaving as the air pumped in and out of her flaring nostrils. Her thighs opened and closed in spasms, like the limbs of some mighty threshing machine. Then she stopped closing them, and left them complaisant, honey-fleshed and delectable.

He lowered himself.

She wriggled and shivered with pleasure. He moved his head, found the inflamed tip of one breast inches from his lips, and then took it in, kissing the firm globe tenderly. She started to make little wordless moans of pleasure.

He found her buttocks again. He held them tight, lifting her body, touched, hesitated for a moment, bodies joined and yet not really joined, and then, with sudden tumultuous vigor, sent himself home as though nailing a stake through a vampire's heart.

Her whole body shook.

The jolt was a terrific one. He closed his eyes and let himself slide forward, down that long runway, into the abyss of pleasure.

Her body moved in slow pivoting swings, up and down, up and down, up and down. There was something wonderfully unhurried about those motions of hers. Other girls, especially their first time with any man, tended to rush things. They were afraid of being left in the lurch, and they tried to wrest all the sensation they could out of the first few minutes. They twitched up and down like overstrung puppets, and the only result was that they brought about the selfsame too-rapid culmination that they were trying to avoid.

Not this girl. Not Avery.

She had confidence in his abilities, it seemed. She brought her body up and let it loll back, up and back long slow swings that assured a perfect meeting of their flesh. Nothing rushed, nothing hurried and jerky.

Slow and calm and deep.

And the passion mounted. High, higher, highest.

Andreas felt the blaze spreading outward from his loins consuming his entire body, and he trembled, and clenched his jaws until his molars ached, and filled his hands with her breasts and his mouth with her tongue and thrust and thrust again, and now they were both moving in a headlong helter-skelter race the final few yards to ecstasy, and he saw to it that they moved at exactly the same pace, so that when the slamming, jolting, numbing moment of pleasure came for him, she was right at his side experiencing its equal.

Up, up, and away!

And then the slow return.

They lay side by side, hand in hand, spent and drained. He grinned at her. Sweat stippled her body. He leaned forward and kissed one nipple, then the other. She ran her hand affectionately over him,

"That was good," she said softly.

"More than good. It was unforgettable."

"For me too," she said.

"Kiss me?"

"Gladly."

Their lips met. There was little passion to the kiss, now. After the journey they had just taken, little passion remained in them. They had expended their supply, and it would be a while before they renewed it. But they kissed fondly, a lovers' kiss, and it was strange to think that only a few hours before they had not known one another.

They rested half an hour. Then he rose, and fixed drinks for them, and they drank slowly, and put their glasses down, and he looked at her, his eyes roving hungrily over the supple contours of her slim nudity He loved the olive hue of her skin, glossier now that sweat bathed her.

She laughed and pointed at him. "Look at you. That's indecent!"

"Is it, now?"

"It sure is. You can't go walking around on display."

He went to her. And the next moment they were rolling around on the bed together, and the old springs were giving out with a symphony of sex, and somebody was pounding half-heartedly on the walls to quiet them, and they paid no attention at all, and after a while the pounding of body loving passion-inflamed body. Then that pounding came to an end too, but there was yet another pounding, that of healthy hearts, and that pounding continued for a long while yet.

She left about one in the morning. He wanted to see her home, but she wouldn't hear of it. He was home already, she said, and drowsy from his workout, and it was absolutely criminal to make him put his clothes on and go out into the dark and the cold.

"You talked me out of it," he said with a grin. "When will I see you again, Avery?"

"Day after tomorrow?"

"So long?"

"It can't be helped," she said. "But I'll be looking forward to seeing you."

"So will I," he said.

She came over to the bed, fully dressed, and kissed him. It was a hungry kiss. He nearly dragged her back into bed with him. But she wiggled away.

"Tomorrow's a working day," she said, smiling.

And then she was gone.

It was a nice, cozy, sweet little deal.

Andreas saw her three, sometimes four nights a week. She was never free two nights in a row, and it was quite clear to him that she was also seeing someone else, but he never let jealousy enter into the relationship. He was content to have her half the time. It satisfied his needs.

As one week and then a second passed, he realized that he was coming to have a real emotional attachment to her. Avery was a terrific girl. In many ways, she reminded him of Tony—her liveliness, her straight-from-the-shoulder honesty, her intelligence, and above all her good looks and her passionate nature.

But he had always felt intellectually inferior to Tony, and he never felt that way with Avery. Part of the reason was that in the eight years plus since his affair with Tony, he had come to be far better read, far more aware of the world; he had developed mentally. But also, Avery was far less dedicated and scholarly than Tony had been. Avery read, she liked to go to concerts and art galleries and museums, but it was more as a consumer of such things than as a scholar. Tony's approach had been the scholarly one. Maybe Avery had been like that in her teens, but not any longer.

Of course, Andreas had no idea of making a permanent relationship with Avery. He had had plenty of opportunity to see that he was not cut out either for marriage or for having a regular mistress. This was strictly a one-month deal. When he left New York, he would end the affair. In later years, when business brought him this way again, he might look her up for old time's sake, but that would be all.

But things never work out smoothly according to plan. There are always hitches.

With Tony, the hitch turned out to be first college and then pregnancy. A lovely romance went down the drain.

The hitch with Avery was something entirely different, something totally unexpected. It hit Andreas hard when he discovered it.

He was in the last week of his New York stay, now. Avery knew that he was leaving in a few days, and she was taking what struck him as a mature, levelheaded approach. She was sad to lose him, naturally, but she was not being clinging or sticky in any way. They had had their fun like adults—and now, like adults, they were going their separate ways.

He had had a good time with her. They had gone through the whole roster of variations, rung the changes. She was inventive and resourceful. It had been a memorable month in every respect.

Now he wanted to show his gratitude.

He picked up a little trinket for her at a jewelry shop on Fifth Avenue. It was a clasp, Japanese-made, cultured pearls set in 14-karat gold. It set him back $90, but he thought that was a small sum to pay for the pleasures Avery had given him in these weeks.

He decided to surprise her.

He was supposed to see her the next evening, and he had been planning to give her the clasp then. But impatience set in. He decided it would be fun to drop in on her early in the morning. He knew that she never had modelling assignments before eleven in the morning. So if he came in around nine, she would be deliciously sleepy and relaxed, and he could give her the clasp and perhaps even grab off a quick one before he started on his daily selling routine.

He took the bus downtown to the Village, and walked over to the quiet street where she lived. She had a little three-room apartment overlooking a lovely back courtyard with trees and a garden and a horde of cats. Andreas had been up there a couple of times. He had met her roommate Elaine once or twice, too—a short, slender girl who did not seem to like him very much, who had seemed to be half a million miles away whenever they talked.

Elaine and Avery each had their own bedroom. The third room of the apartment was a living room-kitchenette affair. Andreas didn't know whether or not Elaine would still be in the apartment this late in the morning, but he didn't much care. They could always go into Avery's bedroom and close the door, if Elaine felt embarrassed.

He took the stairs two at a time. The clasp, bulky in its square box, bulged against his hip.

Reaching their floor, he started to knock, then held his hand. Perhaps they hadn't locked the door, he thought. The surprise would be more fun if he could tiptoe right into Avery's bedroom and wake her up with a kiss. It might startle her, but she wouldn't die of shock.

He tried the door, carefully, quietly.

It wasn't locked. He gently pushed it open, two inches, three, hoping it wouldn't creak and give the show away.

The door opened silently. Andreas put his head inside, looked around, saw no one, opened the door a little wider to admit himself.

Suddenly he froze. Sounds of passion were coming from Avery's room! The color drained from his face, and he stood there, chilled, appalled.

He listened grimly to the pleasure-sounds. The creaking bedsprings, the gasps of delight. The unmistakable sound of body rubbing sensually against nude body.

His first impulse was to turn and get out, fast. He knew he had no business being here. Avery's private life was her own business, and he had assumed all along that she was seeing somebody else, and quite obviously that somebody else had spent the night with her last night and was still here. Which was quite all right with Andreas. In any event, he was going to drop out of Avery's life in a couple of days, so he had no claim on her at all.

He started to leave.

But he waited just one moment too long. It was a fatal moment.

He heard a voice saying, "Well, Avery? Who do you prefer? Me or that salesman of yours?"

It was Elaine's voice!

And he heard Avery—unmistakably Avery—say, "You, darling! You didn't need to ask! You know it's you I love. He's just a sideline. A change of pace."

"I've been so fearfully jealous all month."

"I know you have. But I felt I needed the fling, Elaine. Anyway, he's leaving soon. And then there'll just be the two of us again."

Horror flooded Andreas' brain as he listened to the conversation. A surge of something very close to madness came over him.

Avery a lesbian?

Making love to her roommate?

No, he thought. It couldn't be. Had those lips that he had kissed so fondly also engaged in foulness with another woman? Had those round, coral-tipped breasts rubbed against those of Elaine?

He couldn't believe it.

He had to see with his own eyes.

On numb, tottering legs he moved into the apartment. He crossed the floor step by cautious step, gritting his teeth every time the ancient boards creaked. The door to Avery's bedroom was ajar. There was a mirror facing the bed, he knew. If he glanced in at an angle, he would have a clear reflected view of whatever was going on in Avery's bed.

He peered in.

He saw.

It was just as he had guessed. Avery and Elaine were in bed together. They had kicked the covers to the floor, so that both their nude bodies were exposed to his view, Avery's dark and lean, Elaine's pink and thin, with small high breasts that became visible for moments at a time.

Their bodies writhed. All too clearly, they were both experiencing the heights of passion.

Andreas watched, and a feeling of betrayal crept over him. This was nearly as shattering as that harlot's screamed words had been, eight years ago. To play second fiddle to a lesbian to be almost, but not quite as satisfying in bed as Avery's roommate—

No. No, it was more than he could bear.

Still he watched. He watched Avery slide down her friend's body, and then he saw the other girl coiling up like a pink serpent, pulling herself around so her head rested around Avery's thighs, and the two of them, knotted and entangled, rendered illicit pleasure to one another at the same time, bodies tense with excitement and unnatural desires, minds oblivious to anything but the sensations of the immediate moment.

Andreas thought his brain would explode.

But still he watched.

He saw them lose all inhibition in the grip of their sterile mating.

He listened.

He heard their cries of passion. He heard their whispered words of love.

He trembled in an ecstasy of his own—an ecstasy of knowing that his rage would find release—that the deeper the rage, the finer, the more all-consuming his release would be.

Finally it was more than he could stand. He broke from his freeze, as shock gave way to anger.

He threw open the bedroom door. Like a dark angel of vengeance, he burst into the room.

CHAPTER THIRTEEN

They were so busy with one another that even the clatter of his abrupt entrance failed to interrupt them for several seconds. They went right on, body thrusting against body, breath mingling in an unnatural kiss, until he was hovering above them.

He reached down and caught a soft shoulder. It was Elaine's. Andreas tugged, and the girl came away. With a contemptuous shove he lifted her and threw her to the floor. She landed heavily on her buttocks and sat there with her legs spread, her sweat-shiny breasts rising and falling in agitation, her face blank with shock.

He looked down at Avery.

His lips worked with rage, but no sounds emerged for a moment, until he could master his anger enough to be able to speak coherently.

"Pig! Tramp!" he roared at her.

"Lou—what are you doing here—?"

"I came to surprise you. To give you a present. Trash! Scum! How you fooled me I don't know."

Fury overwhelmed him. He grabbed the girl's arm. She cowered away from him, tried to free herself. Naked, she looked pathetic, defenseless, terrified. She shrank into one corner of the bed. But he maintained his grip on her arm, his fingers digging deep into her soft flesh.

Slowly and inexorably, he hauled her to her feet.

They faced each other in silence. He did not know what he was going to do to her.

Punish her, yes.

But how?

His hand lashed out. It landed in a backhand blow across her mouth. Her full lower lip split, and a trickle of blood ran across her chin. He slapped her again, two, three, four times in succession. Avery's eyes glazed with pain. Her roommate looked on in horror.

Hitting her only made it worse. Contact with her flesh reminded him of the pleasures they had shared, and those memories rendered all the more agonizing the awareness of her true self, her lesbian identity. One blow led to the next, and then to the next.

"Please! No, stop!"

He didn't stop. His avenging hand slammed into her breasts, slapping them so hard they danced, striking across the tender nipples, battering the delicate tissues. Hitting her breasts gave him particular pleasure. He pounded them mercilessly, backhand, forehand.

He had never been much of a sadist before. It had been the simple act of killing that gave him delight, not the process of rendering pain. He had always taken care to see to it that his victims died as quickly as possible.

But this was an entirely different situation.

He had no intention of killing Avery—at least, not at the outset. He simply wanted to punish her. And punishment meant inflicting pain. By hurting her, he would make her see how deeply she had hurt him.

So he hurt her.

He slapped her until slapping lost its novelty, and then he turned to punching. That was it. Bruise her, maul her until she quivered in a little heap.

He punched her breasts. She whimpered in pain as the tender fleshy globes were struck. He smashed his fist into her belly, and the taut muscles gave only half-hearted resistance. She was not trying to fight back. She looked dazed and bewildered by the sudden intensity of his onslaught.

He struck her again, just below the heart, and she collapsed onto the bed. Curling up in a fetal ball, she tried to present as little of herself to him as was possible. But the areas of her vulnerability were still great. Her buttocks, her back, her shoulders these were exposed no matter how she tried to hide.

He struck her in the buttocks with his knee, a solid blow to the base of her spine. She hissed in agony. As she started to uncoil, he threw himself on her, pummeling her, clubbing her with his fists.

It was hard to remember that there was a human being underneath him, that he was hitting a sensitive and beautiful girl who had given him great pleasure. In that moment of madness, it seemed to him that he was at work venting his anger on some sort of punching bag.

Ribs crumpled under his onslaught. She turned her face to him piteously, and he smashed his fist into it, and pearly white teeth splintered. Her sleek lovely lips were bloody ruins now. One eye was hideously swollen.

Part of his mind urged him to stop. He had already inflicted fearful damage on the girl. But there was no pulling back, now. Avery confronted him, body bruised and battered but still sexually magnetic, and he thought of the emotions he had felt for her, and was unable to halt his punishment now.

He drove his fists into her again and again. She fell to the floor, rolled over and over, looking for someplace to hide from him.

But there was no place to hide. None at all.

He kicked her, now, lashing out with the points of his toes. One kick caught her in the groin, and she let out a terrible howl and doubled up, her hands going to her loins. As she writhed in pain, he continued to rain kicks on her. Now his foot connected with a sweetly curved breast, now with the softness of her belly, now with the fleshy rounds of her buttocks.

The writhing, bloody thing on the floor bore little resemblance to the Avery he had kissed and caressed, the Avery he had clasped against his throbbing body, the Avery for whom he had bought a gleaming trinket in a Fifth Avenue shop. She looked now like some nightmare thing, a dismal ruin of the sleek beauty that had been.

Still he kicked and spat and cursed at her.

Then, as she turned and twisted in what was by now only a reflex attempt to escape his punishing blows, Andreas landed one kick that he had not intended at all.

It struck her on the temple. His shoe smashed against her skull with the short-range impact of a baseball bat.

There was a strangely sharp sound as it hit.

Her body recoiled, stretched out to its full length for a moment—

And then went limp.

Andreas stared down at her in fear and wonder. He had known, the instant he had felt the impact, that the kick would be a fatal one. But his mind clouded at the awareness that he had killed her.

"Avery—" he murmured, as the haze of rage cleared from his brain. "Avery—"

She didn't move. She lay on one side, her arms dangling like strands of spaghetti. Her body was horribly bruised, with purplish welts forming in fifty places. Her ruined lips gaped open, blood dripping from the shattered and nearly toothless gums. Her face was ghastly to behold.

Andreas began to tremble. He had never done anything like this before. The savage, unmitigated cruelty of it, the sheer animal bestiality—the power of the forces that had been unleashed in him for those five minutes of fierce destruction frightened even him.

And there had been a witness.

A witness!

Elaine. The roommate. Throughout the whole beating, she had crouched in terror on the floor, huddling up against the wall, too frightened to come to Avery's defense, too frightened to call the police or to rush naked into the hall to summon help. She had done nothing.

And now she sat there, her eyes wide, her face a mask of sheer disbelief and horror.

"You killed her," the girl murmured in a voice that was as flat and emotionless as a child's. "You beat her to death. She's dead. You killed Avery. You killed her."

Andreas turned to look at her. She seemed tiny in her nudity, a small, fragile girl, fair-haired, pink-skinned, slender. She clasped her hands over her small pale breasts, as though by hiding them beneath her fingers she would in some way be less nude before Andreas.

A great sadness came over him. He had no quarrel with this girl. He did not even know her. He had nothing against her except that she had been Avery's partner in perversion.

But he was going to have to kill her too.

He had no choice. What else could he do? She had just witnessed his beating Avery to death. There was no way of swearing her to silence. Killing her was the only way to be certain that he was safe.

He had taken nearly forty lives, now. But this was the first time that he felt he had killed in cold blood. He went to her.

"Get up," he said.

"What are you going to do to me?"

"Get up."

She shrank away from him. He reached down for her, caught her by her thin wrists, hauled her to her feet. She was more than a foot shorter than he was. It would seem as though he could break her in half with a single blow.

Her lips moved. She was trying to scream. But she was too frightened, too numbed by the monstrous thing she had just witnessed.

He put his hands around her throat.

Squeezed.

Comprehension came into her eyes, and for one instant there was a look of fear and bewilderment in them. Then his grip tightened, and her eyes bulged forward, and her head lolled limply, and she dangled from his grasp like a marionette without strings.

He let go of her.

She fell backward across the bed. Andreas stood over her, and as he looked down he saw that her breasts were rising and falling, that a spark of life still remained in her. He knew he had not killed her. He had only just begun to throttle her when she had fainted.

He looked down at her slim nudity, and a sudden surge of passion came over him. The violence that had been raging in him transmuted itself to lust.

He wanted her.

It would be the final revenge against this pair of lesbians, he thought.

With trembling hands he dropped down on top of Elaine's limp form. She stirred, but did not return to consciousness. His hands went to her cool, smooth thighs.

He readied himself.

He struck.

There was sudden resistance. The thought came to him with stunning impact: Elaine was a virgin! Never before in her life had any man had her!

Her first man would be her last, then.

The pain of being taken brought her back to consciousness. She stirred. Her eyes opened. She moaned feebly.

She said, "No—don't—please don't—"

"Too late," he said. With a fierce thrust he drove himself against the obstruction like a battering ram, and burst through it. Elaine gasped in pain, and her entire body quivered as if live current had jolted through her.

His hands returned to her throat.

They tightened.

This time he completed the job. As his body moved in short urgent strokes, as his body made a woman out of her, he choked the life from her.

She died without a word.

In the moment of her death he experienced his climax, a fierce and intense one. He lay still for a short while afterward, drained of passion, a little dazed by the enormity of the acts he had committed on this peaceful morning.

Finally he rose, and adjusted his clothing.

The bedroom was a shambles. Everything had been overturned. Perfume bottles and toy poodles and combs and brushes had been swept to the floor.

He glanced at the naked girl on the bed. She looked relatively peaceful now. Only the mottled look of her face and throat told of the violence that had been committed on her.

But Avery—

Andreas shuddered. Not since his first murder, years ago, that brutal clubbing with a bottle of gin, had death looked so frightful to him. He could hardly bear to look at his own handiwork. He felt sickened.

On watery legs he started to leave the apartment. As he stepped over the bedroom threshold, he noticed something small lying on the floor.

A jewelry box.

The clasp he had bought for Avery. It must have fallen from his pocket during the struggle. Breathing a little prayer of relief, he stooped, snatched the box up. If he hadn't noticed it, he would have signed his own death warrant on the spot, he knew. The box had the store's name on it, and the police would be able to trace the purchaser, and only a shrewd lawyer would be able to save him from the electric chair once they had located him.

He pocketed the box. He took a last look around, and shuddered again. He left.

No one saw him on the way out. His traditional luck in leaving the scene of a crime held. It was more important than usual, he realized. The police were certain to devote intensive effort to solving this particularly brutal double murder. He had not cut off the lives of anonymous tramps, this time. He had struck at two girls who were members of the community, good citizens, and all that.

He knew that his position was more precarious than it had ever been before. There were people who could link his name with Avery's. He might be pulled in as a suspect in the case, and possibly prolonged questioning might break him down. For the first time in his career as a murderer, he had taken the life of someone whom he had known for more than a single night, and so there was a trail that could be traced.

He tried to stay calm despite his fears. Hurrying back to his hotel, he checked himself over, found no scratches on him, no telltales that the police might want him to explain. He quickly made a few telephone calls, set up business appointments for himself that might be useful as alibis for the time of the murder, if matters came down to that.

He could do no more.

He could only hope that his luck, which had been so good for so long, would not fail him now.

The next morning, he left New York on a train bound for Atlanta. No one intercepted him at the station. The morning papers were full of screaming headlines about the sadistic murder of two girls in Greenwich Village. Andreas bought all the papers in sight, and read the newspaper articles with diligence as his train chuffed southward.

It was a long time before he fully recovered from the Avery episode. Avery's bloody, mutilated face haunted his dreams for weeks afterward. He roamed the country like a man obsessed, deliberately asking his company for the most wide-ranging of assignments, taking him from St. Louis to Tacoma, from Tacoma to Grand Rapids, from Grand Rapids to Mobile, from Mobile to Chicago.

But the dreams traveled with him.

What he had done to Avery and her roommate seemed altogether different from the killings he had committed earlier. Those had been executions, eradications—the removal of human vermin. But these killings had been murders. What business had it been of his that Avery and Elaine were Lesbians? Were his feelings hurt that he had been sleeping with a girl who was not quite what she seemed to be? Was that a motive for a brutal murder, he asked himself?

Andreas had never liked to do much digging into the things that motivated him. He did what he did, and tried not to think about it. But he began to think now.

He was starting to see himself as a monster.

He had been happy with Avery, really happy, in the normal sense of the word. But he had fled from that happiness. Instead of asking Avery to marry him, as another man might have done when he met such a girl, he had coolly decided to drop out of her life when the appointed month was up. And then he had killed her hideously when the nature of her true self was unexpectedly revealed to him.

He had been happy with Tony, long ago. He had not killed her, but he had stepped out of her life with a cruelty and a bluntness that had been not far from murderous. Perhaps Tony had salvaged some happiness in her life over the years, but not thanks to him.

As the months passed, Andreas came to a new understanding of himself. All the old rationalizations about extermination and eradication dropped away, and he saw himself with chilling clarity, as a psychopath, as a creature who was less than human in all the ways that counted.

It was not a comforting realization.

But he managed to come to terms with it, just as he had come to terms with every other crisis of his life. *If that's what I am*, he told himself smugly, *then that's what I am, and no sense wasting time worrying about it.* It was a relief to have come to this acceptance of himself.

After that, things became a little easier for him again. The dreams went away. Avery's death receded into a closed compartment of his mind.

It remained there, biding its time.

For eight months after the double murder, Andreas did not kill. Those were the months of his crisis. But, when he came to terms with himself again, he decided that the best way to show his independence from humanity was to return to his killing ways.

He felt a little awkward about it at first. He was more or less out of practice. For eight months he had lived a virtuous, responsible life. He had worked sixteen, eighteen hours a day, and he had had little sex to distract him, and no thoughts of murder.

He was in St. Petersburg, Florida, when he managed to make the return to his old ways. He picked up a girl, a sallow blonde with thin lips and a skimpy, bony body, and he made love to her in her dilapidated little room in a creaking frame boarding house, and then he put his hands to her throat and choked the life out of her with the same practiced ease that a concert pianist employs when he joins his talents and experience to the proper instrument for coaxing a Beethoven sonata into glowing tones.

It was very easy to kill, he discovered once again. Easy and marvelously pleasant. It was a great little relaxer, this business of strangling.

He was back in business again. His private war with the female sex was resumed.

It was a great feeling to be killing once again. It was like coming home after a long absence.

CHAPTER FOURTEEN

Having rediscovered the joy of killing after the temporary derailment of the Avery business, Andreas lost no time catching up.

He began to slay with joyful abandon and the roll of the dead mounted.

He was in San Francisco when he scored his fiftieth kill. That was an important occasion, he felt. The girl was only a semi-professional, a beatniky trollop who probably gave it away as often as she sold it, but that didn't trouble Andreas anymore. He throttled her in her North Beach flat, and then treated himself to a handsome dinner at Fisherman's Wharf later the same evening.

The kills kept mounting.

Fifty-one, fifty-two, fifty-three.

Number fifty-four was a girl in Little Rock, slim and sweet and stupid, who kept "you-alling" him right up to the moment that he put his hands around her throat and closed off her windpipe.

Number fifty-five was a honeybunch from Salt Lake City with the most astonishing breasts Andreas had ever seen, two big swollen round things like basketballs. She was so amazingly stacked that he felt a little hesitant about killing her—it was like demolishing one of the Seven Wonders of the World—but after they had made love, she made what sounded to him like a wisecrack about his virility, and even though she protested loudly that she hadn't meant to insult him, her doom was sealed from that moment on. He choked the life out of her and took one last unbelieving look at her enormous boobs before clearing out.

Number fifty-six was registered in Buffalo. Number fifty-seven in Schenectady, two weeks later.

Number fifty-eight in New York City. It was the first time he had been in New York in almost two years, since the Avery murder, and he felt a little queasy about it even now. He took care to stay away from Greenwich Village. He didn't want to be reminded of that scene of carnage.

The day after his fifty-eighth kill, he was on his way to Cleveland.

He was coming home.

He hadn't been in Cleveland for a long, long time. The company gave him a certain amount of leeway in choosing the route he was going to follow on each sales trip, and he had always managed to map things out so that he skirted around his native city. Somehow he didn't want to go back to the place where he had been born, where he had committed his first three murders, where he had loved Tony and been loved too well by her in return.

He wasn't sure why he had scheduled Cleveland into this trip. He had done it in an absent-minded moment, and then, looking at his itinerary later, he had decided to let it be. Ten years was a long enough time to stay away from your hometown. It was time for another look-see.

It was a warm summer night, and for reasons of economy, he had not rented an air-conditioned room. Air conditioning was a dollar extra. Anything he could peel off his per diem expense account was something he could stash away and make good use of later on.

About nine that evening, after he had rested up and disposed of the New York newspapers with the account of the Marie Raimondi killing, he went down for a stroll.

Euclid Avenue was crowded that night. Every tavern on the street seemed to be doing capacity business. Andreas stopped in one for a beer, listened to a baseball argument for a couple of minutes, and drifted out and onward.

There were plenty of policemen around. He didn't remember there being this many cops in Cleveland before. But maybe he had simply forgotten. In any case, he had nothing to fear from them. He smiled cordially at them as he went past. Some of them smiled back.

He had gone about four blocks, now, toward the lake. The neighborhood was starting to look rundown. The movie theaters were smaller and dingier, and in place of cafeterias and restaurants there were dismal little hash houses, and there were fewer cops to be seen. Andreas was just beginning to wonder how far he would walk before he grew tired and went back to his hotel room, when a girl stepped out from under a lamppost and accosted him with a familiar come-on.

She wasn't really a girl, he saw. She was a woman. She was obviously in her late twenties, perhaps even in her early thirties.

Once, she must have been terrifically beautiful. But a girl fades fast in the streets. She had lost the bloom of youth. But she was still a strikingly handsome woman, he thought, tall and lush and full-blown.

She was wearing a tight maroon sweater buttoned down the front, and the buttons were straining mightily to contain the heavy swells of the breasts that thrust forward against the thin fabric. The ripe, mature curves of her hips and buttocks were outlined plainly and provocatively by her skin-tight, contour-hugging dress.

In a deep, rich voice she said, "Can you give me the right time, mister?"

He was studying her. She was a good-looking woman. Obviously a prostitute. He hadn't particularly planned to make a pickup tonight, wasn't really interested in scoring a kill. The girl he had just taken care of in New York would quench his thirst for murder for a few weeks, at least.

But still, he was in his hometown, and maybe he would knock one off tonight, just for old time's sake.

"It's quarter after nine," he said.

She smiled. Her eyes peered levelly into his, "Thanks," she said. She winked, "Hey, you're pretty good-looking, you know that? You a stranger here?"

"I was born here," he said. "But I haven't lived here for ten years."

He stared full in her face. A nagging memory prodded at him.

She looked familiar. Tremendously familiar.

Was she someone he had gone to high school with? No, He couldn't place her.

Then who—?

No, he thought. *It can't be!*

He stared, and the years dropped away, and a face glittered at him in his memory.

A mocking face.

He had to choke back a gasp of astonishment. The street began to spin around him, and he felt dizzy with disbelief and surprise.

No, he thought. *It isn't possible. Not after all these years.*

"You okay, mister?" she asked anxiously. "You look kind of dizzy!"

"I'm—all right," Andreas said, struggling to recover his control. "Just a passing spell. The heat. It can get you if you aren't careful." He dug out his handkerchief, patted his sweaty forehead. In a husky, quavering voice he said, "I think I could stand a drink, though. You know where there's a good bar around here?"

She grinned. "Just what I was thinking. There's one right down the street."

"Let's go, then."

His heart was beating out a symphony for drums as they walked along the shabby street together. The nearness of her was maddening, the warmth of her body so great that she seemed to blaze at his side.

After so many years, he thought in amazement.

It was almost too far-fetched to be believable. Such a wild coincidence, that on his first night back in Cleveland in almost a decade, he should be picked up by—by the same girl who—

There could be no doubt, though. For ten years he had carried the sharp imprint on his memory, burned into his brain, and he never could or would forget the way she had appeared that night, the fury in her eyes, the smile of contempt on her full lips, the acid in her voice as she mocked his manhood in biting words.

Ten years had passed—and here she was, still plying the same dismal trade. The years had added pounds to her already ample body, but she was still voluptuously beautiful, robustly sensual.

Time had taken the sheen from her hair, and it had added cruel lines to her face. No doubt she had had a hard time of it, he thought. He had had enough experience with prostitutes by this time to know that theirs was a miserable life, even at best. A golden few made it to the big money, and the rest froze in loneliness on drab street corners. If she had spent ten years in the life, she had really been through the mill, he realized.

Everything tallied, though.

The face, the figure, the voice—even the age.

When he had been a callow seventeen-year-old, she had seemed to be around eighteen or nineteen. Now, ten years later, she was on the threshold of her thirties. It added up the right way.

She was the one.

The one whose cruelty had chilled his heart and turned him into something less than human, had turned him into a killer, into even a being beyond the pale of normality. The one whose hated image he had recreated fifty-eight times, and fifty-eight times destroyed.

Through some wild stroke of luck, he had found her again.

Tonight he would have *real* revenge.

She gave no sign of recognizing him. But why should she remember? Why should she have any occasion to recall the unimportant incident of a decade past? It had changed *his* life, but it had been only a momentary annoyance for her, quickly forgotten. She had had so many clients since. She had offered herself for hundreds or perhaps thousands of men, had groaned at their clumsy weight, had waggled her hips to give them their grunting moment of joy.

No, she had forgotten him. In any event, he bore little enough resemblance to that gawky, uncertain seventeen-year-old kid of a decade ago.

He had matured, gained weight and strength. There was only the most incidental of links between the boy that had been and the man that was now. He had almost nothing in common with that vanished, innocent Lou Andreas, nothing but his name.

They entered a bar. The bartender smiled jovially at her as she came in. Obviously she was well known in this part of town, a regular here. He didn't like that much. He knew he was going to kill her, and he didn't want to set up the possibility of being identified.

He averted his face from the bartender. "What'll you have to drink?" he asked her.

"Rye and ginger."

Without looking at the barkeep, Andreas said, "One rye and ginger, one beer."

He didn't want anything stronger than beer right now. He had had a beer a short while ago, and if he switched to hard stuff now, it might tend to blur his brain. He couldn't afford to function at less than full sharpness now. Drunkenness would lead to possible blunders, and blunders would lead to the electric chair or the noose of the hangman.

They had a couple of drinks. She nestled as close to him as the bar stools permitted. She didn't seem to object when his hand grazed her bosom, more on accident than by design. He felt the firm, warm flesh. Her cheap perfume pervaded his nostrils.

He waited for her to pitch a proportion at him, and it wasn't long in coming. Midway on the second drink she said, in the approximate words he had heard so many different times from so many different girls in so many different taverns, "How's about you and me getting out of here? We could go up to my place and have some fun."

He smiled. "I'd love it."

She gulped down the remainder of her drink and set the glass on the counter.

"Let's go, then."

They left the bar. Andreas moistened his lips and tried to stifle the rising tension within him.

How will I kill her, he wondered?

It had to be something special, he knew. This would be a grand occasion, A quick slaying—hands around the throat, squeeze squeeze squeeze and all over with—would not be fitting to the circumstances.

Maybe I should torture her first, he wondered. *To repay her for the ten years of torture she gave me. Peel away her flesh in strips, rip her fingernails out, poke her eyes with my thumbs. And then have her when she's half-crazy with pain, maybe.*

Or perhaps he should make love to her first—just to show her that he was no longer the callow boy she had laughed at way back then—and then, after he had had her, he could kill her.

Yes, he thought. *That's it. I'll take her and then I'll kill her. I'll cut her wrists and bleed her to death. I'll force her to watch while her life ebbs away.*

But first I'll talk to her—

They reached her apartment. It was about what he had expected, and nothing very different from the place she had been living at the other time he went home with her. It was a shabby walk-up, on the third floor of a decrepit rooming house. The building was dark. No snoopy neighbors to worry about, he thought.

They entered. She locked the door.

Turning to him, she smiled and said, "Now we can have some privacy."

"Yes. Privacy."

She stretched voluptuously. The high, heavy mounds of her breasts bulged against the thin fabric of her sweater. Letting her breath out in a sudden whoosh, she relaxed and said, "My name's Lois. What's yours?"

Ordinarily he made up some name when he was with a girl he planned to kill. But he didn't want to do that now. He wanted her to know who he was, who he really was. Not that the name would mean a thing to her. "Andreas," he said. "Lou Andreas."

She walked to the window, peered out, pulled the blind down. Without turning she said, "What kind of line are you in, Lou?"

"I sell. Traveling salesman—heating accessories, strictly wholesale."

"You get around the country, huh?"

"I suppose I do."

"Where was your last stop?"

"New York," he said, "And in two days I'm on my way down to Louisville, Kentucky. I keep busy."

She turned toward him. "It must be a lonely life," she said. "Traveling, living in hotel rooms."

"I survive. Sometimes I feel the need of a little feminine companionship, though."

"Like tonight?"

"Yes," he said. "Like tonight."

"I bet you've picked up dozens of girls, Lou. You must be a real man of the world."

She was a talkative witch, he thought in annoyance. But he maintained an outward appearance of calm. Shrugging, he said, "I've had my share."

"Given them a real good time, too."

"Maybe. I like to think I do."

She smiled lustfully. "You going to give me a good time tonight?"

"I'm going to send you way out of this world, baby," he told her.

She laughed and stretched again, elevating her breasts until he thought the buttons would pop on her sweater. He felt the currents of lustfulness go through him.

She began to unbutton her sweater.

It dropped away. A tight pink bra contained her breasts. She reached around casually, and unsnapped it. He had remembered her breasts as being magnificent, and his memory proved to be accurate. They were superb breasts, high and round and heavy. They swayed slightly as she moved.

"You like 'em?" she asked.

"Guess."

"Come on over. Take a feel."

He nodded. He went to her, put his hands on her breasts, squeezed them. They were hot, and the nipples were growing rigid. He caressed the two heavy globes of flesh, moving them around, pressing his fingertips into them.

And then he decided abruptly that he would not make love to her after all. Not while she lived, anyway. He would kill—swiftly, soon. That would be far more satisfying to him than mere animal lust. And by showing her that he was above the attractions of mere sex, he would repay her for the mockery she had given him. Later, when she lay lifeless at his feet, he might strip her the rest of the way and violate her cooling body.

He released her breasts. His loins throbbed with desire, but he forced himself to ignore the insistent pounding of need, to repress it until he had done what he had to do.

He said, "You know, this isn't the first time I've been with you."

She frowned. "Huh?"

"Really, it isn't. The last time was ten years ago, Lois. Ten years."

She stared at him. Absently, she scratched one of her high, full breasts.

"You're kidding," she said. "Ten years? Nobody remembers a girl ten years."

"I wish I could forget. I was seventeen, then, and I wanted a woman in the worst way, because I was a virgin. And I picked you up on Thirteenth Street, and we went up to your room. It was a little dump of a room, pretty much like this one you've got now."

"Say, you're making all this up."

"No, I'm not," he said quietly. "We went to the room, and you undressed, and I touched your body, just as I touched it now. But I was young and frightened, and nothing happened. You laughed at me, Lois. You called me filthy names and chased me out of your room. And I remembered. You've forgotten all about it, but I remembered. For ten years I've sought out girls like you—punishing them for your laughter—never dreaming that someday I would be granted the chance to punish you yourself!"

She was staring at him curiously. Her bare breasts were like two giant grapefruit, leading him on, inflaming her. He knew now that he would possess her after he had killed her.

"What do you mean, punish?" she asked.

"I punish them with my hands, Lois!" He held them out. "I squeeze, and I tighten, and eyes bulge, faces go purple, pretty faces, painted faces, lying faces—"

"You're out of your head!"

"After ten years, Lois, luck has brought you to me. Laugh now, Lois! Go on! Mock me! Why don't you mock me? You know all the words! Laugh long and hard—until my fingers choke off your breath!"

He advanced toward her, his hands outstretched.

He forgot all about his plan of cutting her wrists, of letting her die slowly. He couldn't wait that long. Choking was more direct. He wanted to feel her body writhe beneath his iron grip, he wanted her to sink to her knees, to turn black in the face as her oxygen-starved lungs cried out.

She backed away from him, slowly, not really panicking. He followed her. The heavy rises of her breasts swayed, like two big bells. His hands reached out, going this time not for those massive breasts, not for the soft flesh of her bosom, but for her throat.

In a moment she would begin to die. This was going to be the greatest thrill of his life, the one unforgettable moment of superb revenge, the climax to ten years of slaughter.

His fingers touched her soft skin.

"Okay, Nick," she said.

The door burst open.

Suddenly the room was full of policemen. Powerful hands grasped him, pulling him away from her. He felt the hard snout of a police revolver pressing into his back. He caught a glimpse of Lois calmly pulling her sweater back over her bare breasts. She wiped sweat from her face and sat down on the bed.

"Whew!" she said. "This guy's really bugs!"

One of the cops said, "I taped it all. It shouldn't be hard to get the rest of the confession from him."

Andreas felt dazed and bewildered and numb. The only thought that he could focus on was that the police had caught him, that they had sprung some kind of trap.

"What is this?" he asked in a blurred, uncertain voice, looking up at the cold faces of the cops. "You locked the door, Lois. I saw you."

She grinned. "You think I'm nuts, buster? Lock myself in here with a creep like you?"

"But—"

"We've been watching you since you came to town," the cop said behind him. "You've been trailed all over the country for weeks. But you've always slipped through our hands. We've been unable to get any solid evidence on you, and we couldn't move till we had it. How many girls have you killed, anyway? Twenty? Thirty?"

"Fifty-eight," Andreas said proudly. It was pointless to try to pretend to innocence now. They had him. He was finished.

"Fifty-eight," the cop muttered. "But we caught up with you finally. You got sloppy in Schenectady. We missed the New York job, but this time we nabbed you."

"I don't understand," Andreas murmured faintly. He looked at the prostitute. The impudent bulges of her breasts thrust forward shamelessly. "This girl—she cooperates with the police?"

Lois smiled and reached for her handbag. "I wised up about six years ago, Andreas. I got tired of being arrested and always in trouble, so I got myself an honest job. With the police force. If you can't beat 'em, join 'em. I'm the Number One decoy on the Cleveland Vice Squad, now."

She opened the pocketbook and took out a gleaming police badge. Her eyes were bright with mockery—just as they had been, ten years before. He heard her silvery laughter. "Surprised, huh? You didn't think you were picking up a policewoman on that corner!"

Andreas made a gurgling incoherent sound deep in his throat. He felt madness close in. Trapped, deceived! It hadn't been any coincidence that she had picked him up. She had been lying in wait for him. Unwittingly, she had begun his career of crime, and now she had ended it!

"Come on, Nick," she said. "Let's take this creep down to headquarters. It's time to call it a day. And it disgusts me to have to look at him. I want a nice hot bath now. To wash the touch of him off my body."

The handcuffs snapped into place around his wrists. She smiled at him again—mockingly, contemptuously. And then they took him away.

THE END

THE EROTIC NOVELS OF ROBERT SILVERBERG

As by Loren Beauchamp
Love Nest (Midwood, 1958)
Another Night, Another Love (Midwood, 1959)
Connie (Midwood, 1959)
Unwilling Sinner (Midwood, 1959)
Meg (Midwood, 1960; reprinted as *All the Best Beds* as by Don Elliott, 1967)
Nurse Carolyn (Midwood, 1960; reprinted as *Registered Nympho* as by Don Elliott, 1967)
And When She Was Bad (Midwood, 1961)
Sin on Wheels (Midwood, 1961; reprinted as *Orgy on Wheels* as by Don Elliott, 1967)
The Fires Within (Midwood, 1961)
Campus Sex Club (Midwood, 1962)
Sin a la Carte (Midwood, 1962)
Strange Delights (Midwood, 1962)
Wayward Widow (Midwood, 1962; reprinted as *Free Sample*, 1968)
The Wife Traders (Boudoir, 1963)

As by Dr. Walter C. Brown
The Single Girl (Monarch, 1961)

As by David Challon
Campus Love Club (Bedside, 1959; reprinted as *Campus Sex Club* as by Loren Beauchamp, 1962)
French Sin Port (Bedside, 1959; reprinted as *Rouge of the Riviera* as by Don Elliott, 1967)
Suburban Sin Club (Bedside, 1959; abridged & reprinted as *The Wife Traders* as by Loren Beauchamp, 1963)
Thirst for Love (Bedside, 1959; reprinted as *Wayward Widow* as by Loren Beauchamp, 1962)
Man Mad (Chariot, 1960)
Suburban Affair (Bedside, 1960)
Campus Hellcat and Other Stories (Bedside, 1960)

As by John Dexter
Stripper! (Nightstand, 1960; reprinted as *One Bed Too Many* by Jeremy Dunn)
Sex Thieves (Nightstand, 1961; reprinted as *Wife in Name Only* by Jeremy Dunn, 1974)
Sin Festival (Nightstand, 1961; reprinted as *The Goddess Makers* by Jeremy Dunn, 1974)
The Bra Peddlers (Nightstand, 1961; reprinted as *The Venus Affair* by Jeremy Dunn, 1974)
The Lust Plotters (Nightstand, 1962)
Passion Bum (Nightstand, 1962)

As Walter Drummond
Philosopher of Evil: The Life & Works of the Marquis de Sade (nf; Regency, 1962)
How to Spend Money (nf; Regency, 1963)

As by Dan Eliot
Dial O-R-G-Y (Ember, 1963)
Flesh Flames (Ember, 1963)
Lust Lover (Pillar, 1963)
Nympho (Ember, 1963)
Sin Doll (Ember, 1963)
Sin Hellion (Ember, 1963)
Sin Mates (Pillar, 1963)

Don Elliott (all published by Greenleaf under various imprints)
Love Addict (1959)
Gang Girl (1959)
Naked Holiday (1960)

The Flesh Peddlers (1960; reprinted as *The Flesh Merchants*, 1973)
The Lecher (1960)
Mistress of Sin (1960; reprinted as *Depravity Town*, 1973)
Party Girl (1960)
Sin on Wheels (1960; reprinted as *The Instructor*, 1973)
Passion Trap (1960; reprinted as *Carnal Cage*, 1973)
Sex Jungle (1960; reprinted as *Jungle Street*, 1973)
Convention Girl (1960; reprinted as *The Man Collector*, 1973)
Summertime Affair (1960)
Woman Chaser (1960)
Backstreet Sinner (1961; reprinted as *The Bed and the Beautiful*, 1973)
Expense Account Sinners (1961; reprinted as *Keep the Clients Happy*, 1973)
Lust Goddess (1961; reprinted as *The Temptress*, 1973)
Lust Queen (1961; reprinted as *The Decadent*, 1974)
The Lust Seekers (1961; reprinted as *Till Love Do Us Part*, 1974)
Sin Club (1961; reprinted as *The Lady from Soho*, 1974)
Sin Cruise (1961; reprinted as *Fifteen Nights of Love*, 1973)
The Sinful Ones (1961; reprinted as *Every Night in Rome*, 1974)
Wild Divorcee (1961; reprinted as *Nowhere Girl*, 1973)
Streets of Sin (1961; reprinted as *The Untamed*, 1974)
Hotrod Sinners (1962)
Kept Man (1962)
Lust Captive (1962; reprinted as *The Game Susan Played*, 1974)
Lust Cat (1962)
Lust Cult (1962; reprinted as *None But the Wicked*, 1974)
Lust for Two (1962)
Lust Lord (1962)
Lust Market (1962)
No Lust Tonight (1962)
The Orgy Boys (1962)
Passion Thieves (1962)
Roadhouse Girl (1962; reprinted as *No Pleasure So Painful*, 1974)
Sex Fury (1962)
Sexteen (1962)
Shame House (1962)
Sin Bait (1962)
Sin Kin (1962)
Sin Quest (1962)
Sin Sick (1962)
Three Sinners (1962; reprinted as *A Change for the Bedder*, 1974)
Wild Flesh (1962)
Lust Crew (1963)
Passion Patsy (1963)
Sex Bait (1963)
Sex Bum (1963)
Sin Crazed (1963)
Sin Made (1963)
Sin Servant (1963)
Beatnik Wanton (1964)
Black Market Shame (1964)
Flesh Bride (1964)
Flesh Lesson (1964)
Flesh Melody (1964)
Flesh Pawns (1964)
Flesh Prize (1964)
The Flesh Seekers (1964)
Flesh Taker (1964)
Gutter Road (1964)
Lust Burns (1964)
Lust League (1964)
Lust Set (1964)
Lust Spree (1964)
Orgy Isle (1964)
Orgy Maid (1964)
Passion Pair (1964)
Passion Partners (1964)
Passion Trio (1964)
Pickup (1964)
Shameless (1964)
Sin Bin (1964)
Sin Circuit (1964)
Sin Partners (1964)
Sin Service (1964)
Sin Sold (1964)

BIBLIOGRAPHY

Switch Trap (1964)
Wanton Web (1964)
Alternate Wife (1965)
Carnal Carnival (1965)
Escape to Sindom (1965)
Flesh Bigamist (1965)
Flesh Boarder (1965)
Flesh Cry (1965)
Flesh Man (1965)
Good Girl, Bad Girl (1965)
Lust Doomed (1965)
Lust Finale (1965)
Naked She Died (1965)
The Nite Lusters (1965)
Nudie Packet (1965)
Of Shame Reborn (1965)
Only the Depraved (1965)
Orgy Slaves (1965)
Passion Killer (1965)
Passion Peeper (1965)
Passion Pusher (1965; cover listed as by Don Holliday)
The Shame Protector (1965)
Shame Scheme (1965)
Sin for Solace (1965)
Sin Kill (1965)
Sin Spin (1965)
The Sin Switch (1965)
Sin Warped (1965)
The Sins of Seena (1965)
Teaser (1965)
Would-Be Sinner (1965)
The Young Wantons (1965)
All on Sunday (1966)
Big Blast (1966)
Campus Traders (1966)
Cousin Lover (1966)
Diary of Desire (1966)
Every Bed Her Own (1966)
The Gay Girls (1966)
Initiates (1966)
Lust Demon (1966)
One Night Stand (1966)
Pain Lusters (1966)
The Passion Barons (1966; reprint of *Streets of Sin* by Mark Ryan, 1959)
Take My Wife (1966)
The Virtuous Ones (1966)
All the Best Beds (1967)
Carnal Counselor (1967; ghost-written, author unknown)
Diary of a Dyke (1967)
Flesh Fever (1967)
Flesh Tryst (1967)
Orgy on Wheels (1967)
Registered Nympho (1967)
Rogue of the Riviera (1967)
Those Who Lust (1967)
The Wanton West (1967)

As by Marlene Longman
Sin Girls (Nightstand, 1960; reprinted as *The Tormented*, 1973)

As by Dan Malcolm
The Mystery of the Judge's Mistress (*Guilty*, March 1962)

As by Ray McKenzie
The Wild Party (Chariot, 1960)

As by Gordon Mitchell
Immoral Wife (Midwood, 1959; reprinted as *Henry's Wife*, 1961)

As by Mark Ryan
Company Girl (Bedside, 1959)
Streets of Sin (Bedside, 1959; reprinted as *The Passion Barons* as by Don Elliott, 1966)
Twisted Love, (Bedside, 1959; reprinted as *Strange Delights* as by Loren Beauchamp, 1962)
Savage Love (Bedside, 1960)
Illicit Affair and Other Stories (Bedside, 1961)

As by Stan Vincent
The Hot Beat (Magnet, 1960)

As by L. H. Walker
The Lascivious Abbott (Greenleaf, 1967; introduction by L. T. Woodward)

As by L. T. Woodward, M. D.

Sex Fiend (Monarch, 1961)
Sex and Hypnosis (Monarch, 1961)
Sex in Our Schools (Monarch, 1962)
Virgin Wives (Monarch, 1962)
The Deceivers (Beacon, 1962)
90% of What You Know About Sex is Wrong (Parliament, 1962)
Sex and the Armed Forces (Monarch, 1963)
The History of Surgery (Monarch, 1963)
You and Your Sex Life (Monarch, 1963)
Twilight Women (Lancer, 1963)
Masochism (Monarch, 1964)
Sex and the Divorced Woman (Lancer, 1964)
Sophisticated Sex Techniques in Marriage (Lancer, 1967)
I Am a Nymphomaniac (Belmont, 1967)

The Science Fiction Works of Robert Silverberg

Novels

Revolt on Alpha C (Thomas Crowell, 1955; Scholastic, 1959)
The 13th Immortal (Ace, 1956)
Master of Life and Death (Ace, 1957)
The Shrouded Planet (with Randall Garrett, as Robert Randall; Gnome. 1957; Dell. 1963)
Invaders from Earth (Ace, 1958)
Lest We Forget Thee, Earth (as Calvin M. Knox; Ace, 1958)
Stepsons of Terra (Ace, 1958)
Aliens from Space (as David Osborne; Avalon, 1958)
Invisible Barriers (as David Osborne; Avalon, 1958)
Starhaven (as Ivar Jorgenson; Avalon, 1958; Ace, 1959)
Starman's Quest (Gnome, 1958)
The Plot Against Earth (as Calvin M. Knox; Ace, 1959)
The Dawning Light (with Randall Garrett, as Robert Randall; Gnome, 1959; Dell, 1963)
The Planet Killers (Ace, 1959)
Lost Race of Mars (Scholastic, 1960)
Collision Course (Avalon, 1961; Ace, 1961)
The Seed of Earth (Ace, 1962)
Recalled to Life (Lancer, 1962; revised version, Doubleday, 1972)
Blood on the Mink (written in 1959, first published in 1962 as "Too Much Blood on the Mink" in *Trapped* magazine, re-published by Hard Case Crime, 2012)
The Silent Invaders (Ace, 1963)
Time of the Great Freeze (Holt, Rinehart and Winston, 1964; Dell, 1966)
Regan's Planet (Pyramid, 1964)
One of Our Asteroids is Missing (as Calvin M. Knox; Ace, 1964)
Conquerors from the Darkness (Holt, Rinehart and Winston, 1965; Dell, 1968)
The Gate of Worlds (Holt, Rinehart and Winston, 1967; Magnum, 1980)
Planet of Death (Holt, Rinehart and Winston, 1967)
Thorns (Ballantine, 1967)
Those Who Watch (Signet, 1967)
The Time Hoppers (Doubleday, 1967; Avon, 1968)
To Open the Sky (Ballantine, 1967)
World's Fair 1992 (Follett, 1970; Ace, 1982)
The Man in the Maze (Avon, 1968)
Hawksbill Station (Doubleday, 1968; Avon, 1970)
The Masks of Time (Ballantine, 1968)
Nightwings (Avon, 1969)
Downward to the Earth (serialized in *Galaxy*, 1970; Signet, 1971)
Across a Billion Years (Dial, 1969; Magnum, 1979)

Three Survived (Holt, Rinehart and Winston, 1969)
To Live Again (Doubleday, 1969; Dell, 1971)
Up the Line (Ballantine, 1969)
Tower of Glass (serialized in *Galaxy*, 1970; Charles Scribner's Sons, 1970; Bantam, 1971)
Son of Man (Ballantine, 1971)
The Second Trip (Signet, 1971)
The World Inside (Doubleday, 1971; Signet, 1972)
A Time of Changes (serialized in *Galaxy*, 1971; Signet, 1971)
The Book of Skulls (Charles Scribner's Sons, 1971; Signet, 1972)
Dying Inside (serialized in *Galaxy*, 1972; Charles Scribner's Sons, 1972; Ballantine, 1972)
The Stochastic Man (Harper & Row, 1975; Fawcett, 1976)
Shadrach in the Furnace (Bobbs-Merrill, 1976; Pocket, 1978)
Homefaring (Phantasia, 1983)
Lord of Darkness (Arbor House, 1983; Bantam, 1984)
Gilgamesh the King (Arbor House, 1984; Bantam, 1985)
Sailing to Byzantium (Underwood-Miller, 1985; Tor, 1989)
Tom O'Bedlam (Donald I. Fine, 1985; Warner, 1986)
Star of Gypsies (Donald I. Fine, 1986; Popular Questar, 1988)
At Winter's End (Warner, 1988; Warner, 1989)
Project Pendulum (Walker, 1989; Bantam, 1989)
Letters From Atlantis (Atheneum, 1990; Popular Questar, 1992)
The New Springtime (Warner, 1990; Warner, 1991)
To the Land of the Living (Gollancz, 1989; Warner, 1990)
Nightfall (expansion of the 1941 novelette "Nightfall" by Isaac Asimov; Doubleday; 1990; Bantam, 1991)
Thebes of the Hundred Gates (Axolotl/Pulphouse, 1991; Bantam, 1992)
The Face of the Waters (Bantam, 1991; Bantam, 1992)
Child of Time (expansion and revision of the 1958 novelette "Lastborn" by Isaac Asimov; Gollancz, 1991; US edition, The Ugly Little Boy, Doubleday, 1992)
Kingdoms of the Wall (HarperCollins, 1992; Bantam, 1993)
The Positronic Man (based on the 1976 novelette The Bicentennial Man by Isaac Asimov; Gollancz, 1992)
Hot Sky at Midnight (Bantam, 1994; HarperCollins, 1994)
Starborne (Bantam, 1996; Voyager, 1996)
The Alien Years (HarperCollins, 1998; Harper Voyager, 1999)
The Longest Way Home (Gollancz, 2002; Harper Voyager, 2003)
Roma Eterna (Eos, 2003; Harper Voyager, 2004)
The Last Song of Orpheus (Subterranean, 2010)

Majipoor Chronicles

Lord Valentine's Castle (Harper & Row, 1980; Bantam, 1981)
Majipoor Chronicles (Arbor House, 1982; Bantam, 1983)
Valentine Pontifex (Arbor House, 1983; Bantam, 1984)
The Mountains of Majipoor (Bantam, 1995; Bantam, 1996)
Sorcerers of Majipoor (Macmillan UK, 1997; HarperPrism, 1997)
Lord Prestimion (Harper, 1999; Eos, 2000)
King of Dreams (Voyager, 2001; Eos, 2001)

Tales of Majipoor (Gollancz, 2013; Roc, 2013)

Short story collections

Next Stop, the Stars (Ace, 1962)
Godling, Go Home (Belmont, 1964)
Needle in a Timestack (Ballantine, 1966)
The Calibrated Alligator (Holt, Rinehart and Winston, 1969)
Dimension Thirteen (Ballantine, 1969)
The Cube Root of Uncertainty (Macmillan, 1970; Collier, 1971)
Parsecs and Parables (Doubleday, 1973)
Moonferns & Starsongs (Ballantine, 1971)
The Reality Trip and Other Implausibilities (Ballantine, 1972)
Valley Beyond Time (Dell, 1973)
Earth's Other Shadow (Signet, 1973)
Unfamiliar Territory (Charles Scribner's Sons, 1973; Berkley, 1978)
The Feast of St. Dionysus: Five Science Fiction Stories (Charles Scribner's Sons, 1975; Berkley, 1979)
Sunrise on Mercury (Thomas Nelson, 1975; Pan, 1986)
Capricorn Games (Random House, 1976; Starblaze, 1979)
The Best of Robert Silverberg (Pocket, 1976)
The Shores of Tomorrow (Thomas Nelson, 1976)
World of a Thousand Colors (Arbor House, 1982; Bantam, 1984)
The Conglomeroid Cocktail Party (Arbor House, 1984; Bantam, 1985)
Beyond the Safe Zone (Donald I. Fine, 1986; Warner, 1987)
The Collected Stories of Robert Silverberg Volume 1: Secret Sharers (Bantam, 1992)
Pluto in the Morning Light: The Collected Stories Volume 1 (Grafton, 1992)
The Secret Sharer: The Collected Stories Volume 2 (Grafton, 1993)
Beyond the Safe Zone: The Collected Stories Volume 3 (Grafton, 1994)
The Road to Nightfall: The Collected Stories Volume 4 (Grafton, 1996)
Ringing the Changes: The Collected Stories Volume 5 (Grafton, 1997)
Lion Time in Timbuctoo: The Collected Stories Volume 6 (Grafton, 2000)
Phases of the Moon (Subterranean Press, 2004),
In the Beginning: Tales from the Pulp Era (Subterranean Press, 2006)
To Be Continued: The Collected Stories Volume 1 (Subterranean Press, 2006)
To the Dark Star: The Collected Stories Volume 2 (Subterranean Press, 2007)
A Little Intelligence (with Randall Garrett; Crippen & Landru, 2009)
Something Wild Is Loose: The Collected Stories Volume 3 (Subterranean Press, 2008)
Trips: The Collected Stories Volume 4 (Subterranean Press, 2009)
The Palace at Midnight: The Collected Stories Volume 5 (Subterranean Press, 2010)
Multiples: The Collected Stories Volume 6 (Subterranean Press, 2011)
We Are for the Dark: The Collected Stories Volume 7 (Subterranean Press, 2012)
Hot Times in Magma City: The Collected Stories Volume 8 (Subterranean Press, 2013)
The Millennium Express: The Collected Stories Volume 9 (Subterranean Press, 2014)

BIBLIOGRAPHY

Non-fiction

Treasures Beneath the Sea (Whitman, 1960)
Sir Winston Churchill (as by Edgar Black; Monarch, 1961)
First American Into Space (Monarch Books, 1961)
Lost Cities and Vanished Civilizations (Chilton, 1962)
The Fabulous Rockefellers (1963)
Sunken History: The Story of Underwater Archaeology (1963)
How to spend money (as by Walter Drummond; 1963)
Fifteen Battles That Changed the World (1963)
Empires in the Dust: Ancient Civilizations Brought to Light (1963)
Home of the Red Man: Indian North America Before Columbus (1963)
The History of Surgery (1963, as L. T. Woodward)
The Great Doctors (1964)
Man Before Adam: The Story of Man in Search of His Origins (1964)
Akhnaten: The Rebel Pharaoh (1964)
1066 (1964, as Franklin Hamilton)
The Loneliest Continent: The Story of Antarctic Discovery (1964, as Walker Chapman)
The Man Who Found Nineveh: The Story of Austen Henry Layard (1964)
Great Adventures in Archaeology (1964)
Socrates (1965)
Scientists And Scoundrels: A Book of Hoaxes (1965)
Men Who Mastered the Atom (1965)
Niels Bohr: The Man Who Mapped the Atom (1965)
The Old Ones: Indians of the American Southwest (1965)
The Great Wall of China (1965)
The World of Coral (1965)
The Crusades (1965, as Franklin Hamilton)
Antarctic Conquest: The Great Explorers in Their Own Words (1966, as Walker Chapman)
The Long Rampart: The Story of the Great Wall of China (1966)
Rivers: A Book to Begin On (1966, as Lee Sebastian)
Forgotten by Time: A Book of Living Fossils (1966)
Frontiers in Archeology (1966)
Kublai Khan: Lord of Xanadu (1966, as Walker Chapman)
Leaders Of Labor (1966, as Roy Cook)
Bridges (1966)
To the Rock of Darius: The Story of Henry Rawlinson (1966)
The Hopefuls: Ten Presidential Campaigns (1966, as Lloyd Robinson)
The Morning of Mankind: Prehistoric Man in Europe (1967)
The Golden Dream: Seekers of El Dorado (1967, as Walker Chapman)
The Auk, the Dodo and the Oryx (1967)
The World of the Rain Forests (1967)
The Dawn of Medicine (1967)
The Adventures of Nat Palmer (1967)
Challenge for a Throne: The Wars of the Roses (1967, as Franklin Hamilton)
Men Against Time: Salvage Archeology in the United States (1967)
Light for the World: Edison and the Power Industry (1967)
The Search for Eldorado (1967, as Walker Chapman)
Sophisticated Sex Techniques in Marriage (1967, as L. T. Woodward)
Mound Builders of Ancient America: The Archeology of a Myth (New

York Graphic Society, 1968);
reprint (Ohio University Press,
1986) - Silverberg's fourth-most
widely held work in WorldCat
libraries

The World of the Ocean Depths
(1968)

The Stolen Election: Hayes vs.
Tilden, 1876 (1968, as Lloyd
Robinson)

Four Men Who Changed the
Universe (1968)

Sam Houston (1968, as Paul
Hollander)

The South Pole: A Book to Begin On
(1968, as Lee Sebastian)

Stormy Voyager (1968)

Ghost Towns of the American West
(1968)

Vanishing Giants: The Story of the
Sequoias (1969)

Wonders of Ancient Chinese Science
(1969)

The Challenge of Climate: Man and
His Environment (1969)

Bruce of the Blue Nile (1969)

The World of Space (1969)

If I Forget Thee, O Jerusalem (1970)

The Seven Wonders of the Ancient
World (1970)

Mammoths, Mastodons and Man
(1970)

The Mound Builders (1970)

The Pueblo Revolt (1970)

Clocks for the Ages: How Scientists
Date the Past (1971)

To The Western Shore: Growth of the
United States 1776-1853 (1971)

Before The Sphinx: Early Egypt
(1971)

Into Space: A Young Person's Guide
to Space (1971, with Arthur C.
Clarke)

The Realm of Prester John (1972)

The Longest Voyage:
Circumnavigation in the Age Of
Discovery (1972)

John Muir, Prophet Among the
Glaciers (1972)

The World Within the Ocean Wave
(1972)

The World Within the Tide Pool
(1972)

Drug Themes in Science Fiction
(1974)

Reflections and Refractions:
Thoughts on Science Fiction,
Science and Other Matters (1997)

Musings and Meditations (2011)

www.ingramcontent.com/pod-product-compliance
Lightning Source LLC
LaVergne TN
LVHW021810060526
838201LV00058B/3321